Jije is a work of fiction. Names, characters, places, and incidents are the products of the author's imagination or are used fictitiously. Any resemblance to actual events, locals, or persons, living or dead, is entirely coincidental.

D1568861

Cover design and illustration: C. P. Allen

Photography by: Nevaeh Hartley

This book is dedicated to my friends and family. To my loving and supportive fiance, Sheba. When the stress and self doubt threatened to stop me, you kept me going. Also to my dogs Frankie and Bailey for making me stop to take you outside right when I sat down to write. Breaks are important.

A special thanks to Annette Frisby for coming to the rescue in a time crunch. Your spit and polish has made this story shine.

Jije

A novel by:
C.P. Allen

Intro

"This isn't real. Don't scream. They aren't really there." Paul silently repeated his mantra.

The silhouettes that he woke up to were nothing new. Figures beside his bed, as if standing vigil over him. It was always a mix of horror and sorrow that filled Paul when it happened. With all of the recent events, he wasn't surprised to wake up to this. Less than 24 hours ago, he had seen someone die… violently.

"Night terrors," his brother Adam stated the first time Paul awoke screaming.

"Just a bad dream, baby," was the explanation his mother, Frances, had offered.

"God damnit, son!" was the response his father gave him after charging into the room with his 12 gauge at the ready. The ear piercing screams his son had let loose during his first experience with night terrors surely meant someone was killing him in the middle of the night. Finding him safe and screaming in his bed confused and irritated him.

None of that mattered anymore. This was different. Normally the figures were too dark to make out more than the outlines. From the dim light coming off the clock on the nightstand, Paul began to make out details.

Straw-like grey hairs shot from beneath what appeared to be a hooded cloak made out of burlap. A glint of light bounced off of the figure's eyes from under the darkness of the hood. She stood there, motionless, as the others always did. Paul gasped as she moved ever so slightly towards him. A horrible gurgling groan escaped from her.

"NO NO NO!" Paul screamed. Well, he would have if he could have remembered how to operate his body. What actually came out was more like a dog with laryngitis trying to whine.

The figure raised up a bony hand to the footboard of the bed, and rested it just centimeters from the foot Paul left hanging out of the blanket on warm nights like tonight. She curled crooked fingers endowed with dirty; jagged nails on the wood.

Paul began mentally chastising himself. "Sit up goddamn it! Really? You're gonna let this figment of your fucking imagination do this to you?! You are not going to scream you pathetic shit. Sit your ass up an..."

The gurgling changed, transforming into words, cutting Paul's internal berating short. "Mween pa pral jije." Water poured from her mouth as she spoke, splashing on the covers and Paul's exposed foot as the words bubbled forth. It felt like ice as it saturated his skin. The smell was that of a corpse that had been left to rot in the swamp. The stench assaulted his senses. It was so potent he could almost feel the odor permeating his flesh. His stomach lurched, threatening to expel the dinner he'd had that night.

"No. No that's not real. Wake up! Just scream, damn it!" His thoughts were so loud they should have been audible. He sucked in a shallow gasp of air that was all his fear-stricken lungs would allow. The figure dug its fingernails into the wood creating a terrible chalkboard sound. Paul prepared to unleash the humiliating scream that begged for release and would free him from this hell.

All thoughts stopped when the ice-cold hand violently shot out and latched onto his ankle. He felt nails push into the flesh of his shin as the grip tightened. He felt bone threatening to crack in the vice-like grip. His vision flashed to white and the world fell away.

Chapter I

"Paul! Ruben and Madie are here I think," his mom announced from the kitchen following the tell-tale pattern knock of Ruben: three rapid knocks followed by two solid slow ones.

Paul spat out the mouthwash and did one last check in the mirror. Ponytail was good, no boogers playing peek-a-boo, acne was in check, deodorant.... check. Feeling confident he was socially acceptable, he exited the bathroom and forced himself to calmly walk to the door.

Paul was a good-looking 16-year-old kid. He had long brown hair with natural red highlights in it. Taller than average at 6'2", the 175 pounds that sat on his frame bordered between a swimmers build and a Jew from a Nazi death camp. Freckles lightly speckled his cheeks. The most noticeable and attractive features were his smile of perfect white teeth thanks to braces and being OCD about hygiene, and his eyes which were the compliment to that movie star smile. They were a deep brown that hid gold flecks in the darkness. His cousin Sam once described them as wet root beer barrel candies. Yes, that was meant to be a compliment.

Despite the admiration that he received from the local girls, he never saw himself as attractive. All he could see was a zit that had blossomed overnight, the way one nostril was oddly shaped compared to the other, or the lack of a muscular build. Confidence in his physical appearance was not something that was familiar to Paul. While he didn't exactly see himself as ugly, he saw his flaws as bigger than any good features he had.

This led him to rely on a quick wit and suppressed emotions, with the exception of his best friend Ruben. He was the only one that Paul felt didn't judge him and would always shoot him straight. Even when it came to the girl that occupied his thoughts and fantasies more frequently than a fat kid at an all you can eat dessert bar, he hid his emotions.

Ruben was only a few months younger than Paul and almost as tall. He had a lean, muscular build and mocha skin. His head was adorned with short braids dyed blonde at the tips. The two had met in the 6th grade and were fast friends from then on. Both shared a love of Dungeons and Dragons, video games, and WWF. They were a match made in heaven.

Paul opened the side door to find both his best friend Ruben and the girl of his dreams - Madie.

"My honkified negro!" Ruben said as he gave Paul their traditional gangster style hug accented by two sharp slaps to the back to ensure the hug didn't mean they were gay or anything. Unspoken teenage man rules.

"What's up my dude!" Paul replied.

"Just picking up my favorite slut." Ruben smiled.He gave Madie a look. She returned a look of warning. "And Madie, too."

Madie chimed in "Do I need to give you two a minute?"

"No! Just about 30 seconds. Paul has that whole premature ejaculation issue," Ruben sighed to Madie.

Her face turned to shock and disgust with a hint of a stifled smile. He shot Ruben a sideways glance.

"So, what you're telling us is, you like to be the catcher and you want me inside you? I knew you wanted me!" Paul gave Ruben a shove as he laughed.

Madie joined in the laughter and pulled Paul into a hug. She smelled so good. He drank it in as they embraced. He wanted to hold her longer. To bury his face in her soft blonde hair. He caught himself lingering and quickly pulled away.

His heart always seemed to beat in his stomach when Madie came around. She was beautiful in a very subtle way. To Paul, her natural beauty was what put her leagues above the other girls. Heavy makeup was always a turn off to him, like a lie. She didn't wear makeup aside from eyeliner and occasionally lip gloss. She had shoulder length dirty blonde hair and sapphire eyes. She was built with the curves of a woman in her twenties.

Relatively new to the area, she had moved to Delisle about a year ago. She, her little sister Jennifer, and her dad had moved to Mississippi from Ohio after her mother and older sister died in a car accident. She never offered details of the accident and none of

8

them ever pushed the issue. She said her dad wanted a fresh start.

After a rough start at her new school, she met Rachel, Rubens half-sister. An outspoken redhead with a smoker's voice, Rachel was popular with the guys in school and had a bit of a reputation for sleeping around. Seeing the shy new girl struggling through each school day, Rachel took her under her wing. Over the next few weeks, she taught Madie the ins and outs of the high school hierarchy and protected her from the douchebag guys that wanted to be the first to bang the fresh meat. In return, Madie taught her about tarot cards and the occult.

Madie had become obsessed with all things occult after the accident, and was always on the search for a way to communicate with her deceased mother and sister in the great beyond. While she'd had no definitive success thus far, once a few candles flickered after a summoning ritual. While these flickers could be easily dismissed by a skeptic, they were more than enough to further fuel the fires and keep her quest alive.

In time Madie met Ruben. He was only a few months older than Rachel, as their dad had a hard time with monogamy. Fortunately for Rachel, she got to grow up with her mother instead of the monster that was their father. Despite growing up separately, Rachel and Ruben bonded during and after their dad's illness and death. Rachel had come to visit their dad in the hospital a few times after the "incident" as her mom referred to it. After that. Ruben even stayed with them for a few weeks until he went to live with his Aunt Kat.

Alas, Ruben's friendship with Paul would be the beginning of the end of Madie and Rachel's friendship. Madie had met Paul while having a sleep over at Rachel's about 6 months ago. Ruben was visiting with Rachel, which really meant he came over to use her Nintendo 64. Paul had come over to defend his title in Mario Kart while waiting for his brother, Adam, to pick him up. At least that's what Ruben told Rachel. He left out the part about insisting Paul come over because the hot new girl was over there-not that Rachel minded. She loved to flirt with Paul when he was around. She thought it was cute how he would blush and get quiet when she did.

Madie and Paul had felt an unexplainable connection at first sight. After some awkward introductions, Ruben started a conversation including the two of them to get them talking. Before long they were in their own world, while Ruben was grinning as he played solo on Mario Kart.

As fate would have it, Adam's trusty steed wasn't so trustworthy that night, and he broke down in Gulfport. Paul was more than happy to spend the night. Rachel, however, spent the evening trying to win Paul's attention only to be ignored by both him and her friend. This was where bitter jealousy first tore into the fabric of Rachel and Madie's friendship.

Neither Paul nor Madie slept that night. Instead, he and Madie sat up talking on a trampoline outside till the sun began to peek over the horizon. The conversation was effortless, and the connection was intense. Had both not suffered from the same low self-esteem that night could have easily turned into one of teenage hormone-fueled passion. Well. a good solid minute of passion, anyway.

As Madie spent more time with the two boys, Rachel became openly jealous about it. After all, she had dragged Madie up from the metaphorical sewers of the school and helped her fit in - kept her safe from assholes that would have used her and broke her heart. Then Madie just up and ditched her for her brother and his cute friend that she had been crushing on for years. As is the case with most teenage friendships, emotions and fragile egos eventually led to harsh words. Mere months after their friendship had begun, Rachel and Madie's friendship crashed and burned.

"So, what's the plan yo?" Ruben inquired still chuckling.

"The same as every day...destruction and mayhem! Taking over the world!" Paul exclaimed, raising his arms in a victorious pose.

"So, the Quarters it is." Ruben responded with a disappointed sag of his shoulders.

Paul shrugged, "Well not quite as exciting, but I suppose that will work."

Paul grabbed his fishing pole and turned back towards the kitchen yelling, "I'm headed out, Mom!"

"Ok, be back before dinner. I'm making tacos," she hollered back.

"Mmmm, tacos" Ruben swooned as he gathered the fishing gear that he always left in Paul's carport.

"Y'all got a cigarette?" Paul said quietly as he held two fingers up in the universal "give me a smoke" symbol.

Madie pulled a red and white soft pack of Marlboros from the back pocket of her jeans and offered them to him.

Paul stared in horror at the severely flattened pack in his hand.

He jokingly chastised her as he held up the offending pack between them. "Damn it girl! I'm going to have to get you a fanny pack."

"Hey, buy your own then asshole!" She snatched the pack away and gave Paul a solid poke to the ribs.

"No! See what I meant to say...what had happened was...I'll give you chocolate and sing praises of your beauty for one of your perfect, unflawed cigarettes," he pleaded in front of her with his hands together in begging pose. He shot a quick look over his shoulder to make sure his mom hadn't heard.

"Hmmmm. I don't know. I'm thinking you aren't deserving." She put the pack behind her back.

"Oh, I'm the most deservingest guy you'll meet. I ooze deserving! What's it gonna take? You need someone dead? I got you. Need some of that sweet Mexican black tar heroin? I'll make it happen. Need someone's dick sucked? Ruben's got you!" He turned a smirk to Ruben.

"Hey, everything has a price," Ruben shrugged. Madie and Paul burst into laughter.

Madie produced the "perfect and unflawed" pack and handed them back to Paul.

"You're lucky you're cute when you beg," she said.

Ruben rolled his eyes. "Would you two just make out already?!"

Madie and Paul blushed simultaneously. "I have a whole bag of shit you can eat good sir," Paul rebutted, turning away from Madie to hide his reddened cheeks.

Paul fished through the pack and was astonished to find that despite it being the thickness of two Quarters stacked up, none of the cigarettes inside were broken. He pulled one out, and after molding the butt into something that resembled the shape it was supposed to be, placed it between his lips and turned back to Madie.

"All I have is a habit. Gotta light?" Paul grinned.

Madie, with a roll of her eyes and one practiced motion whipped out her Zippo, flipped open the lid, and sparked the flame. She brought the flame to the tip of the cigarette, and Paul puffed until there was a glowing red tip. He took a deep drag, letting the nicotine bring a wave of calm over him. He'd been out since lunchtime the day before and the nicotine fits we're giving him...well, fits.

"You, my dear, are a lifesaver," Paul said as he placed his hand over his heart and gave Madie a dramatic bow. Concluding his bow with a flourish, Paul declared, "Onward my people!" He motioned like a general leading his troops into battle, ending with a finger pointed towards Delisle cemetery.

"You so stupid," Ruben laughed, shaking his head.

"And you love me for it," Paul replied as he stepped out of the shade of the carport into the burning Mississippi sun.

The thermometer hanging under the carport read 93 degrees. Out of the shade, the temperature was at least ten degrees higher. When you added the humidity of the surrounding Bayou, it was like a sauna built in the depths of hell. For anyone not accustomed to the sub-tropical heat, summer was the time to stay indoors until the sun was low in the sky. For the residents of the area, it was just another day. Sweating was one of the traditional past-times for the locals. For Ruben and Paul, the heat was only a minor discomfort. Ruben was a lifelong resident of the area. After about three summers in the environment, Paul had become acclimated as well. Madie, however, came from the mild summers and frozen winters of the north and hadn't quite built up the same fortitude. The humidity was inescapable and only amplified by the rays of the sun.

"Dear God! I am literally dying," Madie whined.

One hand shielded her eyes from the harsh glare of the sun while the other hand grabbed the bottom of her crop top and rapidly shook it in and out to create a breeze. Sweat beaded down her abdomen, creating a seductive sheen on her skin. Every few shakes exposed a hint of the lacy pale blue bra she wore beneath it. Paul took notice and quickly looked away.

14

Occasionally temptation got the best of him, though, and he dared another glance from the corner of his eye.

The trio headed out across the yard to the one lane packed concrete street called Hand Road. At the corner of Paul's yard, Hand Road intersected with Notre Dame Avenue, another one lane road. From that corner if you looked left you would see the main strip, a two-lane blacktop road named Kiln Rd., about a half mile down. Today, they left the yard and headed down Notre Dame Avenue.

This was a familiar trek to the Delisle cemetery, the official hang out of the Rat Pack. The nickname Rat Pack had been unintentionally given to Paul's group of friends by his grandfather.

"Where are you and the rat pack off to today?" was the simple question asked one fateful day. For reasons unknown the name stuck.

Delisle is a small town with one gas station and no traffic lights hidden on the Mississippi coast. The landscape was decorated with bayous and centuries old oak trees adorned with spanish moss hanging sorrowfully from the branches. In the daylight, those giant trees gave a beautiful southern charm to the scenery. In the evening, they had the ambiance of a classic horror movie.

If you were an adult, there were two options for entertainment. Karl's, a convenience store on the main road, hid a small bar in the back. It featured one old unleveled pool table and a jukebox filled with all the hits. Sure, they were hits from ten years ago, but they were hits nonetheless. Paul and his friends frequently utilized the pool table.

Karl's was owned by an elderly couple, Karl and Evelyn Hern, who would allow the Pack to play during the daytime hours. The other option was the Dock, a bar set cozily on the water's edge where the Wolf river flowed into the bayou. A giant oak sat behind it gently draping Spanish moss along the roof, giving it a postcard quality.

The postcard would have read something like "Come to Delisle! Ain't much to do, but the beer's cold."

The patrons at the Dock were generally age 60 and older, most of them veterans. Paul's grandpa, Mitch, was a well-known regular. His name was Donald, but everyone knew him as Mitch from his military days.

He brought Adam and Paul in occasionally when they were little, much to their mom's dismay. The grizzled old vets always brightened when the two young boys tagged along. Something about the horrors of war made the innocence of small children that much more beautiful.

The boys would sip root beer out of chilled mugs and listened to grandpa and his pals talk about politics or share war stories. Paul and Adam would both come to cherish these memories of their grandfather when they grew up.

As for the youth, options were far more limited. As in; you had better have a friend with a car, have your own boat, or have a good imagination.

Paul had a license, but his dad would never let him use his car unless it was a store run. Adam had ruined Paul's open access to a car by getting caught drag racing in his dad's cherished '62 Buick Lesabre. He was supposed to just be going to the river.

Luckily for Paul, his brother had his own vehicle now -an old beat up Isuzu Pup that was held together by Bondo, rust, and a prayer. The stereo system was top of the line, however, and cost more than the truck with a full tank of gas.

When Adam wasn't out of town working, he generally would take Paul and his friends wherever they wanted to go. Usually they went to the Wolf River in the Kiln to go swimming or to Boone's, their favorite spot to hustle at the pool tables. Adam enjoyed the feeling of being idolized by the younger crowd, so he welcomed their company. Plus, he still felt guilty for all the time missed with his little brother and the bond that was lost during his "dark period," as he referred to it.

Today though, the Rat Pack was without transportation, as Adam was working in Houma, Louisiana.

"When's Adam going to be back? Summer is wasting away," Ruben asked.

"He'll be back this weekend. I'm working on Mom to let me take the car up to Boones tomorrow while dad's working. He's on night shifts, so hopefully I can butter her up and put on the puppy dog eyes. Definitely need some

17

fun! Two weeks of summer have been wasted already," Paul said.

Ruben held up both hands and crossed his fingers. "Dear God, I hope so. I love you guys, but the Quarters and fishing every day is getting old. "

"I second that," Maddie said.

The Pack hiked down the old road, crunching gravel under their feet. Madie was thankful for the long arms of oaks reaching over to offer occasional breaks from the rays of the sun as they walked.

A late model brown Cadillac approached from behind. As it passed, Paul looked at the old withered figure behind the steering wheel. He sat hunched over with dark aviator shades on and blue coveralls, the popular garb of local World War II vets since they were comfortable yet left them ready to work on any mechanical issues that might pop up. Mr. Goodrich, a regular at The Dock, was normally a chipper guy. Paul hadn't seen him much since the funeral. Paul gave him a wave and a nod. He didn't wave back. He didn't even seem to be aware of Paul and his friends.

The skin around his face seemed more like a pale white cloth draped loosely over his skull. Normally he sat and stood very erect, like a soldier awaiting inspection. Today he slouched behind the wheel.

'Lifeless' was the word that kept echoing in Paul's head. Like he was dead, but his body was going through the motions. He looked much older than his 78 years.

An ominous aura filled the air as the car passed. The Cadillac continued on its path in the same direction they were headed. The same place Paul and Adam found Mrs. Goodrich almost a year ago. Paul made a pointed effort to not think about that day. Despite his efforts, the memories came flooding in.

It had been just another day of killing time. Adam joined Paul at the cemetery that Saturday because he was out of gas and his check didn't make it to the bank in time. He didn't really spend much time there with Paul anymore since he got into partying.

Paul didn't approve of the recent drug use Adam had taken up. Adam assured him it was just a social thing and nothing to worry about. Paul had noticed the change in him since he started, though. He got angry so fast- seemed disconnected from all the people he used to be close to.

Paul rarely saw him anymore and cherished moments like these when it felt like before - like his old brother that loved deep conversations about the universe, religion, and comic books. The only time he got to see that side of him now was when Adam was out of money.

Once his check cleared he wouldn't see Adam for the rest of the week, if not longer. After the money was gone and the partying was over, he would come home and sleep for twenty-four hours before going back to Houma to work on the barges. Today, however, belonged to Paul, and he was going to make the most of it.

They had spent the day fishing off of the bank behind the cemetery wood line and had just come back to the Quarters. Paul laid on a long limb of Louis, the giant oak that inhabited the Quarters. Adam named it that because he said it looked like a hanging tree and he thought it was fitting to name it after Louis Congo, the freed slave turned executioner. Paul was puffing a cigarette and watching the Spanish moss dance in the wind. Adam was occupied throwing his boot knife into an adjacent tree. He'd had the knife for the last six years and had gotten pretty good at throwing it.

In the distance, Mrs. Goodrich's Lincoln came into view, rounding the turn from the new area of the cemetery. She then continued to turn down the path to the Quarters. This struck the boys as odd. Nobody ever came to visit this area other than grounds keepers and the occasional sheriff's deputy. No one had been buried there since the slave days. Yet, here she came. She turned right after entering the Quarters and drove out of sight just beyond the overgrown area that was home to the oldest of graves. They heard the car being put in park and the engine turned off.

The boys liked Mrs. Goodrich, despite the toothbrushes she gave out on Halloween when they were younger, but it made them uncomfortable having someone outside of their clique invading their sacred hangout.

"What is she doing back here?" Paul asked his brother.

"No clue, dude," He responded.

They heard a car door open and shut, followed by twigs and leaves crunching as she walked away. The two sat in silence; each with one ear cocked to the side trying to hear if she was coming back their direction.

After a few moments, the boys looked at each other in unison and shrugged. Paul opened his mouth getting ready to suggest they head back home, since their sanctuary had been invaded. Before the words left his mouth, the silence was broken. A short, rage-filled scream pierced the air. After a few seconds it was followed by sobs and unintelligible words.

Paul and Adam once again looked at each other, waiting for something to happen, for something to dictate their next actions. If Mrs. Goodrich was in trouble, the boys would not hesitate to rush through the thicket and help. They did not want to act too hastily, though.

Adam motioned for Paul follow him and placed a finger to his lips. Adam carefully chose his steps as he headed in Mrs. Goodrich's direction; Paul mimicked him a few steps behind. After a few minutes of their best stealthy ninja impersonation, they reached a vantage point where they could see the car and Mrs. Goodrich a few yards ahead. To their horror, she was standing next to her discarded clothing with all her 73-year-old naked glory on display. She looked much older than her age. Pale skin hung from her bones. Every rib and vertebra was visible. Bruises and liver spots dotted her flesh. Her shoulders were slumped, and her posture was slouched as if she were exhausted. Her knees were slightly buckled, and her head listed to one side.

"What the fuck!?" Adam whispered.

Paul was silent as his mouth sat agape. To see her in this state was too disturbing.

"Please....don't," Mrs. Goodrich croaked. A round of sobs shook her shoulders.

"Stop....please stop. Stop stop stop stop STOOOOOOOOOOOOOP!" She slammed her hands to her ears as if trying to block out a voice, but the boys heard nothing aside from her.

Paul looked to Adam and whispered, "This isn't OK man. Should we go tell someone?"

"Yeah, go get dad. He will know how to deal with this. I'll stay here and keep an eye on her. Make sure she doesn't try to drive off," Adam replied.

Paul nodded and gave a look back to the old woman. "Damn, better you than me," Paul said as a shiver of revulsion ran through him.

Her hands fell back to her sides and she let a long, defeated sigh. She turned her attention to the tree beside her.

"Ok," she whispered, her voice choked with sobs.

Paul prepared to turn and run to get help. Mrs. Goodrich reached her hand to the side of the tree, out of their line of sight. It came back holding a pump action shotgun. She turned to face the tree and dropped to her knees. Adam stood from his crouched position as the old woman brought the barrel of the gun to rest under her chin. Her trembling hand slowly moved towards the trigger.

"MRS. GOODRICH STOP!!" Adam shouted.

She gasped and jerked her hand away from the trigger. Her eyes found Adam and her expression calmed.

As if the whole situation wasn't creepy enough, she smiled and said, "Oh, hello there, dear."

Her demeanor suddenly pleasant and frighteningly happy. Like she wasn't buck naked with a gun under her chin - as if Adam had just happened along while she was in her yard gardening.

"Mrs. Goodrich...are... are you ok?" Adam asked in the calmest voice he could muster.

"Everything's fine, darlin'. It's going to be just fine." Her eyes shimmered with tears, but her pleasant expression never changed.

Paul stood up next to Adam. Mrs. Goodrich saw him and fear painted her face. She looked back to Adam.

"GET HIM OUT OF HERE! YOU HAVE TO GET HIM OUT OF HERE!" She snapped her head back towards the direction of her one-sided conversation and then quickly back to the boys.

"She saw you." Her voice barely a whisper.

She locked eyes with Paul. "Run!" she commanded, frantically moving her hand back to the trigger.

Her chin quivered, and tears streamed from her puffy eyes, filling the deep lines in her face. Her eyes didn't leave his until the moment the explosion of the shotgun broke the trance. Paul reflexively closed his eyes and flinched. When he opened his eyes again, a cloud of smoke, red mist, and shredded flesh were all that remained.

The world fell silent as both boys stood there frozen in time. Her body stayed in a

23

kneeling position for a few moments- an occasional red geyser erupted from the mass of destroyed flesh and bone that now resided on her neck. Finally, the eternity ended, and her body fell to the ground.

"Shit! What the fuck! Adam! She fucking… holy shit! What the fuck do we… " Paul's stomach interrupted his sentence as vomit shot from his mouth.

After several heaves and burps, Paul stood upright again. For a moment he thought he saw a woman in the distance through the cloud of tears in his eyes. He wiped the tears away and looked again to find nothing more than headstones and the gruesome scene of Mrs. Goodrich's suicide.

Adam took a few steps closer to Mrs. Goodrich's corpse and back peddled to Paul's side. He grabbed Paul's arm and gave him a push towards the path leading out of the Quarters.

"Go! Fucking go! Let's go!" he barked at Paul.

Paul needed no further encouragement. The air felt thick and toxic. The trees seemed to be creeping closer. If he could just get out of here, he could catch his breath. Maybe he would even wake up in his bed. A nightmare. That made sense. These kinds of things didn't happen in Delisle. They especially didn't happen to a nobody like him. They happened to actors in movies, not in real life. Yes, surely if he ran out of here he would awake to find himself at home.

He turned and pushed off in a mad dash for home. Despite Adam's longer frame, Paul was a much faster runner, which was why Adam originally tried to send him to get their dad.

The boys made record time getting to their house. Both felt as though their lungs were on fire, and legs were made of rubber. They breathlessly told their dad what had happened. He pulled his police radio off the charger and called it in. Throwing on his utility belt, he instructed the boys to stay there and took off.

The remainder of the day was a blur for them that consisted of giving statements, cops moving in and out of the house, mom making finger foods and drinks for everyone and Father Mariotti attempting to counsel the boys.

"Catch up, slow ass!" Ruben's statement snapped Paul back to the present. Paul's stride had slowed as that day had played in his mind. Ruben and Madie were turned facing him about 30 feet ahead. Paul got his bearings quickly, trying to come up with a witty come back.

"Well wash your nasty ass more than once a year and I'll be able to walk near you!" He put the memory back into its locker, at the bottom of the ocean of his mind.

"Oh, he got jokes." Ruben shot him a quick middle finger.

Paul did a light jog to catch up with his friends and they continued their journey. The conversation flowed as they walked. Trivial conversation about school and life in general. 15 minutes later, they arrived at the entrance of the cemetery. A wave of anxiety came over Paul as they entered. He scanned the area looking for Mr. Goodrich's car. Nowhere to be found in the main cemetery. The Quarters couldn't be seen from here.

"Please don't be back there," Paul silently mouthed to himself.

He never saw the car come back out and there was no other way to go but the way they had just come, unless he cut down Father Sorin lane. It was an old road that the county had long forgotten. Pot-holes riddled the pavement. The road itself was barely as wide as a driveway and few people took it. His stomach tightened. The door to that locker in his mind creaked slightly and he stopped his stride.

"Mr. Goodrich never came back out, did he?" Paul asked.

Ruben looked to Madie and back to Paul. He shrugged and shook his head, "No, I don't think so."

"No, I never saw him come back through," Madie added.

"Shit" Paul exhaled.

"You don't think he… " Ruben asked stepping up next to Paul. He put a hand up to shield his eyes from the sun as he took his turn scanning the cemetery.

"I don't see his car anywhere out here, only one place he could have gone. Fuck." Paul responded.

Madie stepped up behind Paul and grabbed his arm. "Was that the guy whose wife killed herself back here that passed us?"

"Yeah," Paul's tone had an edge.

"Why would he want to go back there, where it happened?" she asked.

"I don't know but that's pretty damned creepy. He probably just came out and hit Sorin," Ruben responded.

"Yeah… maybe. Did yall see the way he looked when he passed by?" Paul's eyes stayed fixed on the wood line that hid the Quarters.

"What do you mean?" Ruben asked.

"I don't know. He just looked… I don't know… dead...Like a zombie driving a car." He turned to Ruben. "Something's off, man. I have a bad feeling."

He had grown to trust Paul's "feelings" as they had proven to almost always be correct. It was like he had a Spidey-sense that would start tingling when things were about to go bad. Like the time his cousin, Jason, talked him into going to a bonfire. Paul didn't know anyone there except Jason, Ruben, and Adam. All night his gut was shooting him bad vibes about an extremely drunk white thug wannabe. Before the night was over, the kid had tried to pull a gun on Jason after a heated debate over Jason accidentally bumping into him. It ended with Paul cracking the kid in the back of the head with a burning log he pulled from the fire. The thugs four friends had surrounded Paul, ready to pounce. Their plans had quickly changed after Adam dropped the largest one into the edge of the fire with a blistering slap to the ear.

Ruben could see the dread Paul was trying to hide. He knew the toll it took on Paul witnessing Mrs. Goodrich's suicide. He had looked ragged for weeks after that. He barely slept because his night terrors had become so regular. As thin as he already was, he had managed to lose a frightening amount of weight. He would do whatever it took to protect his best friend from going through that again. If Paul had a bad feeling, then Ruben wasn't going to question it.

"Hey Paul. Let's just go fish off the bridge. If he's back there, he would probably rather be alone," Ruben said with one hand on Paul's shoulder.

He turned it into a respect issue to keep Paul from feeling like he had to prove something by continuing.

Paul looked to Ruben. "Yeah. Yeah, I suppose you're right."

Paul offered one last glance in the direction of the Quarters then turned back the way they had come. He couldn't stop picturing the old man back there, wrapping a rope around his neck or putting a gun to his head. A few steps into their long walk, the sound of an engine faded in from the distance. Paul stopped and turned back to the cemetery. The sound of crunching gravel joined in as the hum of the engine grew louder. A few moments later, the brown Cadillac came into view as it rounded the turn coming out of the Quarters.

Paul let out a sigh of relief as he watched the car approach. As Mr. Goodrich came close Paul could see he had the same zombified look to him. The long car slowed as it approached the trio standing on the side of the road. Paul's blood ran cold when the vehicle came to a stop next to them. The automatic driver's window came down and Mr. Goodrich turned to look first at Ruben. His face offered no emotion to read.

He nodded his head to Ruben in a greeting fashion. "Ruben."

Ruben offered a polite nod back and a smile. "Mr. Goodrich. How are you sir?"

"Everything's fine," he answered.

Everything's fine. The words rattled Paul. He heard the echo of the man's departed wife as she had made the same statement moments before turning her head into a jigsaw puzzle.

The old man then looked to Madie. "Madeleine, is our little town still treating you well?" he asked.

"Yeah… uh, yes, sir." She still wasn't accustomed to the southern culture and the religious use of sir and ma'am when talking to an elder. "Everyone has been great. Uh, it's starting to feel like home."

He cracked his undead facade with a smile, "Oh, that's good to hear darlin'. Pretty girl like you, I knew you'd have no trouble fitting in."

His attention then went to Paul, and his smile faded. He stared at Paul for a long moment.

"Are you… how are you, son?" his expression turning sincere.

"I'm fine, sir," Paul answered.

"I just want you to know, I'm truly sorry for what my wife put you through." His face soured when he said "wife."

The statement caught Paul off guard. He stood in stunned silence for a moment before attempting a clumsy response.

"No sir. It's not… I mean… I should be apologizing to you."

"Nonsense boy!" His response was sharp. "You have nothing to be sorry for."

He suddenly appeared to become distracted by something and looked back to the passenger seat of the car. After a moment he looked back to Paul. His expression had gone dead again.

"She saw you…" With those last words, Mr. Goodrich pressed the gas and resumed his drive.

"Ok, that was awkward," Madie broke the silence.

Ruben stepped beside Paul. "Yeah Paul, something's definitely off with him, man. What did he mean 'She saw you'?"

"No idea, man," Paul lied. Despite the pounding heat of the sun, Paul felt a shiver run through him. He watched the tail lights until they disappeared. Just then, he realized his stomach muscles were constricted so tight that they were on the verge of cramping or making him shit his pants. He took in a slow deep breath and allowed them to relax.

"Well, enough of that shit. Can I bum another smoke, Madie?" Paul said.

Madie pulled the flattened pack from her back pocket and handed it to Paul. He didn't bother straightening the butt on this one, slipping it between his teeth. Madie lit the tip as Paul momentarily got lost staring into her deep blue eyes. The snapping shut of the zippo brought him back.

He looked towards Ruben who was wiping the crumbs of the dip he just put in away from his lips. His eyes were studying Paul's face, trying to read if he was ok. Paul was good at hiding his emotions, but his one tell gave him away. The muscles in his jaw clenched and released over and over. It was an unconscious gesture that Paul had not been able to overcome when his mind was heavy with worry, anger, or fear.

At the moment he was struggling with the latter. Images of that day kept popping in his head with the intensity of a camera flash.

"You good, Paul?" Ruben asked.

"Yeah…just fucks with my head sometimes. I'm fine, bro." He shot Ruben a reassuring smile. "Summer is a-wasting, guys!"

Chapter 2

The three continued on their way to the bridge. Paul forced the memories back into their prison and returned his focus back to more important matters. Like staring at Madie when she wasn't looking and making crude jokes with his best friend. After 30 minutes of walking, they finally arrived. It was one of three bridges in the town. Each bridge sat on one of the only three ways in or out of town. The Wolf River separated Delisle from the Kiln to the north, and Long Beach to the east. Kiln Road Bridge crossed it to the north, and Cuevas Road bridge crossed to the east. Whitman Way Bridge, the crew's secondary hangout, crossed south into downtown Pass Christian. This is where they would retreat to when the Quarters were unavailable due to a funeral in the new section.

Paul and Adam had initially been drawn to the bridge because of its history. Grandpa Mitch had told them that it was the oldest bridge still standing in the area.

The three of them were drenched in sweat by the time they came to their destination. They descended the embankment and took shelter from the sun under the cover of the bridge. Madie knelt at the edge of the bayou. Cupping her hands, she gathered the brackish water, splashing it on her face and neck. Droplets of it trailed down her chest and vanished in the cleavage exposed by her shirt as she leaned over to the bank. The water was a refreshing sensation, even at 85 degrees. She let out a moan of ecstasy and went in for another. The two boys stared at the display approvingly.

"Oh my GOD! This heat!" Madie exclaimed as she wet the back of her neck.

Paul pulled his eyes away and chuckled. "You get used to it eventually. Just takes a few heat strokes and a virgin sacrifice to Satan."

"Well Paul you had better watch out before you end up a sacrifice," Ruben said.

"I know right? I'm just glad banging all those dudes has kept you safe," Paul said.

"You guys need Jesus," Madie said shaking her head.

The boys looked at each other and shrugged.

"You may have a point," Paul answered.

Ruben tossed out his dip and began setting up the fishing poles.

"I still don't know how you stomach that nasty shit. Why dip if you smoke too?" Paul asked Ruben.

"I like variety, man. Plus, if I'm gonna get cancer, I'm gonna do it right. Aunt Kat didn't raise no half-ass bitch." Ruben puffed up jokingly.

Paul laughed and shook his head. "No, she raised a dumbass."

"No, that part just comes natural." Ruben smiled as he finished a fisherman's knot.

Paul turned his attention to where bridge's underside met with the ground. He read the red spray-painted tags.

The Rat Pack
Ogre
Paul
Ruben
Sammy
Coon Ass

Paul and his brother were the first to tag the bridge. Adam (aka Ogre) snagged a red can of spray paint from their dad's work shed as they snuck out one night about three years ago and the tradition was born. Anyone that became part of the Pack was immortalized in red paint under the bridge. Rubens name went up the same day. Paul's cousin, Sam, was a week after. The Coon Ass was Adam's Cajun friend that used to hang out with them regularly, until the day he was found hanging from a tree behind his house. Adam said it was over some girl leaving him. He had seemed pissed instead of sad when he found out. Said suicide is for little bitches that don't have the balls to deal with life. That same day Adam came to the bridge and painted a line through his name.

Paul walked a few steps up an incline of large rocks and moved a dry rotted piece of canvas. He snatched up the slightly rusted can with a faded label on it. His eyes moved up to the graffiti then to Ruben. Ruben was just finishing a second fisherman's knot and looked up to Paul. Paul held up the can and motioned his head towards Madie. Ruben looked at her and realized what he was suggesting. He nodded at Paul with a smile. Paul nodded back, and the decision was made. He turned to Madie. She was looking through the tackle box. He put the can behind his back.

"Madie," he said.

"Yeah?" she answered, looking up to him.

"So, you've been hanging with us for a while now."

A confused smile came over her face "Ok…"

"I was just thinking that it's time to take this to the next level."

"Ummmm… wait. What?" She looked to Ruben for answers. He just smiled at her.

"Madie… " Paul dropped to one knee and brought the can out and held it towards her like a man proposing. "Will you tag the bridge and be one of us?"

She laughed. "Paul Allen, you are such a dork. I would be honored."

She took the can from Paul and walked up to the graffitied wall.

She stared for a moment, considering what to leave as her mark. Madeleine was out of the question. She didn't like anyone to call her by her full name. It reminded her of her father when he would get excessively drunk. He took Lithium as well, which was prescribed to him for his mental issues. The two made a horrible combination and turned her already cruel father into a monster. He was never a kind man, even before the accident. After losing his wife and daughter, any remnants of kindness that were in him vanished. She never told anyone about her home life, or her father.

Madie would take her sister and stay gone during the times her dad went on a binge. Usually taking refuge at Rachel's. He never noticed or remembered. When Rachel's stopped being an option, she would stay at Sam's. She was grateful to have made the friends she had here. Back home everyone knew who her dad was and would have nothing to do with her. When they moved to Mississippi, she decided that she would separate herself from her father as much as possible, taking on as many responsibilities as she could. She paid the bills, signed herself and Jennifer up for school, and even did the grocery shopping when she could get a ride to the store from a friend. This all allowed her dad to leave the house as little as possible. Thus, exposing as little of him as possible to the outside world. Yet as much as she hated the man, she still loved him for the man he was before. She knew it was foolish to hope that he would go back to the old him one day, but she held onto that hope. While he may not have been the best man before, it sure beat the hell out of who he was now. She shook the can a few times and nodded to herself. After a few swift motions, her mark was left.

MaJiK

Paul cocked his head to the side, confused.

"MaJiK?" he asked.
"Yep." she replied. "Madeleine June Kane," she said pointing to the M, J, and K in the name. "And, I'm pretty magical," she said as she turned back to Paul with a smile.
"Well there ya go. It's perfect," Paul said returning the smile.

The remainder of the day was spent catching croakers and the occasional eel. Once the sun dropped to a sliver on the horizon, they all went back to Paul's house for dinner. His mom always made enough to feed the neighborhood kids; just in case. Ruben and Madie left around 11, after a 3-2 victory by Ruben in Madden. After seeing them off, Paul grabbed one of the cinnamon rolls his mom had made for dessert and went to his room.

With a mouth full of pastry, he plopped down on his bed, and lay back to stare at the ceiling. His meeting with Mr. Goodrich played through his mind. The dead eyes behind the windshield bore into him. A phantom gunshot blast in Paul's head as Mr. Goodrich's imagined eyes rolled back in their sockets. He shot up to sit on his bed and shook his head.

Paul let out a stiff huff of air in irritation. Forcing the memory from his mind, he scanned his room. Desperate for a distraction, he evaluated multiple sketches he had drawn that were tacked to his wood paneled walls. He intentionally focused on the drawings of Wolverine and the medieval scenes of knights battling fantastical dragons and beholders. He studied them, criticizing shaky lines and botched shading. His eyes kept begging to drift to the other drawings that cluttered the dark corner of the room. The idea of looking at them filled him with a cloud of misery. Gooseflesh popped up on his arms. The dark figures that filled the pages would haunt him tonight; he could feel it in every fiber of his being.

"No... no. Fuck off," he ordered.

He continued back and forth through the drawings without seeing them. He could resist no longer; his eyes crept over to the corner. The charcoal sketch was a point of view image from one of his night terrors. He was laying on his back looking down towards his feet, which were hanging out from under the blanket. Moonlight was shining brightly through the bedroom window. Two shadow figures stood on the side of the bed, their unseen eyes staring through the page into his. A shiver shot up his spine and he pulled his eyes away to the thin green carpeting of his floor.

"Quit being a bitch," he mumbled to himself.

He would draw things he could remember from his nightmares. He felt it somehow gave him power over them. Hours would be lost in the pages as he drew. Most of them wound up crumpled in the waste basket next to his desk, but the ones he deemed worthy of keeping; those hung on his walls as a way of making himself face them. Before Mrs. Goodrich, the terrors had become less regular and much less intense. No new nightmare drawings had been hung in at least a year until that day. The anxiety caused by staring at them had all but disappeared. Since watching her blow her head into gorish confetti, however; they brought back all the fear and dread that he felt before. The newest drawing was of Mrs. Goodrich's tear covered face smiling with a shotgun barrel under her chin. Still, he refused to take them down. Something inside of him wouldn't let the dreams have that victory. Not here in the real world.

He forced his eyes back up to face his demons again. He would not let them win. He would not allow them to turn him into everything he despised about himself again. Not tonight. This time, he looked at the sketch of the female figure standing in the corner, beside his dresser. Paul glared at the drawing. He stood from the bed, walked to the offending wall, and put his face inches from the page. Fear shook his abdomen slightly, and he took in a slow, calming breath.

"Fuck you," he said sternly. Then he raised a middle finger and pressed it into the paper. His knuckles ground into it until they hurt.

"Fuck you. Fuck. You." He went through each drawing on the wall and presented it with the same salute and statement.

His eyes went back to the now smudged sketch of the female figure.

"She saw you," Mr. Goodrich's words replayed in his head.

Paul stepped back from the wall and felt a cold breath against the back of his neck. He froze. His eyes began to burn, and tears pooled in their corners as fear gripped him. An inaudible whisper came from behind him. His whole body began to tremble. His lungs constricted as he tried to gasp. A cold hand gently came to rest on his shoulder, followed by a gurgling moan. Paul shot up from his bed with a scream caught in his throat. Relief, and irritation, came over him and he pushed the scream back down.

"God damn it!" he whispered.

Another night terror. The torture of these regular horrors waking him were becoming too much. A touch of hatred for Mrs. Goodrich trickled into his heart. Everything was going so well. He had been relatively happy for the longest period he could remember. Then the old woman went and shot herself. That same night, he'd had the worst one ever. There were no memories of what had happened, only what he felt. There was so much pain. The fear that he'd felt that night was something that he couldn't imagine possible. The terrors were almost every night now it seemed. There were very few reprieves from waking up to terrifying images around his bed, and it was driving him mad.

He got up and walked to the kitchen. Grabbing the ashtray off the windowsill above the sink, he sifted through the butts until he found one his dad had put out halfway through. After lighting it on the blue flame from the gas stove, he went back to his room and opened the window. He checked the clock as he took a pull from the cigarette. 2:22 AM.

"Make a wish," he said to no one.

His wish was always either for Madie to fall in love with him or for the terrors to stop. Once or twice it was to be dead. Not to die...just be dead. Done with this life.

A few more drags and he tossed the butt out of the window. His nerves were firing overtime. Sleep wouldn't be finding him for a while, though. Surrendering, he went to the living room and clicked on the TV. Flipping through channels he settled on a rerun of

Beavis and Butthead. After a few episodes, his eyes grew too heavy to stay open.

Paul groggily rubbed his eyes and got up from the couch. After a short stumble through the living room and down the hall, he found his bedroom. He flicked the light on and sat on the edge of his bed with a big stretch and yawn. As the yawn came to an end, he opened his eyes to find himself staring at the sketch of the woman in the corner. Smudges streaked the page. Four knuckle sized dents rested across the middle of the page. An icy chill raced up his spine. The hairs on his neck and arms stood at attention. He lifted a hand to his shoulder. The skin was tender like a healing sunburn.

"What the hell?" he said.

He half sprinted to the bathroom. Once there, he pulled his shirt off and turned to get an angle to see his shoulder. There...Barely visible. Four pink welts. Like fingers that had been hot enough to burn his skin.

"No. Bullshit!" The last word came out much louder than he intended.

He heard movement from his parent's room next door. Quickly he threw his shirt back on just as the knob on their door turned. His mom stepped out in her pastel blue robe, her red hair a tangled mess of sleep.

"What's wrong, honey?" she asked, concern in her puffy eyes.

"I...nothing. I stubbed my toe on the shelf," he said, motioning to the metal shelf that housed the towels.

She let out a relieved sigh, "Oh, ok. Watch your mouth and go back to bed. Love you."

He blushed as a guilty smile came across his face. "Sorry, Momma. Love you too."

His mom gave him a quick kiss on the cheek and retired back to her bedroom. Paul turned back to the mirror and stared at his reflection, as he rubbed the tender skin on his shoulder. He fired up his logical brain and began the process of debunking how he wound up with these marks.

"Did a ghost really decide to get fresh with me before scalding me with its frozen fingers? No. Yet…" He paused his internal dialogue to pull the collar of his shirt and expose the welts. "Here they are. So, since we know ghosts most likely aren't real, that leaves...." He brought his fingers up and matched them to the marks.

"And there you have it. Flailing around like a scared little girl, you scratched yourself mid night terror. And the knuckle prints on the drawing? Sleepwalking? Maybe." Unconvincingly convincing himself that he had solved this mystery, he gave his reflection an approving nod.

"And I would have gotten away with it too, if it weren't for you meddling kids," he gave his best Scooby-doo villain impersonation to the mirror.

With his faith somewhat restored that supernatural forces were not trying to take his sanity before killing him, his anxiety dropped down to normal levels. He reinforced the lock on the cell in his mind, where all the horrible monsters and evils were imprisoned. He studied

42

the welts one last time before going back to his room. Climbing into the bed, he still debated internally about what had really happened. Lack of sleep didn't allow for the dialogue to continue very long. After a few minutes, exhaustion kicked in, and Paul was fast asleep.

Chapter 3

Paul knew he was dreaming. He saw himself standing in a spotlight that shone down from nowhere. There was nothing but darkness outside of the beam. He looked exhausted. Hair, greasy and unkempt, posture slouched, knees slightly buckled, and worst of all, he was naked. His shoulders shook occasionally with a sob. Inaudible whispers escaped his lips as he stared into the darkness. Paul began to approach his dream self. The naked version of him didn't notice as he continued his hushed conversation.

As Paul drew closer to himself, his foot caught on something and sent him sprawling to the black floor. He braced for the jolt of impact and was surprised to collide with nothing. His equilibrium was thrown off as he found himself standing again. After the world stilled once more he looked back to see what he had tripped on. A woman's hand was latched onto his pant leg. Tracing the arm down he found the face of his mother pleading to him. Blood trickled from her red hair, down her forehead, tracing the lines of her face.

"Paul please don't!" she screamed.

A sickening sound of bone crunching under skin accompanied a dent forming in the side of her skull just above her temple.

"Mom!" he cried out.

Her body rapidly decayed decades worth in a matter of seconds.

"NOOO! MOM!! MOM!!" Paul had lost the thread of realization that he was in a dream. It was all too real now.

Wheeling around he came face to face with the disheveled version of himself. There was madness in his eyes. Blood spattered his face, and he clutched a pole like a wrought iron fence rod. The dream Paul flinched, as a bony hand reached from the blackness and grabbed his shoulder. The madness in his eyes turned to pure horror. His chin began to quiver. Violently, he was snatched into the blackness by the hand.

"Mine!" an inhuman voice roared.

Paul reflexively threw his hands up to cover his ears from the blood chilling sound. He welded his eyes shut in fear that whatever those words belonged to would show itself. He didn't want to see it. It would be more than his mind could bear.

Electric chills of fear rippled through his body. His entire being trembled as he urinated on himself. The warm wetness pooled up his side and abdomen. He could hear the cartilage of his ears crack under the pressure he was applying with his hands. Somewhere in his mind, pain and the feel of the warm urine registered, but it was not acknowledged by the rest of his brain. Fear and the flight instinct were the only things Paul was conscious of. Bile burned in the back of his throat. He could not stay like this. He had to run, yet his body felt frozen and encased in ice that held him down. The notion came to him that at some point

he had fallen to the floor in the fetal
position. The floor was soft. Paul became more
aware of the warm wetness that soaked him. His
mind began to acknowledge the smell of piss.
There was also the smell of sweat. Paul rallied
the courage to move. He pulled his hands from
his ears. The release of pressure made his ears
throb like unclamping a clothespin off a
fingernail. Daring to open his eyes to small
slits, he saw light and the fuzzy outlines of
shapes. They were not human shapes. After a few
moments of them not moving, he opened his eyes
enough to make the shapes out: a dresser, a
flat black writing desk, wood paneled walls,
and an old brown wooden door. He was in his
room. Relief flooded him. Swinging his legs off
of the bed, he sat up. The wetness of his
boxers and mattress turned his relief to
humiliation.

     "Goddamn it…" his voice was weak and
trembling.
     In this moment Paul realized just how
little control and power he had - even over
his own mind and body. Whoever had control was
a sadist hell bent on driving him mad. His eyes
drifted to the rifle hanging over his bed. He
worked his jaw as he considered the gun. He
reached out and pulled the rifle down. With a
slow motion, he worked the lever to open the
chamber slightly. The brass of the 7.62 round
glinted in the light from the ceiling fixture.
     "It wouldn't even hurt," he reassured
himself as he rested the barrel under his chin.
"Just a quick squeeze and no more of this
shit."

His thoughts went to his mom. The scene played out in his head of her rushing in after the shot. There she would find her son. A large exit wound in the top of his skull. Brain matter covering the wall. She would scream. Fall to her knees. That one short, selfish moment would hurt her for the rest of her years. His mom was the kindest soul he had ever known. Then there was Adam. He would hate him for the rest of his life. Adam's thoughts on suicide were very blunt. Pussies kill themselves and make everyone else suffer for their weakness.

With force, Paul quickly worked the lever over and over, ejecting the bullets until none remained. He laid the gun on the bed and stared at the discarded rounds on his lap.

Sobs overtook him. Deep painful sobs. All pride and sense of control were abandoned. A knock on the door startled him.

"Just a second!" he barked.

He quickly grabbed the bullets and tossed them under the bed. Sliding his wet boxers off, he scanned the room for his sweatpants. He tossed the wet underwear under the bed with the bullets. Clumsily, he worked on his sweats while hopping on one foot to the door. With a final tug he got them up and grabbed the doorknob. Opening it just far enough to see who was on the other side, he found his best friend's face smiling back at him. Upon seeing Paul's face, his expression turned to worry.

"You ok man?" Ruben asked.

Paul wanted desperately to tell his most trusted friend that he wasn't ok, that he needed help.that he was going mad and wanted to die.

What would it help though? Ruben could no more help him than Paul could help himself. Why worry him? Why become a burden?

"Yeah, I'm fine. Just a rough night of dreams," Paul replied, unable to make eye contact while telling a lie.

Ruben looked his face over. His eyes were swollen and red. Sweat beaded down his brow from his soaked hair. He was pale aside from the flush that comes from a fresh cry. He was not okay. Ruben knew this. Yet, he didn't want to embarrass him by pushing the issue. He would find his moment to bring it back up.

"Ok, well get your lazy ass up and moving, cracker." Ruben put a smile back on.

"Yes dad," Paul replied, shooting him a middle finger as he closed the door. He looked back to his urine-soaked bed and sighed.

"Like a damned toddler," he mumbled. "Well, no wallowing in self-pity today."

Quickly, Paul gathered up the soiled bed coverings into a ball and tossed them into the closet. He would have to wash them when nobody was around. It was embarrassing enough that he had pissed the bed at his age. Anyone finding out about it would be the highest form of humiliation. Grabbing an outfit for the day, Metallica Ride the Lightning T-shirt and black cargo shorts, he darted to the bathroom to shower off the night of sweat and piss.

Ruben was in the living room watching TV with Paul's mom and eating a plate of pancakes.

"These are amazing, Mom," Ruben said with a mouthful of syrupy goodness. He had come to call Paul's parents his own and they viewed him as an adopted son.

"I put a little cinnamon and clove into the mix," Frances said.

Entering the bathroom, Paul turned on the shower then studied himself in the mirror while the water warmed up. He looked like shit. The bags under his eyes were amplified by the pallidity of his skin. His hair was an oily mess from the night's sweating.

"Nope," he said to the dark thoughts that tried to crawl into his mind.

He turned from the mirror and stepped into the shower. The water was blissfully hot, right at the point between pleasure and pain. He put his face into the stream of the shower head and let the water wash it all away. After a moment, he bowed his head and let the stream massage his neck. A small sigh left him as he let his thoughts focus only on the comfort of the water caressing him. Once he felt at ease he grabbed the bottle of shampoo and lathered up his hair. Satisfied it was clean he returned his head to the flowing water.

After washing all cracks, crevices, and appendages, he rinsed off and stepped out of the shower. He felt better. Funny how a shower can do that, he thought. Quickly throwing on his outfit he went out to the living room to join Ruben and his mom. He stopped in the threshold and looked at his mom. The moment of her death replayed for an instant in his head. He blinked rapidly to force the vision away.

"Hey hon, you sleep okay?" his mom asked.

Paul shrugged and plopped down on the couch next to Ruben. "I slept," he said.

Concern creased her face as she looked her son over. "You were making some awful noises this morning."

"I'm ok, Mom. Just dreams. I promise." He smiled as he tried to ease his mother's mind.

"Well, I talked to your grandma about it. She said my sister used to get them too. Ms. Swanier would make this herbal tea stuff for her. Said it made her sleep like a log. I haven't seen Ms. Swanier for a long time, she's probably long gone by now. Hell, she seemed ancient when I was a little girl. Grandma is going to talk to her daughter to see if she passed the recipe down. If she can get it, I want you to try it."

"Yes ma'am," he replied and turned his attention to Ruben. "So, my brother, what shall we do today?"

Ruben was hypnotized by a rather portly middle-aged black woman on TV preparing to spin the giant wheel on the Price is Right.

"This lady is gonna break the wheel if she puts her weight behind it." Ruben said.

Paul looked at the screen and found himself also mesmerized by the rippling of cellulite in the woman's beefy arms. For reasons Paul could not fathom she had decided to wear a tight sleeveless shirt with "I Love Bob" embroidered on it. To compliment the top, she had on leopard print spandex that highlighted every dimple, roll, and crease of her backside.

"Dear god, man!" Paul exclaimed with a chuckle. "It's like a train wreck… I can't stop watching."

They both sat with eyes fixed to the screen until the woman gave the wheel a disappointingly weak spin that didn't even make a full turn.

"Well that was anticlimactic," Paul said.

"Yeah, I was expecting the wheel to spin off the base and take out Bob and a few people in the crowd. Very anticlimactic," Ruben agreed.

"You boys aren't right" Paul's mom chuckled.

"Well you made me, Mother,' Paul said nudging his mom's arm.

"I'm pretty sure I was a victim of a Rosemary's baby ritual with you," she responded.

"Ouch!" Ruben laughed.

"You cut me, Mother. You cut me deep," Paul said clutching his chest.

"Yeah, yeah. So, what are you guys getting into today? "she said.

"Probably going to shoot some pool. Maybe fish," Paul answered.

"He meant to say get spanked at some pool by the pool god, Ruben," Ruben chimed in.

"HA! You're just mad 'cause I beat you like a red headed step child last time," Paul replied.

The reigning champ title regularly swapped hands between the two of them. They were equal in skill and, aside from Adam, there were not many who could challenge the boys in their age range. They had learned most of their pool skills from Jack, the owner of Boones.

Ruben looked to Frances, whose eyes were fixed to a commercial about a face cream guaranteed to take 10 years off your skin. Confident that she wasn't looking, he switched to Paul and cleared his throat. Once he had his attention he mouthed the word "Boones" to him. Paul nodded in acknowledgment.

"So, speaking of pool, Mother, I would be willing to offer you six souls of the innocent and doing the dishes in exchange for the use of your motor vehicle to embark on a journey to Boones. What say you?" Paul said in his snobby British voice.

She stared at him, pursing her lips in contemplation.

"Pleeeeeeeeeease," Ruben pleaded with a pouty face.

"Make it dishes, and floors, AND be back by three. I have enough not so innocent souls to take care of as it is. You can keep those," she said.

Paul lunged, wrapping her up in a hug and planting a kiss on her cheek. "You're the best, Mom!"

Ruben came up behind them and turned it into a group hug.

"You're crushing me!" she grunted under the weight of the boys.

"Sorry," Ruben chuckled, standing up.

"Keys are on the hook. Nowhere but the pool hall," she said.

"Yes ma'am!" Paul and Ruben said, as they stood to go to the kitchen.

"No speeding," she said stopping Paul in mid stride. He turned to face her.

"Yes ma'am," he said and did an about face to the kitchen.

"Do not blow out my speakers again!" she said, bringing the boys to another halt.

"Yes ma'am," they said again.

This was beginning to feel like a game of red light, green light to Ruben and it made him laugh.

"Green light!" Ruben said as they resumed their race to the key hook. Ruben edged out Paul and snatched the keys from the hook.

"Hell has not frozen over, Ruben. Give the keys to Paul," Frances said from the couch.

Ruben deflated and held the keys out to Paul.

"Tell Jack hi for me, and to come over Saturday for shrimp," she said.

"Yes ma'am," Paul said.

The boys shoulder-checked each other as they raced through the door and out to the carport. Ruben flung open the car door and jumped into the passenger's seat. Paul's progress was cut short by something in the distance. He studied the figure that was standing in the middle of Notre Dame road, facing the cemetery. She was too far away to make out any details other than she had on a knee length off white dress and long silver hair. There was something… not right about the scene. A sense of foreboding crept into the air around Paul. Ruben honked the horn, making Paul jump. He looked through the window at Ruben to give him a quick middle finger, then back up to an empty street. She was gone. After scanning the area, he dismissed it and climbed into the car.

Paul parked the car in the small lot behind the plaza and got out. The smell of coffee and bread filled the air, reminding Paul's stomach that it had skipped breakfast. He would have to remedy that soon.

Boones was an all ages pool hall and arcade one town over, in Long Beach. By design, it drew in mostly teenagers and younger. It shared space about 500 yards off of the beach in a small plaza with Gilligan's bar, Beachside Subs, and Chicory coffee shop. The owner, Jack Ritter, aka Popeye, was a middle-aged man with sandy colored hair, hazel eyes, and a wicked sense of humor. In his prime, women swooned at his Elvis-like good looks. For 44 he still wasn't hard on the eyes even with the beer gut. The most unique feature he possessed were his forearms, hence the nickname Popeye. While the rest of his body was that of an average middle-aged man who enjoyed a daily beer or six, his forearms were double the size of his biceps. Years of turning oversized tank wrenches and boxing in the Army had forged them into something similar to coiled steel encased in flesh. He and William, the boys' dad, were high school friends who drunkenly joined the Army near the end of the Vietnam war. Fortunately, they were still in boot camp as the war ended, so neither of them ever left American soil. Jack served for about 4 years before opting out and moving back home. After a decade of working at the local textile plant he took his savings and opened Boones. It was an immediate hit with all the local kids and teens. Initially he was going to open a bar but opted for a safe haven to give the kids something to do away from the ever-growing drug scene. William, on the other hand, would have served till the end had it not been for his wife's insistence that he retire so the boys could have some sense of normalcy. Shortly after his deployment in Operation Desert Storm, he had hung up his army greens for a police uniform. Jack treated the boys like a cool Uncle, offering questionable advice, and a place to relax and have fun. He also allowed them to smoke without telling his dad. Coolest unofficial Uncle ever.

Pool was always free for the boys, as were the sodas. They looked forward to the tales of Jack's youth and growing up with their dad as much as they did playing pool. Jack was a great story teller. He had the ability to make you feel like you were watching the events unfold in front of you. Paul had a lot of trouble believing the stories of his father's youth. Drugs, alcohol, partying, and fighting were things that just didn't come to mind when he thought of his dad. These days, he was all about order, structure, respect, and self-discipline.

It was well known that drugs and trouble were not allowed in the hall. Still, an occasional hormone infused kid would test Jack, not knowing what all the regulars knew. They would come in starting trouble of some kind. Most commonly it was some jackass trying to sling drugs. Jack, like the boys' dad, was a take-no-shit kinda guy. He just had a better sense of humor. Where their dad would just take to throwing punk kids out on their ass at the first violation, Jack gave everyone the benefit of one warning. If you didn't heed the warning, however, he ensured you left with your ego thoroughly detached. Since most of the customers were minors, he couldn't just break jaws when things got out of hand. Instead, he would box them around open handed. There was something so much more degrading and humiliating about the sting of a slap to the cheek, let alone many of them in rapid succession. It always seemed to be a better lesson to force someone to give up than to knock them out. Not once, in all of the altercations they saw Jack get into, did anyone ever land a punch on him. He was something of a living local legend to the youth.

Paul and Ruben especially liked coming to Boones because Jack would allow money games, so long as nobody got rowdy or bet more than twenty dollars on a game.

The boys opened the glass double doors and the bells hanging over the door chimed.

"Hey pal, we don't allow your kind in here," came a familiar voice as Paul and Ruben entered Boones.

Paul turned to find Jack tying off a large black bag of trash and smiling at him.

"But we have hookers and hardcore drugs!" Paul pleaded.

"Well why the hell didn't you say so, kid?!" Jack laughed.

Jack dropped the bag and gave both boys a firm, edging on bone crunching handshake.

"How ya' been, bucko?" he asked Paul.

"I can't complain. Woke up on top of the dirt again" Paul replied. A saying he learned from Jack.

"Can't ask for more than that. How's your momma an'em?" Jack asked.

"They're good. Mom said to tell you to come over Saturday for shrimp." Paul replied.

"Oooooooo dat woman know I can't say no to dat!" Jack gave his best Justin Wilson impression while rubbing his pot belly. "I gotta run this trash out, you know where everything is," he said hoisting the large black bag over his shoulder. "Don't rob me blind while I'm out, kid!" he shouted as the door closed behind him.

The pool hall was relatively empty. There was a chubby kid, maybe 10 or 12 years old, playing the Nightmare on Elm Street pinball game. Another older, fatter boy was playing Mortal Kombat next to him. They shared the same blonde hair and bowl cut style. Paul assumed they were brothers.

The town goth kids were shooting pool at a table in the back corner. Tristan, Ryan, Summer, and Katrina. Ryan was 16 and the others were 15.

Summer was Tristan's and Katrina was Ryan's. The goth culture hadn't quite caught on in this area, so they were basically each other's only options if they wanted to maintain their lifestyle and have a romantic life.

Rumors always floated around about them being Satanists and having ritualistic orgies in the Delisle cemetery. When several local strays came up missing last summer, there was talk that they had been sacrificing them. Paul and Ruben had known all of them since elementary school and knew better than to believe the hype. Summer was an avid animal lover and volunteered at the wildlife refuge over the summer vacation. If any of them tried to hurt any of nature's creatures, they would face the wrath of a really pissed off closet hippy. She was a very pretty girl that suffered from very low self-esteem thanks to an abusive mother and absent father. Sadly, she hid her beauty behind a mask of pale makeup, heavy black eyeliner, and black lipstick.

On a few occasions they had all gotten together and played D&D with Paul and Ruben. They were good people, just different.

"Hey guys!" Katrina said with a wave to the two.

Ryan walked up and gave Paul a handshake "How's it going, man?"

"Eh, you know. Murder and mayhem," Paul replied with a smile.

Ryan was wearing a sleeveless Cannibal Corpse shirt and long baggy black shorts with a dog chain as a belt. The shirt showed off his DIY tattoo of what was supposed to be a skull on his left shoulder. Homemade ink and a sewing needle left it looking more like a misshapen alien head. He was about a head shorter than Paul, with a farmer's build. If the goth group had a leader, he was it.

"Well, I wasn't invited?" Ryan chuckled.

"Sorry man, I figured you guys would be busy with animal sacrifices and orgies in the graveyard. I didn't want to disturb you," Paul replied.

Ryan laughed again. "Yeah, yeah. That's what us Satanists do I guess. So, we need to hang out sometime. It's been too long."

"Yeah man. It has. Well, swing by this weekend. We are always getting into something. Maybe not the summoning of the Dark One that you guys are used to, but it's still usually a good time."

"Speak for yourself! Me and the Dark One are boys!" Ruben chimed in.

Ryan threw up devil horns to Ruben with a smile. "Alright, well I'm gonna get back to my game. Maybe I'll see ya this weekend." He gave Paul a firm slap on the shoulder and went back to his group.

Paul went behind the counter to the drink cooler, grabbed two Barq's root beers out, and handed one to Ruben, who was already racking up a table.

Ruben held a cue out to Paul. "You're the current champ, break em."

Paul set his root beer down on a nearby table and did a royal strut up to the table, waving to his imaginary subjects. "Bow peasants!" he exclaimed in a noble accent to the room. "The King of Poolandia demands it!"

In unison the four goths bowed with middle fingers extended in front of them.

"Yes! The royal salute, as commanded by law!" Paul exclaimed as Rubens face turned deep red with laughter.

Paul wasn't normally comfortable with making a spectacle of himself, but this place was like a second home to him. Even the goths let out the rare laugh. Ryan continued laughing as he walked to the jukebox and began dropping in quarters.

Dropping the persona, Paul placed the cue ball on the table and lined up the break. Two solids dropped, and he set to looking for his next shot.

Once recovered from his laughing fit, Ruben considered how to work into a conversation about what was going on with Paul. If he came straight at him with it, Paul would just shut down and pretend everything was fine. He had been down this road with him before, although he could tell this time was different.

He wasn't up for visiting his best friend in the loony bin or at a graveyard. Tact was never his specialty, however.

Metallica's One began to play from the jukebox as Ryan continued searching for songs. The music was loud enough to make conversation private from anyone not standing close.

The direct route it was. If he had to beat it out of him, he would. Paul would just have to forgive him later. Ruben stepped up to Paul as he was setting up his shot. He grabbed the chalk and absently worked it on the tip of his cue while he waited for Paul to shoot. The 7 dropped smoothly into the corner pocket. Paul immediately began looking for his next shot.

"Go ahead and get a few in so I can run this table," Ruben said.

"Uh-huh. Keep telling yourself that," Paul smirked.

Setting the chalk down, Ruben said, "So, I know you don't like to talk about it, but I'm getting worried about you, bro."

Paul's jaw muscles tensed as he pretended to still be studying the table. "I'm fine man. Same old nightmare bullshit I've been having for years. It's no biggie," he said unable to meet Rubens eyes.

"Nah man, it's not. You looked bad this morning. Real bad. I've never seen you like that. And mom said she was scared with the things you were saying and the noises you made." He took a step closer to Paul. "You know I got your back. Always have. You gotta trust me and tell me what's going on."

Paul studied a scuff mark on the white tile floor in front of his foot. "Things I was saying?" Paul asked.

"Yeah. She said you were crying. Saying something about you didn't kill her. Then… I don't know man, she said you were growling. That you didn't sound like you," Ruben said.

He watched Paul's face as he spoke, spotting the signs. He could feel the tension building in him. The fear and frustration threatening to boil over. It was a thin line between pushing him into opening up and just pushing him. He didn't fear Paul. They had fought in the past for one stupid reason or another. Aside from a few bruises and a busted nose or two, neither of them really tried to hurt the other, even when they were pissed. Usually after it was over, and they were too exhausted to fight anymore; they just laughed at themselves and went about the day as if nothing had happened.

Ruben had never pushed this issue though. It was always a taboo subject and he respected

Paul's wish not to talk about it. On occasion, when it all got too heavy for him, Paul would come to him and let it all out. Other than that, Ruben left it alone.

Ruben liked that Paul trusted him to help shoulder that load. Even if he couldn't physically do anything for him, it always seemed to put him at ease. Watching the decline Paul was going through, he had assumed that any day now he would talk to him about it. It had been weeks, though, and he was still bottling it up.

"It's just my crazy head. There's nothing you can do to have my back. Stop stressing, Mom." Paul tried to sound humorous, hoping to end the conversation.

"Bullshit. I'm stressed whether you let me know or not. So, how 'bout throwing me a bone," Ruben snapped at him.

"Just drop it, man," Paul said, meeting Ruben's eyes.

Ruben saw a deep anger there. It almost made him look away. Ruben never backed away from a challenge, though, and he sure as hell wasn't about to start now.

"Not gonna happen. You're my best friend… my brother. I can't just sit back and watch you go through this. I'm sorry it scares you and makes you feel weak or whatever. Doing this shit alone is stupid. Not fair to you or any of us that love you, man. So yeah, fuck you, I ain't dropping shit."

Paul began to lunge at Ruben and stopped himself. He bowed his head and took in a slow deep breath. He was fighting the strong urge to punch his best friend in the mouth to make him stop talking about it. The fear of it was so strong that he wanted to hurt his truest friend. He hated himself for that.

"You want to hit me then hit me. It isn't gonna make me stop trying to help. We will just end up wore out and bloody and I'll still keep at it 'til you start tell me what the fuck is going on."

Paul tossed his cue on the table and started towards the front door.

"Paul," Ruben said grabbing Paul's shoulder.

Paul spun to face him. His eyes were a mix of rage and panic.

"Just stop!" Paul shouted as the songs last note played.

All eyes turned to the two of them. Jack was checking a delivery of drinks outside the glass front doors and looked to Ruben upon hearing the shout. Ruben smiled and waved at him. After a moment he returned to counting cases.

"Lover's quarrel," the older of the two blonde boys quietly giggled to the other.

Ruben turned his attention to the portly boy. "Don't make me kick the Twinkie filling out of you, kid," he said matter of fact.

His giggling stopped and the two quickly returned their attention back to their games. Another Metallica song filled the awkward silence. Ruben looked back to Paul who was fighting back a grin causing him to give a confused tilt of the head.

"Fucking Twinkie filling?" Paul was overcome with laughter.

Paul's laughter was infectious and the two were caught in a brief fit of it. Paul's face dimmed back to a serious after a moment.

"I'm sorry Roob. I'm being a dick. You're right. I just don't like to think about it when I don't have to. I have to deal with it every night. Hanging out with you is my escape. I don't think about it much when we are out doing shit. Plus, I mean I'm not exactly a fan of spilling my soul in front of a crowd."

Ruben sighed and rubbed his hand through his braids as he scanned the room. He caught several people trying to do that awkward quick look away like you do when you get caught staring.

"Shit. Yeah. I guess I didn't think the whole timing thing through. My bad. Alright, I'm sorry. Let's just get back to pool. But, we WILL finish talking about this later. Deal?" Ruben held out his hand.

Paul hesitated… "Deal," he said, giving Ruben's hand a shake.

Paul glanced at the table and the cue he had tossed on it. "Well, gonna have to re-rack em. I kinda messed up the balls."

Ruben set about the task as Paul lit a cigarette and took a swig of his drink. After the table was set, Paul set the cue ball and broke. No balls went in this time. He stepped back as Ruben examined the table for his shot. As much as he hated being forced to think about it all, he realized how grateful he was to have someone like Ruben as a friend. He really did have his back no matter what. He was loyal to a fault. Paul truly believed that if given the opportunity, Ruben would take a bullet for him and not think twice about it. A rare thing, indeed. He smiled. If there were actually evil spirits out to get him, he felt better having Ruben at his back, even if he couldn't do anything to stop them. At least they would be subject to a profanity-laced onslaught as they tore Paul to shreds. That's gotta count for something, right?

Ruben won the next two games. Paul was distracted and missing shots that would normally be a cakewalk. Beating Ruben was a challenge on a good day, so being off was a guaranteed loss.

A few more kids had come in and the place was starting to get full. The crowd was making Paul uncomfortable for some reason. He checked the clock on the wall. 1:51.

"Hey champ, let's grab a sub before we head home. Gotta be back by three," Paul said.

Ruben checked the clock as well. "Yeah, guess we don't really have time to make any cash today."

Paul began gathering the balls into the tray. His eyes fixed on the 3 ball in his hand. A shiny red ball. It gleamed from the fluorescent lights. Jack took pride in his place. It was so clean and polished it looked wet. Like the top of a skull drenched in blood. His thoughts went back to the dream and his Mom's dead face. A twinge of the same unfiltered fear he felt in the dream tugged at his stomach.

A hand clapped him on the back, startling him. He spun with one hand cocked back, half ready to run, the other half ready to fight. His eyes found Ryan standing with a surprised look on his face.

"Woah, sorry man!" Ryan said with his hand up like he was being held at gunpoint. "I said your name a few times, man. Didn't mean to scare you."

Paul dropped his hand and swallowed hard. He let out the breath he realized he had been holding. "Shit, sorry man. I was somewhere else in my head I guess." He let out an awkward chuckle. "What's up?"

"Yeah, it's cool. No worries." Ryan said nervously, hands still in the air. "Um, I was just gonna see if it was cool if I brought the rest of the crew with me this weekend."

"Huh? Oh, yeah...yeah. Of course, man. Mom's cooking up some shrimp Saturday if yall wanna come eat. We can go get into something after that." Paul asked.

A big grin spread across his face. "I know exactly what we can get into."

Paul raised a curious eyebrow. "I'm not sure I like the look you gave with that statement."

Ryan's grin grew. "Well, I got a jar of blueberry moonshine I jacked from my uncle's stash. I figure we can make a little bonfire to sit around and get drunk. Maybe bust out the old D&D dice and get nerdy?"

"Ha! Now you're speaking my language. Minus the shine. Reminds me too much of lying next to a puddle of my vomit by the river, praying for death," Paul said.

"Oh god. Yeah that was a rough night for you. I tried to warn you. Shine is no joke," Ryan said.

"Yeah, for sure. But, the most valuable lessons are the hardest learned. I now know what alcohol poisoning feels like and have learned the lesson to stay away from Satan's water," Paul said.

Ryan laughed heartily. "Satan's water! I'm gonna have to use that one."

"Well I expect a cut of the profits if you start marketing your uncles shine under that name. I can see it now. Satan's Water! Guaranteed to make you regret being born!" Paul said.

"It's a deal," Ryan said.

Katrina came up and planted a kiss on Ryan's cheek. "Your shot, babe."

"Alright. Well, I'm gonna get back to it. See ya Saturday," Ryan said as he walked back to his group.

Paul could tell by the expressions he was sharing the plans with them. Smiles all around it seemed.

Paul finished clearing the table and placing the balls back in their tray. He got up to the counter and caught the tail end as Jack was telling Ruben the story about when he and his brothers accidentally set farmer Buddy's hay fields on fire. He had heard the story a half dozen times before, but still enjoyed hearing him tell it.

"We were picking rock salt out of our asses for a week." Jack stopped the story as Paul walked up.

"You outta here pal?" Jack asked as he stood.

"Yes sir. Gonna grab some lunch and head home," Paul said.

Jack studied his face for a second. "You feeling ok, kid?"

"Yes sir," he said.

"Your dad was here a few days ago. Got to talking about how he's worried about you, with those dreams and all. I gotta say… you look like shit, kiddo," Jack said patting Paul on the back.

Paul sighed, "Well it seems I'm the talk of the town." He shot Ruben a look. "I'm fine, Uncle Jack. Just not sleeping good lately. Mom's supposed to be getting some voodoo tea or something for me to try," he said.

"Voodoo tea?" Jack asked.

"Yeah, some stuff Ms. Swanier used to make that's supposed to help me sleep," Paul replied.

"Oh hell!" Jack laughed. "Not the Swanier stink bomb?!"

Paul laughed. "I don't know. You have experience with that I take it?"

"Oh man. Momma used to get it from Swanier's grandma. Was supposed to be for if we were sick to help us sleep. But she would make us drink that shit at bed time if we wouldn't keep quiet. Like drinking the sweat from a camel's asshole. It will knock your dick in the dirt though. Could use that stuff in surgery," Jack chuckled.

"Greeeeeat," Paul said.

"Well I hope it works. Just tell your ma, open all the windows when she makes it. I'll pray for you, boy," Jack chuckled.

"Well thanks for the confidence boost there, Uncle Jack," Paul laughed.

"Motivational speeches are my specialty," Jack shrugged. He studied Paul for a moment and placed a hand on his shoulder. "I know your Pop isn't real good at showing it, but he loves you, boy. I also know your old man isn't a worrier, so if he's worried… I'm worried."

Paul felt awkward in the moment and examined his shoes. "I know he does. Honestly, I just wish everyone would quit worrying. I'll be fine. I promise."

Jack sighed. "You can't bullshit a bullshitter. I get that you don't want to talk about it and bother anyone with it. I'll leave it alone. Just don't forget that I'm here if you need me, kiddo. Your folks, too. And apparently this goofy bastard." He gave Ruben a friendly pop in the shoulder.

Paul was disappointed to find a fray beginning in his right shoelace. He would have to ask his mom to get some new ones for him soon.

"I know. I appreciate it." As much as he usually enjoyed conversations with Jack, he desperately wanted this one to end.

Jack gave a firm squeeze to Paul's shoulder and paused. He stared at Paul as if he had something more to say. He let out a sigh. "Alright, well get trucking then. I'll see y'all Saturday."

"See ya later, Mr. Jack," Ruben waved and headed out the door.

Jack gave a wave back and watched the boys leave and turn towards the sub shop.

"Fuck!" Ruben said as he rubbed his shoulder once they were out of Jack's view. "That old fucker hits so haaaard."

Paul chuckled and opened the door to Beachside Subs. He swooned at the aroma of fresh-baked bread. It was a small shop with four tables filling the small dining area and two small black wrought-iron tables outside the front of the store. There were a wide variety of seashells hanging from the ceiling by thin fishing line. The walls were painted with beach scenes, seagulls, pelicans, and crabs. The counter was decorated to resemble a Tiki bar. The owner's daughter, Ella Ladner, was working the counter today in the Hawaiian shirt and khaki shorts uniform. Currently, she was flipping through a fashion magazine and looking somewhere between bored and irritated.

She was a year older than Paul and ran in the rich kid circles, so Paul didn't really know her. Her father, Jason, owned three beachside subs across the coast, and while not actually rich, he didn't do bad. He spoiled his daughter. She got a brand-new Mustang for her sweet sixteen, and while the other popular kids were still using pagers as a status symbol; she had the latest Motorola cell phone. All of her clothes were name brand. She wanted for nothing. Looking up from the magazine, she offered a smile. "Hey Paul. Ruben."

Paul was a bit surprised that she actually knew their names. He knew who she was simply because of her level of popularity in

71

school and the stories he heard of the epic parties she had on her birthdays.

"Oh, hey Ella. Didn't realize you knew who we were," Paul said smiling back.

Ella laughed. "How could I not know who you are. You dented a locker with my cousin's head."

Ruben laughed. "Well! You're famous!" He gave Paul a slap on the back.

Paul blushed a bit. "Shit. Freddy is your cousin? I'm sorry. He just…"

"Don't be. Freddy is an asshole. Unfortunately, he's family, but it doesn't mean I have to like him. I think most of the school was cheering for you on that one," Ella said.

"Oh... ok. Good. Whew. Thought you were about to spit in our subs." Paul chuckled.

"Nah, I save that for the special customers. The principal, the mayor, my step mom. You know, the real shit heads," Ella smiled.

"Well alrighty then," Paul said.

"So, what can I get yall?" she asked.

Paul ordered "The Beach Bum," a foot-long version of a club with olive salad on it. Ruben went for the J Birds meatball sub. After watching Ella expertly construct the lunches, they filled their drinks, said goodbye to Ella, and took a seat at the outdoor tables.

"Alright, so a deal is a deal. Talk to me. What's going on in your dreams now." Ruben said.

"Like a damned crab on a pube, isn't ya? Just won't let it go." Paul chuckled as he unwrapped his sub.

"That's a disgusting way of putting it… but yeah," Ruben replied. "So, spill it, yeah?"

He hesitated "Yeah. I…" Paul found himself hesitant at the idea of reliving last night to tell the story.

"Out with it, bitch," Ruben pushed.

Paul sighed. "Ok. Right. Well… It's not so much that I'm dreaming, but, and don't fuck with me about this, but I think the dreams are starting to happen when I'm awake."

Ruben furrowed his brow, considering what Paul had said. "Run that by me again? Your dreaming while you're awake?"

"It feels like it. Last night I was standing in my room and I put a mark on one of my drawings. When I did someone grabbed my shoulder. The hand was so cold that it hurt." Paul's stomach muscles and fists clenched as he let the night play through his mind. "I could actually feel the cold and the pain. Then I passed out. Or so I thought. But I woke up on my bed like I had just been dreaming. That mark was still on my drawing though. And…" He pulled down the collar of his shirt, showing the welts to Ruben.

"I found these… right where it grabbed me. I know what you're thinking. I scratched myself in my sleep. I came to the same conclusion and went back to bed. When I finally got to sleep, I had this crazy dream that another version of me killed Mom and then whatever had grabbed me before took the other me away. It all just felt too real, man. Like there's a line that separates real from dream but it's getting blurry as hell." He left out the part about the gun.

"Shit," was all Ruben could say.

"Yeah… shit," Paul replied.

Paul's hand trembled when he lifted his cup to his mouth. Before Ruben noticed, he forced it to stop.

"Was last night the first time that happened?" he asked.

"Yeah," Paul said as he took a drink, "but the dreams had been getting worse before that."

"Something happen that triggered that?" Ruben asked.

"Not that I can think of. It got bad after Mrs. Goodrich. Then it started calming down. Then a few months ago it started amping up. Damned if I know why."

"Maybe you should see a doctor?" Ruben suggested.

"They will just say the same thing they said when I was a kid. Night terrors… some past traumatic event… take these sleeping pills… Blah blah blah. The pills don't help. They just make me fall asleep faster. I'm in no hurry to visit my nightmares," Paul said.

"Maybe…" Ruben began.

"No. There's nothing that doctors or anyone else can do." Paul cut him off. "That's why I don't talk about it. I don't like reminding myself that I'm screwed, and I don't want to burden anyone else with this shit. I'll just deal with it like I always do," Paul said, cutting Ruben off.

Ruben felt frustrated , because he didn't have a solution. He wanted to fix this for him. He began slowly running his fingers through his braids, letting the gears turn in hopes of having a eureka moment. The moment never came.

"Well, then I guess your bitch ass is stuck with me as a roommate for the summer," Ruben declared.

"Huh?" Paul exclaimed through the bite of sub in his mouth.

"I'm moving in for the summer. I'm sure your mom won't care and Aunt Kat sure as hell don't care. Hell, I practically live there, anyway," Ruben said.

"Dude, Adam isn't going to let you have his room," Paul said.

"That's why I'm sleeping on your floor," Ruben grinned.

"What? No." Paul objected. He felt panic. He didn't want Ruben to see him in a night terror. Or God forbid, waking up covered in piss.

"Hey, if I can't help you, then I can at least be there for you. And if there is some ghost shit going down, then I want to be there beat the shit out of it for fucking with my boy," Ruben said.

"I can't," Paul started.

Ruben cut him off this time. "I've seen you have them before when we were little. It ain't nothing new. Stop with the pride shit,"

"You don't understand," Paul pleaded.

"Well I guess I'm about to," Ruben insisted.

Paul knew he wasn't going to talk Ruben out of it and his mom wouldn't object to Ruben staying. He was like a tick once he set his mind on something. Only way to stop him was pull his head off.

"God damn it! Fine. No making jokes about anything I say or do when I'm sleeping though. Swear it," Paul said.

"Of course, man. I wouldn't make fun of you," he said. Paul shot him a look.

"Well not about this, anyway," Ruben chuckled.

"You are a pain in the ass, Roob," Paul said.

"It's what makes me so loveable," Ruben said. "I'll pack some shit up tonight and crash at your house tomorrow."

"Fine." Paul answered in defeat.

Ruben swallowed down a bite of his sub. "So, what if this is something besides bad dreams?"

Paul raised an eyebrow at him.

"I mean, like… spirits or ghosts or something," Ruben shrugged.

Paul snorted, "Right. Well I guess I'll call a priest."

Putting his hands up, Ruben said, "I'm serious, man. I know you don't believe in all that shit… but what if?"

Ruben and Paul had different takes on the supernatural. Ruben believed he had encountered a spirit in his grandmother's house when he was ten. Paul was sleeping over that night, and Ruben swore he saw an old woman standing over Paul staring at him while he slept. He had wanted to wake him up but was frozen in place with fear. At some point, he had either passed out or fallen asleep. The next morning, he shared what he'd seen with Paul, who thought it was a cool dream but never really bought into it.

"Well it's not that I don't believe. I just haven't ever seen proof. I'm somewhere between skeptic and believer, I suppose," Paul said.

"I don't know about you, but waking up with ghost handprints on me would be kicking me a little more to the believer side," Ruben said.

Paul sighed and contemplated for a second. "It's just as likely that I scratched myself, and I'm just losing my mind. A lot more likely, actually. I just find it hard to believe that if there are ghosts and evil spirits and shit, that nobody since the invention of the camcorder has managed to catch any definite proof. People tend to see and believe what they want to in my opinion. Where some folks see a glass that was moved by a ghost when they left the room, others realize they just moved it and forgot. Some hear ghosts walking around their house at night. Others hear the house settling or branches banging on the side of the house."

"First off, your mind has been lost for many years," Ruben smirked. "But for real though. After all these years of dealing with the dreams and weirdness… and now this. You don't think there might be more than science and head doctors can explain?"

"I suppose there is a small part of me that wants to, but no. I mean the idea of being crazy and it getting worse isn't appealing either, but I'm not special. People go crazy all the time. Just because it's me doesn't mean I am the chosen one and not just another lunatic. Bad shit just happens sometimes. This is just the bad shit for me, ya know?" Paul absently slid the straw up and down in his drink while he spoke. "Really I don't know which would be worse. Would I rather be haunted by asshole spirits that want to drive me insane… or just be nuts?"

A small part of him wanted to believe that was the case. That he wasn't just crazy and getting worse. That there was something that could save him from himself. This thought hit him. 'Save me from myself…' That's the road he felt he was on. One of these mornings, he wouldn't be able to talk himself into ejecting the bullets from the gun. He could feel how weak his will had become. The draw of nothingness seemed disgustingly appealing. Ruben, he supposed, was one of the only influences that gave him hope. After all that Ruben endured as a boy, he still seemed generally ok. He had been through things more horrible than most people ever will. He had been forced to do something few could understand. Yet, he never sat around feeling sorry for himself. Paul never once heard him cry about it or wish for death. He seemingly just accepted it and moved on. Paul deeply admired this about him. He felt pathetic for thinking about death so often lately. Yet, that little voice in his head, the one which tried to rationalize how much better it would be to simply give up and die, had been growing louder.

"How do you do it man?" Paul asked.

"Do what?" Ruben looked at Paul confused.

"Everything you went through. You know, with your dad. It doesn't seem to bother you.

Yet here I am on the verge of being committed to an insane asylum, because I have nightmares," Paul said.

Ruben smiled and thought about it for a moment. "I don't know man. I mean, I can't change anything that happened. Doesn't mean I don't think about it every day. But, way I see it, that fucker took enough from me that day. He got what was coming to him. I ain't giving him anything else. I think about it, I deal with it, I move on. It is what it is, as aunt Kat likes to say."

"You gotta teach me how to do that one of these days," Paul absently smiled.

"I can't teach you how to be amazing, man. It's a gift I was born with." Ruben popped his nonexistent collar up.

"You're a fucking dork," Paul laughed.

"Anyway… like I was saying. If it's something supernatural, though, maybe there's something that can be done."

Paul sighed in frustration, "And if I'm just nuts and can't be helped?"

Ruben sat briefly silent. "Then I guess I'll be visiting your crazy ass in the mental ward. Way I see it, the meds haven't helped. Doctors haven't helped. Therapists haven't helped. What the hell do you have to lose by at least giving it a shot? It all just seems too odd to be a coincidence."

"What does?" Paul asked.

"Okay. So, things were never this bad with you until Mrs. Goodrich. I mean yeah, you had night terrors, but never anything that got to you like lately. It is physically affecting you this time. Your weight. You always look like you are on the tail end of a stomach bug. You always look exhausted. Everything you told me about what happened just sounds like there was something more to it than her going insane. She was always a nice, God-fearing woman. Never saw her get mad. Never heard her raise her voice. Then suddenly without warning she just decides to strip down and kill herself? And her reaction to seeing you. It's like she was trying to protect you from whatever it was that made her lose it."

Paul had often thought the same thing, but the skeptic in him always came out on top. "People snap out of the blue all the time. How many times have you heard people being interviewed about a guy that shot up a post office or killed his wife? They always say the same thing. Oh, he was such a nice guy. I never would have imagined. Blah blah blah. Who's to say she didn't have Alzheimer's or dementia or something. Hell, go visit a nursing home. Those people go from normal to freaking out all the time."

"Yeah but I haven't seen too many teenagers in nursing homes. As for shooting up post offices, they always find that there was a history of mental illness or drug abuse. You don't have either. Hell, you can't even smoke weed without having a panic attack. So, I know you ain't doing any hard shit that would make you crazy." Ruben paused to take a swig of his drink. "You just want to sit and do nothing? Just keep doing the same shit and hoping something different will happen? The definition of insanity is doing nothing and expecting results."

Paul let out a burst of laughter. Ruben cocked his head at him quizzically. "That's funny to you?" He said.

"You really gotta start paying better attention in Mr. Bollings' class," Paul said, still laughing. "With your trying-to-quote-Einstein ass."

"What?" Ruben huffed, seeming a little embarrassed and offended.

"I think you were shooting for, the definition of insanity is doing the same thing over and over again but expecting different results," Paul said.

"You know what the fuck I mean, bitch," Ruben said somewhere between smiling and scowling.

Paul grinned. "Don't be mad at me 'cause you is a dumbass."

"Excuse me if I can't give a shit about Social Studies. That man could put a wild Tasmanian Devil to sleep." Ruben threw his arms up.

"You being a dumbass aside…" Paul shot a crooked grin at him. "You have a point, I guess. Nothing else has worked. Not like I have anything to lose. Well, except my mind, and it seems I'm well on my way to that already."

A look of surprised relief came over Rubens face, "Thank you! About time you stopped being a little bitch and listened to me!"

"Hey, I learned how to be one from the best," Paul said holding both hands out to Ruben like a model that was showing off an item on the Price is Right. In reply Ruben tossed a chip at him, sticking it to his shirt.

Paul swiped the chip away. "Okay, so what's the plan?"

"Well, I figure the only ones we really know that is into all that supernatural shit would be Madie and Mrs. Swanier. Which one you want to start with?" Ruben asked.

Paul immediately thought of Madie as the first choice. However, her knowledge in the matter seemed more teenage fascination than actual knowledge. Ms. Swanier was in her late 80's and came from a long line of Creole ancestry. She was rumored to practice voodoo, witchcraft, or Satanism, depending on who you asked. Paul's grandmother often got tinctures and remedies from her for varying issues that came with age. As a child, she once forced Paul to suffer these concoctions when he fell ill. As foul as it tasted, he couldn't deny that it worked. Better than the prescriptions he was taking at that.

"I suppose Ms. Swanier is the obvious choice. I think Madie just dabbles in it. Better to go to the seasoned pro," Paul said.

Ruben nodded. "I was thinking the same thing. See if your grandma can get her to talk to us and we will go from there."

"Alright, I'll ask Madie too. Maybe she has some books or something that I can check out 'till we do get to talk to Mrs. Swanier," Paul said, popping the last bite of his sandwich into his mouth. "But don't think any of this means you get to keep the pool champ title."

Ruben snorted, "Biiiiiiiiiitch! Don't hate. You got spanked!"

"Hell naw! You got my little bitch side all flustered and distracted. Basically cheating. It's in the rulebook," Paul replied.

"Cracker please!" Ruben scoffed. "Alright. Meet me at Karl's tomorrow at 1. I'll beat yo' ass again. Loser sleeps on the floor for the summer."

"What? You invited yourself over for the summer. I ain't sleeping on the floor in my own damn room!" Paul said incredulously.

"Look at you, already know I'm gonna whoop dat ass. Being all scared and shit." Ruben crossed his arms over his chest with a grin.

Paul's face flushed a light shade of pink. "Oooooh. I see what you did there. Alright, it's on ho!"

Ruben checked his watch. "Oh shit, we gotta go."

Paul checked his watch as well. 2:38. "Shit!" he exclaimed as he crumpled the paper his sandwich came in.

The two dumped their trays in the trash and took up a brisk pace to the car. After breaking a few speeding laws and a dash into Winkie's (the only store that would sell cigarettes or dip without checking ID), they pulled into Paul's drive with six minutes to spare.

"I'm gonna go ahead and get home. Get some shit together for tomorrow and check on my aunt." Ruben said as they got out of the car.

"Alright cool. Don't be late for your ass whippin' at Karl's tomorrow," Paul's smiled.

"You ain't gotta lie to yourself like that, man. It's not healthy. But for real, let me bum a smoke for the road," Ruben replied.

"Sure dude. Least I can do before humiliating you tomorrow," Paul said as he pulled the soft pack of Marlboro reds out of his pocket.

He thumped the pack on the bottom, making three cigarettes pop out of the opening on top. Ruben grabbed two and said, "Uh huh. You keep telling yourself that."

The boys gave a quick gangster-hug to each other. Ruben grabbed his bike. Paul watched as he peddled down the drive and hooked a right towards the main road.

The woman in the road earlier entered Paul's mind. He gave a quick glance towards the distant cemetery. To his relief, nothing was there. Letting his eyes drift further down the road toward the cemetery, he pondered their meeting with Mr. Goodrich yesterday.

What had he been doing in the Quarters? He could understand visiting a loved one's grave… but not the place where they so tragically met their end. Curiosity tugged at him. There was no way in hell he would go investigating on his own, but the next time the crew all went; he would have to look around. While they all still hung out in the Quarters, Paul avoided the section where Ms. Goodrich died. Next time, though, he would face that demon and look around.

Chapter 4

"Paul is that you?" his mom's voice called from the living room as he walked into the carport door.

"Yes ma'am," he said and hung the keys on one of the hooks next to the door.

"Cutting it close, huh?" Paul could hear the couch give a squeak as she got up.

"Nah, I had several seconds to spare!" he laughed.

He noticed one crumpled paper sack on the dining table. Picking it up, he gave it a quick shake. It was light, whatever it was. The shake also puffed a foul odor from the bag. Sort of like fermented cabbage, with some type of sweet smell mixed in. His nose crinkled, and he dropped the bag back on the table.

"Mom? What died in this bag?" Paul asked as his she came into the room.

She rolled her eyes "Oh, it doesn't smell that bad. It's the tea from Ms. Swanier. Your grandma and I went to see her today."

Paul's eyes went wide. "That's the tea I'm supposed to drink?! It smells like you stuffed dead cats and old fruit in that bag!"

"It does not, Paul. Quit being dramatic. You are going to drink this stuff before bed tonight, like it or not." Her tone grew stern on the last sentence.

Paul studied the bag on the table. "Fine… but I want witnesses and a pre-signed confession that you are making me drink this stuff. That way when I wake up dead tomorrow, they know who to blame."

"Well if you wake up then you can't really be dead. And if you do die, your dad's a cop and will know how to dispose of the body and cover up the crime. Plus, if you don't drink it, I will kill you," she said with a grin.

"So, I have no say in this?" he asked.

"Nope." she responded.

Paul let out a long, dramatic sigh. "Fiiiine."

"Did you see Jack?" she asked as she took the bag off the table.

"Yes. He is excited about the shrimp," Paul said as he watched his mom sniff the bag and flinch away from it.

She waved a hand in front of her nose and walked to the kitchen sink. She placed the bag down and opened it. "I've never known a man that gets more excited about food." She turned her head away as the opened bag released the full glory of odors.

"What's wrong mom? The tea smell too good for you to handle?" Paul chuckled.

"Uh huh, keep it up and I'll make you drink two glasses," she said as she pulled an old tea kettle from the top of the cabinet.

"I'd like to retract my last statement," Paul quickly said.

"I thought you'd see things my way," she said.

As she began to fill the kettle, Paul raised an eyebrow at her back. "Um, mom. It's a bit early for bed. The suns still up."

"Oh, no, Ms. Swanier said it has to steep for a few hours before you drink it." She finished filling the kettle and placed it on the stove. With a turn of a knob, the blue natural gas flames whooshed to life underneath.

"So, Mom. You think I could meet her?" Paul asked.

"Who?" she said.

"Ms. Swanier," he said.

She turned around to face Paul with an odd look of surprised worry. "Oh. I didn't figure that was something you'd be interested in."

"Yeah, I'd definitely like to meet her," he responded a little more eagerly than he meant to.

"Umm ok. Why the sudden interest?" his mom asked, raising an eyebrow at him this time.

Paul opened the fridge and busied himself looking for a snack. "Well… it's kinda dumb."

"It wouldn't be the first dumb thing you've told me. Go on," she said.

He raised up from the fridge with a shocked look on his face "Mother! I'm your son! How could you say such things?!" he said as he clutched his chest.

"Yeah Yeah. Come on. Out with it," she said.

Paul snagged a yogurt and shut the refrigerator. "Ok, so Ruben has this idea about my night terrors. He thinks that since the meds don't work, therapy hasn't helped - and in his opinion, they are getting worse - that there might be something… supernatural to it all. So, he said I should go to see Ms. Swanier since she is all into that kinda stuff. He wouldn't lay off the idea and you know how Ruben gets when he has an idea in his head. To shut him up, I agreed to go." Paul made sure to place all the blame for this idea on Ruben's shoulders, so his mom would lecture Ruben instead of him.

Instead, she nodded. "Ok" was all she said.

"Ok? That's it? No speech about how stupid or dramatic he is being?" Paul said stunned.

She chewed the inside of her lip for a moment. "No."

"Really?" Paul said as he peeled to top off his yogurt.

She looked to the floor and back up to him. She sighed, turned to the stove and watched the kettle.

"She was actually wanting to meet you, too." she said reluctantly.

"Huh? Why?" he asked.

"She was interested in your dreams, I guess," she said busying herself with wiping the clean counters.

"You told her about my dreams?" he said, feeling slightly irritated.

"Yes. The one you had last night… worried me," she said.

"Why is that? They are just dreams, Momma," he said dismissively.

She hung the rag on the faucet. "It didn't sound like you were alone."

Paul swallowed hard. "It didn't?"

"No. Someone was talking to you. At least it sounded that way." she said, still not looking at Paul.

A chill ran through Paul. "What?"

"I heard it through the walls, so it might have been my ears tricking me. I just thought I heard a woman in there with you. At first, I was thinking you snuck Madie into your room and you guys were talking. But then you started making the sounds you always do when you're having a bad dream. This time though, you started growling and laughing. Then you started crying I think. I was getting worried. I was about to go check on you but then I heard you get up and go to the bathroom. I thought that was the end of it but then you started again this morning. You were cussing in your sleep. Saying you were going to kill someone. Just terrible things."

Paul began piecing the noises she described what had happened in the "dream" the night before. He hadn't said or wanted to kill anyone in the dream from what he could remember. The rest he could place, but not that. He was going to ask questions when the kettle began to come to life with a light whistle that steadily increased in pitch. Frances pulled the kettle off the burner, placing it on a cold one, and turned off the flame. Pulling a large coffee mug from the cabinet, she placed it next to the bag of rancid smelling herbs. Paul watched silently as she pulled out a cheesecloth bag, filled with a mixture of dark leaves. The bag was stained with atar like resin up to a thin string that held the bag closed. She dropped the bag into the mug and grabbed the kettle. A cloud of steam swirled around her face as the piping hot water flowed into the mug. The aroma became intense as the steam circulated through the kitchen, pulling Paul from his thoughts.

"Oh, Jesus! Mom, that's so bad!" Paul exclaimed.

She placed her hand over her mouth and nose. "Shit. Yeah, that's bad. Oh my God!"

"Mom, I really think that's body parts, not tea leaves," Paul said as he pinched his nostrils shut.

Frances grunted in disgust. She grabbed the mug and walked out the side door into the carport.

"Fucking voodoo tea!" Paul heard his mom mumble through the window.

"Mother!!!" he hollered.

"You weren't supposed to hear that!" she responded.

"Ooooooh, I'm telling grandma!" Paul chided.

"Boy! You will find yourself drinking three glasses of this crap," she warned.

Paul walked out to the carport with a grin, and watched his mom frantically looking for a spot to set the mug down. Finally, she placed it in an empty flower pot and took a few steps back.

"Oh my God! Who ever thought that would be safe to put in your body." she said. "Ok, well. We will just have to let it steep out here."

"Yeah, probably a good idea. That smell might become permanent if you don't," Paul replied from the doorway.

"Momma," he said.

"Yes?" she answered.

"I was dreaming about this terrible old woman last night. And there was another version of me there too. He was insane looking. All dirty and stuff. Looked like he had been killing people," he confessed.

Frances stood in silence, contemplating what he said. "You should go see her tomorrow. She said to come anytime."

"Ms. Swanier?" he asked.

"Yeah. Just… be careful," she said.

He thought it odd that she would tell him that about visiting a woman older than his grandma. "Um… ok. There something you're not tell me Momma?"

"Just go see her. I don't know what else to do. Maybe she can help." Her voice trembled as she spoke.

He walked up and wrapped his arms around her. "Hey, it's ok. I'm gonna be fine, Momma."

"I love you, baby. I'm sorry I can't fix this for you," she said with a sniffle.

"Mom. Stop. I'm fine. None of this is your fault," he squeezed her.

They stood like that for a few seconds before Frances pulled away. "Ok. I'm gonna go get dinner started," she said, wiping her eyes.

"Ok. I am gonna be ok, Momma. Stop worrying." he smiled at her.

She gave a half smile back and went inside. Paul sighed and walked to the side of the house to smoke out of view of his mother.

Before he figured out which pocket he had his pack in, a figure coming down Hand Road caught his eye from the direction of

Madie's house. Still several hundred yards away, all he could tell was it was walking at a very fast pace. The kind of pace you would walk for exercise or if you were storming away from an argument. He squinted at the person, trying to make out details. As she drew closer, Madie's features grew clearer. A smile crossed his lips. She stopped, still a good distance from his house. Crossing her arms, she turned back towards her house, took a few steps, and stopped again. She then began pacing from one side of the small road to the other, stopping periodically to look back towards her home. Paul furrowed his brow. Something didn't seem right.

He started towards her at a slow pace, studying her body language as he walked. Her shoulders shook like a person that was crying. She hadn't seemed to have spotted him yet. Unsure if he should bother her right now, he slowed his pace. He knew he didn't like to be seen when he was having a meltdown, if that's what was going on. But, what if she needed someone… needed him? He felt silly for that thought. Wishful thinking. Yet, if something was wrong, he would do his best to be there for her.

She was facing her house again. Slowly approaching her, he pulled out his pack of smokes. He shook two out of the pack and cleared his throat. She jumped in surprise and spun to face him with bloodshot eyes and cheeks wet with tears. He was conflicted on what to do next. Make a joke? Hug her? Turn and run?

"I got cigarettes and a shoulder to lean on. Both are on special today at the low cost of free," he said.

Madie laughed and sobbed simultaneously. "I'm sorry," she said. She turned her face and wiped the tears away.

"You ok?" Paul asked. He placed both cigarettes in his mouth and lit them while he watched her. She rubbed her shoulder and stared at the ground before answering.

"Yeah. Yeah, I'm ok. Just my dad. He's drunk as always," she said.

"Did he hit you?"' Paul asked.

"It's nothing to worry about." She pulled in a hitching breath and wiped her eyes again. "You gonna smoke both of those?" She motioned to the two cigarettes in Paul's hand.

"I was considering it," he said and then handed her one of them with a smile.

She took a long pull off of it. "Thank you."

"Welcome. So… you want to talk about it?" he asked.

She sighed and shot another look towards her house. "No. If that's ok. I'd really rather talk about anything else."

Paul could relate. "Ok. Well, I'm here if you change your mind."

"I appreciate it," she said.

They stood there in an awkward silence. Paul's mind raced with things he would like to say but knew he wouldn't. Then through things to talk about to break the silence. Something funny? Something serious? Something cool? Madie cleared her throat and took another long drag.

She thumped the cigarette into the ditch. "I better get back."

"Oh… ok," Paul said nervously. Kicking himself for his insecurities.

"Thanks for the smoke," she said.

"Yeah, anytime. God knows you've supported my habit enough," he chuckled.

She gave a false half smile and began walking back to her house.

After a few seconds Paul called out "Hey Madie!"

She turned back to him. "Yeah?"

"I mean it, I'm always here for you if you need a shoulder… an ear… a smoke." A kiss, he wanted to say.

She gave a real smile this time. "Thanks Paul," she said and continued on her way home.

It did raise her spirits some, and made butterflies in her stomach. The smile remained with her until her house came into view. It should have been a nice place to live. A deep blue two story, four-bedroom three bath house. The unique feature of a large deck on the roof had made Madie excited when she first saw the home. She regularly went up there to escape her dad and get some sun. Stained glass windows decorated the front doors. Sadly, in the short time they had lived there, her father had already turned it into a hoarders paradise. Fourteen cats lived on the front porch, two of which were pregnant. A wide variety of useless items, trash, and empty cases of beer littered the porch and front yard, along with several bags of open cat food. Inside was worse. Junk filled every unused area of the home. The dining room table was stacked high with children's toys, unused clothes, full cases of beer, and mail. The house smelled of cat urine and shit. If not for Madie, the kitchen sink would be overflowing and there would be no clean dishes to eat from. She stopped at the edge of the yard and looked back down the road to where she met Paul.

Initially, she was going to Paul to cry to him. She was going to tell him that her father had just shoved her down the stairs, and all the things he said… such horrible things. She was going to run away. For some reason she felt like she owed it to him to tell him she was leaving. As the emotions calmed and Paul's house came into view, she had thought of Jennifer. How bad things would be if she was left alone to face her father's wrath. Madie knew she was the only thing keeping him from subjecting Jennifer to the beatings and humiliations she suffered. She couldn't do that, no matter how bad it got. She also had no desire to show Paul, or any of her other new friends just how messed up her family was. Her instincts told her she could trust Paul, but she would not risk it. This fresh start was the best thing to happen to her and she wasn't going to let her depraved father ruin it this time.

With a slow calming breath, she reinforced her mental armor and took the final steps to her back door. She placed her ear to the door, listening for hints of her father still on a rampage. A low growl came from somewhere on the other side. Madie took a step back, staring at the door. A dog was one of the few things her father hadn't allowed into his trash palace. He always despised dogs, and they seemed to share the sentiment. Slowly, she stepped back to the door, resting a hand on the stained-glass pane. Holding her breath, she placed her ear back to the door. Silence.

"Mother fucker!" Her father's voice shouted from inside, followed by a loud crash. She took several steps back this time and turned to run.

"Madie!" A small voice came from behind her.

She turned back and found herself face to face with… nothing. The only thing behind her was a dirty stained-glass door. Two cats resting under the edge of the house, whose names she couldn't recall, if they even had names. She had lost track after the first five.

"Jennifer?" Madie said.

"Up here," Jennifer half whispered from above.

Madie looked up to find the terrified eyes of her sister staring down at her from the deck on top of the home.

"You ok?" Madie asked.

"What's wrong with dad? He's scaring me," Jennifer squeaked.

"It's going to be okay. Just stay up there until I come get you." Madie told her.

"Ok," she said before disappearing.

Madie took in a deep breath and opened the back door. The sound of someone talking on the TV was the only thing she could hear. Seconds dragged by as she stood in the doorway, waiting for something to happen. Nothing.

"Ok." She steadied herself before walking in.

"That you?" Came Jim's slurring voice.

She stopped in the hall, "Yes."

"We are out of what I need to make dinner. I want to make us dinner tonight. That would be nice wouldn't it? Make a list and run to the store," he said stepping into view. His demeanor was frighteningly calm. Madie looked deeper into him, seeing his mood. He was calm at the moment. A drastic difference from 15 minutes ago.

"Ok. Tell me what you need," she said.

He smiled at her with rotten teeth. "You are such a good girl. You know that? You take such good care of me."

"Yes, dad. What do you need?" She hated when he would get like this.

"I don't know why I get that way. I don't mean to hurt you. I need you to know that. I love you. You and your sister are all I have left. I don't know what I'd do without you guys," he slurred.

She had heard this 'woe is me' apology bullshit more times than she could remember. It used to make her feel bad for him. Over the years, it had lost its effect. The only thing it made her feel now was disgust and anger.

"I know, dad. Tell me what to get from the store," she said shortly.

He stepped uncomfortably close to her. Close enough for the burning mix of alcohol and sour breath to waft up her nostrils.

"You look just like her sometimes," he breathed at her.

Feeling completely repulsed, she turned her head to the side. With great effort, she hid her feelings and smiled. Talking to her dad in moments like these were like trying to defuse a bomb. One wrong move and everything went up in flames.

"Please, just tell me what you want from the store. The sooner I get there the sooner we can have dinner. I'll help you cook."

Jim pressed his forehead against hers and sighed. "Ok," he said. "Milk, angel hair pasta, cheese…"

Madie scribbled it all down on the back of an envelope and snatched the keys from the counter. "I'm going to get the check book and see if Jen wants to come."

"Uh huh," he said. A predator's grin was on his face. Stumbling to the recliner, he fell into the seat with a grunt. "Just like her."

Madie hurried upstairs and got the checkbook, and Jen. Opting for the balcony stairs so as to avoid further contact with her dad, they piled into the car and left for the store.

Chapter 5

Ruben rode his bike down the familiar, bumpy, dirt road that led to his Aunt Kat's trailer. His thoughts drifted to his childhood. Not many of the memories there were pleasant. He remembered sitting in the back of his aunt's car, pain in his back. The bumps in the road pulling his stitches. He remembered the trash bag on his lap and back pack on the seat that held all his belongings. He remembered wearing his first suit. The rose pricking his thumb before setting it on his mom's casket. CPS workers visiting. Therapists. Tears that he would only shed in private. Anger. Sorrow. Hate. Loss. Is that all there was? He dug through his memories for something good. His mom smiling as he opened a He-Man action figure for his 6th birthday. Meeting a fat, shy kid in elementary school that would become a brother to him. Laughing as that kid bit a bully in the face for taking his cinnamon roll at breakfast. Kissing Sheila Burke behind the bleachers in 7th grade. That same fat kid, flying through the air like some professional wrestler, and drop kicking one of the three guys that were jumping him in 8th grade. A smile spread across his face at that flashback.

Making the turn into the drive, he sighed at the brown single-wide trailer he had called home for the last seven years. It was a scene right out of a movie set in a white trash backwoods town. Most of the skirting was gone or littered with holes. The three wooden steps going to the front door had a distinct lean to the right and were in dire need of repair. Two rusted out trucks sat in the front yard with weeds and small trees growing up through them. An old refrigerator leaned against the front of the home. A burn barrel resided in the side yard with holes rusted through in several spots. Two dirt covered mutts, Grump and Molly, barked before crawling out from under the trailer to greet Ruben. Grump was a thick, medium sized dog. His coat of short fur was a mix of browns, blacks, and white. Molly, a much larger dog, wore a long, matted coat of solid black fur. They yipped excitedly as they crisscrossed in front of his bike, tails working overtime.

"How are my bitches doing?" Ruben said as he dismounted the bike and let it fall.

Dropping to one knee, he allowed the dogs to sniff and lick him. He gave them both hearty pats on the back and a generous helping of scratches behind the ears. Aunt Kat came around from the back yard carrying an arm load of tree limbs. She dropped them into the barrel and dug a pink leather cigarette case out of her pocket.

"I didn't know if you were coming home so I didn't make no dinner. There's some hot pockets in the ice box if you hungry," she said, pulling a cigarette from the case.

She was a portly woman with ebony skin the color of night. Most of her black curly hair had gone grey. The skin around her double chin was sagged and wrinkled. She was 15 years older than Ruben's dad, though most would think she was twice that. She lived a hard life and worked the same way. Most of her life she had been a welder at the shipyard in Pascagoula, since 'decent work' for a colored woman was hard to find in her day. When she retired from there, she busied herself with her large garden, or making knives and welding metal artwork to sell at the local flea market.

"Hey, Aunt Kat." Ruben smiled as he walked toward her. "I already had a sub while I was out with Paul. It's fine." He gave her a peck on the cheek.

"You home for the night then?" she asked as she lit her cigarette.

"Yes ma'am, but I'm gonna' go stay with Paul for a while," he replied.

She took a long pull from her smoke, her eyes fixed on the burn barrel. "Everything ok with him?" she asked indifferently.

"Yes ma'am, just been having those dreams again," he said.

She pondered for a moment. "You boys ain't gay, are ya'?"

"Jesus Christ, Aunt Kat! No!" Ruben exclaimed.

She let a harrumph. "Just saying. You boys spend more time together than most couples I know. Can't blame people for wonderin'."

He felt his face flush as anger swelled in him. "Well, I apologize to the world for having a best friend. We ain't gay. My friend needs me and I'm gonna be there for him, if that's ok with the world."

"Boy, don't sass me!" she yelled as she stuck a calloused, meaty finger in his face. "I asked you a simple question! Sorry if that hurts your delicate feelings, but you give me anymore lip and I will slap the taste clean out of yer' mouth, you understand me?!"

Ruben ground his teeth and stared down at the dirt between them.

Kat dropped her finger and took in a long slow breath. "I'm sorry, boy. I lost my temper." She sighed, "Curse of the family, that damned temper."

Ruben looked back up to her. She was looking to the cloudy, gray-washed sky. Grump came and nuzzled against her thick thighs. Looking down with a sad grin she gave him a quick pat on the head.

"I don't mean to lose my temper like that. But you know you don't sass your elders like that." Kat said.

"Yes ma'am. I'm sorry," Ruben said.

He understood the temper. It really did seem to run in the family. God knows he had his troubles due to losing his cool on several occasions. Plus, he was being a shit. He knew better than to talk to her like that. She had taken him in without a second thought. He was truly lucky to still have his lips intact after snapping at her.

"Thank you for letting me keep my sense of taste, Aunt Kat," he said with a grin.

She snorted. "Well don't let it happen again. You'd look a mite funny walking around with my foot up yo' ass. Plus, I'm too fat to be hoppin' around on one leg."

Rubens laughter quickly spread to Kat. The two sat there laughing at the image of her trying not to fall over, as she hopped around with a foot wedged in Rubens ass.

After the laughter subsided, Ruben said. "Damned family curses."

He often wondered if short fuses were a genetic thing. There was a lingering fear that he might become like Mike, his father. Ruben and his mother had faced multiple beatings by him, when he came home from a few days of being drunk and high. It only took a tone or glance that he deemed offensive, and all hell would break loose. He remembered the evil in his dad's eyes that last night.

As if sensing what Ruben was thinking, Kat squeezed her hand on his shoulder. "You ain't like him."

He looked at her and smiled. "I know. Just scary to think about sometimes."

"I won't let you go down that road. You start acting like him, and I guess we'll have to see how long I can hop my fat ass on one leg," Kat said.

They shared a laugh and headed into the trailer for the night. Ruben gathered up some clothes in a faded green duffle bag; his toothbrush, two cans of wintergreen dip, his hunting knife, and a book on demonology he had snagged from the public library a few days ago. After double checking his inventory, he lay down to sleep for the night when his stomach gave a rumble of protest. Perhaps, a Hot Pocket wasn't such a bad idea.

Walking into the living room he found Kat asleep in her recliner, with the local news still on the small television. He quieted his steps and went to the kitchen. He pulled a frozen ham and cheese Hot Pocket from the freezer. As quietly as possible, he removed the noisy wrapper and slid the pocket into the cooking sleeve. Kat began to snore loudly as the microwave started. A minute and a half later the microwave beeped. He juggled the steaming hot meat pastry from hand to hand, as he swiftly walked back to his room. Unable to take the pain in his fingers, he dropped it on the bed to cool and blew on his fingers.

"Son of a bitch!" he muttered.

Realizing it would be a bit before he could eat, he decided to pull the demonology book from his bag and skim through it. After flipping through the first few dozen pages, an image caught his eye. A drawing of a frighteningly thin old woman covered in shadow, standing over a small boy in his bed. He panned down to the caption underneath it.

: The Night Hag, or Old Hag, is a creature claimed to have been sighted by individuals of many nationalities. Frequently, the Night Hag is used to rationalize the phenomenon of sleep paralysis. Sleep paralysis occurs when upon waking, a person is incapable of voluntary movements, and may even be unable to breathe anything more than shallow inhalations. Additionally, the affected individual attests to feeling the presence of a supernatural malevolent being that immobilizes the person as if sitting upon his/her chest or the foot of his/her bed. The word "night-mare" or "nightmare" was used to describe this phenomenon prior to the term acquiring its modern, more general meaning.[1] Various cultures have various names for this phenomenon and/or supernatural character. See also Mare, Bahtak, Jinn, Mohra, Succubi, Incubi, etc..."

His thoughts went back to the night he woke to find an old woman standing over Paul.

He dog-eared the page and put it back into his bag. After devouring the Hot Pocket, his stomach gave an approving gurgle. Satisfied, he lay down and quickly drifted off to sleep.

Chapter 6

Paul awoke the next day feeling surprisingly refreshed. He lounged in the bed for a moment, enjoying the peace. His head was quiet. The details of his dream escaped him, however the emotions from it remained. It was a feeling of tranquility, fulfillment, and love. He closed his eyes, and let it wash over him like an ocean. The warmth of the wave, pulling him out into a blissful riptide.

"Paul, you plan on getting up at some point today?!" The loud knock on the door and his father's voice snatched him back to the shores of reality. Tension erased the moment as he flinched.

"Yeah, yes sir." He sat up in the bed and looked at the clock. 12:48.

"Shit!" Paul harshly whispered.

He was supposed to meet Ruben at Karl's in 12 minutes. It was about three miles away, which took Paul around fifteen minutes if he rode his bike casually. With his dad being here, he knew borrowing the car was out of the question.

He hurried out of bed and dug an outfit from his dresser. A pair of faded blue jeans with a hole in the right knee, boxers, socks, and a Marilyn Manson shirt he got at his very first concert. Forty-five dollars and threats of eternal damnation from Bible thumping Christian protesters outside of the venue, were totally worth it.

After brushing his teeth and grabbing a pop tart for the road, Paul kissed his mom's cheek and rushed out of the door. His dad, William, was in the carport washing his car.

"Where are you off to in such a hurry?" He asked Paul.

Paul came to a halt before answering. His dad viewed walking away while answering him as disrespectful. He did not care to raise his dad's ire right now, as he was already running late.

"I am headed to Karl's to meet Ruben. I have to try to win my pool champ title back from him."

"Ah. Well I know it's summer, but you can't sleep all day like that. Leads to laziness," his father said.

"Yes sir. I'm sorry. That swamp tea mom got must have put me in a coma," he assured him.

William studied his son's face for a moment. The bags around his eyes weren't so heavy today. It eased his mind slightly, but he still worried about him. The concern for him stayed hidden behind the military stone face. When the dreams first started he had just chalked it up to Paul being scared-natured and weak. As the years went on, he had watched him grow into a respectable young man, despite the girly long hair. He was proud of him, although he rarely let a compliment like that be known. Even though Paul had turned out to be what he considered a tough kid, the night terrors continued to torture his boy. He felt helpless. Helplessness turned into frustration.

"Ok. Make sure it doesn't," William said.

"Yes sir." Paul said, meeting his dad's eyes.

William gave him a nod. "Tomorrow get the grass cut before you take off."

"Yes sir." Paul hid his irritation. He was grateful that his dad at least didn't make him do it now.

"Go get your title back, boy." He granted Paul a smile and a wink.

That smile lifted Paul's spirits back up. For so long all he got from his dad was criticism and emotionless lectures. In the last year or so, that had begun to change. While he was still strict and drill sergeant-esque, he'd started to treat Paul more like a person than a nuisance. He had even told him that he was proud of him for the first time in his life. This was after Paul got suspended for three days for denting a locker with Freddy Ladner's forehead. Freddy had decided a new freshman that weighed in at 125 pounds soaking wet needed some bullying. Paul decided he didn't. The locker helped Paul win that debate.

Smiling back at his dad, he said, "Yes, sir!"

Paul snatched up his bike and darted off down Hand Road. Setting a new record of six minutes, Paul came skidding to a stop in front of Karl's. 1:21 pm. The new record was partially thanks to a little extra motivation from Mr. Moran's pit bull, Puss. Seemed the old man had forgotten to latch his gate, and Puss encouraged Paul to reach speeds he didn't know were possible as he chased him to the end of

Hand Rd. After a short chase and a near miss with a pickup truck, Puss lost interest.

Paul took a second to catch his breath before going in. The gravel parking lot had only two vehicles in it. One was Mr.Hern's old blue pickup. The other, a black Mercedes sedan that Paul had never seen before. Laid against the side of the dark brown wood of the store was Ruben's purple 10 speed. He took one last deep breath and slowly let it out. After using the bottom of his shirt to dry the sweat dripping down his face, he crossed the finish line into the store. The cool blast of the window unit AC was blissful as Paul passed in front of it.

The store was very fitting to the small country town - very simplistic. Most of the walls and floor were nothing more than unpainted plywood. The interior smelled of lumber and cigar smoke. Paul grabbed a root beer out of the cooler and rolled the chilled bottle across his forehead. After a few rolls, he brought it to the counter.

Mr. Hern was in his usual post behind the register. He was kicked back in his oak rocker, puffing on a large cigar; while reading through the newspaper for the third time. Paul loved the smell of the smoke. Often, he would sit with his grandpa on the porch, as he puffed away on a giant stogie and told stories of the war. Paul loved the stories, but the smell of the cigar smoke was the compliment to the tales that he looked forward to.

"Hey, Mr. Hern." Paul greeted him, placing a dollar bill on the counter.

"Heyo, boyo" Mr. Hern gave his traditional greeting. "He's waiting on ya." He motioned his head to the bar area.

"Yes sir. Gotta win the championship back," Paul smiled.

"Seems y'all might have a challenger today," he said with a grin.

"Oh? You coming out of retirement?" Paul asked with interest.

"Oh no. Not me. New kid came in today. Him and Ruben have been shooting for a bit now. From the language coming from back there, it sounds like it's getting serious," Mr. Hern chuckled.

"New kid?" Paul asked.

"Mhmm. Think it's the son of that doctor that just moved into the old Dedeaux house," Mr. Hern said as he thumped ashes into the large ashtray on the counter.

"Hmm," Paul's curiosity was peaked. He looked to the door of the bar area. "Well, I guess I better get to work, then."

"Yep." Mr. Hern gave Paul and nod and went back to re-reading the paper.

Paul went to the doorway to find Ruben leaned over the pool table lining up a shot at the one ball. He was so intently focused on his shot; he hadn't noticed Paul yet. There were five solids left on the table and one stripe. Irritation creased his brow as he slid the stick back and forth, preparing to shoot.
The back of the new challenger was all Paul could see, as he stood at the opposite corner of the table watching Ruben set up his shot. His broad shoulders stretched the red t-shirt he wore. Scruffy red hair poked out from under

110

the black baseball hat he had on. Love handles pushed out at the fabric of his shirt, and thick muscular calves were exposed by his khaki cargo shorts.

"Either a farm boy or a jock," Paul thought to himself.

The clack of the cue ball striking its target brought Paul's focus back to the table. The yellow ball sped to the corner pocket opposite the stranger, then out of Paul's line of sight. He heard the thump thump of the ball hitting the nipples of the pocket, a pause… and finally, the sound of the ball dropping in. Ruben exhaled and stood from his leaning position. He immediately began studying the table, allowing Paul to remain a fly on the wall just a bit longer.

"Only four to go, chief. Don't choke," the stranger said, with cockiness dripping from his words.

Ruben looked up ready with a comeback when he spotted Paul standing in the doorway.

"There that bitch is!" he said with a smile.

The new guy turned to face Paul and looked him over. His eyes lingered for a moment on Paul's long hair. He was pretty sure he saw a glimmer of disapproval in his eyes.

"My bad, dude. I overslept, and then dad wanted to lecture me before I could leave," Paul said, looking back to Ruben.

Ruben made his way around the table and gave Paul the gangster hug. He then looked to the new guy.

"This is Brian. Brian, Paul. My best friend I was telling you about that is late as hell." Ruben gave Paul a friendly pop in the shoulder.

"My baaaaad! Damn." Paul looked to Brian.

Beneath the Black Saints hat sat a chubby yet intimidating face. His hazel eyes were narrow and held a constant look of mild anger. The type you see on those guys that are always starting fights at parties. A faint speckling of freckles dusted his cheeks. His bottom lip protruded from the wad of dip behind it.

"Good to meet ya, dude" Paul said, and stuck his hand out to Brian.

He grabbed it in a vice like grip, and tightened down a little more before giving it a stiff shake. Paul gave no hint of the pain he felt in his hand. The awkward eye contact with Paul dragged as he held the grip a few more seconds. Paul gave a friendly smile at his attempt to establish alpha status. It was pretty clear Paul wasn't going to be best friends with this kid. He despised alpha types, as they were most commonly the bullies at school.

Brian released his hand just beforePaul devised a smart-ass comment about liking to be bought dinner before holding hands. He decided to let it slide and just try to enjoy the day. A good night's sleep had him feeling better than he had in a long time, and he wasn't going to let this guy ruin it.

Turning his attention to the pool table, he said "So Ruby, looks like you're letting the new guy spank you a little bit."

Ruben gave a shrug. "He's not bad." He then flicked a quick wink at Paul.

A hustle? Mr. Hern had a strict rule about hustling. Unlike Jack at Boones, Karl had no tolerance for money games. This guy must be a real dick if Ruben was willing to face Karl's wrath.

Sensing Paul's concern, Ruben gave him the 'Don't worry I've got this under control look.'

"Not bad?" Brian chimed in. "I been whippin' yer ass for two games now. 'Bout to be three, son!" His deep southern drawl oozed arrogance.

Yep, Paul didn't like him. It was official. All concern over breaking their hustle rules was replaced with a giddy excitement at the idea of watching Ruben destroy this kid's over inflated ego.

"Well damn, Roob. I was hoping to take the title back from you today, but it looks like the new guy has that handled," Paul said as he took a seat on one of the weathered bar stools.

The cracked green faux leather cushion dug into his leg through the fabric of his jeans. causing him to squirm as he attempted to get comfortable. Mr. Hern spared no expense.

Brian held his arms out in a welcoming pose. "You are welcome to lose too, kid."

'Kid? Oh, this is gonna be good,' Paul thought.

"Hey, if you can beat Ruben that easy, then I don't suppose I really stand much of a chance. My dad always told me never walk into a battle you can't win," Paul said.

Brian sneered, "Sounds like a smart man."

"Yep." Paul laughed wryly.

Ruben returned to the game and pocketed one more of his balls, only to scratch on the cue ball's rebound.

"Damn it!" he grumbled.

"Damn, son! I told you no more chances. Now you just hand me the win? Ha!" Brian said, as he stood at the ball return waiting for the cue to drop.

"Can't catch a break, man!" Ruben said with frustration.

Brian placed the cue on the table while watching Ruben. "A break ain't what you're missing. It's skill, son," he chuckled.

Had Paul not known what was coming, he may not have been able to resist the urge to talk his way into a fight with this guy.

"Whatever, man. I bet you can't make this next shot," Ruben said with feigned irritation.

"Right, man, I got the ball in hand." Brian looked to the table. His last ball was blocked against the rail by two of Ruben's. Unless he suddenly became some kind of trick shot wizard, there was no possible way he was going to legally make the shot.

"Bet you five bucks you can't," Ruben said still pretending to be mad.

"Well, shit no I can't, but it don't matter none. You'll get one more shot and blow it just like you keep doing, kid," Brian replied.

"Fine, bet I run this fucking table then. You can't be lucky that long!" Ruben exclaimed. He was really putting on a show. Paul was struggling to keep a serious face.

Brian quickly evaluated the table. Nothing was lined up for an easy shot. The three remaining balls would either require covering a lot of green or walking the ball down the rail. From what he had seen from Ruben so far, he was fully confident that there was no chance he could make all three shots plus the eight ball without missing.

"Ha! A'ight, son." He laughed as he pulled his wallet. He took a five out and slapped it onto the edge of the table. Paul couldn't help but notice an excessive amount of other bills in his wallet. Most notable was the fifty-dollar bill poking out. A grin crossed his face.

Ruben pulled out a crumple of bills and produced a wadded up five. He set the bill on the edge next to Brian's.

"That's what's up! Easy money." Brain continued his boisterous display of ego.

Ruben turned to Paul with a mischievous grin. Brian opted to go for defense and lead the cue ball to barely tap his last remaining ball. This left Ruben with no other shot than banking the three off the rail into the side pocket. Keeping up the facade he stood rubbing his hair and staring at the difficult shot.

"Shit," he sighed. "Well, here goes nothing."

Brian laughed, "You're fucked bro. You can just forfeit and save yourself the embarrassment. Nobody has to know. Well, except hippy over there," He nodded towards Paul.

'Oh, this mother fucker!' Paul barely kept from saying.

"Nah, I got this," Ruben said.

After a quick measure up of the shot, Ruben hit the bank shot and the three went cleanly into the side pocket.

"OH! NOTHIN BUT NET!!" Ruben celebrated.

Paul watched Brian's face turn a pinkish shade of red, and his lips thin. The joy of watching Brian get hustled and humiliated was worth more than the bet, and more satisfying than knocking him on his ass.

"Yeah yeah, even a blind squirrel finds a nut sometimes. Two to go, kid," Brian said.

This whole calling everyone kid thing was really starting to feel like sandpaper on Paul's ass. Like when you get stuck sitting next to the kid at lunch that smacks as he chews and makes loud slurping sounds when he takes a drink. Bobby Lanham came to mind. His incessant smacking had once driven Paul to momentarily lose his sanity.

"FOR FUCKS SAKE! CLOSE YOUR FUCKING MOUTH WHEN YOU CHEW FOR THE LOVE OF GOD!" he hollered as he slammed his tray down, sending the mystery meat of the day through the air and into Ruben's lap across the table.

There was a moment of silence while Ruben stared in disbelief at the gravy covered meat product in his lap. He laughed and launched his own back at Paul. Ruben missed, and hit the kid behind him. Thus began the great food fight of Delisle Middle School. Luckily none of the teachers were able to figure out the source of profanity or the origin of the food fight. Ultimately, that day had cured Bobby of his poor eating habits.

Ruben made short work of the last two solids and then the eight. With a triumphant "BOOYAH" he snatched up his winnings. Brian was scowling at the back of Rubens head as he did. His right hand balled into a fist. Paul slowly stood from his chair, preparing to pounce if Brian was about to make the horrible decision that he was hoping he would.

"Well, hello boys," a female voice said from the doorway.

Paul turned to find his cousin, Sam, standing there with a Barq's root beer in one hand and a cigarette in the other. She was a pretty girl. She was tall compared to most girls, at 5'9". She had shoulder length sun-bleached hair and dark tanned skin. Her almond eyes, full lips, and high cheekbones ensured no man would easily resist her, but she was always more like one of the guys to those closest to her.

"SAMMY!!!" Ruben and Paul cheered simultaneously.

Paul scooped her up in a huge bear hug. Ruben followed suit after Paul put her down, though he hugged her a bit longer than Paul.

He'd had a crush on her since 4th grade and had been shot down by her on many occasions. This, however, never discouraged him.

"Don't you have band camp today?" Ruben asked.

"Nope. Mr. Holland's wife was in an accident, so they cancelled today," she replied.

"Oh, shit! She ok?" Paul asked.

"She broke her arm and ankle, but nothing serious from what they told us. Just has to stay in the hospital for a few days," Sam said.

Mr. Holland was always a student favorite, and his wife regularly sent him to school with treats for his class.

"Damn, that sucks. I hope she's back on her feet soon," Ruben said.

"I'm sure she'll be fine. So, who's this?" she asked, turning her attention to Brian.

Paul looked back to Brian who was leaning against the pool table. His expression had gone from one of outrage to what Paul assumed was his cool face. He was posturing to appear relaxed and confident. A laser like gaze was fixed upon Sam, more like what you'd expect to see from the lead singer of a boy band aiming at the swooning girl in the front row of his concert. Paul grinned and stifled a laugh as he returned his attention to Sam.

"This is Brian. New guy in town," Ruben replied.

"Sup." Brian said to her with a flick of his head. He maintained his verging on creepy gaze.

Sam looked him over for a moment then smiled. Paul knew that smile. Feeling Paul looking at her, she flicked her eyes at him to find an expression of stunned disgust on his face. With a roll of her eyes, she walked up to the bar and snuffed her cigarette out in one of the dirty ashtrays. Once it was out, she turned her attention back to Brian.

"Well Brian, what brings you to our little town?" she asked.

He adjusted to face her. "Well, my mom and dad got divorced. My dad has money and a prenup. Mom had a habit and was a whore, so I had to go with him. He wanted a fresh start, so he bought the old plantation house up the way and had it fixed up."

"Oh. That blows," Sam replied. "Like it here so far?"

He gave her a slow look up and down. "I definitely like the scenery," he said as he locked eyes with her. Sam giggled and brushed her hair back behind her ear.

Ruben and Paul looked to each other, both wearing the same look of shocked revolt. Paul dropped his head and shook it. He stepped closer to Ruben and spoke in a hushed tone.

"This fucking guy? Does she just have douchebag radar or something?"

"I was thinking the same thing. Now not only do I have to watch my future ex-wife flirt with him, but I'm not even gonna get to finish taking all of his money," Ruben said.

"I've put up with her dating some real winners, but I don't think I'll be able to stomach this sack of shit for long," Paul said looking back to find Brian now standing at the bar next to Sam. His jaw muscles began working overtime.

"Maybe I can at least fix the taking his money part," Paul said.

He pulled two Quarters out of his pocket and set them on the table.

"Hey Sam, Ruben just beat Brian. You want to play him for the table, or can I?" he asked.

Sam opened her mouth to respond but was cut short. The blow to Brian's ego in front of her was not something he was going to stand for.

"Oh hell no, kid! He didn't beat anything. Getting lucky one game ain't winning." He pointed his cue at Ruben. "I beat yer ass twice. You're gonna put that money back on the table and let me win it back, son!"

Paul turned to Ruben and whispered, "Like a moth to a flame."

Her expression became one of confusion and slight disdain as Sam watched the events unfold. Paul shot Sam a "SEE?!" look as he walked over to sit next to her.

"Woah, easy there killer," Ruben chuckled, as he put his hands out in front of him. "Ok, fair is fair. One more game. This time, though, let's make it worth all the fuss since I got my groove back now."

He pulled the crumple of money out once more. After straightening the bills out, he counted out forty dollars and tossed it on the table.

He was no longer trying to put on a facade. "Forty bucks. Winner takes all."

Brian studied the money for a second. "Shit yeah! 'Bout time you man up!" he laughed as he got his wallet from his back pocket.

After slamming his money on the table, Ruben grabbed it and placed it on the bar next to Sam.

He gave her a wink. "I'll buy you lunch after I get done winning."

She gave him a smile and a wink in return.

"Winner breaks," Brian said.

He placed himself against a wall and leaned back with a smirk on his face.

Ruben chalked up his cue and placed the cue ball in position. His face had gone to stone. There was no emotion other than business at this point. He sent the cue ball flying into the rest.

After a storm of balls bouncing and clacking together, the four dropped into the side pocket. He immediately lined up and pocketed his next shot. Then the next. Brian stood from the wall. His expression changed from cocky to stunned. Another ball dropped. Brian's neck and ears reddened. Giving Brian no chance to shoot, it took less than three minutes to win the game. Snatching up the money he walked over to Brian and extended his hand.

"Good game," Ruben said.

Brian slapped his hand away, cueing Paul to ease his way towards them just in case Brian could actually back up his mouth.

"You fuckin hustled me?!" Brian growled.

Ruben looked down to his stinging hand and stared at it a moment. Then slowly looked back up to Brian. Visions of his father flashed in his mind. The respect for Mr. Hern was the only force keeping him from wrapping his hands around Brian's thick neck.

In a stern, yet hushed voice he replied, "Yes. And if you ever put your goddamn hands on me like that again, you won't get them back."

Paul saw Brian's hands once again ball into fists and prepared to pounce. In the next second, he had formulated a fight plan if he had to get involved. He would kick the back of Brian's right knee to stop him from advancing on Ruben. As soon as his knee was on the floor, he would follow up with a rear choke if he stayed on his knees. If he fell all the way, he would simply drop on top of him and hold him in a neck crank or arm lock.

He was halted by a strong hand grabbing his shoulder and pulling him back a step. The hand spun him around to find Mr. Hern, holding him in place. For an old man he had one hell of a grip. Karl's eyes went to Ruben and Brian.

"Y'all cut that shit out. Ain't gonna' have you boys breaking shit in my store," he barked.

Ruben turned to face Mr. Hern with wide eyes.

"Yes, sir. Sorry," he said, taking a step away from Brian.

Brian didn't move, his eyes still bore into Ruben. Brian's face was filled with rage, and his fists were still balled tightly at his sides. Paul feared he was going to take a cheap shot on Ruben while his back was turned.

"Boy, I suggest you turn those fists back to hands before I take it as an insult," Mr. Hern said to Brian.

Brian's expression became conflicted. After a second of looking from Ruben to Karl's old yet sturdy frame, with a baseball bat resting on one shoulder, he relaxed his hands with a huff.

"That's more like it. You're new here, so this is your one get out of jail free card. You don't start trouble in my store. You do, you leave with an ass whippin' and don't come back," Mr. Hern said to him.

He then turned Paul to face him and pointed for Ruben to come stand in front of him. Reluctantly, Ruben joined Paul.

"As for you boys. You know the rules. You don't hustle in here. Friendly games only. I get that the kid has a big mouth and probably deserved it, but rules are rules," Mr. Hern said, looking from one to the other.

Brian scowled at Hern.

Mr. Hern was a very by-the-book, black and white guy. There was no grey area. You either did right or you did wrong. He had begun the no playing for money rule after a local biker pulled a gun on a guy for winning $300 from him.

"Ruben, you give that boy his money back," he said.

Ruben hung his head and sighed, "Yes, sir."

He took his money back and tossed the remaining forty bucks on the table. Brian quickly snatched the money up and put it back in his wallet.

"Alright. Now you're square with your money. In the future, I would consider being a little less of an asshole when you're new in town. Acting like that will get you hurt, boy. You're lucky it was these guys you met here today and not some of our less patient folk," he said, giving Ruben and Paul a hearty slap on the back. "Game's over for today. Go on home and cool off," he instructed Brian.

Brian shot Paul and Ruben a death glare as he walked past them. Paul offered him a smile in return. He gave half a pause as he fought down the urge to bounce Paul's head off the door frame.

"Shit ain't over by a long shot, kid," Brain said, locking eyes with Paul.

Mr. Hern gave a firm smack to the back of Brian's head. "Don't test my patience, boy! Only one you got to be mad is your damned self for not knowing when to shut that shit hole you call a mouth."

"You can't hit me!" Brian yelped. "You'll be hearing from my dad and his lawyers, old man."

Hern gave him another, harder smack to the back of the head.

"Well I just did, didn't I? I don't give two squirrel turds who your daddy is. I will whip your ass like you were one of my own. Apparently, like your dad should have. If he doesn't like it, he knows where to find me. Now quit that puffing-up macho bullshit and git on before I get mad!"

Brian looked to be on the verge of tears as he stormed past Karl and the rest. Everyone stood silently until Brian was out of the store.

"Sorry about all of that, Mr. Hern," Paul said.

Mr. Hern sighed and chuckled. "I get it, boys. If ever I met a spoiled little shit that needed a good humbling, that was it. BUT, y'all know the rules. Don't let it happen again. You boys keep your heads on a swivel though. I get the feeling that kid ain't the type to let things go easy."

"Well, sir, that would be a bad day for him," Ruben said, watching out the window as Brian got into the Mercedes that was parked outside.

The tires kicked up gravel as the car sped backwards. The brakes slammed on and a middle finger shot out of the window before it disappeared in a cloud of dust.

"Eh, the little guy probably just needs a hug," Paul smirked.

Brian actually wasn't very little. Yes, he was about five inches shorter than Paul. However, he had about forty or fifty pounds on him. While he didn't have a bodybuilder physique, he was a very solid kid. Physically, Paul knew that if it came to a fight he wouldn't be able to match him in strength. Hopefully the four years of martial arts would pay off if that was where things led. Those were problems for another day, though.

Mr. Hern went back to his place behind the counter and resumed his 5th read through the paper as Sam walked up to the boys.

"That went well," she laughed.

"Right? Ruben and I take our jobs as the Delisle welcome committee very seriously. As you can see, we have just created another satisfied customer. I wouldn't be surprised if we got medals and a raise!" Paul said.

"Oh, absolutely! You two are beacons of hospitality," she said.

"Well, from what I saw you were wanting to give ole short, squat, and emotionally unstable a VERY warm welcome."

"What? He's cute. AND has a nice car. Well, he was cute until he spoke. But, he fucked with my family and Sammy don't play that," she said, and hooking her arm in his.

"Family first and always," Paul said with a wink.

He looked at Ruben, who was still staring out the window. One hand was lightly rubbing the back of the other. His jaw was clenched, and his body was tense.

"You good man?" Paul asked.

Ruben turned to face him. "Yeah. Just hard to let a man slap me and not put him in the ICU. I mean at least have the courtesy to punch me. Something so insulting about a slap, ya know? First person that got away with hitting me since my biological sperm donor." He gave a half smile.

"Well, I wouldn't worry about it. I have a pretty good feeling that you will have your payback real soon. Mr. Hern is right. Dude isn't the type to let things go," Paul said.

"I hope he's not," Ruben said looking back at the window.

With the jovial mood thoroughly ruined, Ruben lit a cigarette and hoisted up his duffle bag from the corner. The three bought an ice-cold root beer and headed out into the blistering summer sun.

"Well, Madie won't be home for another hour. Shall I beat your asses in some Street Fighter till then?" Paul said.

"Biiiiiiiiitch! I will spank you like an albino midget Eskimo hooker," Ruben replied.

"What? What the hell? I don't even know if I should be offended by that," Sam said.

"Sounds like a good time to me," Paul laughed.

Paul became distracted by a sound approaching in the distance. It sounded like music… almost like heavy metal. There wasn't anybody in Delisle with a sound system that listened to anything other than rap or country, except Adam. He wasn't due back in town for a few more days, though. After a moment, the sound registered. It was the savage cords being shredded out by Slayer. Paul hurried to the edge of the parking lot and shielded his eyes from the sun to look down the road. A small white pickup truck a few hundred yards away began beeping its horn in the Shave and a Haircut pattern.

Paul's excitement covered his face while he held both arms out as if asking, "What the hell?"

Adam slid the Isuzu PUP into the parking lot, coming to a stop beside the three.

"What is up, bitches!" Adam exclaimed as he opened the driver's door. Hefting his large, 6'6" frame out of the small truck, he scooped Sam up into a bear hug. This was followed by the traditional handshake/man-hug to Ruben and Paul.

"What the hell are you doing back so soon?" Paul asked, the smile still on his face.

"Storms rolled in and caused some problems on the barge. They sent all the contract crews home, while the guys that make the money actually earn it for a change," he replied.

"Well fuck yeah! Welcome home, ya' big bastard," Ruben said.

"Always good to be home. So, what is the plan today, kiddos?" Adam asked.

"We were going to shoot pool until Madie got off work. Brian fucked that up for us, though. So, we were headed to the house to play some Street Fighter," Paul said.

"Who's Brian?" Adam asked.

"New guy in town. He's a piece of work. Cocky redneck type," Ruben chimed in.

Adam twisted the tip of his scruffy beard, as Paul filled him in on the day's events. "Sounds like I need to introduce this kid to our humble little town," he said after Paul finished.

"I got dibs on beating his ass first," Ruben said.

Adam chuckled and slapped Ruben on the back. "Absolutely, my man."

"So, you up for going to the river, brother-man?" Paul asked hopefully.

"Yeah. Just gotta drop by the house to unpack and change," Adam replied.

"My hero!" Sam said as she dramatically fell into Adams arms like a damsel in a 1950's movie.

He laughed, "Yeah yeah. Alright, load the bikes up and pile in."

"Sweet! Mind if we swing by and scoop Madie up from Save-A-Lot before we go to the river?" Paul asked.

Madie worked part-time there during the summer. Having the extra money was nice, but it also kept her away from her father.

"Alright, lover boy," Adam jabbed at him.

"What? She wanted to go the next time we all went. Plus, we were all supposed to hang out when she got off," Paul said.

"Uh huh. Doesn't have anything to do with seeing her half naked and wet, does it?" Adam gave him a little shove.

Paul rolled his eyes. He felt his cheeks beginning to flush. "Whatever man… she does look pretty good in a bikini, though."

Adam, Ruben and Sam burst out into laughter.

"Damn right she does!" Ruben said grabbing Paul by the shoulders and giving him a shake. "That's my boy. We'll make a man of you yet."

Paul bowed his head and shook it. "If we are done with the 'Give Paul Shit Show', let's go," he said, motioning to the cab of the truck.

Still laughing, they crammed into the small cab of the truck. After a stop at Paul and Adam's house, they were on their way to get Madie.

Chapter 7

As if they had synchronized their watches, Madie was walking out of her workplace as they were pulling in. Adam laid on the horn, startling her and causing her to drop her smock and keys. After going through the emotions of fear, embarrassment, and ultimately laughing at herself, she scooped her things off the ground and ran up to the passenger window where Paul was sitting. Ruben was squeezed in the middle with Sam sitting on his lap. He had no objections to this seating arrangement.

"Jesus! You scared the crap outta me, Adam! What are you doing back so soon?" Madie asked.

"Storms rolled in. Couldn't do any work," he replied, still chuckling at her expense.

"Nice! So, what are yall up to?" she asked, turning her attention to Paul.

"Coming to get you to go to the river," Paul said.

"Still got your bathing suit in the car?" Sam asked.

"Yeah, but I need to get Jennifer," Madie said.

Madie had brought Jennifer to Sam's the previous night so she wouldn't be alone with her dad while she worked. After the incident last night and his steadily declining demeanor, she decided that Jennifer would not be by herself with that man anymore. Sam was the only one she had to reach out to, although she had hated to ask. Thankfully, Sam was more than happy to help. When Sam wasn't hanging with them she was playing mother to her younger siblings while her mom worked. She assured Madie that adding one more wasn't a problem.

"She's at my house still and having a blast with my sister. She didn't want to go home and she's welcome to stay. Stop worrying, girl, my house is basically a halfway home for the neighborhood kids," Sam said.

"You sure?" Madie asked.

"Girl, get your bathing suit and let's go!" Sam said.

"Ok," Madie said, as a smile grew on her face. She could use some responsibility-free fun for a change.

Paul watched Madie do a light jog to her car, admiring every inch of her. Something caught his attention just ahead of the car.

An old woman in a white nightgown was standing a few feet in front of the car as Madie dug through the back seat. The front of her gown had some type of red design on it. Her posture was hunched, and her head was bowed. The hair atop her head was matted and dirty. The base of her night gown appeared to have been drug through muddy water. Slowly, her eyes raised to meet his. A chill ran through him causing goose-flesh to cover his arms and legs. The design on her nightgown became clearer to him as he stared...blood splatter. Her lower jaw was missing, and shredded flesh hung from the exposed bones of her cheeks.

"Mrs. Goodrich?" he whispered. Tears of fear welled up in the corners of his eyes.

"Huh?" Madie said as she jogged back to him. She felt the emotions coming off of him.

Paul looked towards Madie and then quickly back to where Mrs. Goodrich was. Nothing. Just asphalt and white lines marking the parking spots. He looked to Madie again, then to the others.

"You didn't see her?" he asked, trying to hide the panic in his voice.

Adam leaned forward with a look of confusion. "See who?"

Paul took in a breath and closed his eyes. Just as slow, he let it out. Forcing his brain to return to its natural method, logic. 'Not getting enough sleep. It's starting to mess with your head,' he thought.

"See what, Paul?" Adam asked again. A tone of concern in his voice.

"Sorry, just… Haven't been sleeping much lately," he finally said, "It's nothing, man. I'm good." He feigned a smile.

"What did you see?" Ruben asked.

"It's nothing, man. It's stupid," Paul replied.

"Dude, you can't just leave us hanging like that. The suspense is killing me," Ruben chuckled.

Paul sighed. He was frustrated with himself for letting his emotions slip in the moment. Now, here he was, the center of attention. The vision of her old frame was vividly fresh in his mind. It was so real. It wasn't something out of the corner of his eye. He wasn't sleeping. "I think it was Mrs. Goodrich. Just standing right there, in front

132

of Madie's car. Face was all mangled, just like…except she wasn't naked."

The silence was audible in the truck. All eyes were on Paul except Adam's. He stared at the steering wheel. His mind went somewhere else. To the day at the graveyard. Mrs. Goodrich's frail naked body. The gunshot. The chaos that ensued. Finally, to the day of her funeral, when Mr. Goodrich pulled him to the side and warned him.

"Woah. That's fucked up, man," Ruben said, leaning past Sam to see out the windshield.

"You saw her?!" Madie said with a mixture of fear and excitement.

"No. I mean, yeah, but no. It's just lack of sleep messing with my head. Really. Let's just go to the river." Paul was becoming agitated and wanted to change the subject.

"My dear cousin, you have to start getting more sleep. That's not healthy," Sam said.

"You good?" Adam cut her off. His eyes were still fixed to the steering wheel.

"Ye." the expression on Adams face cut Paul's answer short. Fear. Almost. Fear mixed with anger. It was not a look he was used to seeing on his brothers face.

"Yeah, man. I'm good." He paused a moment, studying Adam's face. It was the face of someone with a secret that was tearing them up inside. It was too uncomfortable to see him like that. He decided it was time to drop the subject and find a new spot in the locker of 'Shit He Didn't Want to Think About' to place this moment.

"Alright. Good. Then let's go have some fun. No more talking about bad shit." He seemed to perk up a bit after giving the order.

Paul didn't find it difficult to distract himself from what he saw. Adam's rule for his truck was that women always got to sit in the front. Guys in the back.

"Well Madie, you either gotta kick Paul out or sit in his lap," Adam said.

"Aw, I can't make him ride by himself," she replied.

After some contorting, she made her way into Paul's lap and shut the door. Paul began a silent plea to his penis not to embarrass him.

The ride was filled with idle chat about Brian, school, tales of the insane coon-asses Adam worked with, and plans for the summer. After the half-hour ride, they turned onto the bumpy red dirt road that led through the woods to the river bank. A few ball-crushing minutes of bouncing down the hole laden trail later, they arrived.

Adam stopped where the red dirt became mixed with sand a hundred feet from the river. The crew piled out of the truck and stretched a moment. Ruben and Paul rubbed cramped muscles out of their legs.

"Sam, come with me. I gotta change," Madie asked.

"Ok. No peeking, boys," Sam scolded mockingly.

While the two went off behind a cluster of bushes, Adam grabbed a small cooler from the back of the truck. Ruben and Paul stripped off their shirts and took off in a race to the bank of the river. He watched his little brother get tackled into the water by Ruben after winning the race. Coming up laughing, Paul lunged at Ruben and the two began wrestling. Paul's face looked so happy and carefree in this moment. Adam grabbed a beer from the cooler, cracked it open, and leaned back against the truck.

He had forgotten about what Mr. Goodrich had said that day, chalking it up to a man on the verge of insanity from grief. The way he made Adam tell him every detail of what happened that day still baffled him. Why would a man want to know the gruesome details of his wife's suicide? The old man had become enraged when Adam didn't seem to believe the story he had told him. He recalled how strong the old man's grip was on his wrist when he turned to walk away.

Goodrich had dropped his tone to just over a whisper through gritted teeth. "I'm not fucking with you. I'm not fucking crazy. We will all be there soon. Starting with your brother!" His finger pointed to his wife's casket.

"BEER!" Sam's exclamation snapped Adam back to the here and now.

"Oh. Yeah. Help yourself," he told her, motioning to the cooler.

She and Madie grabbed a beer and started towards the water.

Sam turned back to him. "You coming?"

Sit here and relive that day over and over, or enjoy the day with his brother and friends? He stuffed the memories away and chose the second option.

Madie and Sam sat on the bank with their feet in the water, sipping on their beers as Paul and Ruben continued their battle. It was never an alpha issue or an attempt to show off for the opposite sex. The two genuinely loved the friendly competition. Paul pulled off an impressive leg sweep on Ruben as Adam approached the bank. Ruben was up in an instant and scooped Paul up in a belly to belly suplex. Had Adam not known the two were friends, he would have thought they were really fighting by the ferociousness of their wrestling bout. However, after each slam and sweep they both came up laughing. Adam managed to come up behind Paul unnoticed. In a swift and effortless motion, he snatched him into a fireman's carry and then pressed him straight up and above his head with both arms.

"Oh, fuck me!" Paul said as was sent flying through the air into the deeper part of the river.

Ruben, Madie, and Sam cringed as the slap of Paul's stomach against the water filled the air.

"Holy shit, Adam!" Sam laughed.

"Oh, damn," Adam said with a look of worry.

Paul shot up from the waist high water. His long hair a wet sloppy mess on his face. The skin of his stomach was already turning a deep shade of pink. Adam honestly hadn't intended to throw him that high or far. He was a little surprised at his own strength at times. While he had always been naturally strong, months of turning wrenches and heavy lifting on the barges had taken that to new heights. It wasn't just that, though. Paul was lighter. He noticed his ribs and spine were more pronounced as he came up from the water.

"Diiiiick!" Paul chuckled through the sting. He pushed his hair back from his face and rubbed his stomach as he waded back to the group.

"Damn it, man. You need to eat a sandwich or something," Adam said.

Paul gave him the one finger salute.

"My bad, my bad." Adam laughed.

Paul shot a quick look to Ruben, who was slowly working his way behind Adam. The sloshing of Paul trudging through the water masked Ruben's movements.

"You need to lower the dose on the roids, ass!" Paul said still laughing.

As Paul got within arm's reach, Ruben wrapped both arms around Adams right leg. Paul immediately followed suit on the left leg. Before Adam could drop his weight to stop them, they had him lifted in the air and sent the giant crashing down into the waters.

"OOOOOOOH!" the two exclaimed as they high fived each other.

Adam shot up in an explosion of water, and a two versus one battle began. The girls watched as Ruben and Paul's bodies flew through the air. Adam got toppled on occasion, though not in the same dramatic fashion as Paul and Adam soared.

Sam took a sip of her beer and watched as Paul desperately hung onto the Adam's legs to keep from being lifted. Ruben came sailing in from the side with a solid tackle, and the three of them disappeared momentarily under the brown waters of the Wolf River. Paul was the first to pop up, sucking in a deep breath of air. He looked over to Madie and Sam with exhausted joy on his face. His eyes fixed on Madie and he smiled as he straightened himself.

"Come on i…" He was cut off as Adam and Ruben pounced on him, pulling him back into the fray.

The girls laughed till their stomachs ached. Sam watched Madie as she kept her eyes on Paul, as she always did when he wasn't looking. Quickly averting her eyes if he turned to face her. It was cute. Sam was far more experienced in the ways of love. Well, sex anyway. No, she couldn't say she had really ever been in love.

To her it was like watching two children. The innocence of it made her smile. She wanted them to be together, and she had been quietly waiting for one of them to make a move for months. Leaving it up to them, however, didn't seem to be working.

"So Madie, you ever gonna piss on Paul and claim him as yours?" Sam asked bluntly.

Madie blushed and nervously laughed for a moment "Good Lord, Sammy!"

"I'm just saying. You two have been flirting and beating around the bush for months now. It's no secret that you are crazy about each other. You guys would be great together! Clearly my dear cousin doesn't have the balls to make the first move, so why don't you? I mean, it's the 90's. All that 'men have to make the first move' crap is old-fashioned nonsense. Plus, just to be honest, he is a gorgeous man. You wait too long, and you might lose him to some unworthy skank," Sam said.

Madie fidgeted a bit, "Well I'm just old-fashioned, I guess. Besides, I don't think he really wants to deal with all the drama that would come with me."

"HA! He would take a cup of fire ants in his pants to be with you, let alone dealing with your drama," Sam laughed.

Madie laughed and continued to fidget. She watched Paul as he continued the friendly battle. The sun glistening off his wet skin was alluring. She took in the kindness that poured from his eyes. He deserved better than the train wreck that was her life. The thought of her father began to invade her mind. She closed her eyes and shook her head. Trying to expel the mood-dampening memories.

"You ok?" Sam asked with a look of confusion. Madie's facial expression had gone from happy and laughing to dark so quickly it had surprised her.

"Yeah. Yeah, I'm fine. Sorry," Madie responded, forcing a smile. She began to speak again but was stopped by Ruben landing hard in the water just in front of them. A large splash of water covered the two girls. Sam's cigarette was ruined by the wave.

Paul and Adam stood with their hands still locked around the other's forearm, creating the platform that Ruben had stood on as they launched him into the air.

Ruben sprang up, spitting water. "Told you I know how to get the ladies wet!" He laughed making finger guns at Adam and Paul.

As Ruben performed his victory dance, a glob of wet sand smacked him in the back, followed by another to his forehead as he turned towards the direction of attack. Madie and Sam were already scooping up more sand to pelt him with.

"Shit! Retreat!" he hollered as he dove under water.

The air was filled with laughter as Ruben tried to evade the volley. Adam and Paul's minds were free of the memory of that day for this short time. No flickering of ghosts standing by his bed came to Paul's mind. No apparitions waiting in the distance. They were truly happy and lost in the moment. Playing and laughing like teenagers were supposed to do. Carefree and enjoying life. Sadly, this would be the last happy summer day for all of them.

Chapter 8

The sun began to get low in the sky, and the horseplay had finally settled down. Everyone retreated back to the truck to have a beer and smoke. Adam loaded his one hitter with some especially skunky smelling weed and fired it up. He and Sam shared it as she was the only other one that smoked it.

Paul plopped down onto the tailgate, working the butt of his cigarette between his teeth and taking in the scene. The shadows were starting to get long, the world took on a dark orange glow from the setting sun. He hated this time of day, as it filled him with a sense of foreboding and sadness. It meant that the night was coming, and he would have to sleep soon. Sleep was rarely pleasant. He would wake some nights to find silhouetted figures standing beside his bed. They never moved or made sound. They would just stand there, filling him with paralyzing fear. Despite the fact that he had awakened to these apparitions countless times, he never got used to it. Every time was a shock, as if he had never seen them before. When it first began, he would scream uncontrollably. The kind of screams that have forgotten pride and ego. They were all-consuming, fear choked screams that woke everyone in the house. Through the years and humiliation, he had conditioned himself not to scream. He found that if he just forced himself to sit up and confront them, they would no longer be there. It didn't make it any easier, though. So rare, was a night of good sleep. The other night was a first, however. A dream within a dream? Did something really grab him? Was he sleepwalking? He had never done it before, that he was aware of. Was it getting worse? He wasn't sure if he could handle that. Then today, seeing Mrs. Goodrich while he was awake. That was new as well. He was going crazy, just like he thought. The familiar nausea and heaviness began to come over him. His lifted spirits began to fall. He closed his eyes and took in a deep slow breath, desperately trying to find room to lock away the recent horrible visions. But the cells where he placed such things were overcrowded and its inhabitants threatened to fight their way out. He looked back at the dirt, and using his big toe began to doodle the rough outline of an eye.

Madie was watching him as Ruben and Sam chatted. Adam was gathering some loose wood and piling it up to start a campfire. Allowing the peculiar sensation to tingle in her head, she opened her sight to see the light that flowed around Paul. A swirl of sad colors poured out of him as he bowed his head, making her heart ache. In the short time she had known him, she had seen him silently struggle with this darkness over and over. People's 'glow,' as she had called it as a child, was something she always remembered being able to see. She later discovered what auras were but felt silly calling them that - like one of those annoying pagan wannabes that had become so popular lately. If she focused on someone, the light and color of their glows would come into view. She never told anyone that she could see them for fear of being labeled crazy or a liar. The night she had met Paul, his aura hypnotized her. It was a beautiful swirling blanket of blue, indigo, violet, and red. Amidst the swirling, she would see an occasional wisp of black, like a puff of smoke caught in a strong wind. In recent weeks, the wisp had become more of a small dark cloud. It laid over parts of his aura, smothering the light from those sections. She could feel it sinking into him. How she wished she could just sweep it away, like cobwebs from the ceiling.

She sat there, watching him in his silent torment. Watching his bare chest, still slightly damp with river water, slowly heaving and collapsing with his deep meditative breaths. A glow from the freshly born campfire caught his attention. His eyes became locked on the flames while his mind was far away. The soft fire light began to dance on his skin. She became mesmerized by the shadows it cast on his frame and the flickering reflection in his eyes. He was tall and lean, yet something in the way he moved exuded a hidden strength. She noticed the shape of his back, the angle of his face. She was becoming as lost in his features as he was in the dance of the fire.

Her trance was broken as the ugly dark cloud swam into view across his neck and rolled up and around his face. It stopped there, masking Paul's features in its foggy darkness. That was different. It never went anywhere beyond his torso. It almost seemed to be… looking at her. Like a jealous lover that had

143

caught her staring too long. To her surprise, she found her core tense. A flicker of fear flowed through her. Did this thing have a consciousness? Was it alive and aware of what it was doing to him. Intentionally tormenting him? The fear changed to anger.

"No." she whispered.

The cloud sat unmoving. Taunting her. The anger turned to rage, burning in her abdomen. The sensation flowed into her chest, then spread throughout the entirety of her body. She stepped towards Paul, glaring at the monster.

"No!" she silently screamed.

The entity flinched and seemed to shrink slightly. It swirled chaotically for a moment on Paul's face then retreated back down to his torso. It coiled around his body and faded to a transparent mist.

She took a stunned step back. Did she somehow do that? Could she make it go away completely? She refocused on the entity.

Paul quietly gasped as if startled by something. A look of confusion was on his face. Wetness glistened in the corners of his eyes.

Relief flooded him. Sudden and complete. The feeling was foreign to him. It was as if a veil had been lifted from his eyes, allowing him to see the world around him for the first time. The beauty in the final glow of the sun setting behind the silhouettes of the tall pines touched him with fresh clean light. The serenity in the sound of the flowing river whispered in his ears. The playful crackle of the fire brought him peace. Then a twinge… a smudge of ash on the beautiful canvas of the world, and the veil began to lower back into its place.

Madie's blood iced as the cloud phased back into view. It constricted around Paul's chest greedily.
She tried once more to order it away. Nothing. It sat, unmoving.

Paul stiffened as if he had heard a noise. Looking to his right, then his left, and then behind, he finally met her eyes. He smiled at her, and she returned the gesture. She closed her sight as the awkwardness of the moment took over. She scrambled for something to say.

"Can I join you?" she said, nervously motioning to the empty spot on the tailgate.

"Yeah of course!" he replied, a little more excitedly than he intended. He always felt better when she was close.

She hopped onto the tailgate, opened the flip top of her pack of Marlboros, and offered one to Paul.

"Thanks," he said as he slid one out of the pack.

She smiled and locked eyes with him for a moment. The features around his eyes had darkened. He had taken on a look of melancholy. No, the pinching around his eyes was more like despair. Somehow, she thought this made them even more beautiful. They sat there lost in each other's eyes for endless seconds. She felt something deep for him. Love? She had never really known love outside of the love she had for her siblings. While she did love her father, it wasn't a pleasant emotion. It was more of a love from genetic bonds. There were no good feelings that came to mind when she thought of love for her father. Fear, shame, humiliation, those were closer to what she felt for her father. Not what the story books say a daughter should feel for her father. When she was with Paul, and more so than ever in this moment, this is what she wanted love to feel like. His skin still glistened with the river water. She wanted to touch him. To feel his lips with hers. He truly was beautiful, inside and out. She swallowed hard, as she tried to muster up the courage to seize the moment and grant her desire.

'This is your fault!' Her father's voice shouted in her mind. Anger and self-doubt flared in her chest, stilling her fluttering heart and scorching the butterflies in her stomach. She looked away and took in a deep breath, accepting defeat as the moment slipped away in its final death throes. Paul felt the awkwardness as well and looked to his cigarette, studying the glow of the burning tip, as if it held the secrets of the universe.

Feeling the silence becoming more awkward by the second, Madie struggled for something to talk about. "So… you really saw that lady in the parking lot?" she asked.

The gore-filled moment played in his head. He looked to Madie, then at the ground. She saw the muscles in his jaws ripple.

"Nah. It's just my head being messed up. I haven't been sleeping good," he answered.

"You know, Paul, you can talk to me. I won't judge you. God knows I've been through enough of that." She gently placed a hand on his shoulder.

He closed his eyes at the sensation. A warmth radiated from her touch that let down his defenses. He opened his eyes and stared at the dirt beneath the tailgate.

"I just, I think I'm going crazy," he said, surprised at how easily it came out.

"What do you mean?" she asked.

"I have these dreams. Well they don't feel like dreams. I'm in my bed, in my room. I wake up, and there are… people standing around my bed. They don't do anything. They just stand there."

Madie studied his face for a second. "They scare you?"

"Yeah. It's embarrassing. Used to make me start screaming. My dad would get pissed off and tell me it was all in my head. I could see in his face that he was disappointed in how weak his son is. He would never say it, but I knew. I've trained myself not to scream over the years. Just doesn't change the fact that it's terrifying. And I know they aren't real, which just makes it that much more humiliating," he said.

"I can imagine. Finding people standing around your bed in the middle of the night doesn't sound very pleasant," Madie said.

"I'm sorry" he said, feeling foolish.

"For what?" she asked.

"I don't know why I just told you all of that. I don't tell anyone that stuff. I'm sure I sound like an idiot," he said looking away.

She sighed and squeezed his shoulder. "Not at all. I mean, I do summoning rituals and stupid stuff all the time hoping to talk to my mom or sister."

"Yeah, but at least it's something you want to do. I don't have any say so over it. Plus, something's different," he said as he ran a hand over his damp hair.

"How so?" she asked.

"Well, last night I was awake. I was in my room messing with my drawings. I felt something behind me, like a cold breeze on my neck. Then it grabbed me." He looked down to his shoulder. The welts had mostly faded but were still visible upon close inspection. He turned to face her and pointed to the marks. "Here."

Madie leaned in and looked closely. Three faint marks were on his shoulder. They resembled fingers. She lightly ran her index finger across them. Her fingers tingled as they traced the marks.

"So, you were awake? You're sure?" she asked.

"No, I'm not sure. That's why I feel like I'm going crazy. I thought I was awake but shot up in my bed when it grabbed me. So, I figured it was a dream. Then I found these. And then today… I WAS awake, and I saw Mrs. Goodrich." His eyes pleaded to her for help. His gaze moved to the fire for a long moment as he contemplated his next confession.

"Paul?" Madie said.

"If I tell you something, do you promise to keep it between us?" he asked.

"Of course," Madie said.

Paul considered the fire a moment longer, and said, "I wanted to end it last night. Just make it all stop."

Madie grasped his hand tightly. "No, Paul. Don't say that!"

"I can barely remember what it's like to feel normal anymore. There are small moments that I feel happy, but it's always there. When those moments are gone, it's worse than before. I get the brief glimpse of normal and happy and then it's gone. It's just, constant. Like I'm wearing glasses that hide all the color in the world. They just suck all of the beauty out of it. All of the joy."

"Paul, no," she said as she took his other hand. The warmth came again as their hands joined.

Paul looked into Madie's eyes, that were now filling tears as well. His heartbeat raced.

"Well, not all of it. You're the one thing that it hasn't been able to take the beauty from," he said, a little shocked at his own boldness.

Yet, in this moment, he didn't care. In this moment she was a shining beacon of hope that he had to swim for. His insecurities washed away. He released one of her hands and placed it on her cheek. She closed her eyes and sighed as she leaned into it. He caressed her cheek with his thumb and wiped a tear away. She opened her eyes and met his.

"Paul, I…" He pulled her into him and gently placed a kiss onto her soft lips. He pulled his head back and locked eyes with her again.

"Well it's about fucking time!" Ruben's voice bellowed.

This was followed by a round of applause from Ruben, Adam, and Sam. The two blushed. They had become so lost in the moment that the others being close by hadn't even crossed their minds. Quickly, they let go of each other and began to fidget awkwardly. As the contact was broken, Paul felt something dark coming over him.

Adam wrapped an arm around Ruben and crushed him against his side. "My little guy is becoming a man!" he declared as he dramatically wiped away make-believe tears.

Madie giggled and bowed her head. "Ha, ha, guys," she said.

Paul, on the other hand, found himself enraged. This one moment of bliss and being ok for just a second was ripped away by their need to be immature assholes. He heard his teeth grind. He felt heat radiate in his cheeks. A tire iron across the mouth would stop their laughter. All of them. He would make sure they never laughed again. All he wanted was to feel goddamn happy, and they fucking took that little piece of it from him! They didn't know how horrible it was to be this way. He would make them understand! Adam first. Biggest threat out of the way, the rest would be easy. He would cut.... Paul heard his thoughts. They weren't his, yet they were. Much like the person he saw in his dreams wasn't him. "Just fucking shut the inconsiderate fucks up for good!" his voice hissed behind his ears.

Madie looked up at Paul to find the cloud had moved up the back of Paul's head. Tendrils of black were caressing the canals of his ears. Paul's gaze was fixed on the group at the fire. He had murder in his eyes.

"Paul?" she said cautiously.

He didn't respond. She reached out and touched the side of his face, intentionally pushing her fingers into the blackness around his ear. Her fingertips turned icy as they entered it. The cloud quivered and slowly retreated to its resting place on his torso. He jerked away, his face changing to one of shock as he looked at her.

"Paul, what's wrong?" she asked.

He began to tremble. He looked from Madie to the three at the fire and then back to Madie. The trembling became more intense.

He stood from the tailgate. "I'm not ok," he whispered, voice quivering.

"It's ok, Paul. What happened? Did you see something?" Madie's worry was obvious.

He looked back to Adam. He was staring at Paul smiling. The smile quickly faded as he saw Paul's face. Paul looked as if he had just awoken from one of his night terrors. He handed the joint he was smoking to Sam and began to make his way to Madie and Paul.

"Shit." Paul hissed as he hopped down from the tailgate and started to walk away from everyone. "I don't want to do this," he said.

Madie jumped up and followed after him. The light of his aura was dancing wildly around him. All of the colors swirling around him represented negative emotions. The black wisp moved to his back… looking at her. It twitched and squirmed. At times it seemed to grow. Madie caught up to him and wrapped her arms around him from behind. It felt as if she grabbed hold of a running jackhammer. She pushed her torso forcefully through the cloud. Nausea ripped through her. She persisted until her skin touched his. He stopped and took in a quivering breath. He felt her warmth seep into his skin. A calm flowed from it, pushing the sense of panic away.

"Paul… its ok. I've got you." She focused on those words and repeated them in her head. Trying to force them into Paul's mind. To make him ok.

Adam took a quick pace over to them. "What's going on?" he asked loudly as he approached.

Madie let loose her grip on him and he turned to face his brother. Adam's expression was one of angered concerns.

Paul looked to Adam, desperation in his eyes. Adam, once within reach, grabbed Paul by the shoulders.

"What's wrong?" Adam said sternly.

Paul gave a weak smile and answered with a tired voice, "I'm good. I'm ok."

"Nah. Don't bullshit me. What's going on?" Adam asked.

Paul looked to Sam and Ruben who were becoming aware something was wrong. They began to walk towards them as well. The idea of everyone making a scene over him made him sick. He didn't want this attention. He didn't want everyone to see him as a drama queen, begging for attention. He closed his eyes and drew in a deep breath, letting it out slowly. He opened his eyes and looked at Adam. A sheepish grin crossed his face.

"I'm good man. Just need some sleep. Sorry if I worried you." He looked to Madie. "I'm sorry I scared you, Madie. I'm good. Really."

Adam let go of Paul's shoulders and studied him.

"Don't fuck with me, man. You sure you're ok?" he asked.

"Yeah dude, I'm good. I'll chug some of that god-awful tea tonight and get some good sleep. I'll be fine." Paul smiled.

"We working on an orgy over here or something?" Ruben's voice came from behind Adam.

Adam ignored him as he watched the tremble fade from Paul's hands. Simultaneously Madie saw the entity fade from view.

"Yeah, Ruben, you're gonna be the pivot man," Paul chuckled.

Madie was awed by Paul's ability to put on a convincing mask of being ok, knowing what was going on inside him. She looked to Adam. His eyes were filled with questions, hers glistened with fear. Paul wrapped an arm around Ruben's shoulders and they walked back to the fire.

Sam spoke up. "Is everything ok?"

"I don't think so," Madie responded quietly.

Adam stepped in front of her "What happened?" He matched her hushed tone.

She considered telling them about the dark cloud. How it seemed to be whispering to him. They would just think she was crazy.

Instead she offered what she felt was safe. "I don't know. We were talking. He said he thought he was going crazy. Then we kissed. After he kissed me, and you guys messed with us, he looked… really angry. Like he wanted to kill you guys. Then he got upset and started shaking, saying he isn't ok."

"That's all he said?" Adam asked.

"Yeah. He was trying to tell me what happened, but it was like he couldn't get it out," Madie answered.

"And now he seems like nothing happened," Sam said, looking back to Paul and Ruben as they stoked the dimming campfire. "I worry about him. It's been getting worse lately. He always looks tired. He spaces out sometimes."

Adam looked to Paul and sighed. "Yeah, he looks like shit. Here's the deal, y'all have to keep an eye on him when I'm not around. I'm going to go see about something tomorrow. Maybe, I can get some answers. Y'all just don't leave him alone. Ruben is staying at the house tonight, so he's good for now."

Adam was not one to get worked up about much other than a fight. Upon seeing his concern, Sam saw the situation in a more serious light. The girls nodded.

"Tell Ruben to come here," Adam instructed.

The girls nodded and went to the fire. Sam pulled Ruben to the side and whispered to him. He looked to Adam slightly confused and shrugged.

"What's up Ogre?" he said as he came up.

"You noticed anything off about Paul lately?" Adam asked.

Ruben glanced to the fire and back to Adam. "Yeah, definitely. He's been telling me things lately. His night terrors have gotten worse. Says he feels likc his nightmares are happening while he's awake. The other night he said something grabbed him, and he has these welts on his shoulder that look like fingerprints. Said it was so cold it burned. Then, he dreamed that he killed y'alls mom, but it was another version of him. Crazy shit, man… So that's really why I'm crashing at y'alls house this summer. I think it's breaking him, and I'll be damned if I just sit back and let some ghost shit fuck with my boy. I got him to agree to look into some supernatural shit going on. Supposed to go see Ms. Swanier."

Adam gritted his teeth. "I appreciate that, man. Good to know he's got a friend like you."

"He didn't want me to tell any of y'all. Don't tell him I told you that. Ok?" Ruben pleaded.

"You're good, man. Look, you don't leave him alone, ok?" Adam said.

Ruben nodded. "That's the plan."

"I gotta go talk to Mr. Goodrich tomorrow about this shit," Adam said.

"Mr. Goodrich? Why?" Ruben asked.

"Just gotta finish a conversation with him. I'll fill ya' in if it turns out to be anything," Adam said.

"Um, ok. Well, I'll keep my eye on him. You got my word," Ruben said.

The two watched Paul talking with the girls by the fire. Aside from the exhausted look he always had lately, he seemed fine. He was smiling about something Sam said. Madie did not seem fine, however. She was watching Paul intently. Her eyes moving from one part of his body to the next. Her brow furrowed on occasion. Paul looked behind himself into the dark outside of the campfire light. He seemed to be scanning for something. After a moment, he gave his head a slight shake and returned to the conversation with Sam.

"Alright, let's get the fire out and head home," Adam said to Ruben.

"Ok sure," Ruben answered.

Adam and Ruben walked back up to the others. "It's 'bout time to get going, guys," Adam said. Everyone agreed and started towards the truck. Adam and Ruben used their feet to push mounds of sand onto the fire until the burning coals were completely buried.

Chapter 9

The ride home was quiet. Paul and Madie rode in the back, while the others squeezed into the cab. The evening was humid and hot. The whipping winds felt cool on their skin as they traveled the winding country road. Paul could feel Madie staring at him. He felt so awkward after his bold move at the river and ensuing freak out after. He didn't regret kissing her in the least. He just didn't know how she felt now, with all that happened after. She saw his weakness come out. He felt humiliated.

He felt her hand grab his forearm. "Paul?" she said.

He glanced at her and back to the road being left behind as they drove on. "Yeah?"

"I'm glad you kissed me." She squeezed his arm. The feel of her touch was so warm and soothing. Almost medicinal.

He blushed and smiled. "Even after my little drama spell?" he said, looking down at the bed of the truck.

"Yes, even after that," she said sincerely.

Paul raised his head and met her eyes. He sighed. "Madie, I'm a mess. I mean, like I might end up in a looney bin one day messed up. You sure you want some crazy drama queen kissing you?" He smiled, despite the tears welling up in his eyes.

Turmoil swirled in her. She wanted to tell him what she saw. If she could make him believe, he would understand. She knew she couldn't, though. As much as she wanted to trust him, she knew how it would go. An awkward silence. A chuckle. He would try to act sincere as he pretended to listen and believe her. Then he would start to fade away. The rumors would start about Crazy Madie. In the end, she would find herself an outcast. If the rumors found their way back to her dad… No, she wouldn't go through that again.

Instead, she took his hand in hers and squeezed. "I'm sure," she said, and gave him a tender peck on the cheek.

She rested her head on his shoulder and Paul laid his cheek on her soft hair. It was a blissful silence. Somehow, when the two were together everything seemed smaller. Their problems shrank. The world stilled, and a sense of calm engulfed them both.

Adam watched the two in the rearview mirror from time to time. A smile crossed his face as he saw them leaning on each other. Tomorrow he would have to pay Mr. Goodrich a visit. It was not a visit he was looking forward to. He played the conversation he had with him over in his mind.

"I wouldn't listen to her. She begged me to listen and I wouldn't." Mt. Goodrich's voice echoed in Adams head.

Adam turned on the radio and cycled through the CDs in the multi compartment CD player. After the fifth tap of the button, he landed on Metallica's And Justice For All album. He skipped through to Dyer's Eve and maxed out the volume. The truck vibrated with the bass drum and grinding chords of the guitar. The lead singer's voice drowned out the thoughts in Adams head.

The ride to drop Madie at her car was without conversation. Madie and Paul shared an awkward kiss as they said goodbye, feeling the eyes of Ruben and Sam on them.

"Paul, you're gonna be ok. Ok?" Madie said, trying to convince herself as much as him.

He couldn't look in her eyes. "Yeah."

"I'll see you tomorrow?" It felt more like a plea than a statement.

"Yeah," he said with a smile, meeting her eyes this time. It was genuine.

Madie gathered her bag and belongings. She hopped over the tailgate, gave Paul one last smile, and was off to her car.

"You gonna jump up front?" Ruben asked through the passenger window.

"Nah. Just gonna sit back here and enjoy the view," Paul replied.

"Um, alright then." Ruben said, giving Adam a look.

Paul leaned around to Rubens window. "Hey, someone let me bum a smoke!"

"You non-cigarette havin' bumming bitch!" Ruben said with a feigned look of disgust. "Sorry man. All I got left is dip."

Adam reached down under the driver's seat and produced a carton of Marlboro lights. He pulled out a pack and tossed it to Paul.

"Thanks, man!" Paul said.

Adam just nodded. He reached back under the seat and produced a small black plastic bag, which he also tossed to Paul. "Happy early birthday."

"Dude, my birthday isn't 'til September. You're about two months early," Paul said, a bit confused.

"Well, then happy late birthday," Adam said.

"Man, you don't need."

"Just open the fucking thing, would ya?!" Adam exclaimed, a bit more harshly than he intended, "Jesus Christ!"

"Alright. Ok. Shit." Paul said, opening the bag.

He found a small black box with Zippo printed on the front. He excitedly pulled the box out and opened it. Inside was a brass Zippo lighter, just like their grandpa's that Paul was always fascinated with

"Oh wow, man! That's so cool!" Paul exclaimed.

He pulled it out of the box and flipped it open. It smelled like Adam had already filled it with fluid. He struck it one time and a flame came to life. In the motion he had practiced on his grandpa's lighter so many times, he flicked his wrist, causing the lid to slam shut and extinguish the flame. He rolled it over in his hand and found an engraving on the other side. "Brothers don't let each other wander in the dark alone."

Paul fought down a swell of emotion. "Thank you, bro," was all he could say.

"Yeah, man. Don't lose it," Adam said with a nod.

Paul studied the lighter a second and nodded back. He sat back into the bed of the truck and began packing the cigarettes. The truck lurched forward, and the ride home began. His thoughts drifted to the kiss. It was everything he thought it would be, plus some. Everything in that moment was perfect. A smile crossed his lips as the sensation played in his mind again. Then the others laughter creeped in on the memory. Those assholes had to ruin it. They ruined it with their unyielding need to be immature children. Why couldn't they just let him have that little reprieve from his daily torment? His eyes went to the tire iron bouncing around the bed of the truck. Images of him standing over his brother's bloodied corpse flashed in his head. A blood-soaked tire iron shaking in his hand. Then Ruben. He saw his hands holding Sam's head underwater as she struggled. The clang of the lighter hitting the truck bed between his legs brought him back. He had stopped packing the cigarettes at some point and was simply holding the top of the partially crushed pack against his other hand. He gave his head a quick shake and peeled the cellophane off the top. He removed the foil cover and pulled out a slightly deformed cigarette, placing it between his teeth. After setting the pack next to him, he fished the lighter from his crotch. He ran his thumb over the engraving.

"I'm lost in the dark, big brother." he quietly said.

After battling the wind, Paul finally lit his smoke. Leaving it clenched in his teeth, he rested the back of his head against the rear window, and let the music's vibrations rattle his thoughts away.

At some point during the ride, Paul had drifted off. He awoke with a jolt as the truck' tires struck the large dip from the drain at the corner of their road. The cigarette was still dangling between his lips. The wind had blown the cherry out, leaving about half of it unsmoked. Adam pulled the truck into the dirt drive on the side of the house, and everyone began piling out. Paul stashed his lighter and smokes in his pocket and jumped out of the bed.

"Dude, I'm whooped," Ruben said as he stretched.

Paul twisted left then right, popping his back. "Yeah, battling ogres and fairies has me pretty worn out too."

Adam slapped a meaty hand on Ruben's shoulder. "Those fairies put up a fight, don't they?"

Sam and Adam laughed as Ruben tried to get the joke. A confused expression changed to an eyeroll and middle fingers as it hit him. This led them to laugh harder, except Paul. He felt the earlier anger return at the sound of their laughter.

'What the fuck, Paul? That was funny. Quit being a moody bitch!' He scolded himself internally.

"Alright, boys, I'm headed home." Sam announced. She gave hugs to Adam then Ruben. After, she came to Paul and looked him in the eye.

"I love you, cousin," she said sincerely, and wrapped him in a tight hug.

"I love you too, Sammy," Paul said in a slightly confused tone.

She released the hug and said, "See ya around, guys."

Paul watched her until she stepped out of the illumination of the streetlight. A horrible smell carried on the slight breeze hit his nose.

"Oh! What the hell is that?" he said, clapping his hand over his mouth and nose.

He turned to see Adam and Ruben both holding their noses. His mom was standing in the carport with a mug in one hand and a kitchen towel over her mouth and nose with the other.

"Oh, sweet Jesus, Frances! You dumbass!" came her muffled voice through the towel as she berated herself.

"Good God, mom! What is that?!" Adam said. The odor seemed to be bringing out the religion in everyone.

She set the mug on the windowsill. "Tea. I forgot to brew it outside."

"That's the stuff y'all are making Paul drink?!" Adam said, appalled.

"I'm not MAKING him. It helps him sleep," irritation creasing her brow as she walked away from the offending mug. Seeing her mood, Adam left the matter alone.

"Love you, Ma." He walked up and pecked her on the cheek, followed by Ruben and Paul.

The boys piled into the house. The smell of the tea was in the house as well, although it was not as pungent. As they went from the mud room to the kitchen, the smell was finally buried by the aroma of spaghetti and garlic bread. Ruben's mouth watered. Frances had the dishes and silverware stacked next to the stove, waiting to be used.

"Can we go ahead and eat, Mom?" Ruben shouted.

"William will be home soon. Wait for him," she replied, walking in from the mud room.

Ruben let a defeated sigh, "Ok."

The boys changed out of their wet clothes and into bed clothes. Adam opted to take a shower.

"Hey, babe," Paul heard his dad's voice coming from the kitchen.

He hurried to the kitchen with visions of dinner dancing in his head. He stepped into the room in time to see his parents at the end of a kiss.

"Hey, dad," Paul said.

"Hey, son. You win that title back today?" he asked.

Paul sighed, "No sir. Some new guy in town ruined my shot."

"New guy?" his dad asked as he removed his duty belt and draped it on the back of a chair.

"Yeah, some rich redneck kid. His dad's a doctor or something. He's got some anger issues," he said.

His mom stopped in the middle of setting a plate. "You didn't get into a fight, did you?"

"No ma'am! No," he quickly said.

"That guy needs a good a... butt kicking," came Ruben's voice from behind Paul.

"What's his name?" asked his father.

"Brian," Paul and Ruben said simultaneously.

They told their dad the tale of what happened at Karl's as they helped finish setting the table. Adam came out of the shower and joined them as the story finished.

"This the kid and his dad that just moved into the plantation house?" William asked.

"Yes sir, that's what Karl was saying," Paul answered.

"Hmm. Well y'all steer clear of that kid. Nothing good comes from keeping company like him," William said.

"I'm not gonna hide from him," Ruben said, almost defiantly. Paul's eyes went wide.

"I didn't say hide from him. If you see him, though, you don't approach him. Don't give him a reason," he said sternly.

"What if he approaches us?" Ruben asked.

Paul shot Ruben a look, begging him to drop it.
William finished twirling spaghetti onto his fork as he contemplated. He worked his jaw.

"I'm going to say this once. You boys retain it real tight in your heads. You stay away from the little shit. If that means not going into Karl's because he's in there, then that's what you do. Got it?"

Ruben squirmed in his chair, wanting to argue how unfair that is.

"Now, if the kid wants to be a dumbass and come after you… well, self-defense isn't a crime. If you see him hurting anyone else… defending someone else isn't a crime. But going after him like some half-cocked retarded badass with a hurt ego will get you, and us, into serious shit. Understand?" William's last word left no room for further discussion.

"Yes sir," Ruben said with a bowed head.

The irritation in him was outweighed by the respect and fear he had of Paul's dad. He was generally a calm guy, but he had seen him lose his shit on Adam once; and he'd decided he never wanted to be on that side of his temper.

"Sometimes you just have to let karma take care of people like that," Frances chimed in. "You do the right thing and everything else will work out. I don't want you boys hurting anyone, getting in trouble, or getting hurt. Hot heads like him don't learn from getting beat up or embarrassed. Especially ones that have rich daddies to bail them out. They just make excuses and find someone else to take it out on."

"Yes ma'am," Paul said as he sprinkled parmesan on his spaghetti.

"If he gives you anymore problems, you let me know. Understood?" William said.

"Yes, sir." Ruben and Paul said in unison.

William turned his attention to Adam. "And you are an adult in the eyes of the law. So, don't go getting any ideas of doing anything stupid that will get your ass landed in jail."

Adam sighed and nodded his head while chewing on a mouthful of noodles. "Yef, fir," he said around the food.

"Alright, enough about all of that. How was everyone's day aside from rich bullies?" Frances asked everyone.

"Eh, just spent it driving. Then took these chumps to the river," Adam said, motioning his fork to Paul and Ruben.

"Ok, well I'm glad your home," she said smiling at him. "How about you, babe?" she said as she patted her husband's elbow that was resting on the table.

He shot Paul a quick glance before sliding the offending elbow off of the table and responding. "Nothing special. Traffic tickets and welfare checks on elderly people."

His eyes went to Paul again and quickly away. Paul caught the look and his brow furrowed. He mentally shrugged and went back to his spaghetti.

After dinner, the boys cleared the table and put away the leftovers while Frances did the dishes. The remainder of the evening was spent watching old B rated horror movies. Adam went to bed halfway through the second movie, planning to get an early start tomorrow. Everyone else followed suit after it was over.

Paul went outside and guzzled the foul tea that his mom had left to steep on the carport. Normally any drink left outside would have a layer of bugs floating on it. This stuff was apparently too disgusting even for the pests that inhabit swamps. After a series of burps and half gags, Paul went inside and vigorously brushed the taste out of his mouth.

He felt it was worth it if he got another good night's sleep without nightmares. Sleep found him quickly once he laid his head on the pillow.

"PAUL!" a familiar woman's voice startled Paul awake.

He opened his eyes and found he was lying on his side, facing the wall. He tried to say, "Who's there?" but only managed a raspy exhale. It reminded him of dreams where no matter how hard you tried, you couldn't run. His muscles hadn't caught up to his brain waking up yet. Frantically, he tried to will his muscles to move. The feeling of someone watching him was overwhelming. He slung open the door to his logical brain to fight down the fear swelling in him. He had been here before. Just breathe and give it a second, he thought. There was nothing in the room with him, aside from Ruben sleeping on his floor. He would probably see someone standing at his bed, but they weren't real either. His fingers twitched and moved slightly. After a long minute of willing it, he gained control of his neck muscles and slowly turned his head to scan the dark room. Nothing beside his bed. He sighed in relief as he plopped his head back on his pillow. As he drew in a breath, a foul scent violated his nostrils. Recognition hit him, and his eyes went wide. Ice ran through his veins and a boulder manifested in his stomach. He slammed his eyes shut, and a grunt of fear danced in his throat.

"No," he whispered.

Sweat began rolling down his forehead and back. His breath sounded ragged in his ears, and he tried to calm it. He did not want to open his eyes again. If he didn't look, then perhaps she would have no power.

"Mween pa pral jije." A gurgling voice whispered into his ear.

That night rushed back into his mind. He hadn't remembered it happening until now. A few days after Mrs. Goodrich, she had come. She had hurt him, hadn't she? Black glistening tentacles flashed in his memory. They had tried to burrow into his chest. Then...it was blank.

Every muscle in his body shook. Mostly they shook from pure fear, yet there was a tiny ember of anger mixed in somewhere deep down. He saw that as his anchor and reached for it. The years of humiliation. Nights of staying awake out of fear. The dark cloud that sucked the color out of everything in his life. It was all from this. She was the source of everything wrong in his life. The ember grew into a flame. She made him want to hurt the people he loved the most in this world. She wanted to drive him mad. She had come close on so many occasions. He opened his eyes to small slits, leaving the world around him blurry enough that it would filter out the terror of whatever was at his bed.

"Fuck you," He rasped quietly.

"I...will not...be judged!" It screamed into his ear.

Cold wetness dripped onto his cheek, filling his nose with the familiar, wretched stench. He opened his mouth to breath and felt a bead of that contaminated moisture dance towards his lips. His stomach threatened to heave. He had to do something. He refused to just lay here and be a victim. Holding his breath and gritting his teeth, he chose fight over flight. There would be no screaming tonight. Willing every ounce of courage and anger he could muster, he shot his torso upright, and threw everything he had into a left hook at the area he thought she would be. Connecting with nothing, his momentum carried him to the right and to the edge of his twin sized bed. His center went too far over too fast for him to do anything aside from fall off the bed. His cheek made contact with the thin carpet first, sliding under the weight of his body as it finished it's decent. The skin tingled and burned, but he took no time to feel it beyond his subconscious. For the briefest of seconds, he considered feeling humiliated for the fall. No, the ember had grown into a blazing fire, and he was giving his body to it as fuel. As soon as his body stopped falling, he sprang to his feet and spun to face his bed. His fear was almost non-existent at this point. If the bitch was there, he was ready to throw down. He raised his shaking fists into a sloppy fighting stance, forgetting to properly set his feet. His breath heaved as he scanned. Nothing. Just a twin bed with the blanket strewn half on, half off the bed. He stood, waiting.

"What the fuck?" a voice quivered from behind him.

Paul whipped around, and his eyes found a shadow hunched in the corner by his door. With no hesitation, Paul thrust his rear leg forward and crashed into its torso with the ball of his foot. He felt his foot sink deep with the impact. It felt good. Payback for all the years of being driven mad. A grunting exhale released from the shadow. It attempted to form words, but they didn't sound like the chilling voice he had heard before.. Only pained grunts and...gagging? The sound of liquid pouring onto the carpet was accompanied by the smell of vomit. Paul stepped back, still ready to fight, but now confused as he tried to process what was going on. Again the sound of splashing liquid hit his ears, and was followed by burps, retching, and spitting. Paul's stomach churned at the smell. He was never able to handle people vomiting around him. Did spirits vomit? Ruben! It hit him like wet shit in the face.

"Ruben?" he barked.

"Goddamn it," Ruben wheezed out, barely a whisper.

Paul darted to the light switch and flicked it on. He found Ruben laying on the floor clawing at his stomach where the diaphragm would be. The wall behind him showed a dent where his body had slammed against it. His face was red with pain as he desperately tried to pull in a breath. A large puddle of half-digested spaghetti was inches from his face. Wide eyed, he stared at Paul mouthing words. Paul assumed they were probably something to the effect of "what the fuck, you fucking asshole?!"

"Oh shit!" Paul said pressing his knuckles on either temple. All the rage drained from him. "Fuck! Shit! I'm sorry dude! Shit!"

171

Loud footsteps double-timed down the hall outside his door.

"Paul?!" His dad's voice boomed as the door flung open, slamming into Rubens knee. William had his service pistol in a ready position as he spotted Paul.

"What the hell was that?" He said loudly.

Paul stood there frozen with fear and humiliation. As his dad stepped into the room, his face twisted with disgust. He released one of his hands from the pistol and pinched his nose shut.

"Are you ok? Where's Ruben?" He fired off.

"Here." Ruben gasped from behind the door.

William stepped past Paul and swung the door away. A look of confusion joined the disgust on his face. His eyes went from Ruben, to the crack in the wall, then to Paul.

"What in the hell were you doing?" William shouted.

More footsteps could be heard coming down the hallway outside the room.

Ruben got to his hands and knees, "He didn't do..."

The door swung open again. This time it struck Ruben in the side of the head.

"Fuck!" Ruben shouted.

Frances flinched away from the door she had just forcefully opened. Ruben fell over, catching himself on his elbow. Unfortunately, his elbow caught his fall in a puddle of vomit. Paul and William winced at the sight. Adam came up behind their mother looking at Paul with the same confused expression everyone entering seemed to get. Paul could only stand there helplessly, recoiling from the horrible sight of his best friend floundering his way out of the putrid mess. Frantically, Ruben pushed out of the puddle and into a kneeling position. He held his saturated arm away from him. William turned and opened his mouth to continue the interrogation of his son.

"He didn't do anything, Mr. William. I was getting sick and tried to jump up to run to the bathroom. I fell and wound up puking all over myself and the floor. I'm real sorry about the floor. I'll clean it." Ruben said with exasperation. He looked back at the wall. "I can fix that too, sir."

The room was quiet as William looked from Paul, to the floor, to the wall, to Ruben, and back to Paul. He knew he wasn't getting the real story. The hard-ass in him wanted to revert to police tactics of verbal judo, and work the truth out of them. Slowly he looked at the faces of everyone in the room. His wife was in despair. Her sleepy eyes were wide and held sadness in them as she stayed fixated on Paul. Adam stood behind her, anger creasing his brow. Finally, looking at the horrified expression on Paul's face and the pathetic state of Ruben, he allowed the loving father and husband to take control.

He looked at the gun in his hand and set it on Paul's dresser.

"Come on, go get cleaned up." He said, holding a hand out to Ruben.

Ruben took his hand with his clean one and William hoisted him up. Another jolt of pain shot through his abused abdominal muscles as he straightened. He did his best to play it off, as to not give away the real story. Fortunately, he supposed, Paul had hit him in the gut as opposed to breaking his ribs. Not that it was any consolation to his screaming stomach.

For all of the "fights" they had been in, they had never really tried to hurt each other. The force Paul had kicked him with was shocking. He had never imagined that someone so skinny could hit that hard. He had felt the impact all the way into his spine.

Frances quickly came up and grabbed Ruben's clean arm and helped him towards the bathroom. Paul watched the scene with a feeling of separation from it all, almost as if he was watching a movie. He wasn't a fan of the main character for what he had just done to the guy that was supposed to be his best friend.

Adam watched Paul with mild anger. William was studying the damage to the wall, while covering his nostrils with the back of his hand. He turned his neck to look back to Paul.

"That's what happened?" He asked.

Paul opened his mouth to speak, and a sob threatened. William, seeing his son close to breaking, looked back to the wall. Handling others being emotional was something he only knew how to address as a cop and soldier. He knew that wasn't what Paul needed right now. Sadly, he also knew he had no idea what Paul needed. Something he was sure he couldn't give. He would let Frances handle this part. Instead, he assessed what materials he would need to patch the wall. The cheap wood paneling shouldn't cost much, and it would cover the cracked drywall behind it. It would be a quick and inexpensive repair. He gave a curt nod to the wall, then turned his attention to the vomit. That would probably take longer to clean and remove the odor than the wall repair. William sighed.

"Alright. Well. Let's get this cleaned up. I'll get the gloves and bucket," He said.

Adam stepped in the room as their dad stepped out. "You good?" he asked.

Paul, not wanting to risk another sob escaping, nodded his head. He couldn't meet Adam's eyes.

"Ruben's story is bullshit isn't it?" he asked quietly.

Paul looked at him and quickly away. He harshly rubbed his head as he considered his options on what to say.

"Yes." he decided on.

"Well, you want to fill me in on what the fuck happened?" Adam said impatiently.

"It's just my stupid brain again, man," Paul said in a quivering whisper.

"So… your brain slammed Ruben into a wall and made him do that shit?!" Adam said, pointing at the offending puddle. "You're gonna have to be a little more specific, man."

Paul let a low growl in his throat and turned his back to Adam. His embarrassment was fast becoming irritation.

"Fuck it. Be a bitch about it then. Tryin' to fuckin' help you and you just wanna act like a little cry baby ass fucktard about

175

it. Fine. Fuck it then!" he said in a harsh whisper.

Paul spun hard to face Adam. Instead of having a giant to spew profanities at, he found an empty doorway. With his pulse audible in his ears, he shot two middle fingers at the empty space. Veins throbbed in his neck and temples as he stood there shaking. Paul didn't ask for any of this. What kind of brother would chastise him for something that was out of his control? He had no idea how hard he fought every day to seem ok. To try to BE ok. He waged a war against it every day of his fucking life! How dare Adam, or any of them?! They didn't know what it was like.

He started for the door to go after his brother, to… he didn't know what. So, he stopped in the door. He turned back to the room and took a few steps. He spun back to the door. A low roar emanated from his throat. The images flooded his mind again. Gore and visions of death. Sun kissed hair swirling in murky waters as she fights to come up for air. He gasped and brought his hands to his temples.

A hard corner smacked the peak of his left eyebrow as he did. Flinching his head back, he saw a hand, his hand, holding his dad's 9mm service pistol. He flexed his wrist back, verifying it was indeed his hand. Using his right index finger, he tapped the barrel. It was indeed his father's pistol. He rewound the last few seconds in his mind. He had no recollection of how he came to have the gun.

Footsteps were coming back towards his room and panic rushed over him. Hurriedly, he set the gun back on his dresser and took two large steps away from it. His dad came into the room carrying a black bucket that smelled of Pine sol. He wore a yellow pair of rubber gloves and had a bundle of rags under his arm.

William stopped and looked Paul over. "Why don't you go see if your mom needs any help. I got this."

"Ok. I mean, yes, sir." Paul answered.

Frances was coming out of her room with a freshly lit cigarette between her fingers. Her face showed fatigue as she took a pull from it. The bathroom door was closed at the end of the hall. Paul could hear the shower running. The smell of her cigarette awoke Paul's cravings for one.

"You ok, sweetie?" she asked.

"How's Ruben?" he said, tired of thinking about how not ok he felt.

"He's fine I think. Said he thinks he got it all out," she said.

Paul nodded as he stared at the closed door. "Why don't you go back to bed, Mom? I can wait on him."

"I'm gonna throw his clothes in the wash first. Don't want it stinking up the house," she said, and took another drag.

"I'll do it," he replied.

She furrowed her brow, "You remember how to use the washer?" One side of her lips curved into a crooked smile.

Paul forced a weak chuckle, "Yeah, I think so."

Her smile turned to a yawn, "Ok, let me see if your dad needs any help first." She leaned in and kissed him on the cheek.

Paul rested his head against the door frame. The muffled sound of the shower running and an occasional belch or grunt from Ruben could be heard. He tried to replay what had happened, only to find that the details were fading, much like after waking from a dream.

A wave of anxiety tensed his stomach. He could clearly remember falling out of the bed. Then Ruben had scared him, and he kicked him. Everything after that was clear as a bell. Something had happened before that. Something important. He sighed in frustration. Then there was the gun. How in the hell did he wind up having that in his hand? Why did he have it? He felt himself going deeper into a rabbit hole he didn't want to go down.

His attention went to Adam's bedroom door. The words Adam said were VERY clear. Paul knew he was a burden to everyone close to him. Adam just had the balls to say it. Perhaps he'd had his dad's gun in his hand to do everyone the solid of taking away that burden. Sure, everyone would be sad for a bit, but in the long term it would be better for them all. The stinging of tears made him close his eyes.

Adam sat on the edge of his bed, elbows on his knees, and hands clasped under his chin. He hated himself for what he had said to Paul. He knew it was the situation and helplessness that had made him so angry. Paul just happened to be in the way when it came boiling over. There was nobody to hurt to make this stop. For all his size and strength, he was helpless. Tomorrow he would hopefully find some answers.

In the meantime, he had an apology to give… as much as he hated apologizing. But, his moral code dictated that when you really fuck up, you man up and own it. His shoulders slumped, and he got up off the bed.

"Goddamn it," he muttered.

He pulled open the door and almost crashed into Paul, who had his back to him. Paul startled but kept his back turned. Adam could hear Paul sniffling and saw his hands wiping at his face. Guilt twisted Adam's insides.

"Man… Look, I'm an asshole. I didn't mean that shit I said," he told Paul's back.

Paul's posture straightened, but he said nothing. "I just get frustrated because I want to help ya out with this. Then you clammed up and I didn't know what to do. I'm used to being able to smash somebody's face when there's a problem. I got nobody to put my hands on for this one."

Paul nodded, still not willing to risk his voice quivering.

"That shit I said, that was some dirty coward shit. I know you try. I can't imagine what it's like in there," Adam said, tapping a finger to his head. "I ain't asking for your forgiveness. I fucked up. You want to slug me? I'll stand here and give you one. I deserve it. Anywhere you want."

"Nah. You're good. I know I'm a burden to y'all. I don't mean to be," Paul choked back a sob.

"Don't say that," Adam replied.

"It's true, man. You know it is, even if it makes you feel bad. It's just a fact. Whatever is wrong with me is getting worse and it's a burden on all y'all. Mom and Dad worry. You worry. Ruben has upended his summer to be over here. It's bullshit. I feel everyone pitying me. Walking on eggshells. It's not fair to any of y'all," Paul said, keeping his back turned and voice low.

Adam lowered his head. "Dude, a burden is having a few hundred bucks stolen from your bank account. Then having the bank show you video feed from the ATM, of your son using your card to steal that money. Then, finding out he developed a drug addiction that has him fiending hard enough to steal from his parents. Having a son that did all of that of his own free will is a burden. YOU are not a burden. You didn't choose any of it. You fight against it and try real damned hard not to bother anyone with it. Don't give me that burden crap," he said.

Paul had turned to face him midway through his statement. A confused expression on his face.

"What are you talking about?" he asked.

"I fucked up. That period where I was always gone and partying. I was into some hard shit. Started out selling coke and weed. Started using my own stuff to show I wasn't a cop. Turns out I liked it. A lot. Started using more than I was selling. One time I put my whole paycheck up my nose. I figured I could take the money out of Mom and Dad's account, flip the stuff, double the money and have it back in the account before they noticed.

Somewhere in my geeked out brain it made sense," Adam said. Shame showed in his eyes. He couldn't look at Paul as he told the story. There were so many things he had done during that time that he couldn't tell anyone. If he ever got caught for it, they would be better off knowing as little as possible about his sins.

"That was you?!" Paul asked.

"Yeah. That was my dumbass," said Adam.

"Fuck. I remember them saying someone got into the account. I never really thought anything else about it. Shit. That's messed up," Paul said.

"Yes, it was. So, don't tell me you're a burden. There is much worse shit than trying to help someone who is trying," Adam paused, finally meeting Paul's eyes. "You're my brother. My family. Being there for you is never a burden. Dick." He emphasized the last word with a light punch in the shoulder.

Paul chuckled, "Yeah, I suppose that gives me some perspective."

"That's why I started working longer rotations. I was embarrassed and had to make the money to pay them back. In the end I guess it was a good thing. I dropped it all… well except weed and a beer here and there. We'll get you through this. You'll come out better in the end. Stronger." said Adam.

"Hell yeah, I'll give the Incredible Hulk a run for his money at this rate," Paul said, wiping his eyes. He forgot he'd been crying till he felt the moisture on his hands. "Fuck, I hate crying."

Adam clapped a meaty hand on his shoulder and promised, "Secret's safe with me."

Paul nodded his head. "Thanks," he said.

"We good?" asked Adam.

"Yeah," Paul said. "I gotta tell you something."

"That would be a nice change," Adam said with a smile.

"I made Ruben puke," Paul said switching his gaze to the floor.

Adam raised an eyebrow, "Say again?""

"I don't remember why, but I was out of the bed. Ruben was-," Paul cut his sentence off at the sound of the bathroom door opening. Ruben stepped out, wrestling with a shirt around his neck. Paul immediately saw the angry red and purple welt on Rubens abdomen. He hurriedly pushed his arms through the sleeves and tugged it down over his body. After a quick look and wink to Paul, he started towards Paul's bedroom.

"You ok?" Paul and Adam asked in unison.

"Meh, I'm fine," he said, turning back to them. "Just something I ate I guess."

Adam pursed his lips. "I appreciate you lying for your boy, but y'all don't do me like that. I'm not stupid. Plus, Paul was already telling me what really happened, I believe."

"Right. My bad," said Ruben sheepishly.

Frances and William came out of the bedroom together, William holding the bucket away from him like it might bite. He turned towards the kitchen, while their mom came to them.

"How ya feeling, sweetie?" she said, rubbing Ruben's arm.

"Much better, ma'am," answered Ruben. The smell of vomit had saturated her while she was helping her husband clean up. All three boys crinkled their noses as the smell drifted to them. She noticed their expressions and sniffed at the sleeve of her robe.

"Oh damn. I smell horrible. I'm gonna go wash up and change. You boys need to get back to bed," she said.

They all gave her a 'yes ma'am' as she went into her room.

"Y'all need to fill me in tomorrow," Adam said, looking at Ruben and Paul.

"Alright, man," Paul responded.

Paul turned to Ruben, "I'm so sorry dude."

"I know you said you didn't want me staying over, but that was a bit overkill," Ruben said, gently rubbing his aching stomach.

"No, it wasn't like that," Paul said emphatically.

"Dude, I'm fucking with you," Ruben said with a laugh. His smile faded after a few seconds. "I saw that bitch," he said.

Paul cocked his head, "You saw what bitch?"

"The woman floating over your bed," Ruben said. The pallor of his face telling Paul he wasn't just messing with him again.

Paul's blood went cold. The part he couldn't recall came flooding back to him. His skin turned to goosebumps. His mouth moved, but no words to speak would come to his mind.

Thoughts raced through his mind too fast too process. It was all a blur of cold fear.

"You…," Paul weakly hissed.

"Yeah," Ruben nodded. "I'm not crazy then, right? That's what had you jumping out of bed swinging, right?"

Still unable to formulate a sentence, Paul nodded. Ruben gave a mischievous grin, "Then I'm right, and you're not crazy."

Paul processed that statement for a long second. There was a somewhat relieving truth to it. If Ruben did see her, then he wasn't crazy… right? Or it could just be some trick of mind. Maybe he had mentioned seeing her to Ruben before, and his brain just manifested the woman when Paul startled him awake. He couldn't recall ever mentioning it to him. It had only happened that one time a day or two after Mrs. Goodrich offed herself. Would it be better to be haunted or crazy?

"I need a smoke," Paul stated, matter of fact.

"Me too. And a beer. A joint or three. Sedatives would be nice," said Ruben. His tone not entirely joking.

William came back into the hall, having discarded the offending bucket and gloves. The bags under his eyes were heavy.

"Alright, guys. Party's over. Back to bed."

"Yes sir," said Paul.

After breathing in the smell of vomit poorly masked by pine cleaner, Paul opened his window and wedged his box fan into the frame to pull fresh air into the room. Glancing at the red light of his alarm clock, it read 3:44 AM. His thoughts were still buzzing, and fear prickled his skin. Sleep would not find him. He resigned himself to that notion. He fished out a pack of cigarettes hidden under his bed. After spinning the fan around to pull air out of the window, he lit one, keeping it held up to the fan. Ruben plopped down next to him on the bed, and they shared the cigarette in silence for a moment.

"Guess we are making a trip to see Ms. Swanier tomorrow. Well, today technically." Paul finally broke the silence.

"Yep," said Ruben, as he passed the smoke back to Paul. "I don't think I'm getting back to sleep."

"Nope," Paul sighed.

Chapter 10

The rest of the early morning hours were spent in idle conversation. Occasionally, they found the conversation going back to the night's events and changed the subject to the plans for the day. Around 8am, the two ate quick breakfast and hit the road.

Adam crawled out of bed just as the two were leaving. He had intended to be up with the sun and on his way to see Mr. Goodrich. However, all of the excitement of the night had left him without the willpower to get up the first time he'd he opened his eyes at 5:00. He went to the kitchen window and watched Paul and Ruben peddle their bikes down Hand Road. Still feeling like he was walking through a thick muddy fog, he opted to make a pot of coffee before getting the day going. After hitting the brew button on the machine, he went back to his room to fetch his smokes. He thumped one out of the soft pack, placing it between his teeth. A quick search through the pockets of the jeans he wore the day before produced his zippo with a filigree design etched in the metal. The lighter showed signs of abuse from riding in his pockets during hard days of work on the barges.

A quick pit stop in the bathroom for a morning piss, and he stepped out to the smell of coffee brewing. He saw his dad sitting at the kitchen table, reading the paper, and smoking his morning cigarette. He lit his own before walking down the hall to join him.

"Morning, Dad." said Adam with a quick nod.

"Mornin'." William said, not looking up from his paper.

The coffee maker started making its final gurgles. Adam pulled two mugs from the cabinet. One was a plain off-white mug. The other, his father's, a New Orleans Saints logo mug.

"What's your plan for today?" William asked.

"Actually, I was gonna go visit with Mr. Goodrich. See how he's doing. Haven't really seen him since the funeral. Figured he might like some company," Adam said. He pulled the pot from the coffee maker and began pouring the two of them a cup.

William closed the paper and set it on the table with a sigh, "I don't think you'll be going to see him."

Adam placed his dad's mug in front of him and sat down across the table from him. "Why is that?" he asked cautiously.

William rubbed his face before picking up the mug. He sat pondering for a long moment before saying. "He's dead, son."

Adam stopped the mug at his lips. "What the hell? When did this happen?"

"I got called out to do a welfare check on him yesterday. Ms. Sanders said he had been out of sorts and wouldn't come to the door when she went to check on him. I found him dead at his dining table," said William.

A pit grew in Adam's stomach. He suddenly didn't want or need the coffee anymore. This revelation had him wide awake.

"How did he die?" he asked.

William took a slow sip of his coffee, calculating how much of the truth he should share. "Suicide, from the looks of it. Shot himself,"

"Shit," said Adam.

"Yes. Shit. Don't tell your brother about this. Understand me?" William said firmly.

"You know he's gonna find out eventually, Dad," said Adam.

"I know. But you're not going to be the one to tell him. I'll handle it. He's been… on edge lately. Gotta be tactful how we handle this," said William.

"On edge is an understatement. But yeah, I'm good with not telling him. Putting things delicately isn't really my specialty. To be honest, Dad, it's not yours either," Adam said.

"Yeah. I suppose I'll let your mom tell him. I worry about him. Whatever is going on with him is getting worse. His nightmares got so bad after that day in the graveyard. Thought he was getting better, but it seems to have come back with a vengeance. I'm worried he is going to do something stupid if it keeps up," Said William.

Adam nodded in response before taking a pull of his cigarette. He thumbed his eyebrow as he contemplated what his next step would be. All of his eggs, were in the basket of getting answers from a dead man. Dead by his own hand, no less. Frustration thumped at his temples, and concern for his brother churned in his stomach. He was back in a helpless void where he had no path to choose and no power to wield. He slumped back in his chair, exhaling a long breath.

Chapter 11

Ms. Swanier's daughter, Constance, ran their small convenience store a few miles up the main road from Paul's. If you didn't know the area, you'd easily mistake the old brown and white checkered brick building for an abandoned business. The Swanier's sign was about 20 years overdue for a fresh coat of paint, as was evident by the barely legible lettering. Not having any gas pumps, they mostly sold beer, cigarettes, and snacks.

The store was on the predominantly black side of the rural town and catered to their community. It had been their family's business for over 50 years. Started by Ms. Swanier's father, Barnabe, it was a central hub for goods in the area from the 40's through the late 70's. As modern gas stations and department stores became more prevalent in the surrounding towns, business had slowed.

Despite falling behind the times, local residents still frequented the establishment enough to keep the lights on. Something about the history of the place and the times it had seen seemed to provide a sense of home to them. Plus, many still relied on Ms. Swanier's home-brewed remedies and elixirs for what ailed them. They were cheaper than a doctor's bill, and in some cases more effective.

Ruben and Paul stood in the parking lot under the gazes of two elderly black men sitting in lawn chairs in front of the large glass pane window of the store front. The boys shared a quick glance to each other, conveying their discomfort.

"Well… I guess let's go in," said Paul. Ruben gave a nod to the two men as they walked in the propped-open front door. The larger of the two men raised a gnarled hand holding a large cigar, and gave a quick wave.

The hum of multiple fans filled the store. They seemed to do little more than push the hot air around as opposed to cooling, like a sauna with a breeze. There were four large metal shelves filling the middle of the small store. The shelves were sparsely stocked. Most of the items were canned goods and household items. The coolers lining the back wall housed milk, eggs, sliced cheese, cold drinks, beer, and a surprisingly large variety of meats. Many of these meats would be considered exotic in other parts of the country. Alligator tail, deer, shrimp, every consumable part of a hog, multiple cuts of beef, and frog legs. The aroma of the store was pungent, although not entirely unpleasant. A mixture of butchered meat, herbs, aged wood, and a few smells neither boy could identify.

Constance was a light-skinned middle-aged black woman of obvious creole ancestry, as was every Swanier in the area. The older generation referred to them as 'high yellow'. She gave the boys a smile and nod.

"Mornin', boys," said Constance. Her southern accent turning it into "Mawnin'."

"Mornin', ma'am." the two said together.

She raised a curious eyebrow. "Anything I can help ya wit? Y'all don't really seem like the chitlins type."

"Um, yes ma'am," said Paul. "Well see, my mom came and got some tea to help me sleep. She said Ms. Swanier was wanting to see me after she told her about me."

"Oh, you dat Allen lady's boy. Yeah, Momma was sayin' she wanted to talk wit you. She's in the back room. I'll tell her y'all here," Constance said before disappearing through a curtained doorway.

Paul stuffed his hands into his pockets and examined a collage of black and white pictures behind the counter. The first one his eyes fell on was of a well-dressed man standing proudly in front of a much newer looking version of the store. He had one arm resting on the roof of a brand new 1953 Buick Skylark.

"That was my granpappy, Barnabe." Constance said, startling Paul. "He opened this store many moons ago." She held the curtain open. "Come on, Momma ready for y'all."

Ruben and Paul rounded the counter and went through the door. A cool breeze hit them as they entered, causing goosebumps to pop up on Paul's arms. An ancient looking woman in a mumu sat on a wooden rocker next to a window AC unit. The room was small. The little coffee table, a 19" TV on a short dresser, and three chairs made it feel cramped. Paul wrinkled his nose at the smell of stale urine and mothballs.

192

Constance motioned to the two empty chairs before going back out into the store. The elder Ms. Swanier gave Paul a toothless grin and patted the chair next to her. Reluctantly he sat, and Ruben took the other chair. Grabbing the remote off her lap, she turned off a soap opera.

"Paul, ain't it?" Ms. Swanier croaked. Her voice reminded Paul of gravel and broken glass. Her accent had much more Cajun in it than her daughter's.

"Yes ma'am," he responded.

"Ya momma tells me dat you havin' problems. Cain't sleep? Feel like you losing ya mind sometime?" she asked.

Paul squirmed in his chair and looked at Ruben before answering. "Um, yes ma'am. Something like that."

"Mmhmm. All yo life?" she asked.

"I'm sorry?" he asked. Having trouble understanding her through her heavy accent and harsh voice.

"Ya been havin dem problems all yo life?" she said a little louder.

"Oh, yes ma'am. Not as bad as it has been lately, though," said Paul.

"Dat tea I send yo momma wit. It help?" she asked.

"I think it did the first night, but last night it was… bad." answered Paul.

"Mmm," she grunted. She grabbed a can of snuff from the coffee table. After placing a pinch between her lip and gum, she continued. "After Mrs. Goodrich it get worse, huh?"

"Yes," he answered.

She looked to Ruben. "What kinda man he is?" she asked, motioning at Paul.

"Uh, he's a good guy. I don't know. What do you mean?" Ruben asked.

"He a fair man?" she asked.

"Yes," said Ruben.

"He do da right ting usually?" she asked.

Ruben nodded. "Yes ma'am."

"He like to protect da little guys? Hurt da bullies?" she continued.

"He has a bit of a reputation for it at school," Ruben said grinning.

Looking back to Paul, she said. "You see people when you wake up at night, ya momma tells me. Dey scare you, yeah?"

Paul picked at the skin around his thumbnail, feeling very uncomfortable in the old rickety chair. He nodded to her.

"Why dey scare you?" she asked.

Paul shrugged. "Well, because I'm waking up to people standing around my bed that don't belong in my house," he said with a nervous chuckle.

"No, boy. I mean what you feelin' when you see dem?" She tapped a crooked finger to her heart.

Paul shrugged again. "Scared."

"Gotta go deeper den dat boy. What you really feelin'." She reached over and placed her palm on his chest and closed her eyes briefly.

Her touch was surprisingly warm. A wave of something vaguely familiar came over him, a sense of safety and calm. The weight of his anxiety lifted. He didn't feel as much fear at the idea of delving into his memories. Why did that feel familiar? Madie came to mind.

"Sadness. I feel completely terrified and alone. Because I am alone. I am defenseless when it happens. Nobody can protect me. I don't know what they want or what they will do. They never do anything but stand there, but I'm always afraid they will. Like something bad is waiting for me, you know? Then one night… something bad showed up. That's when it got the way it is now. A day or two after Mrs. Goodrich died," Paul said calmly, almost as if he was talking about someone else.

She furrowed her brow. "What showed up?"

"Well, I had actually forgot it happened till last night. It was a silhouette of a person, like always. This one was different, though. Normally the others are beside my bed. They don't move or make a sound. This one was at the foot of my bed. I could see her more clearly than the others. Like, I could see details instead of just a silhouette. She moved, and spoke before grabbing me. I've never felt a fear like I did with her that night. It really felt like it was going to kill me or make me lose my mind. In a way, I think I did. Lose my mind, that is." He looked at Ruben, who was sitting on the edge of his seat. His face showed concern and interest.

"I saw her last night too," Ruben said. Ms. Swanier perked up at this. "Well, just for a second. When you fell out of bed or whatever, it woke me up. I saw her and then you kicked the fu…" Blushing he dared a guilty look at Ms. Swanier. A mischievous smirk crossed her lips. Ruben continued, " Sorry. Ahem. You kicked me.

I couldn't really make anything out. Like a black cloud floating over him. I felt like it was a woman maybe."

Looking back to Paul, she asked. "What she looked like?"

"Uh well. It looked like she was wearing a cloak, or something made out of the stuff like potato sacks are made of," Paul said.

"Burlap?" asked Ruben.

"Yeah. Yeah that's it. Um, she had this wild grey hair poking out from under the hood all over the place. She smelled like something that died in the swamp. That's all I really could make out. That and she said something that I couldn't understand. Like a different language," Paul said.

"What it sound like, what she said?" asked Ms. Swanier.

"I dunno. It's sounded French maybe?" he said.

"Mween pa pral jije?" asked Ms. Swanier.

Paul's eyes widened as chills ran down his back. "That's it! Yeah that's it! What is that? What's it mean?"

She bowed her head and sighed. "It don't mean nothin' good. Roughly, it mean 'I will not be judged' in Haitian."

Paul and Ruben shared a confused look. "Huh? Who will not be judged? I don't get it," said Ruben.

She closed her eyes and leaned back in her rocker. It let a long slow creak as she settled in. "I don't know who she is, but you not da first to see her. My Jonas thinked she was an angry spirit of a slave woman dat was a pwoteje what lost her jij. Seems she got no interest in going back to where she belong. She got hate in her heart. Gone mad wit grief. When Jonas talked of her, she was more just a presence. Never said nothin' 'bout her hurting nobody. She was just a sad soul what wouldn't leave."

She grabbed an empty coke bottle hidden beside her rocker and spat into it. After staring at the bottle for a bit she inhaled sharply. "Many tings have been lost over time. Many tings. Stories. Knowledge. Magic lost. Not like what dey show in da films. Dey ain't no lightnin' fly outta people hands. I hate dis path for you, boy. It ain't right dat da powers dat be make dis a burden for you. Could at least give a map or instruction book to da poor souls dey curse wit dis!" she said shaking a fist at the ceiling with the last sentence. Emotion put a slight tremor in her rough voice.

"I'm sorry?" Paul said, breaking a long silence.

Ms. Swanier huffed and tapped Paul in the center of the forehead. "You gotta have an open mind, boy. I'm old and don't like to waste what time I got left. You gonna listen when I talk?"

"Yes ma'am," he said.

"No matter how crazy it sound, you gotta open ya mind to it. Understand, boy?" her expression was deadly serious. Paul nodded.

"Now, I don't pretend I have all da answers. I don't. Don't know dat anyone ever has. What I gonna tell you is what was passed down to me and what I learnt on my own." She paused to cough. The cough quickly became an all-out fit of rattling lung butter trying to get out.

Constance entered the room with a mason jar full of a golden colored liquid. Worry lined her face. What looked like coffee grounds sporadically drifted through the concoction. Ms. Swanier took the jar and greedily chugged down half of the contents. She took a few deep breaths,coughed once more into a handkerchief, and after a very productive sound, spat into it. After folding the kerchief, she placed it into the breast pocket of her mumu, causing Paul's stomach to roil. She then turned back to Paul as if nothing had happened. Constance returned to the front of the store after studying her mother.

"Now, everyone got dey own takes on God, evil, the hereafter, and so on. Ain't nobody all right or all wrong 'bout it. I won't sit here and give ya a bunch of preachin' and snake oil. I'm just telling ya what I know. So far back as anyone know, dere been people like you. Like my Jonas. Like da Goodrich's. Da world try to tell you ya crazy. Modern doctors tell ya 'take dis medicine and you be fine.' When da medicine don't work, you tink you crazy. But, listen to me, you not crazy, boy. Dat I can promise you. Quite da contrary. You are special."

"Short bus special," snickered Ruben. From somewhere unseen and with speed not becoming of a woman that appeared to be close to a century old, Ms. Swanier produced a flyswatter and had popped Rubens leg before he could flinch.

"Quiet, boy!" she yelled. "Ain't got no time for foolishness! Dis more serious dan you can imagine. You go on an wait wit my daughter. Go on!" She barked.

Ruben looked at Paul like a wounded puppy and back to Ms. Swanier. "I'm sorry ma'am," he said.

"Save ya sorrys for a priest and get!" she said with another swat on his leg. Ruben leapt from the chair and swiftly left the room.

"Sorry boy, but like I said, I'm old and don't have time for wastin," she said. "Now, as I was sayin, you're special. You are a jij… a judge. You know how you always know when someone a good or bad person da first time you meet dem? Da way you always know when sometin' bad gonna happen? Why you always feel drawn to serve justice to dem bullies? It's part of who you are. What you were born as." She paused to take another gulp from the mason jar.

"I'm sorry, I don't follow. What am I a judge of? What does that even mean?" Paul asked.

"So best as I can 'splain it, there's good and evil. Most folks is a little of both. You got dem some dat are all of one or de other. People always know when dey meet one of da good ones. Da good ones just make you feel warm and safe. Always tryin' to do good for people. Dem bad ones? Child, dey da tricky ones. Always hiding who dey really is. Some can't hide it. That's them ones dat always loud and looking for a fight. Stealing. Killing. Gangbangers and the like. Dey ain't all bad, but dey definitely ate up wit it. But dem ones dat wear a mask of bein good or just in between. Dat's da dangerous ones. Dat's da all bad ones. Like dat man on da news a few week back. Dat one dat dey found all dem bodies where he been raping and killin those kids. Nobody could believe it. He seem so nice. So normal. But he was pure evil… wearing a mask." She paused for another drink. "Good ting bout bein a jij, you always know. Right away, you know. Ain't dat right, boy?"

Paul reflected momentarily, realizing he couldn't say she was wrong. He always got a vibe from bad people when he met them. Not like most people when they base it on how someone looks. It was almost like an audible alarm inside his head. Jeremy Lynch, he knew he was a deranged kid at first sight. When he was sent to a mental institution for running over his little brother's leg with a riding mower and laughing at "how cool" it looked, Paul had felt guilty. Like he should have told someone about his feeling. His logical side knew that was ridiculous and nobody would have listened. Yet, he couldn't help but feel as though he failed somehow. Looking back to Ms. Swanier, he nodded. She smiled and did the same.

"Ok, but I still don't understand what being a judge means or what any of this has to do with me," Paul said.

"Patience, boy," she said before hacking and spitting into her kerchief again. Paul winced as she once more crammed the mucus laden cloth into her breast pocket. "So, you know heaven and hell, yeah? Everyone does."

"Yes ma'am," he said.

"Most folks think its golden streets in a mansion for all eternity in heaven. 72 virgins. Hell a fiery pit of weeping and gnashing teeth and what not. Yeah?" she said. Paul nodded.

"I tink it's not quite like dat. I can't say fo sho what da other side gonna be like till I get there. What I know from my life and what my granmama taught me is, we all part of de same ting. A big ball of energy. Life force. Souls. Whatever you want to call it. When we die our energy go back to it. Our bodies just a shell. A play ting for dat energy maybe? Maybe it's a way for it to experience tings what can be done dere. My granmama believed dat before time and life came to be, dat energy… God, was all dere was in a great big nothing. Back then it was perfect ting. But you can't appreciate anyting till you experience de opposite, or absence of dat ting. Can't appreciate wealth if you never been poor. Can't appreciate health when you never been sick. Ya see? God wanted to know what he wasn't. So, he blew himself apart to create all things. Dis way he could know more den just a perfect lonely existence. He created chaos and life so dat he could experience what he was not. Everyting in dis universe is a piece of God. Even you and I. Granmama didn't believe God was da all knowing, all seeing ting like what most religions tink. She believed he had to truly let go of all he was to do what he did. You can't have a true experience if you control every aspect of it right? It would be like winning a game of cards because you loaded da deck. It's not really winning. Understand?" she asked.

Paul nodded again. His mind was slowly starting to wrap around what she was saying.

"Good. So, way she saw it, dat real bad energy get sent away from da rest. A place absent of good. No light in dat place. Hell, what some folks would call it. It not fire and brimstone. It an inescapable void dat got no pleasant feeling or emotion. Hurt, anger, sorrow, grief. Dat's all dat is in dis place. Now, as for what you are. Gran-mama said that to make sure he would not be forever changed to something evil, he put guards in place. You. Parts of his being to act as filters for da energy what turned bad. For most folk, dat just mean dey bad side get flushed out and da rest go back to da whole. Dem what are all bad got nothin' good to send, so everything dey are go to da bad place. Which why I tink dis one dat torment you don't wanna go. She know what waitin' for her over there and is fightin' to stay."

Paul creased his brow and nodded. It made sense.

"A jij purpose was to separate the good and bad energies when people died. Send dem to da proper place. As you can imagine, this can take a toll on a human body. Specially when you get one dat don't wanna go to da dark place. Many a jij have gone mad and become evil demselves. Those are usually da ones what don't find dey pwoteje and got no help to fight. Dem jij what get turned bad...dey da worst. Dictators, dem dat want to do genocide, Klan leaders, terrorist leaders. Dey know how to get power. Dey use it to hurt people and make chaos in da world." Ms. Swanier paused to give Paul

202

an opportunity to ask any questions he might have.

"So… this seems a little far out there. I don't mean any disrespect. Just a bit much to take in, ma'am," Paul cautiously said, keeping his eye on her flyswatter hand.

She gave Paul a soft smile. "Well of course it do. So did da world not being flat way back when. Just because it's hard to believe don't make it not true. Look inside yaself, boy. You know there's more to it den being crazy now don't ya?"

"Ma'am, I don't really believe in God or any of that stuff," he said.

"You believe in science, yeah?" she asked.

"Yes ma'am. Science is factual. There is evidence to back it up. Religion is just stories men tell. It's used for power. Plus, I have a hard time with the concept of an all loving and forgiving God that will smite you and let you burn for all eternity if you don't worship him. I mean, why would God create life just to have it worship him? Seems like an egotistical brat that I wouldn't care to follow." Paul found himself, as he always did with religious discussions, getting passionate about the subject. His eyes went to the flyswatter again.

Ms. Swanier chuckled. "I ain't gonna hit ya for havin' a brain, boy. You gotta realize though, all science was crazy talk until it was prove right. Just because it ain't been prove yet, don't mean it ain't real, boy. You a thinker. It's a good ting. It's also part of

203

bein a jij. Many good tings about being a jij. You got a knack for knowing when trouble coming. You can sense what people gonna do, so you mostly always have da upper hand in a fight? If your head's clear, dat is."

Paul reflected briefly on the fights he had been in. It did always feel like he knew what was coming. This led to him being able to end most fights pretty quickly and rarely ever get hit. Even when he was new in his karate class, he was able to beat the higher belts pretty easily. As he learned more techniques, even his sensei had difficulty sparring him. Paul took up martial arts at 10 due to relentless bullying for being overweight. Till Paul hit a massive growth spurt at 14, he was a squat fat child. Round faced and jiggly. Over the summer of 1991 he went from 5'7" and 200 pounds to his current frame. His father insisted he join after Paul got suspended for finally standing up to his 5th grade bully, John Niche.

John liked to run up behind Paul in gym class and pull his shirt up with one hand while vigorously shaking Paul's soft midsection with the other. He dreaded gym class and looked forward to the small reprieves from the humiliation when John would be absent.

After a particularly bad day of bullying that involved getting pantsed, jiggled, and pushed down face first by his tormentor, Paul's brother had told him to "just go beast ape shit on him." He assured him that even if Paul lost he would never get bullied again. "If you don't kick his ass, I'm gonna. Then I'm gonna kick yours." Well, that sealed it. Better to take an ass kicking from John than his much larger brother.

So, the next morning at school was spent trying not to vomit before gym class. He prayed John would be absent today. God was apparently not listening. John walked up to the table where Paul was eating breakfast with a shit eating grin on his face.

"Morning, fatty!" John leaned over the table, placing both hands in front of Paul's tray. Paul reflexively pulled his hands away.

"Leave me alone," Paul mumbled.

"What fat boy?" John sneered.

"I just wanna eat my breakfast," Paul spoke up.

"I know you do. That's why you're so fat. All you do is eat. I think you need to diet, fatty," John chuckled as he took Paul's cinnamon roll.

They only served those once a month and they were Paul's favorite. He looked forward to the second Tuesday of every month for that very reason. Adam's threat be damned, that was the last straw.

It wasn't that his dad was concerned with the scrapes and bruises he came home with. It was the description of the fight his principle gave. He couldn't imagine his passive, weak, fat son doing those things. That, and the lawsuit that John's parents filed for the stitches and retinal damage to their son. Paul honestly didn't remember the fight beyond John punching him in the temple for snatching the roll back, and him telling John to "go eat some poop and leave my food alone, ass mouth!" A rather brash statement for a 10-year-old.

From what he was told, he had tackled John after taking a few shots and stuck his thumbs into his eyes while biting his face. John had to wear thick coke bottle glasses from that day on. So, Paul's dad had decided he needed something to channel his anger and give him discipline.

Secretly he was proud of his son for so effectively eliminating the threat, but his pride was overshadowed by the days spent in court. Ultimately, the case was declared self-defense after student statements were admitted and several teachers testified to the countless times Paul was bullied by John. Life in Delisle elementary and on into high school for him was profoundly better after that day. Permanently damaging someone gives you a bit of a reputation.

Paul nodded to Ms. Swanier. "Yeah. Ruben calls it my Spidey-sense."

"I'm not telling you dat any religion got it right. I'm not sayin dey got it wrong. All of em have bits of truth, I 'spose. All of em were tainted by men at some point as well. Power over people will always corrupt. Granmama thought it's part of da reason a jij don't know he's a jij. It keeps dem honest and humble. At least until they are old enough to understand. In old times, a jij was nurtured and trained. Cared for by people dat knew what dey was. Dem and dey pwoteje. As time went by and de world got modern, dat custom faded. Those dat knew da most, died as did da wisdom dey had."

"What's a pwoteje?" asked Paul.

"It's a jij's soulmate. Keeps dem grounded. Heals dem as de bad energy pass through. Dey can see a person's inner light and sometime commune wit da dead. Witout dey pwoteje, most jij go mad or die by dey own hand in one way or another. Witout dey jij, pwotejes feel no sense of purpose. Dey are empty and usually don't have very long lives. Destiny ensures dey paths will cross. Sometime da bad will get in da way and try to keep dem apart. It's getting easier to do, it seems, wit nobody believing or knowing about any of it these days. Now it just gets labeled as mental illness and dem doctors throw medicine at it like beads to a big tittied woman wit her shirt up at Mardi Gras."

Paul couldn't help but laugh at her last remark. He had so many questions to ask her that they were crowding each other.

Pulling a random one from the swirling thoughts, he said "Wait, so you mean the 'evil' has a consciousness and actually fights against judges?" he asked.

"Sure seems dat way. It's what happened to the Goodrich's. But I never heard of it happen dat way before," she said.

"What? Going nuts and killing yourself?" Paul asked.

"No. Like I say, dat happens a lot to a jij if da jij and pwoteje are kept apart. But dey had been together for over 40 years. Don't make no sense. 'Sides, pwotejes don't never get attacked by da spirits far as I know. If dey kill demselves, it's just from loneliness and grief," she said.

"So she was Mr. Goodrich's pwoteje?" asked Paul.

Ms. Swanier slowly nodded. "Yes. It always be dat way. Men are jij and women are pwotejes. Granmama said it's because women have nurturing and healing in dey natures. Pwotejes and jij appear random. Dey don't stay in family lines or what not, for da most part, anyway. Sometimes a family line makes one or two in ten or twenty generations. No real rhyme or reason, really. What is constant is how many dey are. Every area keeps 7 pairs of pwotejes and jij at all times. All within 'bout 1000 miles of each other." She paused and looked absently out the small window. "When one pass, another jij and pwoteje wake up to take dey place."

"So… when Mrs. Goodrich died. That's why it got so bad?"

She nodded "Yes. You woke up. You seen da dead all ya life, but dey was just drawn to you cause what you would become. You weren't a jij yet. Now you is. Well, you should be. Sometin stoppin you from wakin up all da way. I should be able to see you, but you mostly just look like any other boy. Cept your aura. It's da only ting what let me know you special."

"Stopping me? How can that happen?" he asked.

"I don't quite know yet, boy. I will though," she answered.

"And my pwoteje?" Paul said.

"Well, wit pwotejes, dey awake since birth. Just don't have a job to do till dey jij wake up," she said and spat into the bottle again. "Shame how dem Goodrich's went. Without her, it was just a matter of time at his age. I am honestly surprised he lasted as long as he did." A tear filled the corner of her eye.

"What do you mean? You're talkin like he's dead." Paul said, a tinge of caution in his tone.

Ms. Swanier's eyes shot wide to Paul. After a moment she closed her eyes, rubbed at her temples with both hands. "Damn my old mind."

The muscles in Paul's abdomen clenched. "Is he dead?"

"Yes, boy. I'm afraid he is. Wasn't my place to tell you," she said, still rubbing slow circles on her temples.

"How? I saw him just the day before yesterday?" Paul said.

He recalled Mr. Goodrich's appearance. His mystery trip to the scene of his wife's suicide. He supposed it didn't seem that far-fetched that he offed himself.

"When seeing someone just before dey die ever stop them from bein dead, boy?" She let out a long sigh. "Seem dat same ting what been after you finally got him. Made him mad. Speakin evil in his mind till he snapped an kill himself. Either kill yoself or kill others. Dat's how it go." She studied his face. Watching lines of fear and sadness crease his forehead. "I'm sorry, boy." she said, resting a hand on the back of Paul's head.

That familiar sensation trickled through him again. Not nearly as intense as when Madie would touch him, but the same. Sort of like when gum loses its flavor. You can still taste it, but it's not as good. He looked up to her.

Feeling dumb for taking so long to put it together.

"So if Jonas was a jij, then that means you're a pwoteje?" he asked.

"Yes, I was." she said with a smile.

"What do you mean 'was'?" he asked.

"I got no jij. I'm just an old woman now," she said with a forced smile. Sadness in her eyes would not lie, however.

"I'm sorry," Paul said.

"You killed my Jonas?!" she exclaimed.

Startled, Paul sat upright and rigid. "What?! No! No ma'am! I never even knew him!"

Ms. Swanier burst into a hoarse fit of laughter that ended in another phlegm filled cough. To Paul's dismay, she once again producing the disgusting cloth from her pocket and spat into it. It appeared thoroughly saturated at this point. He was screaming inside for her to throw it away. She studied the kerchief momentarily. Paul's stomach celebrated as she tossed it into the small waste basket next to her rocker.

"Den what you sorry for? It's da nature of tings. We all live and we all die. Less you killed someone what dead, you got no reasons to be sorry," she said, fishing a clean handkerchief from a wicker bowl on the small table.

Nervously, Paul chuckled. "Oh, sorry."

He thought about his next question before asking, trying to figure out how to word it. "So… you said pwotejes don't live long without their judge. You seem to be doing pretty good, though."

"Yes. We was lucky enough to have knowledge on these things passed to us. Makes it easier when you know what is happening. Keeps you from feeling like you is crazy. I had family kept me sane when he passed. It was a hard time fo sho. Many nights spent wantin to join him. Thankfully, my granmama had taught my folks about all dat. Dey weren't neither of em jij or pwoteje. Dey sho saved me during dat time, though," said Ms. Swanier.

"How did he die?" asked Paul.

She chuckled, seeing the boy already imagining Jonas in fantastical battles with spirits or going mad and killing himself. "Time, obesity, and diabetes. Jonas couldn't say no to food or sweets. Even after he got put on insulin. Most jij have a 'envie' like dat."

"A what?" Paul asked.

"Something dey obsess over that helps keep dem centered or at least distracts dem from what goes on in dey head. He took to food. Your momma tells me you used to draw all da time, yeah?" she said.

"Yes ma'am," nodded Paul.

"You get lost in it when ya did it, huh? Like you wasn't hearing your thoughts, or you was releasing some kinda pressure?" she asked.

He had never thought about it before, but she was right. He would sit in his room, sometimes for hours, filling sheet after sheet in his sketch pads. turning his thoughts and feelings into images. Some were escapes into fantasy realms of magic and mythical beasts. He would feel transported as he drew, becoming completely absorbed into his works. Other times, he drew what he saw in a dream, or what he woke to find standing around his bed. Those drawings were more like popping a boil that had grown too large. It was a need. Putting pencil to paper was the only way to relieve the pressure.

"Yeah, I suppose you're right, ma'am," he finally said.

Leaning forward, her expression became serious. "So, boy, you found ya pwoteje yet?"

After a moment of thought, he half smiled. "I think so."

"Dat's good. She needs to learn what she is, so you can stand a chance. You tell her come see me. What her name is?" she asked.

Raising an eyebrow Paul asked, "A chance?"

"Boy! Ain't you been payin no attention? You are in danger. You gonna end up like dem Goodrich's you don't get ready!" she exclaimed.

Her expression and tone conveyed to Paul all he needed to know. There was no hint of humor. To her, this was deadly serious. Paul was still having trouble believing all of it. He hadn't believed in God or anything supernatural for a very long time. Well, a long time for someone who hadn't seen 20 years yet. Now he was faced with accepting that not only was the supernatural a reality, but he was some type of supernatural entity himself. Wait, is that what she was saying? I mean he didn't actually DO anything. He just unknowingly filtered energy. Basically, the equivalent of a supernatural drain screen. Catching solid waste while the water filtered through. He supposed if he was supernatural, that was pretty fitting. He wasn't anything special.

"Boy!" she snapped.

"Sorry, sorry. Madie. Her name is Madie," he answered.

"Dat new girl what moved here a while back?" she asked.

"Yes ma'am. That's her," he nodded.

"I ain't laid eyes on her yet. Explains why I didn't know. Tell her come see me soon as she can, hear?" her finger wagged at Paul while she spoke.

"I will. I should see her today. Maybe she can come then," he said.

"We can talk more after I meet wit her. I don't know wat dis is dat been after you, jij. It seem bad. I need to seek some wisdom tonight. You see her today, tell her come by tomorrow, first ting," she said, and took Paul's hand in hers. Her features softened. "You go on wit dat friend of yours out der now. Keep him close. He might can be helpful to you. He got a strong will and don't spook easy. A strong sense of justice. Be mindful of all tings in da coming days, boy. Be on guard."

She released his hand and he stood. "Thank you, Ms. Swanier," he said sincerely.

She nodded and made a shewing gesture with her hand. Paul stepped out of the room to find Ruben leaned against the counter looking at some pictures that Constance had laid out for him. They both turned to him as he came out. Looking around, Paul felt as though the world looked different. As if he had stepped into a movie. His brain was trying desperately to digest everything. The logical part of his brain was at war with the other parts. However, even the logical side was having trouble believing its own arguments. Too much of what she had said made sense. It just felt right. It was like a light had been turned on in a room that had been dark all his life. A room he hadn't even known was there that was storing secrets about who he really was. Part of him wanted to forget about all of it. If it was true, he had much more to be afraid of than being crazy.

"So?" Ruben asked.

Paul looked to Constance. "Thank you for your help, ma'am."

She nodded. "You take care of each other, hear?" She looked from Paul to Ruben and back.

Paul returned the nod and started for the door.

Ruben threw his hands up in frustration. "WELL??" he exclaimed.

Paul's face showed no emotion. "I'll tell ya on the way back. Let's go."

Constance watched the boys hop on their bikes and ride away. She turned and went into the back room with her mother. She slowly rocked in her chair with her eyes closed and head laid against the arched wooden back of the rocker. Constance leaned against the door frame and folded her arms.

"They in trouble, ain't they momma?" she asked.

"Yes. Dat boy. My heart hurt for him. Not right he should have to be da one. He strong, though. Stronger than any I've seen. Dat ting done got hold to him. I fear might be too late to get him as ready as he need, though. We shall see," the elder Swanier said, keeping her eyes shut. "Bad days ahead for him I fear. Maybe for all of us."

Chapter 12

Brian dropped the heavy cardboard box on the wooden floor of his bedroom, wiping his sweaty brow. Boxes cluttered every corner of the room and filled the closet. He surveyed the room, trying to make a plan of attack for unpacking his belongings. The air in his room was stifling since the AC had gone out a few hours ago. A repair man had been at it for about 45 minutes but had to leave for parts. Brian took a deep inhale. The air smelled musty and of old wood. He rubbed his scalp in frustration.

Brian had procrastinated unpacking, taking advantage of the fact that his dad barely noticed him anymore. Unless he was mad, he didn't speak more than a sentence to Brian in a day. All he had to do was keep his head low and he was basically a ghost. The AC dying seemed to put Brian back on his radar today, however. After a long berating about what a disappointing piece of shit son he was, Brian was informed that he was to have the room finished by the end of the day. Brian wisely offered no argument.

Absently rubbing his stomach, he decided where to start. He popped open boxes in the closet, finally opting for the box containing his photographs and football trophies. He lined the wall shelf above his bed with the trophies and a team photo from last year. Grabbing a few thumbtacks from his dresser, he began sticking action shots of himself above the dresser. Returning to the box, he found pictures of his mom and dad together. His blood pressure rose as his teeth gritted. His eyes stung.

"Nah, fuck that. Y'all ain't worth crying over," he said, and kicked the box across the room.

He emptied out a few more boxes before the heat became unbearable. He hurriedly broke down the empty boxes and stacked them. After gathering them up, he went down the hall to the stairs. Making it to the bottom of the flight, he found the front door stood open, allowing a light breeze to blow through this level of the house. Setting down the boxes, he grabbed the bottom of his shirt and pulled it up to wipe the sweat from his face. Even the circulating air was stifling. It felt more like the air whooshed out of a hot oven than a breeze.

Brian heard footsteps coming from the kitchen and started that way. He found his dad standing at the island with a manila folder opened on the countertop in front of him. Kurt was rolling a glass of cold sweet tea across his forehead as he read.

"Dad, I got a few boxes done. It's too hot to stay up there anymore," Brian said tentatively.

Kurt looked up without moving his head, giving him a menacing appearance. "Should have thought about that before you kept putting it off while the AC was working. Go finish." His tone was even and emotionless.

"But dad! It's gotta be 110 degrees up there! I'm gonna get a heat stroke!" Brian whined.

Kurt deliberately closed the file in front of him, not taking his eyes off his son. He carefully placed the sweating glass of tea next to it. Standing up to his full height, a good three inches taller than Brian, he rounded the island, stopping uncomfortably close to his son.

Switching his eyes to the floor at his feet, Brian took a cautious step back. "Sorry, I'll get back…"

Kurt's fist crushed Brian's diaphragm, cutting his words off as the air left his lungs. Brian folded over grasping his abdomen. Strong fingers viciously laced into his hair. A forceful yank brought him nose to nose with his father. Kurt's foul breath seeped into Brian's nostrils as he gasped and wheezed. The other hand locked painfully onto Brian's chin and forced him to look at Kurt in the face. He saw his father's gritted teeth. Ice blue eyes bore into him. A light yellow stained the whites of his eyes. Both hands flashed to Brian's throat and squeezed. Freezing waves of fear pulsed through his body. Before he had time to process what was happening, the pressure released.

"Understand?" Kurt seethed.

Still unable to speak, Brian vigorously nodded his head. Brian understood completely what his father meant in that one simple word. His father glared at him for a long moment, an endless moment, to Brian. All he wanted to do was breathe and run away. Currently, he could do neither.

Kurt's features suddenly softened, and he moved both hands to Brian's shoulders. "Ok, just take a slow breath. One at a time. You're ok," he said, taking slow breaths and exhaling them with Brian. Once he had caught his breath, Kurt stepped back and looked him over. With a firm slap on the back, he said "I need you to go get some things from the store."

His face etched with fear and confusion, Brian nodded. "Ok."

Kurt strolled over to a small basket on the counter next to the coffee pot and snatched a set of keys out. He tossed them to Brian. The keys striking his chest startled him. Fearful that not catching them was going to bring back Mr. Hyde, he scrambled to get them off the floor. When he stood, his dad's back was to him leaning over the counter. Brian's diaphragm finally released and let him draw a full breath.

Nervously shifting from one foot to the other, Brian asked, "What do you need me to get, sir?"

Kurt didn't respond for a few seconds. Finally, he straightened and dropped a pen into the small basket. Tearing a sheet of paper off a notepad, he turned to Brian.

"It's all on here. Should be able to get it all at the K-mart." He handed Brian the paper while digging his wallet out with the other hand. He fished a hundred dollar bill out and handed it to him as well. "Ok, get going."

Brian nodded and turned to leave. He was suffocating in the house. He wasn't sure if it was from the heat or the fear. With a quick pace he started for the door.

"What?!" his dad's voice boomed from the kitchen.

Brian hesitantly turned back towards his father. He was standing in the archway of the kitchen. The look of rage had returned to his eyes. His shoulders heaved with angered breaths.

"I… I didn't say anything, dad," Brian stammered.

Kurt stared him down, unmoving. Just like before, his expression went soft again. "Hmm… ok. Get going."

Brian double timed it to the front door. Stepping outside, he imagined his dad's hand latching onto him and pulling him back inside, like a scene from a horror movie. His father would start stabbing him. Later, he would dump his body in the swamp for the gators to dispose of. Or, perhaps a demon would start speaking through him as he devoured Brian's soul.

Instead, Brian continued his brisk pace to the Mercedes. No monsters pulled him back into hell. After closing the door and starting the engine, he gripped the steering wheel with both hands. His fear transformed quickly to anger. The tears burning his eyes fueled that anger further. The leather of the wheel creaked under his grip. Muffling a scream through gritted teeth, he shook the wheel violently. "FUCK! FUCK YOU! PIECE OF FUCKING SHIT!!!" He screeched through his teeth. The humiliation and fury clawed at his insides. He struck his temples with his palms repeatedly, letting the pain tame the other emotions. Closing his eyes, he took in several deep breaths. The last one he held in, before slowly releasing it. Opening his eyes, he forced a look of calm on his face, and put the car into gear.

He took the long winding drive slowly. He was in no rush to finish this errand and get back to Dr. Jekyll. He should kill him, he thought. It would have to be in his sleep… or poison. He wouldn't stand a chance coming straight at him. He was a former amateur boxer as well as a division champion wrestler in his college days. He had already made the mistake of bowing up to his father once. It was in the midst of divorce proceedings and his mother moving out. Days passed before he could take in a deep breath without feeling on the verge of passing out from the pain. The problem with having a large father that is a doctor, has fighting skills, and a horrible temper? He can hurt you without leaving much of a mark. And hurt him he did.

Generally, his dad kept a calm façade. Brian had never thought of Kurt as abusive. While a very disciplined man, he wasn't cruel or violent. He wasn't the type that came home drunk, beating everyone in the house. He rarely drank before the divorce. He had only hit Brian with an open hand, as called for when he misbehaved. Never in the face, just swats on the ass. Occasionally, a smack to the back of the head. Nothing that bad. That all changed in the days since his mom, aka "the whore," left.

Perhaps Brian asked for that first beating. Telling a man whose world is crumbling that you 'see why the whore had to stay high and fuck around,' when getting grounded for poor grades would test anyone's patience. Teenage angst was a bitch.

That moment, however, seemed to awaken something in Kurt. Some sleeping leviathan, with a lust for violence and a hatred for Brian. In the last few months it became easier and easier to incur his wrath. While none of the beatings had been as severe as that first one, he grew more terrifying with sudden switches from Kurt to an ice-cold sociopath.

'Understand?' Kurt's words echoed in Brian's mind. He rubbed at his throat, replaying the incident. Understand what? That he would kill him? Yeah, he was starting to understand that. Coming to the end of the drive, Brian let the car idle for a while. He contemplated turning right. He could hit the interstate and never look back. His buddy, Mark, lived in Orange Beach, about an hour or so from here. Brian could crash there for a while. Find some kind of work, maybe. Who would hire a sixteen-year-old runaway, though? Plus, he highly doubted Mark's parents would be cool with being a halfway house. He looked left and sighed. Pressing the gas, he cut the wheel and headed to K-mart.

Not far into his ride, he saw two familiar figures on bicycles pulling out of Swanier's parking lot. Still about 100 yards away, he slowed a bit. The long haired one, he couldn't remember his name, glanced back at him. With a flick of his head towards Ruben, they went to the opposite lane, still going the same direction as Brian. He felt himself becoming giddy at the sight of these two. He was going to get his payback. The hustling bastard and his faggot friend tried to embarrass him in front of that girl. He couldn't let that shit fly. Hell no.

Instead of giving into the temptation to be drastic, he decided to play it smart. Be patient. He eased the car off the side of the road, and watched them.

"Boy! Get that car off my grass!" came a shrill voice, startling Brian.

A frail elderly black man stood in the yard Brian had pulled off next to. Raising the cane he was using to walk, he motioned for Brian to move.

"I ain't in your yard! It's the side of the road. County property!" Brian hollered, quickly looking back to his quarry after he spoke.

"Don't tell me it ain't my yard, boy! I've lived here 52 years and cut that goddamn grass every year! Now get!" the old man shouted back.

Ruben and the fag turned left onto a road, almost out of sight. Brian turned his attention back to the man.

"Don't make me call the police!" threatened the man.

"I'm fucking leaving! Shut your goddamn mouth, nigger!" he screamed and shot a middle finger.

Slamming the gas pedal down, Brian made sure to dig a good gouge in the man's yard as he peeled back onto the road. Brian saw the man cover himself from the spray of dirt and gravel in the rearview. The sight made him chuckle. He was sick of people messing with him. That shit was over. First, he was going to handle these two. Then it was time to sort out his dad and every other motherfucker that got in his way. Whatever it took.

He slowed to a crawl as he approached the road that the two had turned down and read the sign 'Ballpark Rd'. Scanning up a good ways he saw them cresting a small hill. As quickly as he spotted them, they dropped down the other side of the hill out of view. He turned onto the road, keeping the needle around 25 MPH. Out of the corner of his eye he saw movement on the right. Turning his focus, he saw the girl from the store the other day walking up a long dirt drive towards the road. She was wearing a pair of cut off jean shorts that showed off her long tan legs and a white tank top. She was focused on the path in front of her and hadn't noticed him yet.

"Damn!" he whispered as he admired her. His plans for vengeance seemed suddenly less important. Hopefully those two fuckwits hadn't ruined his shot with her. Coming to a stop, he shouted, "Hey!"

Her attention snapped up and she raised an eyebrow at him. Brian waved a hand at her. "Hey, we met at the store the other day. I was shootin' pool with your friends. Yer Sam, right?"

Sam hesitated, considering the boy. Finally, she nodded. "Yeah, I remember." Her expression showed a hint of disdain.

"Look, I know we got off on the wrong foot. I was having a shit day. My temper got the best of me. I'm not like that, really." he smiled at her.

Sam placed her hands on her hips and cocked her head. "Nah, I've known plenty of guys like you. That's what you're like. Hot headed and always looking for a fight. Not really my style," she lied.

That was exactly her style. She was magnetically pulled to every bad-boy douchebag that came within a 20-foot radius of her. In her defense, she was working on that. It wasn't the personalities that she liked, it was just the rugged 'fuck the world' look and attitude that lured her in. How much fun those types were in the beginning. Unfortunately, those traits always seemed to be attached to an asshole and the fun ended with fights, cheating, or both.

Brian fought down the urge to burst into a tirade of cursing and insults. She was just too hot to let his temper get the best of him. "I understand. You're right. I am an asshole. I was way outta line, no excuse for it. It's something I'm working on. Trying to be a better person and all. Sometimes it gets the best of me. I'm sorry. I'll leave ya alone, but, can I give you my number just in case you change your mind about giving me another chance? I don't know anyone around here, and you seem really nice."

She stared at him for a moment. She could relate on trying to be a better person. Maybe he really was just having an off day. Paul was always preaching about seeing things from both sides, always playing the devil's advocate. Perhaps Brian, here, just needed some friends and he sucked at making them. Plus, his parents just got divorced. Must be a hard time for him.

"Yeah, ok." she said.

Brian enthusiastically dug through the console for a scrap of paper and pen. He scrolled his number down and held it out of the passenger window. Sam walked up to the car and took it. After reading the number, she stuffed it into her pocket.

"Need a ride somewhere? No strings," Brian asked.

Sam looked down Ballpark Rd., towards Lechene Dr. "Nah, I'm just walking to meet my cousin and a friend, the guys from the store. Don't think they'd be too happy to see me getting out of your car. You kinda suck at first impressions."

"Fuck what those pussies think" Brian had wanted to say. Instead he held his hands up in surrender and said. "Fair enough."

Sam offered him a smile. "I better get going."

"Ok. Hope to hear from you," Brian said.

Sam smiled and started up the road in the direction of the other two. Brian sat in the idling car, pondering what to do next. He at least had it narrowed down to walking distance of where one of the guys lived. As a bonus, he now knew exactly where the finest piece of ass he'd seen in a long time lived. He wanted to follow her. Find out where these fuckers lived and hurt them.

A thought crossed his mind. Why was he so hell bent on getting these two? Yes, they embarrassed him and tried to hustle him. That didn't seem like justification for the unbridled hate he felt. He had been imagining how he would hurt them, in some cases murder them. Over pool and a girl, though? There was something off in his head all day before he even went to that store. Come to think of it, he wasn't even sure why he went there. Wasn't he going to the beach? Or was it to Beachside Subs? He didn't know, but it definitely wasn't to that shitty little hole in the wall store. It wasn't even on the way, but he had decided to take a different route, for some reason. The drive there was escaping him. Memories of it all started with Ruben breaking for the first game. He was already feeling antsy, like he wanted to find a fight.

Once Sam was out of view he drove forward, still trying to piece together the day. It was like trying to remember a lost dream. He could recall the emotions, but the actual events were a blank.

A streak of fur bolted in front of his car, snapping him out of his thoughts. With both feet he smashed the brake pedal, making the tires scream. Before the car came to a full stop something thumped against the bumper, followed by a yelp.

"SHIT!" Brian shouted as he slung the shifter into park.

He jumped out of the car and bolted to the front. A medium-sized blonde mutt was clumsily trying to scramble to its feet. When it saw Brian, a low growl emitted from its throat and hackles rose to attention. Once on its feet it hunched down and started backing away.

"Hey boy. You're ok. It's ok," Brian said kneeling down. He stuck his hand out as a peace offering. The dog flinched and bared its teeth.

"Woah, easy boy. I'm not gonna hurt ya," he said.

Watching the dog's eyes, he realized the dog wasn't looking at him, but somewhere behind him. Chills ran up his spine as the dog's growls intensified. He pulled his hand back slowly and turned his head to look. Nothing. The growls turned to a whimper and the dog bolted.

"What the hell?" Brian said.

Frustrated and shaken, he got back in the car and slammed the door. "Fuckin' dog."

Pulling the car off the road, he put it in park and took a deep breath. Something was wrong. He needed to remember what happened.

"Yesssss." A voice hissed in his ear.

Brian startled and spun to face the voice. A wisp of black smoke dissipated in the back seat, just as his eyes found it. White noise suddenly poured from the radio speakers. Brian gasped so hard he snorted. He stared in horror at the lighted face of the stereo. Fear gripped him tightly. He wanted to reach out to turn off the power, but his hand refused to let go of the wheel. The white noise warbled, the pitch changing ever so slightly.

"Yessss." The voice came through the speakers this time.

Brian released the steering wheel and clamped his ears shut. Still, the noise bled through.

"Be my justice," it beckoned.

A hand grabbed his shoulder. Icy breath caressed his ear. "Kill for me," the voice rattled.

Brian shuddered at the touch. It was so cold.

"Youuu… are miiiiine." The voice hissed. "Kill… for me."

The hand moved to his face, turning it to the side. "You are miiiine."

Brian snapped his eyes open to look upon a grotesquely withered woman. Her skin was like thin old leather that had been left to rot in filthy water. A black smoke danced around her, obscuring her features. She wore a burlap cloak over a soiled peasant's dress. His eyes were pulled to hers. In them, he found swirling clouds of darkness.

"Kill for me," she breathed, though her mouth never moved.

It hung open, much wider than seemed possible. As if someone had pried it apart with the jaws of life. Foul, dark liquid dripped from her gaping maw. Her cracked lips curved into a smile, showing rotted broken teeth.

The longer he looked into her churning eyes, he found his fear ebbed. She was nothing to fear. She had been wronged, he could feel it. Just like him. She understood and felt sympathy for him. He didn't need to hear her say it. Every cell of his body knew it. She cared for him and would protect him. Unlike his parents. Unlike those assholes from the store. Unlike anyone. Everyone else was nothing. Just evil souls waiting for the opportunity to hurt him. Not her, though. She was… beautiful.

"Juuuudge." she said.

Brian smiled with tears streaming down his cheeks and nodded. She grabbed his jaw and squeezed, forcing it open. Slowly, she leaned into him until their mouths almost touched. Her mouth, unbelievably, opened further. A shiny black tendril crept from her mouth into Brian's. He felt it tickle the roof of his mouth as it felt its way around. Two more tendrils rose from the horrible woman's mouth to join the first. Then five. Before long, there was a writhing mass of them dancing around his mouth. He didn't mind. She wouldn't hurt him. Like a frog in a pot of warming water, he didn't sense any danger. The tendrils gently worked their way down his throat. It wasn't until he tried to draw in a breath and found he couldn't, that panic replaced the trust and love he had just felt. He grabbed the hoard that was pushing its way into his throat and pulled. Pain receptors screamed as the mass resisted, causing his muscles to seize. Releasing the tendrils, he clawed at his neck. His gag reflex screamed, but the tendrils left no room for him to vomit. Pain erupted in his throat as they forced it to expand to accommodate them. He wanted to scream. He tried so hard. So hard that capillaries burst in his eyes and nostrils. Then, suddenly, all sensation left and emotion rushed through him. Sorrow at the loss of his relationship with his mom and dad. Losing his friends and teammates at his old school. Next, guilt came. Guilt for what happened to his mom. The emotions contorted, twisted, and blended into anger. Anger at his mom for ruining everything with her weakness. His dad, for the monster he had become. Sam, for rejecting him. The old black man, for giving him shit over parking there.

230

Paul and Ruben, for scamming him and making him look like a fool. Mr. Hern, for interfering.

"Kill for me," she whispered into his ear.

The pain ebbed and he met the woman's black eyes and shook his head, resisting her influence. She wanted him to kill. He was many things, but a killer was not one of them.

Her thoughts went deeper into his mind, spreading like a virus. She showed him her master's killing her love, leaving him there to rot outside her window. He felt her pain and heartbreak. He relished the scene of her vengeance as she killed the whole family. The bliss flowed through him, as he felt her give herself over to the darkness. There was no more pain. Only anger and desire. He wanted that. Without a word, he consented.

Forcefully, the tendrils pushed their way deeper into him. He felt as though his stomach would split open and spill his guts upon the floorboard. The pain was so unbearable he wanted to die, or at least pass out. Panic flowed through him like ice water. His body twitched and convulsed, but she would not allow him to slip away. The pain tore at his mind, killing off trust, pity, guilt, compassion, and love. The darkest parts of his mind mutated and grew. Any semblance of good that he once held died in that moment. Rage and lust were his drugs, now. Hate was the air he breathed. Revenge was food… and he was hungry.

Chapter 13

Paul and Ruben pulled up to the house to find Madie and her sister standing under the carport with Adam. Both Adam and Madie had serious expressions. Adam was perched on the steps, puffing on a cigarette. Madie studied Paul before wrapping him in a hug. He thought the way she placed her hands was odd. Just… not normal, for a hug. She almost seemed to struggle or be uncomfortable to make her skin touch his. As a warmth spread through him, he didn't find it important anymore.

"How'd it go with the voodoo queen?" Adam asked.

Paul shot Ruben a quick glance. He had filled him in on the ride home. Looking back to Adam, he shrugged, "I don't know, man. Some crazy shit she told me."

"Like?" Adam said rolling his wrist as to tell Paul to continue.

"Well, she said Mr. Goodrich is dead. Killed himself," Paul said.

Adam nodded, "Yeah, dad was telling me the same thing."

"That's insane. We just saw him the other day," Madie spoke up.

"I know. Seems like I should have seen it coming with the way he looked," Paul stuffed his hands in his pockets.

"What else?" asked Adam.

"Seems your brother here is magical," Ruben said with a slap on Paul's back.

Adams brow creased. "Come again?"

Shooting Ruben a "fuck you" glare, Paul began to fill them in on everything that Ms. Swanier had told him. He left out the part about Madie potentially being his pwoteje. It felt too much like implying they were meant to be together and taking things to a very serious relationship level. The whole subject made Paul far too uncomfortable.

"Sooooo… you're a Judge?" Adam said skeptically.

Paul shrugged, "According to her."

"And you send bad people to a bad place?" asked Adam.

"I don't know about all that. I mean, to me it sounded more like I'm a drain filter. Separating shit from water," Paul answered.

"Hmm. Ok then. And how does any of this help?" Adam's irritation was evident.

"I'm not sure. I'm supposed to go back to see her tomorrow. All seems a little nuts to me, but something felt right about what she was saying. I can't really explain it. Y'all know I don't buy into all the supernatural crap, but I can't shake the feeling she's telling the truth. Or at least parts of it," Paul said.

"The part where him and Madie are soulmates probably helped make him a believer," Ruben laughed.

"Goddamn it, Ruben!" Paul hissed at him.

Madie saw the black cloud instantly solidify around his neck as Paul's aura flared with angry colors. Seeing his fists ball up as

233

he turned to face Ruben, she reached out and put a hand through the entity and onto the back of Paul's neck. This caused the cloud to retreat to Paul's torso and gradually fade back into its translucent state. Almost instantly, the tension began to leave his muscles. Everything she'd just done felt like an involuntary response. Much like breathing, it just happened naturally. Realizing how odd the whole thing may have seemed, she pulled her hand away. Paul looked to her, clearly confused.

"What's that supposed to mean?" Madie asked Ruben.

"You're Paul's pwoteje," Ruben said, as if pwotejes were just common knowledge.

"His what?" Adam and Madie said simultaneously.

Paul sighed in frustration. "So, she said that judges have people called pwotejes. They help keep them sane and healthy. Doing the judge thing apparently is hard on the body and mind. So pwotejes… I don't know… heal them I guess?"

"And she thinks Madie is yours?" asked Adam with a cynical inflection.

Paul looked apprehensively at Madie, "That's what she says." He couldn't hide the flush in his face.

"This all sounds like bullshit to me," Adam said with an exhale of smoke. "Fuckin exploding gods, judges, pwot-things, dark places where evil goes. It just sounds like the start of some B rated fantasy movie. Now, what? We all find mythological weapons and some wizards? Band up and go save the day? I mean come on."

"I believe it," Madie said.

The three boys looked at her, surprised. "You do?" Paul disbelievingly asked.

"Yeah. There's something I haven't really told anybody." She paused, forcing her courage front and center, "I..." She paused again. Anxiety nibbling at her insides. "I see auras. Well, when I want to. Not on everyone, though. And I always seem to know what people are feeling and thinking. Not like I can hear their thoughts. Just, a general idea of what's on their mind. Most people, anyway." She spouted the whole thing out in one breath. After finishing, she looked to each of them. Adam's face showed little emotion other than an arched eyebrow. Ruben looked to be trying to solve some type of difficult equation in his head. Paul stared at her with the expression you'd see on someone who just solved the equation that Ruben was struggling with.

"So, you knew what was going on in my head when you grabbed my neck?" he said, more as a statement than a question.

Madie shrugged, "Sort of. That's the other thing. There's… something in your aura that doesn't belong there."

"Say what?" Paul asked.

"Seriously? We are buying into all this shit?" Adam said incredulously.

A familiar feeling of regret and embarrassment came over Madie. She folded her arms and looked at the ground.

"Hey! You don't have to be a dick!" Paul snapped at Adam.

Adam stood from the steps, facing Paul. "I'm being realistic. And who the fuck you think you're talking to?!"

Ruben's eyes went wide as Paul took a step towards Adam and shoved him. He really didn't want to see them fight. He sure as hell didn't want to try to pull Adam's giant ass off Paul to keep him from killing his little brother. "Fuck it." he thought as he stepped between them.

"What the fuck guys?! Y'all are brothers!" he exclaimed.

Madie looked up upon hearing Ruben. She gasped as she saw the entity engulfing Paul's head. The part that truly terrified her was the sight of the tendrils reaching from Paul's head, wrapping around Adams neck. The ends were dancing around Adam's ear canals, much like they were on Paul's at the river. One of them whipped around Ruben as she watched, though it quickly released him.

"No!" she shouted.

She placed a hand firmly on the back of Paul's head. Her entire body felt a sensation of pins and needles as she made contact. Much like a foot falling asleep. Nausea ripped through her. Her body tried to force her to pull her hand away. A will not her own would not let her. The edges of her vision turned dark. The dark spread quickly to encompass the world.

She found herself standing in pitch blackness. Except, she wasn't. She raised her hands to her face. A glow seemed to be emanating from inside them, like a very low watt bulb. She realized that it wasn't actually dark. Instead, there was… nothing to see. No light. No dark. Just nothing, other than her and the light she was producing. She attempted to swallow as fear filled her, but she couldn't.

Nothing was the same here. There was no up or down. No gravity. No smell. No sound. She couldn't even feel her own skin as she hugged her arms around herself. Cold… that was the only thing she could feel.

She startled at the sound of a low growl behind her. While not loud, in the absence of all other sensation it seemed like an explosion. Terror froze her in place.

"Miiiiiiinnnnee…," a hoarse whisper entered her mind.

"You worthless whore!" a scream boomed in the void.

There was something familiar about the voice. Forcing her fear down, she scanned the nothingness. She stopped on a dim light somewhere in the distance. Maybe it was right in front of her? Nothing seemed to follow the laws of physics as she understood them. She focused on the light, wanting to go to it, and then she was there. Did she move? Her vision distorted as her brain tried to catch up. Everything was happening in slow motion, yet, somehow instantaneously. Her mind ached as she tried to understand any of it. She felt like a cave man that was plopped into the pilot seat of a mid-flight plane.

Forcing her thoughts to slow, she willed her eyes to focus on the light. "Paul?" she gasped.

Before her stood a disheveled shirtless Paul. He hunched like a beast prepared to pounce. Spatters of blood and filth covered his chest and abdomen. Greasy hair hung down over his face, exposing one cloudy eye filled with insanity and rage. He was glaring into her very soul. She felt his menacing intent in every inch of her. He was a creature of unadulterated hate and pain. The intensity of his emotions felt violating.

"What's going on Paul? Where are we?" she said, though no words were actually spoken.

"You!" he hissed. "You were supposed to save me from this. Save all of us! You did this!! Now they're all dead!"

"What?" she whimpered. "I don't understand."

"You killed them, Madie. Look what you've done!" Paul shouted, motioning his hand around him.

Figures lay at his feet. Frances stared up at her with vacant eyes. The side of her face was deformed from the crushed bone beneath the skin of her cheeks and forehead. If not for the distinct hair color, she wouldn't have been sure who it was, although there wasn't much of that left unstained with blood.

"No!" Madie whispered.

Next to her, Ruben gagged and coughed up spouts of blood. The hilt of a knife protruded from his throat, bouncing and bobbing with each gag or attempted breath. His eyes found her and pleaded. Unable to bear the sight before her, she looked away.

Adam lay a few feet away. His eyeless sockets looked out into the nothing. His mouth hung open at an odd angle. Where his bottom lip should have been there was only a confusing mash of mangled flesh and broken teeth. His skin was charred and blistered.

"Stop it!" she begged. She wanted to close her eyes but couldn't.

Sam's lifeless form was next. Her soggy hair clung to her face. Blue lips and bulging eyes peeked out from behind the tangled mess of hair. Sam's lips were swollen to the point of almost rupturing. Tattered and wet clothes draped her bloated body. Pieces of her flesh appeared to have been picked at by small carnivores.

"Paul, stop it!" she screamed.

William sat hunched over and limp, a gaping hole in the top of his head clearly visible. Blood still trickled out of his mouth. His service pistol still clenched in the hand hanging limply at his side.

A crushing sorrow, so heavy that it paled her grief over her mother and sister's passing, swept over her tas she looked up to Paul. In his arms, Jennifer sagged motionless. Paul gently set her down.

"You did this," Paul said remorsefully.

Jennifer's eyes were wide with fear even in death. Her lips still curled around her teeth, contorted by pain. Black and purple marks decorated her neck. The collar of the rainbow unicorn shirt she always wore to bed was stretched and torn. The matching bottoms to them were covered in mud at the cuffs of the legs. Filthy bare feet poked out of the pant legs. Her left big toe was bent at an unnatural angle with the middle joint separated and pushing through the skin.

Madie looked desperately up to Paul. Tears streaked his face, though his expression showed no sadness. A maddened smile showed rotten jagged teeth in his head. "I will not be judged," he croaked.

A wet rattling began with every breath he took. Each breath more labored than the last. Paul's throat began to swell dramatically. A slow trickle of thin black fluid began to leak from his mouth and nostrils. His smile gave way to a look of pain. With a twitchy motion, his mouth began to open. It was as if an invisible force was prying his jaws. Wider and wider, it opened. The flesh at the corners of his mouth split under the strain. Gurgling sounds escaped from Paul, followed by a gush of black fluid. Aside from his ever-expanding jaw, he never moved. As Madie watched in horror, ten or twelve slimy black tendrils crept out over his lips. Barely thicker than spaghetti noodles, they brought to mind images of a dog's heart full of heartworms that she had once seen in a medical book. White heart worms were coming out of every aorta in the picture. Paul's face was the aorta in this picture. Unable to look away, more of the horrible worms came out, all still anchored in his throat as they writhed around his face. As more appeared, less of Paul's features could be seen. Before long, Paul's face was nothing more than a mask of the things.

Madie wanted to scream. She did scream, but the only sound was in her thoughts. Unable to close her eyes, she looked back to her friends and sister. Then back to Paul. Paul was Paul again. Well, the maniacal and disheveled Paul, at least. Anything was better than the nightmare he had been a moment ago. He now had his dad's service pistol in his left hand.

Paul smiled at her sorrowfully. "I love you, Madie," he said as he put the gun to his temple and fired.

Raw, pure, unfiltered grief filled Madie. She wept and wailed like she had never known possible. It frightened her how powerful the pure agony felt. Her entire existence poured out of her with each sob. She howled her sister and Paul's names over and over, begged them to wake up. She wanted to reach down and hold Jennifer, but she found herself formless. The light that she had once emitted was fading. Her body was evaporating into a black swirling mist laced with crackling red energy. An absolute feeling of hopelessness, loss, and defeat enveloped her. She released her desire to be. She wanted to feel nothing ever again, and then there was nothing.

"Yesssss," a scratchy voice hissed.

"Madie!" her name exploded in her ears. A slit of stinging light appeared. Sensations began to return. The smell of magnolia blossoms. Dogwood trees. A cigarette burning. The feeling of warm hard ground on her back. Heat. Pain. Her throat and eyes now burned with grief. A sob shook her body, and she was grateful that she could feel at all.

"Jennifer…" her voice quivered.

"Madie!" The voice boomed again. She forced her eyes open slowly. A fuzzy image of the world came into view dominated by a blurred image hovering over her. Far away, voices seemed to be calling her name.

She blinked several times, attempting to clear her vision. The shape of a woman leaned over her. Blurry strawberry blonde hair hung down over a hazy face.

"Madie?!" Frances' voice rang in Madie's ears.

She squinted, trying to make out the person before her. Paul's mother's face came in and out of view as her eyes focused. Confusion screamed questions in her mind.

"Can you hear me?" Frances said with urgency.

Madie's vision cleared and she saw Frances. The sun seemed much lower in the sky now. Behind Frances Adam, Ruben, and Paul stood anxiously. All three looked very worried. Her heart leapt as she found her sister kneeling next to her crying. Madie covered her face with her hand and wept tears of joy at seeing those she had thought lost alive again. Tears of embarrassment. Tears of fear and confusion.

"Hey, hey, hey. You're ok. Shhh," came Frances' voice. A gentle hand squeezed her shoulder. "Just breathe. You're ok. One of y'all go get me the ice pack out the freezer and some water."

The sounds of hurried footsteps and a squeaky screen door swinging open followed the order. Madie sucked in a long shaking breath and exhaled slowly.

"You scared me, Madie!" Jennifer said meekly.

"I'm sorry," she said and burst into another round of weeping.

After regaining her composure, Madie pulled her hands away and began to sit up. "Go easy, now," Frances said as she placed an arm on Madie's back to help.

Paul came rushing out of the door, carrying a half full glass of water and a cold compress. Running up to his mother, he handed her both. His worried eyes met Madie's.

"What happened?" Madie asked as she took in her surroundings. She was still under the carport.

"You fainted, sweetie," Frances answered before Paul found the words. She placed the blissfully cold compress on the back of Madie's neck.

Holding herself in a sitting position was difficult. She felt very sleepy. Curling up under a warm blanket would be heaven. Her muscles were fatigued as if she had run a triathlon. A dull pain made itself known on the back of her head. Reaching a hand back, she found a goose egg on the back of her head. Touching it made her wince.

"You fell pretty hard," Ruben said, noticing her expression.

"Must be this damned heat. You haven't been here long enough to be used to it. Hell, it gets some of us that grew up here on occasion, too. Gotta be careful when it gets like this. Heat index is 112 today." Frances felt Madie's head with her wrist after she spoke. Surprise crossed her face. "Dear Lord!

You're freezing! Come on let's get you inside on the couch. Paul, Adam come help me get her up."

Paul hurried over and hooked an arm through Madie's armpit. With a nod to Adam, they hoisted her up. Madie's head swam at the motion. Turning her head to Paul, she looked him over, searching for the entity. Unable to find it at the moment, she relaxed.

The boys supported her for the first few steps. Feeling her strength and bearings returning, she gently pulled out of their grip. "I'm ok now," she said.

Paul kept a hand on her elbow, ready if she fell. "Ok, let's get you inside, still."

She leaned into Paul and whispered, "Something bad is coming." She hadn't thought about saying it, it was a compulsion that came out of its own volition. There was something bad coming, though. With every fiber of her being, she now knew there was in fact true evil in this world. Worse still, it seemed this evil was targeting in on Paul and everyone he loved.

"I know," Paul whispered back after a few steps.

They shared a look and Madie nodded to him. Paul helped her to the couch, where she took a seat. Frances handed her the cup of water that she had stopped to refill and add ice to. Seeing the water, Madie's tongue begged for the cold liquid. Greedily, she chugged down the whole glass.

"Thank you," she said, handing the glass back to Frances.

"Now, you need to sit for a while. Keep an eye on her, Paul," she said and left the room leaving Paul and Madie alone.

Grateful for the momentary privacy, Paul sat next to her and took her cold hand. The calming he normally felt was diminished somewhat, when he first did. Then, a wave of warmth washed through them. Both visibly relaxed like a full body sigh of relief. After a moment of relishing the sensation, Paul quietly said, "You need to go see Ms. Swanier. She told me to tell you that. She says we are in danger."

Madie nodded and spoke in hushed tones as well. "That thing I keep seeing on you. I saw it when you guys started fighting. It was… grabbing at Adam and Ruben, too. I think it was making you all go after each other. I tried to make it go away like before, and… well. I passed out I guess. But, I went somewhere while I was out. Somewhere horrible."

"What do you mean?" Paul asked.

"It was like I was in this giant… nothing." she said.

Paul raised his eyebrows. "I think I've been there too! In my dream!" he said excitedly.

Barely acknowledging what Paul said, she continued. "You were there, but it wasn't really you. Everyone was dead around you. Ruben, Adam, Sam, your parents… Jennifer." She choked back fresh tears, as she recalled how helpless she had felt seeing her sister's lifeless body, "Like maybe you had killed them. You kept saying horrible things. How it was all my fault."

"I would never do that," Paul said. He partially felt like he was lying after all the thoughts that had been creeping into his head as of late.

"I know you wouldn't. It was just so horrible. It felt so real. And when I woke up and saw all of you alive…," her defenses caved and she put her face into Paul's chest, crying. He pressed her tightly to him, finding tears streaming down his own cheeks. He had brought this onto her. Onto all of those he cared for. Seeing her hurting and scared because of him filled him with guilt.

"It's gonna be ok, Madie," he said, forcing his voice not to quiver. "We will figure this out. I won't let anything happen to you, or anyone else."

After a few calming breaths, she said, "Promise me you won't let this thing take you, Paul. I think that's what it wants. It wants to take you to that place. You can't let it."

"It will have to remove my foot from its ass while I'm skull fucking it, if it tries." Ruben's voice startled both of them. They spun in their seats to find him standing in the entryway.

"Fuck! How long have you been standing there?!" Paul exclaimed.

"Language!" Frances yelled from the kitchen.

Shrinking away, Paul and Ruben shouted, "Sorry!"

After a pause, Frances went back out to the carport, to smoke.

"Long enough. Y'all know I'm down. Don't act like you're alone in this sh…stuff." He shot a guilty glance over his shoulder to the window looking out to the carport. Looking back to them, he cleared his throat, "Yeah it all sounds crazy, but I believe every word of it," Ruben said.

"You do?" Madie said sheepishly.

"Yep," he said plainly.

"Why? It sounds ridiculous," Madie said.

"My boy ain't crazy. That's just a fact. After seeing what I saw last night, I don't need much convincing that some ghost stuff is going on here. Jij, judge, Casper… whatever the fu…hell it is, Imma beat it's ass if it comes after any of my people."

"Ass is still a curse word, dude," Paul whispered with a chuckle.

Ruben gave a roll of his eyes and plopped down on the couch next to Paul. "You ok, Madie?"

She put a hand to the lump on her head. "I'll live. Hurts, though."

"Good," Ruben said. His expression turned to worry. "That you're ok! Not that it hurts!"

Madie let out a genuine laugh, "I know what you meant."

"Dumbass," a smirking Paul said, giving Ruben a friendly elbow in the arm.

In a mocking tone, Ruben said, "Dumbass is still a cuss word, dude."

Adam came in, stopping in the threshold. His posture was slumped and his head bowed. Both hands were stuffed in his pockets.

"Say, guys. Look… I'm sorry. Fuck, I feel like I'm saying that too much lately," he said.

Paul half smiled. "It's all good. I know you don't buy into this crap. You don't want to buy into this, then that's cool. Just don't be shi…belittling us about it man. I don't do that to you, do I?"

"Nah. You don't. I don't know what came over me, dude. I just got so mad. Totally out of the blue," Adam said.

Madie and Paul shared a knowing look. "Kinda like Paul at the river, huh?" Madie said.

Adam contemplated what she said a moment. "I don't know," he shrugged.

The whole concept went against everything he knew to be correct. There was no god. Life is just survival until the shell holding your energy gives out. The only unknown was what happened to the energy that controls your shell, since energy can't be destroyed. Paul and Adam had had many long discussions about that topic. Does that energy have a consciousness after it leaves your body? Perhaps, it moves on to another dimension or state of being.

The Christian idea of God always seemed so ludicrous to him, though. A God that made us with the sole purpose of worshiping him and doing his bidding? Then to add a little spice, because he didn't make life hard enough, give them free will and a built-in nature that goes against everything he demands from them. But wait, there's more. Should you not be able to resist the irresistible urges that he installed in you, you get to burn for all eternity.

Why would anyone want to worship the equivalent of a dictator with a fragile ego? No, Adam just couldn't buy into it. If God was real, the devil sounded like a better option. At least he had the balls to stand up to him, and a sense of adventure.

However, there was something going on here that didn't fall under anything he understood. Not five minutes ago, he was virtually frothing at the mouth with a desire to maim or even kill his little brother. As with any brothers, they had fought before. What he felt at that moment was an entirely different level. Mr. Goodrich had tried to warn him.

"Your brother is in danger. My wife didn't kill herself. That… thing… it got in her head. Drove her mad. She had become angry and violent. So had I. We fought so much in the weeks leading up to… She knew your brother was special. She tried to tell me that she didn't have long. I was so angry and bitter towards her, that I didn't care. I actually liked the idea of her not being around. I said such horrible things to her," Mr. Goodrich had said. Ms. Swanier had been standing at his side with a hand on the back of his head. Adam had thought she was just comforting him in his time of loss. After learning what she had told Paul today, he remembered the strained look on her face. At the time, he thought it was pity and grief. Perhaps it was something more. Maybe she was trying to "heal" him. Adam sighed in frustration. Just the thought running through his head made him feel silly. Like a child that still believed in Santa. Yet…

"Look, I got y'all's backs. Whatever is going on, regardless of what I think, I'll be there for y'all. I'll do my best to keep an open mind," he said. Part of him wanted to share what Mr. Goodrich had told him at the funeral. The stronger part of him, the skeptic, didn't want to feed the fires of this fantasy. Not yet, at least. Not without something undeniable to push him to the believer side.

"Well, I'm sure as shit glad you're on our side, ya big bastard," Ruben said with a grin.

"Me too," Paul smiled.

"Ah, Jesus, we all gonna make out now?" Adam said rolling his eyes.

"I mean… if the price is right," Ruben shrugged. "Didn't know that was your thing though, Ogre."

Adam raised a brow at him, "Don't make me sew your lips shut, Ruby."

Ruben put his hands up, "My bad. My bad… Wait… you know how to sew? I dunno, man…"

"Ruben… I will beat the clothes off of you, oil you up and treat you like a choir boy," Adam said in his best sassy voice.

Hearing the giant make that voice brought a round of laughter from all of them.

After the laughter died down, Ruben asked, "So, we were all dead?"

"What?" Adam asked.

Madie rubbed her forehead and sighed. "Yeah."

"How did I die? Was it heroic and gruesome?" Ruben asked.

250

"You had a knife sticking out of your throat," She reached over and touch the side of his Adams Apple, "Here."

"Damn. I'm gonna pass on that," Ruben said, rubbing at his throat.

"Sam looked like she had been underwater for a few days. She was all bloated and wet." The visions were still crystal clear in her head.

"Something had ripped your bottom lip off and plucked your eyes out," She pointed at Adam. A disgusted look crossed his face.

"Your dad had shot himself. And your mom… it looked like someone had hit her in the head over and over with something heavy," She stopped.

Paul's expression turned to disbelief, "That's exactly what happened in my dream," he gasped. "Some invisible thing caved her skull in right in front of me. Then… I saw myself holding this big thing, like I was the one that did it."

"I think that's what it's pushing you towards. It's messing with our heads and whispering these terrible things into our ears. It's pitting us against each other," Madie said.

"Why?" Ruben asked.

Madie sighed, "I have no idea."

"Maybe, if what Ms. Swanier is saying is true - that it doesn't want to go to whatever's after death for the bad people. Maybe by getting rid of me and the other judges it gets to stay?" Paul's lack of conviction to that statement showed in his voice.

After a silence, Ruben said, "Makes sense. Maybe by getting us after each other it thinks it will make you evil too. Be its ghost homie or something." There was a long quiet, "Shit, I dunno… I'm guessing like the rest of y'all."

Adam moved to the far corner of the room, his arms folded across his chest. He appeared uncomfortable. "So, if I put myself into the role of believing any of this, my biggest question would be, what the fuck can we actually do about any of it?" he said.

When nobody answered, Ruben said, "Well, maybe there's something that is letting it stay here? Like in the movies, where you gotta give it a proper burial or destroy the thing it's attached to,"

"I guess. I think we should just wait and see what Ms. Swanier says tomorrow. Really, we are just walking around in the dark without any other information," Madie said.

Everyone's attention turned as the carport door opened. Frances walked into the kitchen, followed by Sam. A strange look was on his mother's face as Paul met her eyes. Disdain maybe? A shiver ran up his spine.

"Sammy!" Ruben said as he came off the couch.

Sam gave a quick hug to Ruben before sitting next to Madie. "You ok? Aunt Frances told me what happened."

"Yeah, I'm fine," she smiled.

"Damn, girl, you gotta be careful in these Mississippi summers," Sam said.

"So I keep hearing." Madie looked to Paul, hoping for guidance. Did she fill Sam in on the conversation? Would she believe it? He seemed distracted.

"You will never guess who I saw on the way here," Sam said.

"Who's that?" Ruben asked.

"That guy from Karl's. He saw me walking down my driveway and started talking to me," she said with a roll of her eyes.

Ruben felt his blood pressure rise. "Is that so?" he said, with venom dripping from his words. "What the hell did he want?"

"Calm down, dude," she chuckled. "He apologized for the way he acted, surprisingly. Offered me a ride. I told him, no. That was about it."

"Hmm. Yeah, I'll accept his apology... after I kick the dog shit out of him," Ruben fumed.

"Jesus, you boys and your egos," Sam scoffed. "Hey, I can't stay long, I gotta babysit my brother. I just wanted to step out for a smoke and check on you," she said to Paul.

"Been a strange day," he said.

"He's killing her!!!" a voice screamed in Madie's head. Madie, feeling a sudden sense of dread, sat straight up. "Where's Jennifer?!" In all the chaos she hadn't realized her sister hadn't come inside.

"She was out in the carport when I came in," Adam said.

Madie leapt up and dashed for the door. She almost collided with Frances as she rounded the corner, coming into the kitchen.

"You should be taking…," Frances started.

"Where's Jennifer?!" Madie half shouted, cutting Frances off.

"I don't know, I think she walked home. What's wrong, sweetie?" Frances said.

Madie took off without a word, in a mad dash. The three boys and Sam came charging out the door after her.

"What the hell is going on?" demanded Frances as she snatched Adam by the arm. Sam stopped with him.

"I don't know," he honestly said.

Frances looked back to the others in pursuit. "Make sure they are ok, understand?" she said, releasing Adam.

He nodded and took off after the others.

Paul quickly caught up to Madie and slowed his rapid pace to match her. "Where?" he panted.

"My house," Madie answered, never breaking stride.

Paul pushed off into an all-out sprint. He wasn't sure why Madie was so upset at the idea of her sister walking home, but he wasn't questioning it. In light of everything going on, he trusted that there was something bad happening, or about to.

He made it to the edge of Madie's yard and threw a quick glance behind him. Everyone was two hundred yards or so off still. He bounded over the ditch into the backyard and stopped. Unsure what he was looking for, he looked and listened. For long moments he heard nothing but birds chirping and his own harsh breathing, then a crash came from inside the house. With a few long strides he was at the back door.

'Now, what?' he thought. His hand was on the doorknob. What if it was nothing? He didn't know her dad and didn't think bursting into his house unannounced would be the best first impression. Inaudible screams came from down the road and he turned. He cocked his ear, straining to make out what was being said. It was Madie's voice, but he couldn't make out the words. Ring the door? There was no door bell. Another crash came from inside accompanied by a peculiar noise. It started at a high pitch and went to a scratchy… static-like noise. A series of small thumps and a deep muffled voice followed.

Madie screamed again. This time Paul made it out clearly.

"He's killing her!" His veins turned to ice as her words registered. The sound on the other side of the door… gasping. Paul turned the knob but found it locked.

Paul slammed his shoulder into it hard and felt no give. He cursed himself for being so thin. Over and over he crushed his weight against the door. His shoulder throbbed from the multiple impacts. The door was too solid.

Suddenly, he was thrown backwards and landed hard on his ass. Adam's large bulk smashed through the door on the first attempt, splintering the door frame. Ruben charged in right behind him. Paul heard a horrible commotion and screaming as he scrambled to his feet.

"You mother fucker!" Adam's voice bellowed from inside.

Paul ran inside to find Adam and Ruben wrestling with a rather girthy man on the floor. He had never met Madie's father, so he assumed that's who was being restrained.

Madie and Jennifer were not in the immediate area. Ruben had both arms wrapped around the man's legs and had pressed his whole body weight onto them. He looked like a bull rider as he desperately clung on while the man thrashed.

"Keel road!" Madie's voice came from somewhere in the house. "It's the only house on it! Please, hurry! She's unconscious." Paul was unsure of what to do at this point.

Adam, who was perched on the man's large belly, raised up his torso and began raining down blows onto the man's face. Each strike ringing a meaty smack through the air. Still, the man fought. As Paul made his way beside them to help, blood spattered on his cheek from Adam's fist as he drew back. Paul flinched and wiped it away.

"You! Sick! Mother! Fuck!" Adam accompanied each word with another blow to the man. He loosed a guttural roar as he put his entire body into one last strike. The man finally stilled.

Madie's father's face came into view as Paul stepped around. It was a bloody, mangled display of brutality. One eye was deformed with the massive amount of swelling and split flesh. Multiple cuts on his cheeks and around his eyes streaked blood across his face, obscuring his features. Knots and discolorations littered the parts that weren't painted red. Adam reared back as if he was going to strike again.

"Chill! He's out, man!" Paul exclaimed.

Adam hovered his shaking fist in the air for a second, heaving in deep gasps of air. "You didn't see what he was doing!" he rasped.

"Dude, you don't need to go to jail over him," Paul said.

With a huff, he finally dropped his arm to his side.

A snort came from Madie's dad, followed by a long moan as he exhaled. Similar to snoring… but a more frightening noise. Then again. His one visible eye stared blankly at the ceiling. The process repeated over and over. Paul wanted to plug his ears. There was something so disturbing about the sound.

Ruben released his legs and stood. Upon taking in the scene, he said. "Holy shit! Did you kill him?!"

"I fucking hope so." Adam growled. He winced upon unclenching his fist. After flexing his fingers a few times, he looked around the room. They had ended up in the floor of the dining area. The smell of dirty cat litter was heavy in here. Clutter filled every corner of the home. Books, grocery bags, toys, flats of water, and various other items littered every surface. He noticed the strong smell of stale beer coming from the man under him.

"Hand me some of those shirts over there," Adam pointed to a pile of clothes a few feet away. Ruben quickly moved to get them.

"Where's Madie and her sister?" Adam asked, concern coming to his face.

Sobbing could be heard coming from a small door in the hall leading to the back door they had come through. "Madie?!" Paul called out.

"Help me! Please! Wake up! Goddamn it, wake up!" Madie's voice wailed from the other side.

"See what's going on. I'm gonna tie this fucker up," Adam ordered.

Paul was already charging for the door as Adam spoke. He ran to the door and knocked. "Madie?"

"Please help!" she screamed mournfully from the other side.

Paul barged through the door and found Madie sitting on the floor with Jennifer cradled in her arms. She rocked back and forth like a mother trying to soothe her baby. Jennifer's lips had taken a shade of purple. Deep red and purple marks ringed her throat and neck. A small trickle of blood trickled down from her nose to her lip. The collar of her shirt was torn wide and the waist of her jeans sat low on one side of her hips.

"What the fuck happened?" Paul said, shocked at the horrific scene before him.

"Please, Paul. She's not breathing. Please. Help." Madie's words were barely understandable through the weepy tremble in her voice.

"Oh God. Ok. Let me have her," Paul said and scooped Jennifer up. "Adam! Ruben!" he called out as he exited the small bathroom.

Adam was using shirts to restrain her father's legs. Ruben was working on his hands. "Guys, she's not breathing. I don't know what to do!"

"Fuck! Ok set her down there," Adam pointed to one of the few clear areas of the floor.

Paul gently set her down and Madie's heart sank at the sight. Just like in the nothing. Paul's appearance was even similar. Sweat matted his hair to his face. A panicked look in his eye. Jennifer's lifeless body was even in the same clothes.

"No!" she screamed and ran towards them. Ruben caught her in a bear hug and held her while she thrashed and wept.

"She's gonna be ok, Madie! Adam's got her. Please stop!" Ruben begged, holding her tighter.

Adam quickly checked for a pulse and breathing. "Shit!" he hissed and began chest compressions. He did them as best as he could remember from the mandatory First Aid and CPR classes he'd had to take for work. He cringed as he felt ribs crack under the force of the compressions. While the trainer had told the class this would likely happen, no training could have prepared him for the reality of it happening to a 12-year-old girl's ribcage.

Paul watched helplessly as Adam worked. Time stood still for him. He looked to his best friend, consoling the girl he loved. He looked to the bound fat man lying on the dirty floor. His eyes were starting to flutter. Twitches moved his feet and fingers occasionally as his brain tried to reboot. What the hell had that man done to his own daughter? Paul's eyes had become welded to him. He couldn't look away. It felt like a tense scene in a horror flick where any minute, the monster would sit straight up and open a milky eye while letting out an otherworldly roar. The sound of sirens broke the trance. Seconds later powerful knocks hit the front door.

"Sheriff's department! Open up!" a deep voice barked from the other side. Another series of knocks followed.

Paul darted to the door and turned the handle. Finding it locked, he worked the knob on the door handle for the lock. Once unlocked, he turned the knob and pulled but the door didn't budge.

"Goddamnit!" he growled, before turning the deadbolt and opening the door.

He was greeted by a large man with a porn star mustache in a black police uniform pointing a gun at him. "DOWN ON THE GROUND!!" the man screamed. Stunned, Paul didn't respond. "GET ON THE FUCKING GROUND. GET DOWN NOW!" the officer said even more intense.

Paul threw up his hands and laid down on the gritty carpet. The rancid smell of cat piss and shit wafted over him. Not an inch from his face… a fresh, moist turd lay.

"Hey! He's the fucking guy you're after!" Ruben shouted, pointing at Madie's father.

"Help me goddamnit!" Adam said still performing compressions on the lifeless girl.

"Shit!" The officer exclaimed and keyed up his shoulder mic. "Tell EMS to step it up. Have CPR in progress on a little girl."

"10-4. Dispatch to Medical 2, CPR in progress. Code 3." A female voice responded in the radio.

The officer holstered his weapon and dropped to his knees on the other side of Jennifer from Adam. He pulled a pair of black latex gloves from a pouch in his belt. As he worked them onto his hands he said, "Don't stop compressions. How long has she been down?"

"Maybe 5 minutes. I don't know how long, he was choking her before we got here," Ruben answered as Adam silently counted each push to Jennifer's chest.

"Who was choking her?" the officer asked.

"The bloody motherfucker tied up over there," Adam growled before dropping down to give breaths to her. Sweat dripped from Adam's forehead and stung his eyes. He blinked hard a few times and felt a contact pop out.

The officer hopped back up and quickly placed cuffs on the fat man tied up with shirts and shoe lace. "One in custody. Have one juvenile unresponsive. CPR in progress. How far out is EMS?!"

Sirens became louder in the distance. "We are on scene," a male voice came over the radio.

Paul watched everything unfold, feeling far removed from the situation. Grains of cat litter scratched his face as he moved his head to find Madie. Nothing looked right. It was as if a grey lens had been placed over his view of the world. This wasn't real, was it? He ground his cheek hard into the carpet. The sting of carpet burn and abrasiveness of the filth burned his skin. It was real. His lungs constricted, and his next breath was labored. "Can I get up?!" he asked, fighting the panic welling inside of him.

"What? Oh, Yeah," the officer responded and then took over CPR.

Paul sat up as if the floor were turning into a monster. Quickly, he swiped granules of cat litter from his face. Jumping to his feet, he saw Madie crouched in the corner of the kitchen. Her face was buried in her knees as she rocked back and forth. Sobs racked her body. Paul knelt beside her and pulled her into his arms. The air around them felt cold as he pulled her tightly to his chest.

The sirens sounded like they were coming from the front of the house, and more flashes of blue and red danced on the walls. Two paramedics raced into the house. One was carrying a large orange equipment bag, the other was carrying a back board. The one carrying the back board began a barrage of questions to Adam and Ruben while the other started attaching cords and cables to Jennifer.

"Help me…" a weak whisper drifted through the air. Paul and Madie looked up from their embrace to find the room drained of most color. The commotion around Jennifer's body was moving in slow motion like everyone outside of the two of them were moving in some underwater dance.

Movement caught the corner of Paul's vision. Jennifer stood in the hallway, staring in awe at him. Her form didn't seem quite complete. A glow emanated from her partially ethereal body. Every slight move she made left tracers of her image behind that slowly caught up and reconnected. She raised her hand, her arm whisping apart only to come back together, reaching out to Paul.

"Jennifer?!" Madie's voice startled Paul.

She didn't seem to hear her sister. She was entranced by Paul, though she wasn't looking at him like she knew who he was. A will from inside pulled at him. It beckoned Jennifer to him. She stepped closer and the pull grew stronger. An audible hum rang in his ears.

"Judgment." The word flared to life in his mind.

"No! No, you can't!" he stammered. He raised a hand to her, to keep her back. "No, no, no, no!" Paul exclaimed while flailing his arms in hopes of keeping Jennifer from coming to him. He felt it… she was coming to be judged. To cross over and go to a final death. Every fiber of him felt called to do it. He focused every ounce of will he had into stopping her.

"They can save you! Go back!" he pleaded.

She paused and cocked her head. Her face became frantic and she began turning in a slow circle, looking for something. "Help me…" came her ghostly whisper.

"Jennifer! I'm here!" Madie said, breaking from Pauls' grip. As soon as the contact was gone, Jennifer blinked out of existence and the world sped back up.

Madie collapsed to the sticky tile floor, her mouth agape. "Jennifer," she whimpered.

"I've got a weak pulse. We need to move her, now!" barked the paramedic working on Jennifer.

Madie's head snapped in their direction and she scrambled to her feet. "She's alive?!"

Paul was to his feet as well. A feeling washed over him. Something like guilty joy. He knew he had failed somehow, yet he found it hard to care. Did he send her back to her body? Was that even possible? Everything was happening at such a fast pace. A day or two ago, he'd thought he was just a mentally unstable kid who was losing his mind. In that short span, he was entertaining the idea that he could send the spirits of dead people back to their bodies? Paul from two days ago would have laughed at him, and then given him a lesson in logical thinking. Yet, here he was.

The paramedics had quickly retrieved a stretcher, which they then moved Jennifer onto. She still looked lifeless and cold, although Madie could see her chest rise and fall in the moments she wasn't being jostled around. She found herself holding her breath between respirations, waiting on the beautiful sight of her little sister taking in life. The group of four stood on the porch, as they loaded her into the back of the ambulance.

"Please, let me ride with you," Madie pleaded to the larger of the two paramedics. He nodded to her and waved her in. Looking back to the others, she wanted to thank them. Hug them. Scream at them. Blame them. Cry on their shoulders. Reassure them. All she could do was look at them through a tear stained lens.

"Go. We got this. We will get there right behind you," Paul said.

She gave a weak smile before turning and running to the ambulance. She slid onto the small bench seat next to Jennifer and took her hand. The doors slammed, and she offered one last look towards the forlorn group standing in front of her house... the closest thing she had to family besides her sister. Her breath caught as a menacing silhouette slid into view behind Paul, untouched by the light, and lay a hand on his shoulder.

"Wait!" she shouted.

"We have to get her to the hospital 5 minutes ago. You can call your friends to bring whatever you forgot when you get there," the driver said as he was accelerating out of the driveway.

Another county sheriff's car came sliding to a stop in the front yard as the ambulance left. The driver's door flew open and William bounded out. His face was stone, but the wide eyes and frenzy in which he exited the car betrayed his calm façade. He had heard the call come across, and recognized the address. This area was over 10 miles out of his patrol tonight. Even with lights and sirens, and speeds exceeding 100 miles per hour when possible, it had felt like it took him an eternity to get there.

His eyes went to Adam, "Are all of you ok?"

"We are… I don't think Madie's sister is going to be, though," Adam said looking at the ground.

"What the hell happened?" his attention went to Paul.

"I. I. I don't know, sir. I came in after Adam and Ruben had her dad on the floor," he answered.

William looked back to Adam. "Madie... had a feeling something was wrong and started running towards here from our house, saying 'he's killing her' over and over while we were all running with her." Adam paused to light a cigarette with shaking hands. "Well, Paul got here first and I guess he heard something and was trying to bust the door in. So, I moved him and knocked it open. There that sick bastard was. Had that little kid pinned to the floor by her throat, with one hand down her pants. Just squeezing her neck as hard as he could. Her lips were all purple and shit. I just lost it, Dad. I tackled him off her. Ruben jumped on him, too. He starts saying all this weird shit. We get him held down and I couldn't get that image out of my head. So... I start beating his goddamn face in." Adam painfully flexed his swollen hand as he relived the moment. "I hope I killed him, Dad. I'm sorry... but I really do."

"Hey Allen, can you check on that second EMS for this piece of shit?" the officer who first arrived said from behind them.

He was kneeling next to Madie's father, who had been rolled to his stomach, emptying his pockets. Groggy, pained moans were coming from him, though he still didn't appear to be conscious.

William keyed up his mic. "602 to dispatch. Can I get an ETA for the second EMS unit to our location?"

Ruben spun to face Paul. "Where's Sam? I thought she was with us."

Paul looked around then back to Ruben. "Maybe she stayed back at my place?" He double timed it inside and scooped up the cordless phone Madie had left on the floor. He dialed the number to his house and waited through 3 rings before his mom answered.

"Hello?" Frances said.

"Mom, it's Paul. Is Sam still there?" he asked.

"No. She told me to tell y'all she would swing back by after babysitting. Is everything ok?" Frances said.

"Madie's sister… her dad hurt her bad, Mom. They just took her in an ambulance," he stopped speaking as the tremors in his voice became worse.

"The poor girl. I always thought something bad was happening over there. Is she going to be ok?" she asked.

Paul forced his voice to calm. "I don't know. Adam was doing CPR on her. I think he broke his hand on that guy's face."

"What?! Oh my God! I'm on my way there," The line went dead with the end of her sentence.

"Was she there?" Ruben asked as Paul ended the call.

"No. Mom said she went home as we left. Had to babysit." Paul turned to his dad. "I think mom's coming up here." In that moment, Paul realized how numb he felt. He thought he should feel sad and frantic. Instead, he was confusingly calm at this point. Shock maybe?

William nodded. "Ok. I'm gonna help Moran. You guys stay here."

"Dad, I need to go to the hospital. Madie doesn't have anyone and she's freaking out. She needs me," Paul protested.

William stopped and pondered. "I'll drive you there as soon as the sarge gets here. He's only five minutes out."

Frustrated, Paul reluctantly agreed. Frances slid around the curve like a skilled stunt driver. The brakes locked as she hit the driveway.

Chapter 14

Sam wanted to go with them, though she had no idea what was going on. Her mother would have her ass if she wasn't home in the next 20 minutes, though. That was five more than she needed, but not nearly enough to run to Madie's house first. Hesitantly, she watched them dart down the road before she turned the other direction towards home.

"Will you tell them I'll be back later, Aunt Frances? Mom will kill me if I don't get back to watch Jason," Sam said to Frances.

Frances looked from where the kids ran, to Sam. "Huh? Oh, yeah sure, darlin'. What is going on with them?"

"I wish I knew. Love you." Sam gave Frances a peck on the cheek and began her journey.

The sun was almost gone. Another few minutes and the sparse street lamps would be the only light for her walk home. The dark never bothered her. She actually quite enjoyed it. The world was a little quieter at night, which let her sort her thoughts. Home was a good place, but always busy. Her two younger sisters and one little brother kept the house buzzing. These little walks were her therapy.

Not long into her walk a familiar car came into view, idling on the side of the road. "Ok, stalker," Sam mumbled. She thumbed at the folding knife in her right pocket before continuing on. She didn't actually feel like he was a threat to her, but she liked the reassurance. He wouldn't be the first obsessed guy she'd had to set straight. Not that she thought she was all that, but she had a habit of developing "fans." Subtlety not being her specialty, she had hurt a few feelings in the process.

With a sigh, she continued on. Getting closer, she made out the silhouette of Brian in the driver's seat. Something seemed off about his behavior. It looked like he was having a heated conversation, though from her vantage there didn't appear to be anyone else in the car with him. Rich kid like him, probably has a cell phone or something, she thought. She stood where she was, watching.

The volume of his conversation increased to furious levels. Involuntarily, Sam took a step back. Something was definitely off. Brian roared and threw blows at the steering wheel, causing Sam to take another cautious step back. She slid the knife out of her pocket. After thumbing the blade open, she spun it into an ice pick grip. Setting her jaw, she started forward again. She'd be damned if she was gonna be scared on her turf. This was her home. The twinge of fear she had felt angered her. She was supposed to be safe here. He would not take that. No man would ever make her live in fear again.

Forcing herself to keep an even pace, she moved to the opposite side of the road. Her eyes never leaving the car. Brian stilled and sat unmoving. Somehow, this unnerved her more than the rage he was just in. The sound of the engine turning over startled her. The car lurched forward, then stopped again. The driver's side door opened, and Brian stepped out with a cloud of smoke trailing behind him. His eyes looked puffy and red. A madness seemed hidden in them.

"Hey!" he smiled to her and waved.

She did not offer the same greeting. She angled the knife behind her forearm to hide it from his view. "What are you doing here?" her tone oozed with suspicion.

"Just uh, smokin' some bud before I head home," he said, holding up a half smoked joint. "Gotta get my head right before dealing with my pop."

The smell of weed drifted to her, and she relaxed a little. He must have taken a harsh hit and was having a coughing fit when she thought he was losing his mind. Still, something was off about all of this. Why would he stop under a street light to smoke an illegal substance?

"Want some?" he asked.

"Why are you stopped on my street smoking weed?" she asked.

"Just seemed like a good spot to stop," he replied as his expression turned serious.

"Under a street light, where any cop could see you?" she asked.

He pursed his lips. "Yep," he said shortly.

"...okay. Well have fun with that," she said and started walking again.

Brian tossed the joint. "Hey wait. Let me give you a lift home. It's on my way."

"No, I'm good." she dismissed him.

"Come on. I ain't gonna bite," he laughed, hoping to drop her defenses.

Sam spun to face him, "Look! I said no! Most people get what no means, to stop fucking asking! If I wanted to get in your car I would be in it! I'm not in your car and I have said no more than once! How don't you get that I don't want a ride?!" Spinning back around she continued at a much faster pace.

Brian's mouth hung open and his eyes wide with surprise. He truly had not expected such a harsh reaction. Did she know what he was really up to sitting out here? And the nerve of this bitch! Must be scared to seem like the whore she clearly was. He'd seen it in her eyes when they met. She wanted him. Now she's playin' these fucking games?! Trying to hide a knife like she was gonna stick him?! He'd had enough. Enough of people fucking with him. Not taking him seriously. Thinking they can walk all over him. It was time to show them all that they had screwed up… starting with her.

His mouth shut into grinding teeth. He smiled menacingly at Sam's back before getting back behind the wheel.

Sam heard the engine rev, but pride refused to let her look back. She would not give him the satisfaction of scaring her. He was a piece of shit bully, but she knew he was no killer. The impact was hard and sent her tumbling through the air. She was vaguely aware of the sensation of pain and falling before her consciousness faded.

Brian gasped as he watched her fold backwards over the hood. Slamming the brakes, she flew forward several feet. Her limbs flopped like a ragdoll as she hit the pavement and rolled. Her body finally came to a stop, sprawled at an odd angle.

"What the fuck?! No! No!" Brian screamed. He felt as though he had just woken from a dream only to find himself still dreaming. He prayed it was a dream. Why would he do that?

"Oh god. Shit. Fuck me. No!" His words became quivering sobs. The gravity of the situation hit him. He was out in the open. A dead girl was lying in front of his car, which now had damage to the hood. "SHIT!" he exclaimed. "Goddamnit! No!" He slung open the door and ran to her. She was face down with one arm under her, the other twisted behind her back. Her right leg suffered a compound fracture, with a jagged piece of shin bone jutting out of the skin. A small pool of blood was forming under her head. An abyss formed in Brian's gut.

"Sam?" she heard someone say. She attempted to answer, but her body wasn't cooperating. She was so confused. Where was she? She must have fallen asleep. Attempting to roll over, panic slammed into her at the realization that she couldn't move. A searing pain came alive in her back that knocked the breath out of her.

A small squeak of pain came from the pitiful figure on the road. Brian's heart leapt, and he knelt down beside her. Weak cries began to trickle out of her.

"I'm so sorry. I'm sorry. Sam, I didn't mean it. I'm sorry!" Brian wailed.

Forcing every ounce of will she had she croaked, "Help me."

Something must have been damaged bad inside her. The mere act of speaking shocked her body with electric suffering. Muscles in her back seized and twitched. She gasped for breath through the pain.

"Ok yeah! I'll get you to the hospital. Sam, I'm so sorry. Fuck! You're gonna be OK. OK?" Brian frantically said.

He leaned down and gently started to roll her over. Tormenting pain threatened to kill her with the movement. She erupted in screams. Brian quickly pushed her the rest of the way onto her back and stepped away.

"Stop! Shh! You're ok. Please stop screaming!" he pleaded.

The pressure of the road on her spine felt like an elephant standing on her. She found she could move her arms, though her legs still had no feeling. Digging her fingers into the asphalt, she screamed until her lungs had no air left. Brian squatted next to her shushing her. He stood again after she quieted to suck in a breath, looking around for anyone that might see what was happening.

Another round of screams burst from her. In a panic, he knelt down and placed a hand over her mouth, muffling her scream. Snot, sweat, and blood soaked his palm.

"You have to stop! Please! I have to get you in the car!" he hissed.

The muted wails continued, vibrating his hand over her mouth. He pressed harder. Still, she screamed. He held his other hand a few inches from her nose. He had to stop her.

Someone would hear and come to investigate soon. He could just scare her by pinching her nose closed. When she couldn't breathe, she would listen. Then he could let go and load her up and get her to the hospital. But… there would be questions. The doctors would want to know how she got hurt. Sam would tell them what happened. Cops would be called, and he would be arrested.

"Fuck…" he whispered.

He couldn't go to prison. This was her fault, anyway. She didn't have to be like that to him. Her and those bastards from the pool hall. His dad. His mom. All of them caused this. They pushed and pushed, until he snapped. This was on them. He didn't deserve to go down for what they did. He was an honor roll football player. He didn't cheat to get good grades. Never juiced like some of his teammates. He put in the hard work. Went to church kind of regular. Busted his ass to be the best, and just like that, all of these monsters took it from him.

He looked into Sam's eyes and pushed down the guilt and pity he felt. She'd brought this on herself. Clapping his other hand over her nose, he pinched her nostrils closed tight. Her eyes shot to his. Fear and confusion swirled in them. Why was he here? Why was she in the street. What street was this? Why… was he… killing her?

Fight or flight kicked in, and she turned into pure fight. Opening her mouth, teeth found purchase on a piece of flesh. She bit down with every pound of force she could.

"AH! FUCKING BITCH!" Brian jerked his hand away, the flesh breaking free from his palm. He clutched his hand, looking in awe at the hole of missing skin.

Sam spat the coppery tasting chunk out and began screaming for help. With her right arm, the one that seemed to be cooperating the most, she reached up with fingers curled into claws, aiming for his eyes. A vicious jolt of pain threw her aim off, almost making her black out. By sheer will, she latched onto his neck, digging her nails in hard.

"GAH! Goddamn it!!" Brian roared as he jerked away from her attack. Scrambling to his feet, he took a step back from her. He was shocked at the amount of fight she had left. Her body was clearly broken in many places. The skin on her cheek was raw and bloody. A massive knot rose up from her forehead. Her left arm looked swollen, possibly broken. How?!

Sam attempted to roll over to crawl away. Something ground painfully in her spine, like there was gravel between her vertebrae. She pushed through the pain, thrusting her weight to the side. Something gave and popped loudly inside her. A sizzle of agony raced through her. Tidal waves of emotion crashed over her as her muscles shut down and she collapsed limply to the street. Memories of her life raced through her mind. Her 10th birthday… the last birthday before her dad left. Jackson Murphy, giving her her first kiss on the playground. Easter day at her grandmas last year, and her little sister mistaking a rotten chicken egg in the coop for an Easter egg during the egg hunt. She chuckled inside, remembering the chaos that ensued after she dropped the egg in the house. Mr. Landry, forcing her hand on his exposed penis in the storage closet of the gymnasium after staying to help decorate for the 6th grade dance.

She was suddenly aware she was so very cold and tired. So much more tired than she had ever been in her life. Every part of her hurt… but it seemed to be fading. She must have overdone it helping Maw in the fields, yesterday. She would be ok. Did she help her yesterday? She was so confused and tired. She just needed to close her eyes. Swallowing, her throat felt dry and gritty. A drink would make her feel better.

"Momma…" she mumbled. Was she in bed? Maybe her mom could bring her a drink. She was having such a hard time moving or focusing. Some rest was all she needed. Then she could be ready to meet up with Paul and everyone. He was struggling so much, lately. Such a good soul. He deserved better. She hated seeing him suffer like he was. Yeah, just needed to close her eyes. And so, for the final time of her short fifteen years, she did.

Chapter 15

Paul was barely aware of the siren blaring as his dad drove him to the hospital, feeling so far away from everything still. None of this could be real, could it? He kept replaying everything that just happened, but it felt like remembering a movie he had watched. How did they go from being dumb kids having a dull summer, to this? The dull summer seemed so much more appealing now. Jennifer's ethereal face appeared in his mind, mouthing 'Help me' He blinked the image away.

"You ok, son?" William placed a hand on Paul's shoulder.

"Huh? Yeah. I'm ok," Paul said absently. He looked out the window and realized the car was parked in the hospital ER parking lot. Hadn't they just been leaving Madie's?

"Come on. Let's get inside and see what's going on," William said opening his door.

Paul nodded and climbed out of the car. As he walked to the entrance, a faraway voice came to him.

"She will take them all," a feminine voice wisped through the air.

Paul spun to face the parking lot. There, next to his dad's patrol car, stood Mrs. Goodrich. She wasn't a spectacle of gore, as she had been before. No blood. No carnage of bone and brain. Just a pleasant looking woman as she had been in life. Her expression was sad… worried.

"You must wake up," she whispered.

"Paul," Williams voice came from behind him.

He looked to his dad and back to the car. She was gone. Exhaustion was setting in, and he couldn't find it in himself to give Mrs. Goodrich anymore thought. He needed to be with Madie now. She needed him.

"Sorry, thought I heard something," he said and continued to the entrance.

Having a dad in a police uniform helped speed up the process of getting into the back area of the ER. They found Madie sitting on a chair near a nurse's station, with her head in her hands. A large black woman in hot pink scrubs was kneeling beside her with a hand on her back.

Paul rushed over to her and knelt in front of her. "I'm here, Madie," he said and grabbed her hand.

With a sob she lunged from the chair into his arms. He embraced her, wishing desperately to take her pain and suffering away. He wanted to ask her if Jennifer was ok but feared the answer. Instead, he looked to the nurse, his eyes pleading.

She sighed. "They are working on her sister. They will do everything they can."

Paul gave her a thankful nod and squeezed Madie tighter. "It's going to be ok. She will be fine," he assured her.

"They won't let me go be with her!" she cried.

"It's ok. You will get to see her after they have her fixed up," Paul said in a soothing voice.

"I need to see her. I shouldn't be out here just sitting. I can fix her!" Madie pushed off of Paul and grabbed fistfuls of her hair with each hand. She began pacing like a caged animal. After a few back and forths her shoulders slumped, and she plopped back into the chair, bawling.

William placed and hand firmly on Madie's shoulder. The contact seemed to dam the flow of tears. "I know this is hard. I know you are hurting. You have to keep it together right now. Let the doctors work. There is nothing more you can do," William paused, studying her face, "This is not your fault."

The dam burst once again. William gave her shoulder a squeeze and looked to Paul, "Stay with her. I'll see what I can find out."

Paul nodded and took her hand. He sat on the cold tile floor next to her, willing any good vibes and energy he had into her. There was no warmth or calm at their contact now. The touch almost uncomfortable and almost electric, much like touching a 9-volt battery to your tongue. Still, he didn't let go. He closed his eyes and focused on her.

"Madie," he said. She didn't respond. She was lost in her sorrow and guilt.

"Madie," he repeated, this time lifting her chin to make her look at him. Her eyes darted around the room. She couldn't meet his gaze.

"She's going to live, Madie," he said calmly.

Her eyes locked to his. There was a rage burning behind them. It was trying to turn all the other emotions to ash. "You don't know that," she snapped, showing teeth. Her skin grew hot to the touch.

He squeezed her hand, despite the uncomfortable heat. "I do know. I didn't… I stopped her from… leaving. I sent her back," he said, somewhat shocked at his own words.

He believed them, however. It just felt so narcissistic and delusional to claim he had the power to dictate if someone died or not. Yet, he knew he did just that, somehow. She was trying to cross, though. To be judged by him. She didn't see him in that moment. He was something else to her in that moment. She was drawn to him. Drawn to judgement. Guilt riddled him knowing her judgement. She would have been at peace in the 'light' or whatever it is. Joined with all the other once-scattered good-energy… souls. That's what they were. Souls. Which, he supposed, souls and energy were one in the same.

He had selfishly denied her that peace, though. Out of his love for Madie, and grief, and fear. He pushed her away and back into a battered body to awake with the memories of what her father did. Everything was happening and changing so fast.

There was something awakening in him, slowly. Pieces of a puzzle suddenly lining up, helping him see the next fit. All the chaos, however, was blurring his new-found vision and hindering him.

William walked back up, wearing a hint of a smile. Madie and Paul rose anxiously to their feet. "They have her stabilized and things are looking good. Will be touch-and-go for a bit, but as long as she does good over the next few hours, they say she will be ok."

Madie fell into Paul's arms. "Oh, thank God! Oh, my God!"

The familiar, wonderful warmth spread through them both at the contact. They gasped in unison at the sensation and relief. Paul pulled away slightly, and met her eyes. He knew everything Ms. Swanier had said was right. There was no denying this sensation. What happened with Jennifer, that was not imagined. He could see in Madie's eyes, she felt it too. They would have to go see Ms. Swanier tomorrow.

"Can I see her?" she asked, looking back to William.

"A nurse will be out in a few to take you back after they have her situated in a room," he smiled.

"Paul, I have to get back to her house and help with the crime scene. Adam should be up here soon to get you guys. After visitation is over, you guys come home. Madie can stay with us tonight until we sort all this out," William said.

Paul's heart leapt a little at the idea of Madie staying with him. "Yes sir."

William looked to Madie. "Unless you have family or someone, of course. But you are more than welcome to stay with us."

A twinge of self-pity knotted inside her stomach. She didn't have anybody. She was an outcast to what little family they left behind, thanks to her father. Aside from Ruben, Paul and his family, and Sam… she had absolutely nobody.

"What's going to happen to us?" she asked William.

"You'll come stay with us tonight. I imagine tomorrow sometime, someone from the Department of Children's Services will be coming by to assess what to do," he said.

Madie swallowed hard, "They are going to send us to a foster home."

"No, they will try to contact any family you have, first. You have any aunts or uncles? Grandparents?" William asked.

Madie shook her head. "Not that would be willing to help."

William rubbed a hand down his face and sighed, "Well, we will figure it out tomorrow. Tonight, you need to worry about her." He pointed to the direction he had come from while checking on Jennifer. "I will do what I can to keep you guys out of shitty situations. That's for tomorrow, though. Nothing we can do about it tonight. Ok?"

She wanted to scream and cry some more. Paul squeezed her hand, bathing her in calm. "My dad? What's going to happen to him?"

"He's in bad shape. Adam messed him up pretty good. After he is stable enough, he will be sent to jail for processing," William said.

"What the hell?! He's here?!" Paul exclaimed.

"Hey! Watch your tone," William snapped at him. "No. They took him over to the Bay Park hospital."

"Sorry, sir. I didn't mean to…," Paul said sheepishly.

William fished a pack of smokes out of his breast pocket. "It's been a rough night. We are all on edge. I'm gonna go back. Adam and your mom will be here soon. I'll see y'all at the house when I get off."

"Yes sir," Paul said.

Madie stepped up and hugged William. "Thank you, Mr. Allen."

He awkwardly cleared his throat before patting her on the back, "I just showed up. Sounds like Adam did most of the work. But… you're welcome."

With that, he turned and left the ER.

The two watched him leave. Paul placed a hand on Madie's shoulder.

"Bad things are coming," she said.

"I know," Paul agreed.

"Baby, Imma take you back to see yo' sista now," the large nurse from before said. Her voice was kind and her smile reassuring. Paul felt she was made for a profession of compassion and helping. Maybe she was a pwoteje too? He dismissed the thought. Too much crazy for one day already.

Madie looked to Paul. He motioned her on with a smile, "I'm gonna go get a smoke. I'll be waiting."

She smiled, lifting Paul's spirits, and followed the nurse. The nurse put a hand on her back and said, "You have had a rough night, child. It's gonna be ok now, hear?"

Paul sighed and headed for the exit.

Brian stood over Sam's body. He studied the curve of buttock poking out of her shorts, a tan line marking where her bikini hid her skin from the sun on days at the river. His hand went to his crotch and rubbed his hardened shaft. Awareness of what he was doing struck him like a shot. He gasped and pulled his hand away, taking several shuffling steps back. Humiliation flushing his cheeks.

"What the fuck is wrong with you?" he scolded himself.

His thoughts and emotions felt like a strobe going off. Each flash revealed a different scene. A different emotion. Guilt, anger, fear, satisfaction, revolt, arousal. He hated everything about himself right now. Yet, another part knew this was right. He was a victim of a cruel world. This isn't what he wanted. It was what they had caused.

He had to hide her body. Luck was the only thing that had kept anyone from coming down the road so far. He sprinted to his car and took the keys from the ignition. Moving quickly to the trunk, he opened it and ran back to Sam.

Rolling her onto her back produced a stomach churning crunch from her spine. Brian's face twisted in disgust. His fear of getting caught quickly outweighed the revolt. He gathered her up and toted her to the trunk, where he unceremoniously deposited her corpse. One of her breasts fell out of the tank top she was wearing as he did, hypnotizing Brian. Slowly, he reached a hand out towards her exposed flesh. The sound of a car approaching in the distance snapped him out of it. With a quick shake of his head he slammed the trunk shut and hurried to the driver's seat.

"She was supposed to be yours. She still can be," he thought. DID he think that? Were these his thoughts? It felt more like someone was talking to him than anything he would ever think. This was not him. He wasn't a killer. He definitely wasn't into necrophilia.

"This is what they made you," his inner voice responded. "They have taken everything you were and made you into a monster. You will make them suffer for it. Her death is the beginning. Embrace the monster inside you, and everything you desire will be yours. They will suffer. They will beg. You will be happy again."

Brian nodded… his lips stretching into an ugly, bitter smile.

Chapter 16

Paul leaned his head back against the stucco wall of the hospital and blew out a cloud of smoke. Exhaustion was settling in now that the adrenaline was fading. His eyes felt gritty and heavy. Closing them felt so much better. He couldn't remember if he had eaten today, and his stomach was still too knotted to give him any indication.

He was grateful the hospital wasn't busy tonight. This moment of solitude was much needed, even if it was just on a hard metal bench outside a hospital. It was far away from the ER entrance and there was minimal lighting. It felt like a peaceful oasis from all of the chaos. His mind had been overloaded, with no time to process and compartmentalize anything that had happened.

He remembered seeing Mrs. Goodrich on the way in the hospital. Had she meant Jennifer when she said you must judge her? Well that was off the table now, even if that was what she'd meant. Jennifer was on the road to recovery. Seeing Madie's relief washed away the guilt he had felt before.

He thought about Adam wincing as he flexed his hand. He had probably broken a knuckle or two, because of how hard he had hit that man. The noise it made was… satisfying.

A sensation of being watched came over him and he opened his eyes. Out of his peripheral he saw someone on the bench next to him. He turned his head to look at her. A plain looking middle-aged woman sat next to him. She wore a knee length dress, embroidered with off white roses. Her hands rested on her knees and she stared off into the dark. An intense look of focus was on her face.

"Don't be afraid," she whispered.

"I'm sorry?" Paul said. There was something so familiar about her.

"She is trying to take me. She will try to make you afraid of me." Her words seemed to become more strained.

"Do I know you?" Paul asked.

"You must… be brave." With much effort, she turned to face Paul. Blood trickled from her hair line as she did.

"Oh Jesus! Ma'am, you're bleeding," Paul said, reeling back from her.

"Be brave… judge… her." Her words became grunts and gurgles. As she spoke, gashes slowly opened up across her forehead. Her skull seemed to be expanding underneath the skin.

"End… times… if… she… stays."

Paul barely made out the words. He was on his feet, staring at her expanding cranium in awe and disgust.

In a blink, her head exploded, showering Paul in blood and gore. Paul covered his face and fell to the ground. Moving his arms, he saw Mrs. Goodrich as he had in the final moment of her life... a vision out of a horror movie. The only things that remained of what used to be her head were a mangled jaw and sharp shrapnels of bone. A gurgling hiss came from the stump of a head as a shredded tongue writhed in the gory mass. He scrambled to his feet and ran for the hospital doors.

"PAUL!" a voice screamed behind him as he approached the entrance.

He paused but stayed facing the doors. He couldn't see that again. "Ju…dge…mmm…mmm..e…nt," the voice struggled out.

"Hello?" another different woman's voice came, sounding frightened.

Paul whirled, but found only the dimly lit seat he had left a few yards away. After quickly surveilling the parking lot, he released the breath he hadn't been aware he was holding. He could feel his pulse in his face… in his whole body. If he didn't calm down, he feared he might become the youngest heart attack victim on record. He vigorously rubbed his temples while taking in deep breaths. He just focused on his breathing and the blackness behind his eyelids.

"You ok?" Ruben's voice jumpstarted Paul's nervous system into overdrive again.

Paul spun with a fist cocked back. Seeing his best friend's face, he dropped his arm, "Goddamnit! Son of a bitch. Fuck!"

"Woah, woah, woah! What the hell man?!" Ruben exclaimed.

Sharply exhaling the breath from his lungs, he said, "Sorry. Shit. Sorry. But fuck, man! Tonight ain't the night for sneaking up, Ruben! Fuck's sake!" Paul half shouted.

Ruben threw his hands up in surrender. "My bad. I thought you saw me when you were running up to the door. Then you just stopped and turned around."

"No. I didn't." Paul felt unwarranted anger rising up in him and shoved it back down, "You're fine, man. I'm just on edge with all this shit happening. Didn't mean to be a dick."

"Nah, I feel ya man. Tonight definitely goes in the top five of craziest shit I've ever experienced," Ruben said. Ruben briefly allowed his mind to go back to the night he had killed his dad. How he had tried to run away. The sharp stings of a blade slicing his back open. His mom's screams as she took that blade over and over in Ruben's place. The shock in his hands, from the impact of the hatchet into his dad's skull. Watching the last flickers of life leave his mother's eyes. THAT… would always hold number one on the list of crazy shit he experienced.

"Where's Adam?" Paul said, looking over Ruben's shoulder.

Ruben stuck a thumb at the air behind him, "He's parking the car. He dropped me here, first."

"How's his hand?" Paul asked.

Ruben made a cringing face, "Lookin' like a balloon, man. Still better than her dad's face. Pretty sure that man is going to be eating through straws for a long time."

"Good," Paul said curtly.

Ruben nodded in agreement. "How's Jennifer?" he asked.

"They got her stabilized. They just let Madie go back to see her, so I was grabbing a much needed smoke," Paul said. He saw his brother's large silhouette lumbering through the parking lot. Paul waved a hand over his head. Adam returned the gesture and quickened his pace.

"I saw Mrs. Goodrich, again. Right before you found me," Paul said quietly as they waited for Adam.

"Yeah?" Ruben responded.

"She talked to me this time," Paul said.

"What? What did she say?" Ruben said a little louder than Paul would have liked.

"She said I have to judge someone and to not be afraid. But it was like she was struggling to talk to me. And it looked like her from 30 years ago. Then… her head exploded, just like the day she killed herself. That's why I was running," Paul hurried his words, trying to get as much out before Adam got there. He felt silly talking about it in front of him, after what happened before.

"No shit? That is some kinda fucked up. Who does she want you to judge?" Ruben said.

Paul shrugged. "No clue. She said someone didn't want me to see her, or something. Maybe that's why she was having trouble talking to me. It's like something wants me to be too scared to listen to her."

"Why does ghost shit have to be all riddles and clues? Can't just say, ok, to beat this thing, here is what you gotta do. Nope… gotta solve fucking riddles. Maybe the horror movies knew their shit, huh?" Ruben huffed.

Paul watched as Adam got to the sidewalk, "Right? We can talk about it more later."

"How's the girl?" Adam said once he was close enough not to have to shout.

Paul quickly filled him in as they walked to the hospital entrance.

Adam seemed to untense slightly at the good news. "I hope that fat fuck dies," he said emotionless.

"Yeah, I think we all do," Ruben agreed.

Paul looked to the bulbous shape of Adam's hand. "You jacked your hand up pretty good, huh?"

Adam rolled his hand and briefly examined the misshapen appendage, "It'll be fine. I can close all my fingers, so nothing's broken. Just hurts like a bitch." He wiggled his fingers to set everyone's worried faces at ease, refusing to show the pain on his face.

"I don't know, man. That shit looks weird," Ruben said.

"It's fine," Adam said firmly, ending the discussion.

The three went into the waiting room and sat. Paul found himself shifting frequently in the uncomfortable seats. The sterile smell of the hospital irritated his nostrils and started a dull ache behind his eyes. He'd begun to think the clock was broken after the third time he had checked it knowing it had to have been at least 30 minutes, to find the hand only five minutes further than the previous time-check.

The nurse with the kind features came into the waiting area and smiled at Paul. She walked up and sat in the empty seat across from him. "She'll be out in a minute, baby. Visitin' time's almost up. Little girl is doin' good. She should be right as rain in a week or two."

292

"Thank you, ma'am," Paul said cheerfully.

"My name's Ms. Treese, baby. No need in all that ma'am stuff," she chuckled.

He took in her features. He guessed she was in her 40's. She had a dazzling white smile and golden brown eyes. Her bright pink scrubs matched her cheery disposition. He thought she was pretty, despite being severely overweight. "Nice to meet you, Ms. Treese," Paul said, and stuck his hand out. She gave it a dainty shake. A ripple of grief tugged at his heart. She wasn't long for this world. A vision of her, in the same scrubs she had on, clutching her chest in the aisle of a grocery store shocked him. He flinched and released her hand as casually as he could.

'Come on! I don't want to know that!' he thought. He was still coming to terms with the whole judge thing. Now he won the lottery for premonitions of people's impending demise?! This jackpot really sucked ass.

Should he warn her? Not like she would believe him. Hell, he wasn't even sure if he believed him. He sighed, "It must be tiring doing this job," he said.

"Oh, not too bad. Some days are worse than others. Helping people in their worst moments makes it worth it," she said as her smile lit up the room.

"Well, I really appreciate how nice you've been. It's definitely been a bad night. Not enough people like you in the world," Paul said, meaning every word. "I hope the world repays you for it all somehow."

"Baby, I don't do it for the rewards. I do it because it's my calling. We all have something we called to. Sometimes people don't listen to it. They want more, or less. In the end, those folks end up unhappy. If you do the right thing and listen to that voice inside, everything will work out," she said.

Paul nodded as he contemplated her words. "Besides, I'll be rewarding myself when I get off in the morning. Gonna stop at the store and get me all the fixins for a big ole reward. Nothing says I can't treat myself for a good deed," she laughed heartily.

Paul's heart sunk. She only had a few hours left.

"Ma'am… Ms. Treese…" Paul was hesitant to tell her. What if she got offended. What if she had him sent to the psych ward?

"Yes, baby?" she said.

"Are you feeling ok?" Paul asked.

"I'm fine. A little more tired than usual, but it's been a busy night. Don't you worry yoself about me, child." She patted Paul's leg. The image flashed again. This time she lay on the floor, eyes wide with fear. A heavy sheen of sweat on her face. She was surrounded by faceless people, watching her helplessly.

Paul exhaled with a groan. "Ms.… Ms. Treese. I know it sounds crazy. You need to have a doctor look at you. Please don't think I'm nuts."

She looked at him, concerned. "Child, is you ok?"

"Yes ma'am. I just see… I have a bad feeling," he said breathlessly.

"Oh honey, you've had some trying times tonight. Ain't nothin gonna happen to me, baby. Sometimes when we get too worked up in bad times, we start seeing bad omens and signs that ain't real," she said.

Embarrassment and anxiety were eating Paul alive. He shot his eyes to Ruben who was looking at him with confusion.

"You ok, man?" Ruben asked.

Paul sighed. Perhaps it wasn't his place to interfere when it was someone's time. What was it that Spider-man's uncle had said? 'With great power comes great responsibility.' Besides, for all he knew, it would be like Pet Cemetery if he didn't let people die. At least he had the small comfort of knowing this woman's soul was safe.

"I'm ok, I think I haven't eaten today. All the excitement on top of it has me feeling funny, I guess." He fought back the tears as he spoke.

"Honey, here," she said, reaching in the breast pocket of her scrubs. She produced a small fold of bills and pulled a five out of them. "There's snack machines down that hall, there. Take the second left and walk down a ways. You'll see 'em. I'd go for the Reese's cups. Machine likes to drop two of them sometimes." She held the money out to Paul.

"Ms. Treese… I couldn't," he said, feeling himself about to lose the battle with his tear ducts.

"Baby… I insist. What kinda' nurse would I be if I let you fall out on my floor because you hungry?" she smiled.

Overcome by love and grief for this woman he barely knew, he lost the battle. He took the bill and wrapped her in a tight hug. He saw her leave her body. She was happy. There was peace. Her knees didn't hurt anymore. Missing her blood pressure medicine would never be something she had to worry about again. The sadness of her girlfriend's death 2 years ago, the only woman she would ever love, would be replaced with joy. She would no longer fear being ridiculed for her weight or persecution for her sexuality. To save her, Paul realized, would be pure and unforgivable selfishness.

"You're a good person, Ms. Treese," he wept into her shoulder.

"There there, sugar. It's gonna be ok. Shhhh," she said, hugging him and rubbing his back.

After a long embrace, Paul pulled away. He wiped his eyes and looked at Ms. Treese. "Ok, I gotta get back to work, baby. Y'all be safe out there, hear?" she said cheerfully.

Paul nodded and waved. He watched her walk away, knowing it would be the last time he would ever see her. After she was gone, he looked around the room. He saw his brother looking away uncomfortably. Ruben was still looking at him with questions begging to be asked. The room had faded away in the moment with Treese. Back in reality, shame was trying to take over, but the residual feelings from their hug were lingering. To his surprise, he didn't really care what anyone thought at the moment.

Paul stood and headed down the hall.

"Where are you going?" Ruben asked, standing to follow him.

He held up the bill over his head. "To get a Reese's cup."

Ruben quick stepped to catch up to him. "What was that back there, dude?"

"I… Ms. Treese is gonna die in the morning," Paul said as he continued down the hall.

"Do what?" Ruben said, grabbing Paul's arm.

"She's going to have a heart attack in the grocery store while she's shopping," Paul said with a flat voice. Yet there was a hint of a smile on his face, Ruben noted.

"And you know this how?" Ruben skeptically asked.

Paul looked down to the $5 bill in his hand. "When we shook hands… it just flashed in my head. Then, when she patted my leg."

Ruben was having trouble with this one. He, much like Paul, was just coming to terms with all the other things. This just seemed over the top. He ran a hand through his blonde locks.

"Umm, ok. So, you now have the superpower to see people's deaths?" he asked.

Paul shrugged. "I don't know. I saw hers, though." Pausing, he felt anxiety starting to filter into the peaceful sensation. "I don't want this, Ruben. She's going to be at peace… but I don't want to have this. I don't want to know this shit. I want to go back to being a dumb kid that has night terrors. All my life I've tried to be nice and keep to myself. Do the right thing. What's my reward? Being tormented by dead people and getting to see one of the kindest souls I've met's death? It's bullshit!" Paul's tone grew more irritable and frantic, "And I can't save her. I can't save anyone! What's the fucking point of it?!"

Ruben opened his mouth to speak and closed it, looking behind Paul.

A warm hand gently grabbed his shoulder. "You saved Jennifer," Madie's voice whispered in his ear.

Paul closed his eyes and sighed. "No, that was Adam."

"Stop. You did that. You know you did. I saw what you did back there. I saw what really happened. Thank you," she quietly said before wrapping her arms around him and pressing her body to his back.

Oh, that blessed calm. He sagged in relief at the touch. He had feared he would never' feel it again when she was in the frenzy earlier. He had thought that perhaps that moment had broken their bond. Broken her.

"Well, shit. Let me in on that group hug action!" Ruben said, grabbing the both of them and squeezing. They all chuckled and enjoyed the small reprieve from the chaos of the day.

"She ok?" Adam's voice echoed from down the hall. He was fast-walking towards them.

Madie tensed as she turned to him. His aura was flared with foreboding colors. Anger and grief being the most prominent. Once in arms reach, she grabbed his forearm, willing a calm into him. It wasn't quite the same as with Paul. With Paul, it was natural and effortless, like breathing. Attempting it on Adam was more like trying to breath in a low oxygen environment after sprinting. She watched as the brilliance of the colors dimmed slightly.

Adam looked at her, first in irritation. Slowly, it grew into confusion and a glimmer of wonder. A sensation washed over him, driving calm into his mind.

The only thing he could equate it to was the feeling when ecstasy kicked in, though not that intense. Nor did he want to rub anyone's hair. It was just the wash of peace aspect, that everything was ok with the world.

"What did…" he stammered.

"She's going to be ok," Madie smiled at him.

Adam looked to where she gripped his arm. "What was that?" he gasped.

"I… I don't know. I just get… pulled to do things, lately. I could see your… it doesn't matter." She didn't feel like dealing with his skepticism right now. She had too much swirling in her head and not enough patience to try to get through to him.

Her smile faltered, and she released his arm. "Jennifer's going to be ok. That's all that matters."

Adam grabbed her arm, "You did that?" he asked. "Did you?"

Madie nodded, looking away nervously. "I. I think so. I've been doing it to Paul, lately. When I see that… thing on him."

"What… what is that? It was like a drug or something," Adam said breathlessly.

"I don't know. I just get these feelings. They urge me to do it," she said, fidgeting with her thumbnail, glancing at where he was holding her.

Adam let her go and rubbed at the spot she had touched on his arm. Paul smiled, seeing the gears turning in his brother's head. He was starting to let down his skeptical walls.

"Pretty wild, ain't it?" Paul said, nudging Adam.

Adam looked at him, his mouth still slightly agape, "Yeah. Yeah, definitely wild."

"Still think we are just being dramatic?" Paul asked with a smirk.

Adam ran a hand over his head. "I don't know what to think, man. That… I felt that. Fucking crazy, man. How long have you known you can do that?" he asked Madie.

"About 20 seconds," she chuckled, holding her hands out to her sides. "I mean, I knew it worked on Paul. I never tried it on anyone else."

"Holy shit. That's wild," Adam said in bewilderment. After a moment, he asked Madie. "So, Jennifer is going to be ok? You're sure?"

Madie hesitated. "Yes, she's ok."

"Why do I feel like there is a 'But' coming?" Ruben said.

"I don't know. I wanted to stay with her and… I don't know. Protect her? But they made me leave," Madie said.

"Protect her from what?" Adam asked. "Your dad's not a threat anymore."

"I just… it felt like something bad was in there… in the room with us," she said.

"Pet fucking cemetery," Paul mumbled under his breath.

"What?" Madie raised an eyebrow at him.

"Nothing. Sorry." Paul wasn't willing to talk about it with Adam present. Despite his walls coming down, he didn't trust he would be fully open to EVERYTHING. "I don't think there's anything we CAN do tonight. I say we go back to the house, get some food and rest, then go talk to Ms. Swanier tomorrow. Maybe she will have more answers for us."

After everyone agreed, Paul looked down at the money in his hand. "First, I'm gonna go get my Reese's," he said as he waved the bill in the air.

"I need a smoke," Madie said, patting her pockets.

"I second that," Ruben said.

"I got you," Adam said, pulling a pack out of his jeans pocket.

"Y'all go ahead. I'll meet you at the smoking area," Paul said and continued down the hall to the vending machines.

After what seemed like a much longer walk than Ms. Treese let on, he found the vending area. Scanning the plexi-glass window of the machine, he found his quarry. A quick visit to the coin machine and he pumped two Quarters into the machine. After hitting the numbers for his selection, he watched in anticipation as the metal spirals pushed the orange package forward. It dropped with a thud into the vending slot, yet the spirals kept working a second one forward. Paul smiled and bent down to collect the candy.

"Hello?" a scared female voice called, making Paul jump. He shot upright and spun. He found only an empty room. Still, he could "feel" someone else.

"Hello?" he called back unsurely.

"P… hel… me I …wher…" an ethereal voice spoke. It was coming in waves and he couldn't make any of it out. Fear trembled in his gut. He pictured Mrs. Goodrich's head exploding. Then, he imagined the terrifying woman from his night terror. Any minute she would come shooting into the small room. She would rip him open and eat his innards. He wanted to run.

"Help..." The voice came again. There was something so familiar about it. "Am I dead?"

For reasons he didn't understand, he closed his eyes and stuck his left palm out in front of him. The fluorescent lights shining through his eyelids darkened as he took in a deep breath. A rush of movement flew through him and he was no longer in the hospital. He was… nowhere. He had been here before. He watched his mother die here.

"No!" he screamed. Yet no sound came.

"Is someone there? Hello?!" the voice came again. Recognition of it was just out of his reach.

Paul scanned the nothing for the source. He felt no sense of direction. The voice had come from everywhere, yet nowhere, all at once. He tried to call out again, but nothing happened.

"Who's there?" he heard his thoughts boom into the never-ending expanse.

"HELP!" the woman bellowed. "I can't find you! Please, I'm scared!"

"Sam?" he heard his thought echo into the void.

"Paul? Is that you? I think he killed me, Paul." Sam's voice broke into sobs.

"Who?" Paul asked.

"I… he killed me. I'm dead." Her voice grew louder.

"I'm dead. I'M DEAD I'M DEAD I'M DEAD I'M DEAD I'M DEAD I'M DEAD!!" Sam appeared in front. She looked just as her corpse had before Like it had spent some time floating in the murky waters of the bayou. She screamed those words over and over. Each time louder than the last.

Paul recoiled at the mangled sight of her. Her eyes were wild with fear. She reached toward him. Her feet dragged, dangling in the air as she floated towards him. Anger was slowly replacing the fear in her features.

A hand clapped down on Paul's shoulder, ripping him back to the real world. The sudden sensation sent him reeling and he collapsed to his knees. His head spun. It felt like he had just stepped off a fast turning merry-go-round.

"Paul! What's wrong?" Ruben exclaimed.

Unable to relax his muscles, Paul grunted, "Brian killed Sam." It came out as one word.

"What? Breathe man. What's going on?" Ruben said.

Forcing in a breath, the spinning slowed and Paul was able to loosen his abdomen. "Sam. Was. Here," he said slowly.

Ruben looked around the small room. Then poked his head into the hallway, "Sam? You're sure? Where'd she go?"

"No. Not here. A different place. She…," Paul was flooded with grief at the thought of saying it again. "She said… Brian killed her."

"Nah. No. You were just seeing things, again. Something messing with your head. She's not dead," Ruben said defiantly.

Paul couldn't meet Ruben's eyes. Sam was dead. He didn't want to see the hurt it would bring his friend. Ruben joked about it all the time, but there was truth to the jokes. He loved Sam. More than he ever admitted. Ruben gritted through every shit boyfriend she brought around. He faked smiles and cracked jokes. Inside though, he hurt. Still, he kept faith that one day she would see that they were meant to be together. Her death would devastate him.

"Yeah… yeah. You're probably right, man. Sorry. Tonight was so crazy… My head is just a little messed up."

"Sam's fine man. You'll see. Just gotta have faith," Ruben said patting Paul on the back. He smiled, but it faltered as he watched Paul.

"Yeah. I'm sorry, man. Yeah, Sam's fine. We will find her," Paul said.

Ruben watched Paul's face. Nothing in his body language said he believed anything he had just said. A nagging voice whispered in his head that Paul was right. Sam was dead.

Ruben swallowed hard, working his jaw. "Why would Brian kill her? That doesn't even make sense."

"I don't know. It doesn't. Like you said, it's just in my head," Paul said, still unable to meet Ruben.

Ruben's eyes stung. Sam was dead. He sniffled.

"You uh… squished your candy," Ruben said as he turned to wipe his eyes.

Paul looked at his hand to find it covered in chocolate and peanut butter. The crushed wrappers were on the ground at his feet. "Well, damn," he sighed.

Ruben pushed the idea of her being dead to the back of his mind. No, now was not the time to contemplate anything that horrible. They had saved Jennifer tonight. They had won. That was what mattered right now. The rest… he would deal with as it came.

"Come on, man. Let's go home," Ruben patted Paul on the back.

After a pit stop to wash the mess from his hands, they rejoined the others outside and began the trip back home.

Chapter 17

Brian stood on the muddy bank, staring out at the moonlit bayou. His thoughts drifted to a fishing trip he had taken with his mother when he was much younger. Perhaps it was his first trip. She had hooked a worm to his tiny Spiderman fishing pole. Stepping behind him, she grabbed his hands and helped him cast the line. It was such a bad cast. Barely went 10 feet.

"Good job, baby! You'll be a pro fisherman before long. A real natural!" she had cheered him.

She was so pretty back then. Her eyes had such life in them. In all his early memories, she was smiling and offering kind words. The perfect mom, he had told her one Mother's Day. Back then, he had believed it.

He thought back to seeing how sad he was when she'd brought dinner home and they had gotten his order wrong. He remembered how she hadn't given a second thought about making the trip back to get what he wanted. She couldn't stand to see him cry. He had felt so scared seeing her in a hospital bed after her car wreck. He thought she looked strange. Tubes seemed to come out of every part of her body. Her face was swollen. The top of her head resembled a Q-tip with the massive amount of gauze wrapped around it. Metal rods protruded out of the skin on her leg, attached to some type of metal rings.

When he had touched her hand, her eyes had opened. They were not the kind eyes he grew up with. Rage and confusion filled them.

Listening to his parents fight came next. Sitting at the top of the stairs, hearing his mother call his father such awful things.

"You are a worthless piece of shit. You never loved me. You just loved that you won me. You got me when nobody else could. A little trophy wife to give you a fat cry baby little brat of a son that you don't have anything to do with. You just leave me here all day, raising YOUR son. What do I get in return? A car wreck. Constant pain. And a limp dick husband who enjoys watching me suffer," Dawn, his mother, had yelled.

"Dawn, you need help," his dad had calmly said. "You're taking way more th..."

"WRITE THE GODDAMNED PRESCRIPTION, YOU FUCKER!" a loud smack accompanied her tirade.

There was a tussling followed by his father speaking in the same calm voice, "You have been cheating on me. Forging prescriptions on my pad. Treating me like dirt. Ignoring our son. When you're not, you're telling him what a horrible child he is. Now... now you've hit me. I so want to knock your teeth in right now, woman. Instead... instead, I'm going to give you the option to walk out of this house. You don't get to come back for your clothes. You don't get to say anything to Brian. You get nothing. You give up rights to our son. You never enter our lives again. If I see you anywhere but in a courthouse to sign the divorce papers and give up your parental rights, I'll turn you in for the felony of forging prescriptions. If I can't get that to stick… I would gladly see Brian go live with his grandparents while I rotted away in a cell for feeding you to the gators after beating you to death." There was a deadly tone to his voice.

Brian had not seen his mother since. He had devoted his life to being the best he could be after all of that. He worked out almost every day the summer that his mom left. He went from benching less than 120 pounds to 200 pounds in 4 months. Unheard of, from what he was told by coaches. Several steroid tests followed, and he passed all of them with flying colors. He tried out for the football team, and made the 3rd string defensive line. By the beginning of the next season, he was benching 320lbs and squatting 445lbs. He ran the 40 in 4.9 seconds. Gleefully, the coaches put him as starting tight-end. He broke the scoring record that year. He had ended two opponent's football careers, as well. On top of all those accomplishments, he maintained decent grades.

What his reward for all of this? An absent mother? A father who despised him and blamed him for what had happened to his mother? He had told him as much on several occasions. Had he not been such a spoiled little cry baby, his mother would have never gotten in the car that day.

And just to add insult to injury, he gets ripped away from his teammates and friends at his old school. and nothing but disrespect from the group of assholes that fancied themselves the top dogs of his new town? And now… they had made him a murderer.

Brian looked back to the open trunk of his car. He smiled at the crumple of flesh and bone inside. Well, they had asked for this. He was tired of trying and fighting what the world was pushing him to be. There was no good and no evil There was just life. The creature living in him now? She is a horrible sadistic bitch. She wasn't going to give him any mercy, and no easy roads to travel. He would make his own roads. They would be paved with blood and pain. There was no room for love, or compassion. Those were just illusions. A cruel joke where someone snatches them from you in the end, simply to remind you just how alone you really are in this world.

"At least your suffering is over," he said to Sam's vacant eyes. Leaning down, he gently lifted her out of the trunk. The cold of her skin on his arms repulsed him, but she was still so beautiful. "I didn't want to do that to you. I would have treated you good. You just couldn't control that fucking mouth of yours, though, could ya'? I never did a damn thing to ya'. Just wanted to get to know ya'. Now, look at ya'," he said sincerely.

He stepped to the water's edge, taking in all of her features. "What a waste," he said, and hefted her out into the muddy waters. She flew like a ragdoll briefly, before smacking through the water's surface.

He watched her float on the surface. Panic tingled in his stomach after a minute or so, as she still bobbed on the surface. Why wasn't she sinking?! Isn't that what's supposed to happen? He had read it or seen it somewhere, hadn't he? He should have put rocks in her pockets like they did in mobster movies.

"Goddamn it!" he hissed through gritted teeth.

He scanned the ground around him for a long stick or something he could use to pull her back in. He found nothing. Grunting in frustration, he stepped out in the water to reel her in. Quickly, his feet sucked into the mud. Within seconds, mid-calf deep in it. She had drifted a good 30 feet out. The panic rose up to higher levels upon realizing he would not make it out to her. If he kept going, he would find himself stuck until the tide came in and drowned him.

"Son of a bitch!" he yelled. Immediately regretting it as his voice echoed through the graveyard to his back. He looked at Sam's body, then behind him for any signs of someone coming. Each of the silhouetted grave markers looked like a crouched person bearing witness to his crimes. He became acutely aware of all of the noises around him. Twigs snapping spun his head to the right. The warbling of a bird seemed to be laughter...laughter at his stupidity.

"You just fuck everything up, don't you?" he could hear his father's voice in his head. His heart raced. His breaths came quick. Sweat beaded down his face and back. His mouth was so dry. He had to get out of here. With great effort, he forced one foot from the mud. Then the other. Once free, he frantically got his keys out and stepped back onto the grassy bank. Sand burrs stabbed into his right foot, leaving him hopping on one leg to his car. As he got behind the wheel, the horrible realization that he only had one shoe on hit him. The mud took the other as he broke the suction. "No! No, no, no! Fuck!" Brian banged his hands on the steering wheel.

He sat for a long time, frozen with indecision. Finally, he began a dialogue with himself. 'Ok, let's think it through, boy. That shoe, it's stuck so deep in the mud, nobody will ever find it, anyway. Gators will most likely eat her up before the sun comes up. Even if they don't and someone finds her, there won't be anything to tie me to it. Not like they are gonna bring a backhoe and dig through swamp mud for clues. Ok… you're fine… Just need to get your shit together and act cool.' Brian concluded the conversation with a head clearing breath.

The last matter to deal with for the night would be his father. He had never gone back home, or even made it to the store for that matter. If he went home, he would be in for a beating. No… he would get worse than a beating. The man in his house was not the man he knew as a child. There was something cold and angry inside of him now. If he went home, he wouldn't see another day. He chuckled at the thought that his dad may very well dump him to float next to Sam. The image seemed so much funnier than it should. The irony and poetic justice of the possibility was insanely hilarious to him. Before long, he was laughing uncontrollably as he drove.

As he neared the entrance to the cemetery, headlights shone through the trees that lined the road leading in. They appeared to be some distance away, but he couldn't be seen back here. Trying to control the panic swelling inside him, he looked for some other way to go. There was only one way in and out. He remembered the cutoff that led back into the woods that he had spotted on the way in. Maybe he could hide back there until they were gone. Then again, why would anyone be suspicious right now? He had just thrown her in the water. Nobody knew she was dead yet. Of course… he was in a Mercedes, which was a very recognizable car. Almost everyone in this town drove old trucks or town cars. Once she was found, they would remember seeing it coming out of the graveyard. There was no time for the internal debate. He killed his headlights and headed for the cutoff. The moonlight wasn't really adequate to see where he was going, and the inky darkness forced him to go at a crawling pace.

The approaching vehicle was getting too close. He had to hurry. Throwing caution to the wind, he pressed the gas. The car whooshed into the cutoff. The path was unkempt, and low-hanging limbs smacked and scraped against the car. Each squealing scratch of wood on metal caused Brian to flinch. After a few yards of letting the foliage beat up the car, he slowly pulled the e-brake to avoid the brake lights alerting the rider to his whereabouts. A tree appeared out of the darkness just before crumpling the hood of the car and causingBrian's forehead to bang into the steering wheel. Thankfully, he had slowed enough that it just hurt like hell instead of knocking him out. He rubbed the goose egg that was already forming and winced. He remembered the approaching vehicle.

Brian held his breath as he watched the rearview mirror. The roadway grew brighter as the vehicle got closer. He could hear the humming of the engine and music. After an eternity, the car slowly came into view… and stopped at the end of the path that Brian was parked on.

Chapter 18

Paul, Ruben, Adam, and Madie were met in the carport by Frances. She rushed to Adam and Paul, hugging them both.

She stepped back and held Paul by the shoulders. "Are all of y'all ok?" she asked, trying to hide the fretting she felt.

"Yeah, Mom. All things considered," Adam answered.

"And Jennifer?" she said looking to Madie.

"She is going to be ok," Madie smiled.

"Oh, thank God!" she exclaimed, and pulled Madie into a tight hug. "I'm so sorry all this happened to you and your sister. But, you don't have to worry now. You are safe here. Your dad, or anyone else for that matter, will have to get through me and a gun locker worth of ammo if they want you," Frances said.

"And us," Paul said, wrapping an arm around his brother and best friend.

"Gonna be a bad day for anyone that tries," Ruben said with a proud smirk.

Adam nodded in agreement.

"Ruben, will you take Madie and get her set up in Paul's room? You two are on the couch. Show her where the towels are, too. I'm sure she'd like a shower. And there's gumbo in the pot on the stove, if y'all are hungry," she rattled off.

Ruben's eyes lit up at the word gumbo. "Yes ma'am."

Paul and Adam started to follow, but Frances stopped them. "Hey. Deb came over while y'all were at the hospital. She said Sam never came home. Y'all have any idea where she might be? She got a new boyfriend or something?" she asked, looking from one boy to the other.

Paul's blood ran cold and he replied, "No ma'am. She wouldn't just not go home. Especially over a guy."

"No clue, Ma," Adam shrugged.

"Yeah, it's not really like her. I had to ask, though." Frances rubbed her arm and sighed. "Her mom is out looking for her. I told her to put in a call to the police, but she didn't want to cause a fuss yet. Gonna go to all her friend's houses first."

"How long ago was that?" Paul asked.

"About an hour ago. I tried to call her mom right before y'all got back, but just got her answering machine," Frances said.

"Mom… she needs to call the police. Can we get in touch with dad and let him know?" Paul asked.

Frances held up a hand and nodded. "I put in a call with the dispatch to have him call me, but I haven't heard back yet.

"I'm gonna go look for her," Adam said, pulling his keys out of his pocket.

"I'll go with you," Paul quickly added.

"Son, I don't think you should leave Madie alone after everything that's happened. I mean, I'll be here, but I think she needs her friends right now," she said.

"But Mom, what if she's hurt or something? She might need help," Paul protested.

"Then Adam will help her. Or her mom, if she finds her first," she said.

"Mom… it's Sam. I should be looking for her, too," Paul said, almost begging.

"Go be with Madie, dude. I'm just gonna drive around the neighborhood a few times. See if I can spot her. I really doubt anything's wrong. If something is, I'll handle it," Adam said, patting Paul on the back.

Paul ground his molars together, "I'm not useless or weak, you know! I wanted to help at Madie's house. Everything just happened so fast, man. I should have jumped in and helped you. I…" Adams hand clapping down on his shoulder stopped him mid-sentence.

"Hey! Nobody here thinks you are weak OR useless. You did plenty to help. Madie would have gone off the rails without you there. And I am glad you didn't help me. I was trying to kill him. He still might die. You don't want that on your conscience. Not you, man. You're the good one. You don't need to mess yourself up with that. You gotta be better than that. I'm already a lost cause," Adam was interrupted by Frances.

"Don't you say shit like that! You are my sons, and nobody talks bad about my boys. Not even my boys. I will beat both of you if you say one more bad thing about my sons. Are we clear?" Frances barked.

"Yes ma'am," the boys answered in unison.

"Good. Now Paul, let's get inside and check on Madie. Adam, I want you back here in no more than 30 minutes," she said.

"Ok," Adam responded.

"There's something bad in the air. I don't want you doing anything else heroic tonight. You see something, you get home and we will call the police." She watched Adams eyes until he nodded.

Frances and Paul stood in the carport until Adam's taillights disappeared behind a row of tall pines. Paul looked at his mother, who was still watching the empty road. She seemed to have aged a little tonight. The image of her lying dead in the nothing went through his thoughts.

"Mom?" he said.

"Yeah?" she turned to face him.

"Do you think all this might be… something else?" He felt silly asking her.

"Something else?" she furrowed her brow.

Paul kicked at a pebble by his foot. "I just feel like… I dunno. There's something bad doing all this."

"Baby, Madie's dad is just a sick man. Some people are just born that way. As for Sam, I'm sure she's fine," she reassured him.

"I don't think she is, Mom. I think something very bad happened to her," he said with tears welling up in his eyes.

"Paul…," Frances started to say.

"And Mrs. Goodrich… then Mr. Goodrich," his voice was starting to quiver.

"Paul, what happened at Ms. Swanier's?" she asked.

Paul wiped his eyes and cleared his throat. "Nothing anyone would believe."

"Why don't you give me a try," she asked.

Paul stared at her for a long moment, finally shrugging, "Ok, fine. You asked for it. So according to her I'm some type of supernatural being. I basically judge souls after people die. Sending the bad parts to a bad place and the good parts to a good place. She says it's why I see people by my bed at night. I guess that's when they cross, while I'm sleeping. Oh, and Madie is basically my supernatural nurse. She is sort of like a healer for me. Keeps me sane, which is why I have had so many problems most of my life. For some reason we didn't meet up until this late in life. The kicker… there is a soul that refuses to cross that might have once been like Madie and is trying to kill me and everyone around me, it seems." He said all of this in a sarcastic, matter of fact fashion.

He watched his mom, waiting for the 'look'. That look that would tell him how stupid and dramatic he was. He watched her eyes and body language. Waiting. It never came. Instead, to his shock, she slowly nodded. Her eyes were calculating something. Putting together pieces of a puzzle that she thought were missing.

"Does it seem like Madie helps you?" she asked with total seriousness.

"You aren't going to tell me how ridiculous that sounds?" Paul said.

"Does she help you?" she asked again, ignoring his question.

Paul folded his arms across his chest, avoiding his mother's eyes. "I guess. Yes ma'am."

"Like she is nice to be around and listens to you, or… something more than that?" she asked.

"More than that," he answered.

"How so?" she pushed.

Paul was feeling like he was center stage in front of a large crowd without any pants on. "I don't know. When we touch, if I'm… upset, I get this wave that comes over me. Like she's washing it out of me. She calms me down. Helps me focus."

Was his mom actually believing him, or was she just gathering intel for the psychiatrists in the mental ward? He was regretting bringing this up.

Frances began pacing slowly around the carport. "So, Swanier said you were a Jig…juje…whatever it is?"

Paul's mouth opened, and his arms dropped to his sides. He eyed his mother suspiciously. "I never said that word."

Frances sighed and grabbed her pack of cigarettes off the windowsill. She seemed to be choosing her next words as she thumped a cigarette out of the pack. She lit it and took a long drag before speaking.

"I spoke to Ms. Swanier for a long time when I went and got that tea. I honestly wasn't sure that she was still alive 'til I did. It's like Constance knew I was coming. As soon as I walked in, she had the tea waiting on me. She said there was no charge, but that I had to speak to her mom. So I did. She asked me a lot of questions about you and your dreams. I told her what I knew. What you have told me and what I've seen… and heard." She stopped to take another pull from her cigarette before continuing.

"I mostly just thought she was a crazy old woman. But she starts telling me that you are special. That apparently my side of the family has produced one, oh what was it she called them? Protege? No. Crap, what was it?" she tapped her thumb to her forehead.

"Pwoteje?" Paul chimed in.

"That's it! So yeah. She tells me that my family has produced at least one pwoteje every generation. Apparently, that's a big deal because I guess pwotejes are just random and don't follow family lines. She starts talking about my sister, Elaine, and how she had night terrors too. She was always talking about seeing this scary woman in her room. An old lady wearing clothes made out of a potato sack, is how she described it." She paused.

Paul's eyes widened. "That's what I've been seeing! Since Mrs. Goodrich died!"

"I know. I told her about that night you woke up screaming about some scary old woman at your bed. How she dragged you away," Frances said.

Paul didn't remember that happening. Actually, he had no memory of several days following his first meeting with her.

Frances continued. "She got upset when I did. Not mad, worried I guess would be the right word. Then she goes on to tell me that your aunt Elaine became a drunk and addict because she never found her thing... whatever you are." Frances said.

"Jij," Paul told her.

"Right. Said that most times if they don't find each other, they don't do well. Turn self-destructive, or worse. That all sounded about in line with you," she said uncomfortably.

"What do you mean, Mom?" Paul said.

There was a long pause before she asked "Why was your gun on the bed with all the bullets under the bed? The morning I heard you making those terrible noises." She looked sternly at Paul as she spoke.

Paul looked away. "I was just cleaning it." How could he have been so stupid. He was so worried about hiding his piss coated underwear that he forgot to put that up.

Frances glanced at the ground, pursing her lips. "The cleaning kit is in your dad's safe. It hadn't been touched since the last time he cleaned his guns, and you don't have the combination."

Paul shrugged. "It was nothing, Mom. Just messing with it, was all."

"I made Ruben go knock on your door. He was just waiting for you to get up. I walked by your room and heard you making noises. Then I heard you crying. I stood outside your door, listening. I didn't want to embarrass you, so I just stood there. When I heard you cock the gun..." She walked to the butt can and dropped her cigarette in. "I was too scared that if I opened the door I'd see you shoot yourself. So, I hurried up and told Ruben to go wake you up.

God… that sounds so selfish of me, now that I'm actually saying it out loud." She pushed strands of Paul's hair behind his ear, so she could see his face.

"I'm ok, Mom. It was a rough night. I had a moment, but I'm ok," Paul reassured her. He was getting agitated at the questioning. He wanted her to just drop it.

Frances stared off into the darkness outside of the carport for a while. "We all love you, Paul. I need you to know that. You don't ever have to be embarrassed about any of this. You aren't weak. I see you fighting it. I've seen what it's doing to you. And I couldn't be more proud of you for all you still accomplish in spite of it." Her eyes had grown red and puffy. She stepped to Paul and hugged him again.

"You go see Swanier in the morning. Get this figured out. If this ghost bitch is real, I need to know how to kick her ass for messing with my baby," she whispered to him.

Paul chuckled, hugging her back. "Yes ma'am."

"You really think Sam's in trouble? That part of being what you are?" she asked, surprising Paul.

"I… I don't know. I mean. I guess so. I just have a strong feeling she needs help. That she isn't ok," he said.

Frances sighed. "Ok. You can go check the block and the cemetery, if you want. No further. Then straight back. Bring Ruben with you. I'll take care of Madie. She's been through enough today and needs some rest."

"Thank you, Mom," Paul said and gave her a tight hug.

Paul bounded into the house and found Ruben digging in the fridge. Watching Ruben, he allowed himself the hope that Sam might be alive. Perhaps his Spidey-sense was wrong on this one. Paul was surprised to find himself excited. Almost jovial. He didn't feel useless for a change. He needed that hope, even if deep down he knew it was false hope. He would deal with that when the time came.

"Yo, bitchtits! Let's go look for Sam," Paul said.

Ruben placed his hands over his chest. "I have great boobs, thank you very much!"

"Well bring those great boobs, and let's go," Paul said, already heading back to the door.

Ruben closed the icebox and followed. They both gave Frances a smooch on the cheek as the ran by to get their bikes. In no time, they vanished into the darkness.

"Where do we start?" Ruben shouted over the wind as they pedaled down Notre Dame.

"Cemetery. I got this feeling, man," Paul shouted over his shoulder.

"Fuck." Ruben mumbled. His heart sank at Paul's words.

Chapter 19

Adam drove slowly down the road, scanning the tree line with the large Maglite he kept under his seat. He had decided to start with a quick loop through the cemetery. He kept his slow pace, still looking for signs of Sam. When he neared the entrance, a flash of light from his peripheral turned his head to the right. It was gone before he could pinpoint where or what it was. He kept his eyes on the general vicinity that he thought it had come from, as he crept along. The entrance was maybe 200 yards away, still. If someone did have Sam back there, they might be armed, he thought. His right hand went to the sheath on his waist where the large buck knife rested. He'd just have to hope they didn't have a gun. He always meant to get another handgun but partying and being a dumbass seemed to come first, until recently. That, and he lost his desire to own one after using the last one. At least he had just sharpened the knife two days ago. It was sharp enough to shave with, and a bald patch on his forearm was proof.

"Paranoid, and I ain't even smoked yet," he mumbled to himself.

He thought he saw a flicker of movement cross the road near the entrance as he drew closer. It was going from right to left, just beyond the yellow haze shed by the only light on the street. He stopped the truck and watched into the darkness. Nothing. He counted to ten in his head before continuing on.

Pulling through the entrance, he stopped at the cutoff to the left. Where to start? He thumbed on the Maglite and shined it down the cemetery road. He had no clue what he was expecting to see. A van with no windows and a free candy sign? Masked villains holding his cousin at gunpoint? Sam running through the cemetery screaming for help?

He let out a huff and swung the light to the left, shining it down the old path. The beam didn't make it too far in. The path was overgrown on both sides and curved to the right a short way in. He and Paul had walked down that path once when they were younger. A good ways back were the ruins of an old mansion that had been destroyed by hurricane Camille. Parts of it still stood, but everything had been covered thick with wisteria and vines of thorns. Their grandma had told them that it had belonged to a wealthy farmer in the late 1700's. The name escaped him at the moment. Adam and Paul had both mentioned the bad feelings they'd had as they approached the derelict house. A foreboding aura saturated the air, filling them both with dread. Adam had become so overwhelmed with fear, he had started making up horrible stories about the place so Paul would get scared and refuse to go any further. The stories had worked.

That was at least four years ago. Back then, it had already been hard to walk through once you got a hundred feet down the overgrown path. Not to mention the hordes of mosquitoes, gnats, and random hornet nests in the woods. He didn't see that as the ideal place for a leisurely stroll or a crime. Especially not at night, with no light to see the hazards. Chances were, you'd end up snake bitten and dead next to your victim, if you tried.

He checked his watch. He didn't have a lot of time, before his mom would get worried and make a fuss. He decided he would do one quick ride through the Quarters. If he didn't find anything, then he would drive the routes Sam could have taken to her house. Letting off the clutch, he accelerated and turned into the cemetery.

Brian blew out the breath he had been holding as the truck turned away from him and went into the cemetery. His heart was beating uncomfortably fast, and his muscles ached from the stress of the evening. Using the breathing techniques he had learned in football, he slowed his heart rate and relaxed his body. How had he wound up here? This was not who he was. None of it. Sure, he had bullied a few kids in school. That didn't make him a killer. Yet, hadn't he just dumped a girl's body into the swamp? That reality struck him hard.

"Oh god!" he groaned, rubbing his hands over his head. "What the fuck did you do, Brian?" he asked himself.

He felt like he had been in a dream, watching someone that looked just like him. A dream where the other Brian murdered a girl for rejecting him, like some psychotic stalker throwing a tantrum. Yet, he wasn't waking up, and there wasn't a clone of him doing those horrible things.

That girl had a family and friends. People that loved her and would be worried about her. One day she might be found floating in the bayou. They would be devastating, and he was responsible for all of it.

"You worthless sack of shit!" Brian struck himself hard in the side of the head to emphasize the sentence. The pain felt right, so he did it again. Yes, he deserved this and more. He struck himself over and over, until his knuckles ached. His pulse throbbed in the knots left on his head.

"Die for me," a faraway voice said, though Brian didn't register it.

He sniffled and wiped tears away with his forearm. Looking at himself in the rearview mirror, he saw the pathetic fat child that cried till his mom gave in and went on a drive that she would never come back from. Not the mom he grew up with, at least. "I should just wade out there and die with her," he said to the reflection.

Brian resigned himself to that thought. He couldn't go home. He had already been gone for far too long. If he went back now his father would... who knows what he would do. Wasn't he going to kill Kurt? Brian tried to replay the day's events, but found large pieces missing, like that day at the store.

It didn't matter. He was too far gone now. He knew there was no coming back from what he had done. Maybe he would go home, and Kurt would do him the favor of killing him. No. No matter what his father had become, he had too much love for him to use his dad to commit suicide.

He would wait here. Once the truck left the cemetery, he would find a way to pull Sam's body back to land, so her family would at least have closure. Then, he would take one last walk into the bayou. He would walk until the mud pulled him under, and become carrion for the fish and gators. That was better than he deserved.

Brian settled back into the driver's seat, staring off into the woods, waiting to die. He found his peace in that and closed his eyes.

Chapter 20

Paul slowed his bike as he neared the cemetery entrance. His heart was beating harder than it should for riding his bike. The pull he felt to go here was intense now. Growing more intense with every foot closer he got.

Ruben kept pace with him. "You good?" he asked.

"Yeah. Just feeling weird. Something is trying to get me to come here," Paul said before stopping his bike under the large ironwork arch leading into the cemetery.

"Help me!" a voice screamed in Paul's head.

Paul flinched and looked to Ruben. "Was that in my head?" Paul asked.

"Was what in your head?" Ruben gave Paul a quizzical look.

Paul grunted in frustration, as he scanned the area. He felt compelled to close his eyes like he did in the hospital. The idea of going back to that place terrified him though, so he opted to do things the old-fashioned way.

"Someone screaming for help," Paul said.

Ruben cocked his ear, listening close for anything beyond the ambient noises of nature. "Nah. I don't hear anything."

"It… sounded like Sam," Paul told him hesitantly.

"Well which way did it come from?" Ruben demanded.

Paul saw the look on Ruben's face and felt horrible. Ruben was still hanging onto the hope that she was ok. Paul had let him hang onto it. He was feeling more and more sure they would be finding her body tonight instead of saving her.

"Ruben… I. Sam's voice is in my head." Paul left the statement hanging, hoping Ruben would understand.

Ruben's expression turned serious. He shook his head stating emphatically, "Sam's not dead. I'm not going to start thinking that. She's family. We are going to keep looking 'til we find her. Period."

"I know. I'm not giving up," Paul said softly. "I just want us to be prepared… in case, ya know."

"Well you go ahead and get prepared. I'm going to find her," Ruben growled as he started his bike forward.

"Dude. I want her to be alive. I'm going to keep looking for her until we find her. I pray we do find her alive and well…," Paul said.

"Shut the fuck up, dude! Just stop!" Ruben yelled, stopping to look at Paul.

Paul stopped, hearing the anger and hurt in his voice.

Ruben's breaths came heavy and shaky as he tried to calm himself. Deep in his mind he knew Paul was right, but he couldn't let himself go down that road. "Just. Shut up. I'm going to circle down this side," he said, pointing to the left. "You go right. We find anything, we holler. If not, I'll meet you in the Quarters."

Paul nodded. "Ok, man."

Paul watched Ruben ride away before placing a foot on the pedal. He pushed off and headed to the right at a slow pace. He didn't want the wind picking up in his ears and make him miss something. As he scanned the cemetery, he kept feeling the pull to go back to the nothing.

"I'm here," Sam's voice whimpered, urging Paul forward.

"Sam. It's gonna be ok," he uttered.

Letting the supernatural will lead, he found himself speeding up on a course to the Quarters. In moments, he found himself setting his bike down under Louis, the giant oak tree.

"Where are you?" he thought, as he looked into the dark. A rustling in the distance started Paul's heart into a double time beat.

"Sam? Are you here?" he called out.

A figure moved in the dark near the tree line, trying to hide.

"Ruben? You fucking with me?" he called out.

The figure began walking towards him. "No, you don't get to do it, fucker. Not you. Anyone but you," it said.

Paul's blood chilled slightly at the voice. There was something familiar about it.

"Excuse me?" he responded.

"You and that other piece of shit are what put me here. You don't get to watch. You don't get to do it. Matter of fact, I think you are gonna go first, boy," Brian said as he began a full charge towards Paul.

There was only fifteen feet or so between them before Paul realized who it was and what he was doing. He barely had time to hit the proper stance and set for the impact. With a horribly sloppy hip toss that would have brought shame to his sensei, Paul flipped Brian over. Unprepared for the attack, Paul lost his balance and was carried down with him. Fortunately, he landed on top and was able to keep the advantageous position. Brian popped him on the head with a few short shots, but they were only a nuisance as he couldn't get any power behind them at the odd angle. Paul had secured a control while Brian tagged him in the head. Once he felt confident he had control, he raised up far enough to start smashing his elbow into Brian's face. The first hit landed flush on his cheek, opening a small split that instantly leaked a thin trail of blood. Brian tucked his head to protect his face, so the next three strikes hit different areas of his forehead and scalp. More trickles of blood joined the first as the sharp elbows opened his flesh again and again.

"What the fuck?!" Paul yelled. "Did you kill her?! Did you do it mother FUCKER?!"

Paul added an exclamation to his question with another spiking elbow that cracked into Brian's orbital bone.

"DID YOU MURDER HER!" Paul screamed as he crushed another powerful blow into the crown of Brian's head.

A fury rushed through Brian at Paul's words. Visions of Sam begging for help flashed in his mind. The calls for her momma echoed in his ears.

"Kill for me," the hags voice whispered in his mind.

The pain disappeared from the cuts and knots. Reaching a hand up he found purchase in Paul's long hair. With a newfound strength, he jerked hard, pulling Paul up. He sat up as he lifted Pauls weight off his chest with ease.

Paul was stunned by the pain and unnatural strength. He heard hundreds of hair follicles pull from the roots, as Brian man-handled him. He swung blindly with a punch, as his eyes were forced to the night sky. The strike contacted something fleshy but did nothing to slow Brian.

"You made me into this!" Brian yelled.

Brian swung down hard into the bridge of Paul's nose, turning it to a bloody geyser. A flash of white blinked through Paul's vision at the impact. Pain exploded in his face as tears welled in his eyes. The sensation sapped his strength and rolled his eyes back for a second.

Brian stood, still gripping Paul's hair. With merciless force, he yanked him to his feet. He pulled Paul within inches of his face.

"Mween pa pral jije," Brian hissed at him. Black clouds swirling through his eyes.

Paul's eyes grew wide with fear. "No!" he breathed.

For just a split second, a look of confusion came over Brian. The clouds dissipated. A look of someone who just woke up and found they were not where they went to sleep. Just for a second, confusion and sadness peered out of Brian's eyes before everything was obliterated by rage. Black shadows bled into his eyes, turning them into swirling pits of darkness.

Chills ran through Paul at the sight. He tried to struggle but felt like he was being held by a vice.

Paul saw Brian bring a meaty fist all the way back behind him. If he had hurt him that bad with a short shot, Paul knew he wouldn't be awake after this one. Maybe not even breathing. His muscles still felt so weak from the pain.

Mustering every bit of strength and willpower he could find, Paul thrust the webbing between his thumb and first finger into Brian's Adams apple. There wasn't much behind it, but the throat is a delicate thing. With an awful gagging noise, Brian released Paul's hair and grabbed his throat. He sucked in a snorting breath, which turned into another gag as his throat seized up.

Paul stumbled back drunkenly, trying to shake the cobwebs from his head. He wanted to take advantage of the situation and attack, but his arms weighed a ton. He felt like he was moving through thick soup. Brian was so much stronger than he had anticipated. That throat pop wouldn't have a very lasting effect, and all he would accomplish is getting dead if he went after him right now.

Swallowing down his pride, Paul turned and took off in a clumsy jog.

"Fuck." Paul mumbled, realizing he couldn't run any faster at the moment. His body wasn't cooperating.

"RUBEN! HELP!" he screamed.

Before the echo of his scream could be heard, Brian speared into him from behind. His back bent at the impact and cracked painfully. His feet left the ground, and all sense of direction had abandoned him. His arms wind-milled as he sailed forward. His descent was rapid and uncontrolled. Paul's forehead bounced painfully off of a headstone as he fell. A horrible ping noise, like a basketball slamming into a gym floor, filled his ears, and his vision began to blur. Black formed at the edge of his vision and began to rapidly grow, threatening to cover all of his sight. Muffled words were being spoken behind him. They sounded angry. He tried to understand them, but nothing made sense. Paul tried to get up, but the black covered everything except a small pinpoint of light. As the pinpoint vanished, the world fell silent and Paul stilled in the dirt.

Ruben had taken to walking his bike to make sure he didn't miss anything. The headstones and trees cast frightening silhouettes throughout the landscape. Every rustling of leaves held the hope of either finding Sam, or the terror of some horrible creatures jumping out to eat him.

Ruben sighed, "It would have to be the creepy ass graveyard at night, wouldn't it?" he grumbled.

"…murder her?!" an angry scream echoed through the cemetery. It came from the direction of the Quarters.

Ruben was on his bike at full speed in the blink of an eye. At the entrance of the

Quarters, he spotted the outlines of two people standing under Louis. One appeared to be holding the other up. He peddled harder, keeping his eyes fixed on the people. The one being held up struck the other, sending him stumbling back. The one that struck stumbled back as well, but appeared injured and weak. Ruben watched him turn clumsily and start running. The other one bolted after him.

"RUBEN! HELP!" the fleeing one yelled.

"PAUL!" Ruben gasped.

He was close enough now to see their features. The bigger one slammed into Paul's back hard, sending him flying forward.

"NO!" Ruben screamed as he watched Paul's head bounce off a tombstone. He charged full force at him.

Brian whipped his head in Ruben's direction just in time to see him simultaneously leap off the speeding bike and use the handlebars to whip the bike at him without missing a step. There was no time to do anything but feel the impact of a crank arm smacking into his mouth. Teeth broke from their roots behind gashed lips. He fell backwards on his ass with the bike following. Before he had come to a full stop on the ground, Ruben's foot slammed into his balls. As he involuntarily curled into a ball, a stomping blow cracked his ribs, stealing all his breath away. The power he had coursing through him just seconds ago vanished. She had abandoned him… leaving him to die at this asshole's hands.

"Piece of shit!" Ruben roared as he delivered more strikes. He wanted to see his face. To break it into pieces, but the bike was on top of him, blocking the shot.

Reaching down, Ruben hoisted the bike above his head by the front tire. He sneered at Brian's pitiful form, gagging on teeth and blood, cowering in a ball. Somewhere far away, his conscience told him to show mercy, right before he smashed the rear tire down on Brian with all his might. The cogs holding the chain slashed into his forearm while the impact cracked the ulna in multiple places. Ruben slung the bike behind him, breathing in the screams of pain coming from Brian.

"You killed her?!" Ruben asked.

"Please man. I..." Brian weakly started but was stopped by a solid kick to his spine.

"YES OR NO QUESTION! DID! YOU! KILL! HER!!" Ruben bellowed.

Brian felt so much pain. So much of his body hurt. It felt right. He deserved all of it. He needed more.

He uncurled his body and lolled his eyes to Ruben, who perched over him, waiting for the words that would justify murdering Brian.

Would it really be murder? Carrying out a death sentence pre-trial seemed more like it. He hadn't wanted to let either of these two fags do it, but perhaps it was best. They cared for her deeply. This one that was about to carry out the sentence was in love with her. The rage and pain in Ruben's eyes told the tale. Yes, they deserved to be the ones that did it. To get that closure.

Meeting Ruben's blazing eyes, he said without emotion, "I did." Brian closed his eyes and waited for the killing blows.

A titanium weight plummeted inside Ruben's gut, sending him staggering back from Brian as if he had been struck. "No. You're lying. Just trying to fuck with my head." Rubens voice shook and hitched.

"No. She's over there," Brian said motioning his head towards the woods that separated the cemetery from the swamp.

The words he spoke sounded funny to him. They came out with a lisp around the jagged nubs of teeth and swollen lips. It felt as though he might have bitten a hole through his tongue as well. Trying to adjust his body to better see Ruben made him yelp with pain. His body was mangled. He knew for sure his arm and ribs were broken. Something was definitely damaged around his eye, as he couldn't see much out of it. It didn't matter.

"Why… why, man? She didn't do anything. She was a good person."

Brian sighed. He wished he'd just get on with it. "I don't know. It's like it wasn't even me. She said something smartassed to me and the next thing I know I ran her down like a stray dog. Busted her back up. She didn't die right away, though. She begged me to help her. I was going to. I really was. She was so scared and confused. Didn't even know what happened. But, I couldn't see myself going to jail over some bitch."

Ruben drew a fist back at that word, wanting so desperately to end Brian's existence. Something beyond his own will stopped him. Brian smiled. "Almost there," he chuckled. "I tried to suffocate her. She fought, man. She fought hard. So hard, she

338

ended up killing herself. In the end I didn't have to do anything but wait."

Ruben struggled to contain the murderous rage growing in him. "Bullshit!" Ruben exclaimed, refusing to accept that he was telling the truth. Every part of him wanted to kill Brian, but if he killed him for it, that meant Sam was really dead.

"Fuck's sake, man. Go see for yourself. I just pulled her out of the swamp. She's sitting right on the bank, through that cut-in." Brian croaked through a wave of pain. He hadn't pulled her out. She was still floating a little ways off the bank when he saw Paul ride up. He just hoped the words would push Ruben over the edge. Ruben stared at Brian with murder in his eyes.

"There it is," Brian gave a bloody and broken smile.

"I'll fucking kill you if you hurt her!" Ruben screamed.

Brian painfully chuckled. "Well quit talking and get on with it then, boy. Man up."

Brian watched Ruben. Waiting to see that killer switch fully flip on. "She had some nice tits too, man. You ever get to see 'em? That's what made me feel the worst. Her titty flopped out when I was trying to get her into…," he stopped speaking as he finally saw it.

Ruben leapt into him with a primal scream. Keeping both knees bent, he dropped them onto Brian's already battered ribs with all his weight. The agony seared through Brian, as he felt already cracked bones snap in two. He quickly began to regret his decision to provoke Ruben, as another solid blow crashed into his ribs.

The attack from Ruben was vicious… feral. There was no thought to it. Only intent to cause pain and injury. The seconds became eternities under the barrage of strikes. Each one hurting more than the last. Just when he'd learn to accept the pain, Ruben began striking somewhere new, though never to his head. He wanted him to be awake; he wanted Brian to feel every trickle of the punishment he was giving.

An odd noise caught Paul's ears. Something like an animal roaring or screaming. He cracked his right eye open a sliver, trying to recall where he was. Long, skeletal fingers danced above him, pulling in and out of focus. Fear grew in his gut. Was he in his bed having another night terror? No, that wasn't right. He blinked several times, forcing the image to come into focus. Tree branches. Flicking his eyes around, he spotted headstones. He had gone to the cemetery with Ruben and…

Paul shot both eyes open and tried to sit up. A fire infused with electricity shot through his head and down his neck. A choked grunt of pain escaped his lips, and consciousness threatened to slip away again. He lay still, trying to catch his breath. Warmth of tears caressed his cheeks. Even through the fog in his mind, he ridiculed himself for the tears. Swiping a hand over his face he came away with blood-soaked palms. Not tears. He had been in a fight. He had screamed for Ruben, and… he couldn't remember.

He slowly rolled onto his side with great effort and care. The pain was still there, though not quite as sharp. The sounds of meaty strikes began to register.

"Ruben…" Paul tried to shout, but only managed a whisper.

"Mother fucker!" Ruben's voice boomed, followed by a sound similar to a steak being thrown against a wall.

"Ruben," Paul managed a little louder this time. The effort made his head spin. Was he dying? The thought terrified him.

"…does it hurt?! DOES IT?!" Ruben sounded unhinged. Paul had never heard him like this. This was beyond just being pissed off and in a fight. He imagined Ruben frothing at the mouth with glowing red eyes.

Sucking in a deep breath, he braced himself for the pain. "RUBEN!" he screamed.

The force of it felt like an airbag had rapidly expanded in his skull almost to the point of splitting it open. The darkness closed around his sight once more, as his slipped into unconsciousness.

Paul's voice jerked Ruben from his visceral state. "Shit!" he snapped, realizing he had forgotten about his best friend. He hadn't even checked on him yet. There were too many directions. Keep hurting Brian? See if Sam was really lying dead on the bank? Make sure his friend was ok?

He looked down at Brian curled in a ball, gasping and sobbing. The smell of shit and bile stung Ruben's nose. Seeing the pathetic state he was in, Ruben was confident Brian wasn't going to be running away. The idea of seeing Sam dead… he wasn't ready for that. Paul needed him.

Hopping over Brian, he darted to Paul who lay a few feet away. His heart sank, upon seeing the deep eight-inch gash running from Paul's temple to the center of his forehead. His face was covered in crimson and the wound was steadily pumping more blood out of him. Paul's eyes were half open and stared into oblivion, like his father's after he had buried the hatchet in his head.

"NO!" Ruben shouted at him as he dropped to his knees beside him.

Chapter 21

Adam was on his second pass of the route Sam would take to get home. He had considered going down the old path, but he figured that would be pointless. Sometimes she would cut through the woods as a shortcut, but he couldn't imagine she would do that at night. You can't watch for snakes at night. After this pass, he would go out to the main road and do a larger perimeter around the neighborhood.

Kidnappings and murders just weren't something that happened in Delisle. In all his life, only one person had been shot in his town and that was a hunting accident. Sure, they had husbands that beat their wives, and families that fought at holidays or barbeques after too many beers. It wasn't a town of saints. But everyone knew each other and anything beyond a fist fight was just unheard of around here. Well… until recently, anyway. In less than a year, there had been two suicides, and then an attempted murder by a man trying to kill his own daughter. Now, his cousin was missing.

She wasn't at all the type to just disappear. Generally, she was a good kid. A little promiscuous, but a heart of gold. And there was no way she would disobey her mom. Sam held those southern morals strong. Respect your parents and elders. She loved and admired her mom. There was no way she had just bailed. Shit was getting crazy. He couldn't really explain it. Perhaps that's because there was something unexplainable behind it all. It was getting harder and harder to be skeptical about what Paul and Madie were saying. Part of him had been feeling like something was off since the day he'd gotten back to town. Like a bad omen in the air. He had been writing it off as being tired and needing a joint. After what he saw that sick bastard doing to his own kid, though, and what he had felt from Madie's touch, there wasn't much skeptic left in him.

Something glinted in the headlights on the road ahead of him, just past Sam's road. Adam stopped a few feet from it and hopped out of the car. Angling the beam of his flashlight at it, he walked up for a closer look. There hadn't been any rain. No houses that could have left a hose running. Not that it was a big enough puddle for that. He knelt beside it, probing the light closer. The light reflected red on the puddle, knotting up Adam's stomach. He dipped a finger in it and held it up to the light. A crimson smear decorated his fingertip. It was definitely blood. Quickly he stood and scanned the area around him, looking for a threat. After a few sweeps of the flashlight, he examined the road to see if the blood trailed anywhere. It all seemed to be in this spot. Like something laid here bleeding… maybe dying.

"Shit" Adam whispered.

He shined the light around one more time just to be sure. Finding nothing, he got back into his truck. He needed to go tell his mom what he found, and let the cops know. That blood was still fresh. If it was Sam's, she might be hurt. He closed his eyes, trying to figure out his next move.

His eyes opened and were drawn to the wood line to his left. What was over there? The cemetery. The Quarters would be a good place to take a person… or a body. He had already passed through once, but maybe he had missed something?

He checked his watch. He'd been gone for 24 minutes. He'd be a little past the 30 minutes his mom requested, but it would be fine. She had been disappointed in him for worse than that.

A short drive later and he found himself at the T intersection of Father Sorin Lane and Notre Dame Avenue. He looked left. Then right. A woman about a hundred feet away was in a full sprint down Notre Dame and was coming straight at him.

"What the fuck?" Adam mumbled.

As she drew closer, he realized it was a shoeless Madie running down the road. Her eyes were frantic.

"SOMETHING'S WRONG! PAUL'S HURT!" she screamed at him between rapid breaths.

"What?! WHERE?!" he shouted back.

Madie put her arms out to stop herself against the side of the truck. Slinging the door open she said, "Quarters! Go!"

Sending loose gravel through the air, Adam whipped the truck left. With more force than needed, Adam spun the knob on the stereo volume all the way up. Music always helped him focus, especially when heading into trouble.

Adam was rounding the curve just before the gravel path that led to the Quarters, white zombie blaring on his stereo. The woofer that barely fit behind the seat of the cab of his rusted-out Isuzu Pup massaged his back with each bass drum hit. Madie held on desperately to the bar above the passenger door, as Adam sped through the cemetery. She had no concern about Adam's reckless driving. Her whole being was focused on getting to Paul.

A horrible feeling had overwhelmed her as she had come out of the shower. An ache formed in her head, and weakness washed over her body. She heard Paul's voice screaming for Ruben. Then, a sharp pain across her forehead almost dropped her to the floor. She had thrown on the baggy shorts she always wore to bed and a t-shirt before flying out of the bathroom. Unable to find Frances, she took off out of the house towards the cemetery. She hadn't even realized she had no shoes on, until she was in the truck and felt the burn of multiple scrapes and cuts on her soles.

Upon turning onto the trail to the Quarters, they both made out a silhouette standing up and running to the left before dropping down again. As they got closer, something seemed off. It was Ruben crouched down. He stood and frantically waved his arms at them. Something was all over his hands.

"What the... is that blood?" Adam asked.

Adam could make out a terrified expression on his face now. He was motioning for him to hurry, panic in every move. Did they find Sam? Was she hurt… or dead?

"Mother fucker!" Adam growled under his breath.

Paul heard a car approaching and the slide of the tires as the brakes were harshly applied.

"What the fuck?!" he could hear his brother's voice booming from forever away.

A door slammed. Gradually his vision had started to return. The headlights were so bright it hurt his eyes. He closed them. Tried again to remember where he floated away to. What happened?

Adam ran up to where Paul was laying. A wave of terror shot through him as he took in the scene. Paul lay on his back, motionless with a blood coated face. His eyes closed. A large pool of blood outlining his head.

"What the fuck happened?!" Adam demanded.

"Oh GOD!" Madie screamed as she made her way to Paul. "No! Paul?" She placed a hand on his chest and he stirred. A shock went up her arm at the contact and she recoiled. His eyes fluttered behind his lids and a groan escaped his lips.

"That mother fucker!" Ruben said pointing an accusing finger at Brian heaped on the ground.

"Who the hell?" Adam said turning to him.

"That's fucking Brian," Ruben said. Anger and tears plucked at his voice.

Adam stomped up to Brian and looked him over. If ever there was a broken man, he was it. His face was littered with knots and cuts. The damage the bike caused to his lips had given him an inhuman appearance. Irritating whines and whimpers came from him as he lay on the ground, clutching his ribs.

Adam was trying to process everything and choose between hurting this guy, or going back to his brother.

Paul's eyes shot open wide. Feverishly, his mouth began working, whispering words too quickly to understand.

"ADAM!" Ruben belted from beside Paul.

Adam spun around. Ruben and Madie were kneeling on either side of Paul. Ruben was staring at Adam with horror on his face. Madie was holding Paul's hand on the opposite side. Her look matched Ruben's.

"Something's wrong, Adam!" he said.

Adam abandoned Brian to writhe in his own shit and vomit as he hurried over to his brother.

"He's saying things," Ruben looked up at Adam as if expecting him to have the solution.

"Huh?" Adam responded

He shifted his eyes to Paul. His eyes were wide with fear. His mouth was working silent words at a furious pace.

"Paul what's wrong, man? Talk to me!" he said.

"Please…," a whisper came from Paul. "I can't wake up. Help me. I can't wake up."

Adam knelt down next to Ruben and placed a hand on Paul's shoulder. Paul sucked in a sharp gasp at the touch. His eyes never left the fixed point in front of him, as if there was something there that nobody else could see.

"Paul you're ok, I'm here little, bro. You're alright," Adam assured him.

"Please!" the scream from Paul caused everyone to jump.

"Mom! I can't wake up! Wake me up! Please wake me up! There are too many!" A panicked wheeze seeped from his throat, "They're hurting me!" Paul's eyes slammed shut as pain contorted his face. He began to scream while every muscle fiber in his body tensed as one. His arms stiffened at his sides. His fingers curled into claws and locked in place. The scream emitting from him seemed to never end. Madie covered her ears and turned away sobbing. Adam's palm began to grow hot against Paul's shoulder. Not painfully, but enough to make him pull his hand back for a moment.

"Paul!" Adam shouted as he shook his brother's shoulder harshly.

Tears began to blur Adam's vision. Paul's scream cut off, and Paul gasped an inhalation that reminded Adam of the horrible snorting noises he'd heard when their dad's friend, James, died of a heart attack in their living room. His stomach twisted into knots.

Paul's muscles suddenly relaxed. His eyes shot open as he snapped his head over to meet his brother's eyes. The fear was now replaced with desperation.

"Adam....don't let them take me…," he wept.

"Who? Paul who? It's just us. I got you, man. Nobody is gonna fuck with you. You know I'll kill anyone that tries to hurt you," Adam said.

Adam felt a slight relief that his brother acknowledged him. However, seeing him so scared and helpless was killing him inside.

Paul stared at him for a few seconds, then smiled. It was good to see his brother. He had missed him. Was his back wet? He didn't remember it raining. He drifted to another place for a second. Maybe it was a few hours. Something had happened while he was there. It was important. What was it? Trying to remember hurt too much right now.

"I'm good, man," he said.

No sooner had the words left his mouth, his eyes rolled back, leaving only whites showing. Violent spasms took over Paul's body. Blood began to pour from his nostrils, like he'd taken a fast ball to the nose. His breaths became labored snorts. Adam forgot how to breath. His heart threatened to burst from his chest.

"No, no, no, no!" Madie begged.

"Fuck! Adam we gotta get him to the hospital," Ruben said, as he moved around to hook his arms under Paul's shoulder to carry him to the truck.

"Madie grab his..." before he could finish, Adam scooped Paul up. It seemed effortless, as if he were made of straw. The powerful convulsions didn't even stumble him as he stood and sprinted to the back of his truck. Delicately, he laid him in the bed and bolted to the driver's door.

Ruben hopped over the side and slid Paul up away from the tailgate, resting his head in his lap.

"Get the fuck in,"Adam ordered.

Madie hopped into the bed of the truck to sit by Paul. Adam gave one last look at Brian still rolling around on the ground and wailing. He contemplated getting out and stomping his head a few times. Luckily for Brian, the worry for his brother overpowered that urge.

"Better pray he's OK motherfucker!" he roared at him. He slammed the driver's door and turned the key in the ignition so hard the key bent slightly. The engine turned over several times but failed to fire up. "Start, you piece of shit!" Adam screamed at the dashboard.

He drew back and punched the center of the steering wheel so hard it's plastic covering shattered over the horn. Pulling his hand away from the key, he took in a deep breath. With forced gentleness he grabbed the key and slowly turned it with his eyes closed, pleading to a god he didn't believe in to let the truck crank. After a tense moment of the starter whirring, the engine came to life. Wasting no time, he slammed the gear shift into reverse, and whipped the truck around so fast Madie almost went over the edge.

"Dude, I know this is serious but you're going to hurt him more, and us, if you drive like that," Ruben pleaded from the back.

"Right," was Adams's reply through clenched teeth.

While still going at high-speed, he did slow down around the curves leading out of the graveyard. He'd be damned if he was the cause of his brother's death.

Madie stared at Paul helplessly. "Please, Paul." She placed a hand on his chest, feeling the same chilling electricity. She refused to pull away this time.

"Please stop," she said, willing the thought into him.

The convulsions began to ease, and Paul's eyes slowly rolled back to their natural setting. His eyes shifted to the hand holding his. Trying to focus on anything required the effort of Atlas holding up the earth. His eyes followed the hand up to a feminine arm. Further up, there was blonde hair draped over heaving shoulders. Beyond that was the most beautiful face he had ever seen. The mascara streaming down her cheeks oddly complimented her beauty. Her blue eyes glowed against the red streaked whites of her eyes.

"Hey, Madie," he whispered as a groggy smile came over his face.

Sobs and laughter racked her body at his words. "You're ok, Paul. You're going to be ok," her voice shaking as she fought to speak through the tears. She squeezed his hand, and brought the other up to caress his cheek.

Ruben broke at that moment as well. He dropped his head down to rest on Paul's chest and sobbed along with Madie. Carefully, he gathered him up in the best hug he could manage in the awkward angle.

The landscape was exposed by Ruben leaning over. Paul tensed at the scene before him. It was like the night terrors, but so much worse. Dozens, maybe a hundred silhouettes were standing throughout the cemetery. All were standing motionless just like the ones that stood by his bed so many nights. That familiar terror and sorrow latched onto his soul at the sight of them. Then, something happened. In sync, all of the figures turned to face the truck. Their heads bowed as one. as their arms extended to point a finger at him. A slight gasp shot through his lips. Someone in the truck began whispering.

"Run!" a woman's voice exclaimed.

"What?" Paul turned his attention back to Madie. She looked confused by the question.

"What?" Ruben asked back.

"What did you say?" Paul's weak voice quivered. He refused to let his sight go beyond the bed of the truck.

"Nothin. Just relax, brother," Ruben said patting Paul's chest.

Madie felt suddenly drained in this moment as well. As if someone stuck a straw in her and sucked out every bit of energy she had.

The whispering continued. Madie heard it this time as well, though not as clearly or loud as Paul. Paul attempted to refocus his vision and scanned the faces in the truck. Nobody's mouth was moving, all eyes were on him. Eyes filled with concern. Another whisper joined in. Then another. Followed by a gradual symphony of hushed noise.

"Don't listen to them Paul!" Madie said.

Ruben looked at her confused. "Who?"

The whispering voices were talking over each other, growing more intense until it sounded like a stereo all the way up with white noise coming out of it. He brought his hands to cover his ears and slammed his eyes shut. Hands pressed on his cheeks. He opened his eyes to see Madie holding his face, frantically mouthing words at him. The ear-piercing whispers were too loud to allow any other sound in. A figure stood behind her. He switched his focus. A hunched outline of the old woman from his room stood behind Madie. The lone streetlight they passed under did not seem to touch her as she remained just a silhouette. Paul shut his eyes once more and realized he was screaming with all of his might. He hadn't made a conscious effort to scream. He didn't know when he started. A fire in his throat made itself known. The taste of blood was in his spit. He forced the screams to stop.

Adam continued his cautious race out of the cemetery. The entrance was in sight and he eased the throttle a little higher. Adam looked in the rear view to make sure nobody had fallen out. Madie was looking down and frantically speaking to Paul. He slung his head out the window angling his head back to be heard over the crunching gravel and wind.

"What's wrong?" he roared.

Madie looked up with panic in her eyes. "They are trying to kill him!"

While he didn't know what that meant, he didn't pause to doubt her. "Goddamn it! Hang on!" he screamed.

Adam floored it after coming out of the final turn before the exit. Despite going 70, Adam felt like he was barely moving. Time was a monster chasing them, wanting to rip his little brother to shreds if he couldn't outrun it. He pushed it up to 80. With the iron arch right in front of him Adam glanced in the mirror again. This time, just for a second, he swore a monster had taken form and was in the bed of the truck. The figure was gone just as soon as he saw it. He blinked and shook his head.

"The fuck?" he whispered to himself.

The scream of whispers stopped abruptly. The dread and sorrow left Paul's body so suddenly it felt like something physically came out of the pores of his skin. A boil that finally popped, relieving the pressure. He sucked in a deep cleansing breath and exhaled slowly. With the horrors gone, the pain in his skull made itself known with a vengeance. He moaned as nausea set in.

"Gonna puke," he said grasping for the edge of the truck.

"Oh, shit," Ruben jumped into action helping Paul get his head over the edge. As soon as the path was clear his stomach heaved with no remorse. Brownish yellow bile spewed from his mouth and nostrils, turning into a vile mist in the wind. The effort only made his head throb more. It became like a brain freeze that kept getting worse and wouldn't end. He gasped in half a breath before his stomach spasmed again, sending forth another gush of vomit. The pain became all consuming, like jagged hot coals trying to burn their way out of his eyes and forehead.

"I can't…," was Paul's last words before his battered body and soul could take no more. His eyes closed, and he went limp. No snorting or convulsions. He lay utterly still. Ruben rolled him back onto his lap. He watched his chest, holding his own breath. Nothing.

"Paul?!" Madie screamed.

"Bullshit! Paul!" Ruben shook Paul's shoulders. His lips were turning a purplish blue. He couldn't lose Paul, too.

"ADAM!" his voice lost in the wind howling in excess of 80 miles an hour.

When no response came, he pounded on the rear glass and hung his head around to the passenger door to the open window.

"HE'S NOT BREATHING!!!!!" Ruben yelled.

The words caused a physical pain in Adam's chest. His eyes stayed locked on the road, though they saw nothing.

"No," Adam said with an eerie calm. Tears fell from his eyes for the first time since he was a child.

The unshakable mountain that was Adam, shook. His core cracked. His emotions threatened to avalanche into a destructive wave of sorrow, rage, and guilt. Annihilating anyone in their path.

"He is mine…" a voice whispered in his ear.

Adam jerked back to reality at the sound, just in time to see a woman standing in the road next to an old faded green town car, waving her arms frantically.

Adam stomped the clutch and brake, making the tires scream to a stop mere inches from her. Ruben and Madie smashed into the back window of the truck, both using their bodies to protect Paul.

"Move, bitch, or I will run you the fuck over!" Adam roared at her. The threat was not empty. Anger was the one emotion Adam was able to process. It was familiar and felt good in this moment.

Constance flinched and took a step back. "Please listen. We can help your brother. Follow me."

She was back in the car before Adam could throw anymore profanity laden threats at her. The tires of the town car kicked up dirt as they backed up. The brake lights flared to life, and in an instant the car spun around before accelerating forward.

"That's Ms. Swanier's daughter. Follow her!" Ruben shouted. Shock was still weighing Adam down. His reactions and thoughts were slow.

"GO!" Ruben ordered.

Adam put the truck in gear and sped after her. "He will die. You failed him," that voice came again.

"FUCK YOU!" Adam barked.

Madie focused on Paul, allowing herself to see his aura. Terror filled her as she saw the grotesque cloud, larger than she had ever seen it. It smothered most of the light from his already dim aura. Tendrils writhed out of it like a jelly fish caught in a fierce current. It was killing him, more than just physically. Many of the disgusting appendages were slithering into his mouth and nose.

The sight of it brought on an anger that burned through the fear. "You can't have him," she said.

She dipped both hands into the black mass. Pulses of pain and hopelessness rushed into her. With gritted teeth she pushed further. The tendrils began wrapping around her arms, like an octopus ensnaring its prey. The fear began to return, icing the fires of the anger that had burned them away.

"No!" she gasped.

Ruben looked at her through tear filled eyes, only seeing her with her hands hovering over Paul's chest. Her features had suddenly paled as her eyes widened.

"Madie? What are you doing?" he asked warily.

Her eyes darted to his. "I… help me," she said with a shaky voice

"What's wrong?" he asked, grabbing one of her arms.

She watched as Ruben's hand entered the growing pile of tentacles working their way up her arms. As one, the mass shivered and shook. Madie felt revolt coming from it. Something about Ruben's touch disgusted, or hurt, the thing.

Mouth agape, she looked at Ruben. His aura shone as it always did. No signs of any anger or rage. Only concern and sadness. While beautiful, like all decent people's glows, there was nothing spectacular about it.

She looked back down at her arms. The tendrils had released her, and the mass twitched in some discordant dance. Feeling her faculties return, she pushed through to contact Paul's chest. Upon making contact she felt… nothing. Paul was not there.

"What are you doing?" Ruben shouted over the wind.

"I don't know," she responded.

358

She really didn't. Everything she did was acting on an impulse or urge. Something was compelling her to do this.

The two of them and Paul's limp body slid across the truck bed as Adam took the turn onto the main road too fast. Ruben's momentum half carried him over the side. If not for Madie hanging onto his legs, he would have been dumped out head first.

Once back on balance, Ruben pulled Madie down to a lying position on the other side of Paul. This was to allow their bodies to be a cushion against anymore harsh turns, as well as to keep both of them from going overboard.

A hard left turn ended with the brakes hammering down. Ruben held a hand over Madie and Paul's heads, as his cracked painfully into the metal of the truck wall.

"Goddamn it!" he hissed under his breath as he sat up.

Adam was already out of the truck and standing over them. "Move!" he snapped at Ruben.

Ruben complied, hopping out of the truck. Adam scooped Paul up once again and ran to Constance, who was holding the door open to their store.

"Bring him inside. Momma is waiting in the back room," she said, pointing into the store.

Adam saw a slender doorway next to the wall coolers. The door must have been made to be hidden, as he had never noticed it in all the years he had come in here. A golden flickering light came from the other side.

Turning sideways, he maneuvered his way through with Paul in his arms.

Stepping into the room was like stepping back in time. The windowless 15x20 room didn't seem to be part of the store, although they were connected. Like the store was built onto this room, and then the room had been forgotten for a century. It smelled of must and mildew. Faded red paint was now water stained and peeling from the walls. In the center of the room was an old round wooden table with six matching chairs. The set looked to be as old as the room. On each of the four walls hung a rusted iron candle sconce. A different colored candle was mounted to each, providing the only light in the room. The one by the door was red. Clockwise, the next was orange,then blue, and lastly black. A large mortar and pestle sat at the center of the table.

Adam felt the air here was oppressive. The smell of the room turned his stomach slightly. As sweat began to bead on his brow, he turned to an ancient looking creole woman that was seated at the head of the table, eyeing him suspiciously.

"Child, hurry! He will need you too!" Constance said to Madie.

Without questioning it, Madie ran inside. She saw that multiple symbols drawn in white chalk decorated the walls as she entered. Some of them she recognized from the occult books she owned. At the moment she couldn't recall any of their meanings.

Ruben tried to follow but was stopped by Constance's hand on his chest.

"You will be needed out here," she said.

"Bullshit! That's my best friend in there. I'm not just gonna sit out here with my thumb up my ass!" Ruben exclaimed as he pushed through her.

"BOY!" she shouted, causing Ruben to pause. "You must trust me. He will need you out here… to protect him," she said.

Ruben looked at her suspiciously, "From what?"

"Bad things is coming. Trust me. Your role is out here." She gently placed a hand on his shoulder.

With a grumble, Ruben stepped back.

"You feelin' alright big boy?" Ms. Swanier said to Adam.

"My brother. Help him," he said, presenting his brother's limp body. He let his eyes drift to Paul's face. His color was all wrong. Blues and purples were shining through the few spots not covered in blood.

"Set him here," she said, moving the mortar off the table.

Adam placed him on the table with shaking arms. A pain thumped in his head with every beat of his heart, encouraging the growing nausea.

"You gotta help him," he said, feeling short of breath.

The air felt so heavy and thick. Each breath took focus to pull in, as if he were breathing through a small straw. Sweat now steadily trickled down his face and back.

"We will. You should wait out front, big boy. You ain't lookin all dat well," she said.

"I should… be here. With him," he said, though everything in him wanted to step out and get fresh air.

Ms. Swanier stood and looked into Adam's eyes. No… his soul. "You will wait outside and keep us safe, boy," she spoke softly.

Adam swallowed down the bile in his throat. "Yeah. Ok," he said and walked out of the room.

Once Adam was out of the room and shut the door, the old woman turned to Madie. "Look at him," she said, pointing to Paul.

Madie wiped the tears from her eyes and looked at Paul. When no further instructions came, she looked back to Ms. Swanier.

"Not wit yo eyes," she said.

Confused and panicked, Madie pleaded, "Help him! Please!"

"Child, I can't help him," Ms. Swanier said solemnly.

Madie's heart fell. "What? What do you mean?! WHY THE HELL DID YOU DRAG US HERE THEN?!"

"I can't help him girl. You da one dat can do dat. I can only guide you," she said, taking Madie's hand.

A warmth radiated from her hand and crept up Madie's arm. Similar to when she and Paul touched, though different. "You must calm yo'self, child. He don't have long before he too far gone to save."

"I don't know how to do first aid. Adam's better at it," Madie said.

"His outside wounds ain't wat killin' him. You need to LOOK at him," she said as she squeezed Madie's hand.

362

Understanding, Madie allowed her sight to open as her eyes went to Paul. "I see that thing on him. It's grown so much," Madie told her.

"Mmhmm. Now look deeper, child," Ms. Swanier urged.

Madie tried to do what she asked, focusing on the entity that wrapped around Paul's torso. It quivered in response and lashed out with several tendrils. Madie flinched and stumbled backwards. A ragged breath came from Paul, tripling the anxiety in her. She couldn't lose him. The mere thought of it felt like dying.

"I don't know how! That thing is killing him!" Madie sobbed.

Ms. Swanier stepped in front of Madie and grabbed her shoulders, blocking her view of Paul "Shhhh. Calm yoself. Ain't gonna do him no good wit all dat cryin."

"I don't know what to do!" the panic rose in her voice. She buried her face in her hands.

"Pwoteje… look at me," Ms. Swanier said.

Madie raised her eyes to see the most awe-inspiring light spectacle she had ever seen. The old woman's aura was a blinding beacon, every color blending into one. Madie couldn't see her physical form through the intensity of it. The self-doubt and fear washed away as the light reached out and touched her.

"You're… beautiful." Madie said, breathlessly.

"Yes child, and you are even more den I. You are more powerful den you know. More powerful den any pwoteje I ever done seen. You can and will save dis boy. He is your jije. Now come, put away all dem bad thoughts," she said, an odd reverb coming off her words.

Madie sucked in a breath and stepped back up to the table.

Chapter 22

The feeling of illness and thick air lifted as Adam walked out of the room. Confusion coursed through him. Why had he left his little brother in there with that strange woman? Why wasn't he taking him to the hospital? He spun to go back in.

Constance was in front of him and placed a hand on his chest. "You are needed out here, big boy. We will need you to keep people out."

"What? Why would anyone be trying to get in?" Adam asked.

"Because they will want to make sure your brother don't live," she said.

That changed Adam's focus quickly. "Who? Why?"

"Cause he can stop her. It won't be their fault. They will be influenced by that thing what wants him dead. Could be anyone. Your neighbors. Pastor. Mailman. Parents. Anyone that's got too much dark in 'em." She paused and looked Adam over. "Could be you."

"Too much what?" he asked, becoming frustrated.

"Short version is, some people are just ate up with badness and easily manipulated," she said.

"This is bullshit. I need to be in there with him." Adam huffed and pushed her out of the way, sending her tumbling onto her ass.

Ruben stepped in front of Adam, "Easy man! That's a woman you just pushed down!"

Adam balled his hands and stepped closer to him, "Ruben, I'm gonna give you one chance to move out of my way. That's only out of respect for Paul."

Ruben swallowed down the boulder that formed in his throat but didn't budge. "I love him too, bro. I wanna be in there too. Don't mean I get to shove women and be an asshole in general. Fucking stop and think for a second!"

The anger pouring out of Adam was palpable. There was a very long second during which Ruben was sure he was about to have his head popped like a zit. Then, surprisingly, Adam turned away.

"GODDAMN IT!" He screamed. Thunder boomed in the distance.

Like a soldier navigating a land mine field, Ruben took a step towards him. "Me too, man. Me fucking too. This whole night is fucked. I'm right there with you," Ruben said as he looked at his blood-stained hands. "We gotta keep it together, though, man."

Adam's breath hitched as tears filled his eyes, "I can't lose him."

With those words, the walls came down and Adam let go. Painfully relieving tears flowed, as his shoulders shook with sobs. Ruben took another tentative step towards him and placed a hand on his shoulder.

"He's going to be ok. I know he will," he said. The reality that Sam was dead tried to creep back into Ruben's head, but now was not the time to deal with that snake pit of emotions. Instead, he squeezed Adam's shoulder and stood there with him.

Constance stepped back in front of Adam, her expression gentle as she reassured him, "I know this is hard. You don't know us, and your brother is hurt. I promise you, if anyone can save your brother, Momma can. I need you to trust me."

Adam ran his arm across his face and said, "I'm sorry I pushed you."

Constance chuckled. "It's ok, big boy. Just glad you didn't hit me," she said and walked away from him.

Adam scowled at the front door before turning to Ruben, "Guess we are on guard duty."

Ruben shrugged, "Could be worse."

"Could be better," Adam grumbled.

"Quit your crying, big boy," Constance said as she pulled two beers from the cooler. She tossed one to Adam and opened the other for herself.

Adam looked at the beer, then her. "Thanks," he said.

"You don't want to be in that room. Nothing you need to see in there. My momma has her reasons. I've only seen my momma scared twice in her life. The first time was when a man came into this store and held a gun on me. He was sweaty and shaking with withdraws from some drug. She and my daddy was in the little room behind the counter, there." She pointed to the room where Paul and Ruben first met her mother. "He didn't know they was back there. When he moved that gun away from me for a second, daddy shot him right in the heart with both barrels of his shotgun. Momma screamed and cussed and hit my daddy, 'cause she thought it was the man shooting me. She was so scared. She cried so hard when she saw me ok. The only other time I seen her scared was after you all left. She went into that room for hours." She pointed to the small room where they were trying to save Paul. "When she came out you would have thought she was a white woman. Pale as a sheet. Sweating, tears in her eyes, shakin' all over." She paused and opened a box on the counter. She produced a small thin cigar from the box and lit it with a long match. "Bad things is coming. Things all yo bigness and meanness ain't gonna be able to stop. You have a role to play. Not right now, though. So for now, you will sit here. You will wait for them to do what they gotta do. And you will drink with me." She raised her bottle up in a toast.

Adam returned the gesture and took a long pull of his beer. While humility was hard for him, something in him said she was right.

"None for me?" Ruben asked.

Constance stared at him for a moment. She opened the cooler and pulled a bottle out, tossing it to Ruben. Smiling, Ruben looked at the bottle. His smile vanished into a look of insult. "Root beer. Seriously?"

A series of nearby gun shots snapped everyone's attention to the front door. The three stared silently at the door, waiting. A woman screaming somewhere in the night was followed by the sound of a crash.

Madie looked at Paul, forcing her sight to go past the writhing mass encasing his chest. There, she saw it. A core of light, being smothered by veins of darkness weaving themselves over it.

"What is that?!" she gasped.

"That is the hag. She put her hooks in da boy long ago, keeping his true self sleepin'. She don't want him to wake. If he wakes, it's da end of her. If he don't wake… it's da end of us," Swanier said.

"How do I stop it?" Madie asked frantically.

"First ting is stay calm. You no good to no one if you ain't got a clear head. Breathe, child. Still yo heart," Ms. Swanier said.

Madie pushed back the fret that was building in her. Feeling her thundering heartbeat, she took in a long breath, and willed her heart rate to slow. As she exhaled, she imagined all the negativity and fear being expelled from her body. She looked to the old woman.

"I'm calm. What do I do?" she said.

"You gotta find him. She took 'im away from his body. When you find him, wake him up. It will come to you," Ms. Swanier assured her.

Madie looked to Paul, allowing her focus to burn into the darkness smothering his light. She moved her hand over the wriggling tendrils on his chest, and wordlessly demanded they move. Like maggots dropped into hot ash, they squirmed and thrashed, and finally retreated.

She rested her palm on Paul. "Where are you?"

Chapter 23

Adam went to the large window of the store and scanned outside. A flash of light caught his eye to the west. The moon highlighted a dark storm front rolling towards them. Lighting in the clouds strobed in the distance.

"Guess the storms followed me," he said.

Ruben stepped up next to him and looked, "Well that's some ominous shit."

At that moment, a large red pick-upbarreled down the road that passed in front of the store. As it neared, sparks could be seen from a chain hitting the asphalt of the road's surface. The chain passed under a street lamp, and its light revealed a mangled body being drug behind the truck.

"What the fuck?!" Adam and Ruben said in unison.

"It's starting. Stay away from the windows," Constance said, pulling down long blinds to cover the large storefront windows.

"What the hell was that?!" Ruben exclaimed.

"That is why you two stayed up here with me," Constance replied.

Adam unconsciously placed his hand on the hilt of his knife, as the sound of the truck's engine faded into the distance.

"That was Dewayne's truck," Adam said, unclasping the strap that held the knife in its sheath.

"Dewayne that you used to run with?" Ruben asked.

Adam nodded. "Yeah."

"Never liked that guy. Always tried to act gangster," Ruben said.

Adam took another long pull from his beer before fishing out his cigarettes. "It wasn't an act. Used to sling dope for him. Did some bad shit with him. Watched him do some even worse shit that can't be washed off your soul like it was nothing."

Ruben looked at him, curiously, "Like what?"

Adam stared at the front door for a long time before answering, "If what she says is true, I probably shouldn't be here guarding the door."

"What are you talking about?" Ruben demanded.

"I might be ate up with it," Adam answered.

"Man, fuck that. Your big ass is the best defense we have right now. What? You gonna flip out and kill everyone? Kill your brother?" Ruben said.

"You're right. At some point you might be a danger. Not while you're in here, though," Constance chimed in.

"How can you be so sure?" Adam asked.

"Momma has her ways. There's a reason people still come to this old store. It ain't just for the beer and chitterlings. Momma put her soul into this place. Literally." she said.

"Huh?" the boys said.

"You know how old momma is?" she asked. Both boys shrugged. "129 years old," she smiled.

"Damn! How is that even possible?" Ruben asked.

"I don't think it is. You ever seen Momma outside of this store?" asked Constance.

They thought for a minute. "No," Ruben said.

"At Mrs. Goodrich's funeral," Adam said.

"Are you sure you saw her?" Constance said with a knowing grin.

Adam thought back to that day, to Ms. Swanier standing with Mr. Goodrich. Yet, when he looked deeper, she wasn't there. He could feel her there, but that was all. The feeling of her presence was so strong, that he had put her in his memories.

"No… she wasn't really there, was she? Not physically, anyway," Adam said.

"No, just her energy. There's a reason for that. This place is part of her. It's hard to explain, but she used her soul to make this a safe place. It also seems to have given her a very long life," Constance said and took a long drag from her cigar.

"But wait… she would have had to be in her 80's when she had you, then. You can't be but 35 or 40," Ruben said.

Constance laughed. "Actually I'm 47, but thank you. She's not my mother. She's my granmama. She raised me, though. Just always called her Momma," Constance said.

"Oooooh. Well that makes more sense. So, who's your mom?" Ruben asked.

"She died birthin' me," she answered.

"Oh. I'm sorry," Ruben said sheepishly.

"So, what? She is literally part of the building or something?" Adam asked.

"Her soul is," Constance said.

Adam eyed her for a moment, "And that protects y'all from me how?"

"Felt pretty rough when you brought your brother back there, didn't you?" Constance motioned to the small room.

Adam raised an eyebrow at her, "Yeah."

"Think of this place as one of those things you plug into a wall what supposed to keep mice away. Makes some noise that they hear that drives 'em nuts. Instead of mice, it's the badness in folks. Everyone got some badness. A little is ok. You get too much in you… this place starts to make you feel sick. Make you want to leave." She stared at Adam, waiting.

His brow furrowed, "So… I've got too much bad in me?" he asked.

Constance looked at the floor. "Mayhaps. That room is the center of it all. How you feelin' out here?"

Adam did a quick internal assessment. His head had a dull ache. The nausea was still squeezing at the back of his throat. It sucked, but nothing like he felt while in the room with Ms. Swanier. Maybe he would be ok. "I feel fine," he lied.

She watched him for a second, "Hmmm. Ok. Good."

"Guys," Ruben said.

Constance and Adam turned to see Ruben looking at the silhouettes of five people through the blinds. One held a long object in his hands. The one in the center stepped forward and slung something at the window. Glass exploded into the store, as a brick pushed through the blinds and slid across the dirty tile floor to stop at Ruben's feet.

"Shit," Ruben muttered.

Madie poured all of her thoughts and energy into Paul's core. She felt herself moving through her own body, pushing her light towards her hands where they rested on Paul's chest. Her body began to feel like a prison. She wanted to push out of it, and into him.

"I can't. I don't know how to go to him," Madie said frustrated.

A hand grabbed Madie's forearm. "Let me help you, child," Ms. Swanier said.

The world suddenly shifted and spun. A glaring light flashed, and then there was nothing. Madie's senses returned, and she found herself back in that horrible nothing. Alone. Panic threatened to take her.

"I'm wit you, child," Ms. Swanier's voice echoed.

"What is this place?" Madie asked, trying to calm her thoughts.

"Dis is da edge of all da darkness. As close as you can get witout bein lost. Tink of it as Purgatory. Only dis a place only fo bad souls. Da last place dey see before gettin cast into 'hell'. da eternal darkness. Yo jij is still here. He is fightin'. Can you feel him?" Ms. Swanier's soothing voice said.

Madie let her senses travel through the empty void. Horrible emotions ran through her, as she pushed further. She could feel she was nearing hell. Despair tried to tear away her resolve.

Then a light appeared. Paul's light. "I see him!" Madie exclaimed.

"Go to him. Be careful, darlin'. He is close to da edge. Don't let him go in. Don't let yoself go in," Swanier said.

Madie let herself be in front of Paul. He looked so similar to the version of him she'd seen the last time she had been here, but the madness was replaced with fear this time. His eyes darted around as Madie arrived, although he didn't see her.

"Madie?" he called out.

"I'm here Paul!" she exclaimed.

"Anybody? Please? I can't wake up! Mom!" Paul screamed. "Please wake me up!"

"Paul!" Madie amplified her thoughts.

"Who's there?" Paul's words were becoming cries. He was terrified, like a child lost in the dark woods.

"He can't hear me," Madie said to Ms. Swanier.

"You must pull him back! He is almost gone! Let him see your light!" she answered.

Swirls of black mist came out of the dark behind Paul, forming a slow churning tornado around him. Tendrils danced in his ears.

"I tried to save them! I didn't know how! PLEASE STOP!" Paul clasped his hands over his ears.

Madie's heart ached at the scene playing out. The light from Paul started to fade. The color was draining from his skin, leaving a grey wash in its wake. Madie tried to WILL Paul to see her. She tried to make her light brighter, but nothing broke through.

"Now, child!!" Swanier's voice boomed.

Madie felt something grab her hand. A force inside her swelled. Swanier's ethereal form appeared next to her, holding her hand.

"There is no time. Do it!" Swanier commanded.

Madie somehow knew what she meant. Looking at Paul, she screamed and exploded out across the void, burning the mist away from Paul. Light filled the nothing for the briefest of moments. The light revealed hell. An endless wall of swirling darkness with arcs of crimson energy flaring through it. Hell roared back at her, sending a quake through the nothing. Madie's energy slammed back into her, and Swanier was gone. Paul was on his knees, gawking at her.

"You have to come back, Paul," she said, willing him to her.

He smiled with tear-filled eyes, "Madie!" He stood and ran to her. As he touched her, a red arc of energy flared between them and thrust them agonizingly back into the corporeal world.

Chapter 24

"We don't want to hurt your daughter or anyone else, Delphine! Just come on out with that boy and that girl and we'll leave everyone else alone. We know you the one that been causing all this misery to us as of late. Putting voodoo curses on us with the help of that cracker boy!" said the man who threw the brick.

"Who the hell is Delphine?" Ruben asked.

"Momma's name," Constance replied as she stared at the silhouette that spoke.

Adam stepped towards the door. "Come try to get that cracker boy, bitch! Come find out how your guts taste as I pull em out your asshole and shove em back down your throat, mother fucker!" he roared. A dark fire burst to life in him.

"Goddamn!" Ruben said, impressed and amused by the graphic threat Adam issued. He would have to use that one someday. If they lived through this of course.

"Boy, don't make this worse on yoself. I'll make sure they gets a quick death if you just send him on out. We not cruel people like that witch you sided wit," the man shouted.

Adam snapped his head towards Constance. "He talks about killing my brother one more time and I'm going out there. Fuck the protection. Fuck that bitch taking over me."

"That's what they want. Get you to do something stupid," she pleaded.

A low growl rumbled in his throat. He looked back to the silhouettes before turning and walking back to the cooler. He slammed a palm against the glass of the door, bouncing the door open.

Ruben stepped next to Constance, "What do they mean, voodoo curses?"

"I have no idea," she sighed. "I imagine it's just something the bitch put in their heads. Rumors always been she was a voodoo queen," Constance answered. "Ray? That you?" she shouted at the man.

"Don't matter who I am. Send them out," he said.

"Come get em, fucker!" Ruben screamed.

"You all gonna burn, then!" the man shouted.

The glow of a small flame shone through the blinds, held by the person next to the one talking. He took something from the ground and held it to the flame. With a whoosh it flashed to life in a fiery dance. The light evaporated several of the shadows outside.

Adam heard an odd noise from the other side of the door where his brother was. A wave of rage flowed through him seconds later. He drank in the hatred that filled the air. His brother popped into his mind, momentarily pushing the vile blood lust he felt growing in him. He shook his head and looked to Constance.

"Is there another way out?" he asked.

The sound of breaking glass against the front of the store was accompanied by another whoosh of flames, as the Molotov cocktail burst against the brick. Fire exploded to life on the left side of the windows.

"Through the room there," Constance said pointing to the door her mother had led Paul and Madie through. She noticed the look in his eyes and frowned.

"Oh Momma… no," she whimpered.

"Holy shit!" Ruben exclaimed.

Constance yelped as she ducked and hustled towards the back of the store. Adam pulled Ruben away from the windows and charged for the back door. Finding the door locked, he began pounding on it.

"Open up! We gotta go!" he bellowed.

Two more flaming bottles struck against the storefront. One burst into a bloom of flames. The last one broke through the window, the cocktail spewing a shower of liquid fire as the bottle shattered. Flames poured onto the shelf that sat near the window.

"Burn, witch!" a woman's voice screamed from the parking lot. "You killed my baby boy! Burn, goddamn you!"

"THE FUCKING STORE IS ON FIRE! OPEN THE DAMNED DOOR!" Ruben screamed as he gave the door a solid kick. The hinge gave and the door flung open.

Ms. Swanier lay on the floor having what appeared to be a seizure. Madie sat against the far wall. Her skin was pale and sweaty. Her vacant eyes were fixed to a chalk symbol on the wall.
Paul leaned against the table, gasping for breath.

"Momma!" Constance cried, dropping to her knees at the old woman's side.

"Paul?" Adam said with a smile blooming on his face.

"You're alive!" Ruben shouted and slammed into him with a bearhug.

"What happened? Where are we?" Paul said as he pushed out of the hug. His weak legs gave, and he collapsed to the floor before Ruben could catch him.

"No time. Ruben, get Madie," Adam ordered. A fresh wave of unnatural fury burned into Adam's brain. He looked at Constance, and began justifying how this was her fault. Picturing how easy it would be to snap her neck. Then Ruben. Ruben encouraged Paul to do all of this. Fed this insanity. They both needed to die.

"Adam?" Paul said, snapping Adam from his trance.

Sweat poured from Adam as he stood there trembling, with murderous intentions coursing through him. Looking at Paul he pushed the thoughts down again and hoisted him up by the arm, helping him to a chair.

"Can you walk?" Adam asked impatiently.

"I don't know. I feel so weird," Paul responded.

"You don't have a choice. You are going to have to," Adam ordered.

Ruben ran to Madie. Shaking her shoulders, he called her name. "Madie! Hey! You gotta snap out of it. We have to go. The building is on fire."

Her eyes drunkenly moved to his. "Paul," she breathed.

"He's right here. He's ok," Ruben assured her.

"Good," she said as her head rolled back. She was struggling to keep her eyes open.

"Hey! Stay awake! We have to get out of here. The place is burning. Some bad people are out front," Ruben said as he pulled her to her feet. She offered no help, causing Ruben to struggle to lift her dead weight.

"You gotta help me out here, Madie," he said. She only offered a pained grunt.

"Adam! I need your help." Looking back, he saw Adam clawing at the sides of his head. His face twisting and contorting with pain and anger. Paul was watching him with great concern as well.

"Adam!" Ruben barked at him.

Adams eyes shot to him. The look he gave sent waves of terror through Ruben.

"Adam?" Paul said, seeing his brother's face as well. In his eyes, black began to spread from the edges, slowly filling the whites. "No... Adam. Please. Fight it!" Paul begged.

Paul's words were so distant to Adam, but they gave him a beacon to hold onto.

"Run," he hissed at Paul.

Ruben turned his attention back to Madie. With desperation and adrenaline on his side he finally powered through, throwing Madie over his shoulder.

"Constance, is she ok?" Ruben asked.

Constance stood, eyes fixed on her mother's still body. She swallowed hard and wiped her tear-soaked face. "She gone," she said with a hitch in her voice.

"Damn it! I'm sorry, but we can't stay here. We have to go. We will come back for her," Ruben said. "Paul, can you walk?"

"Adam, please," Paul whimpered. He could see the tendrils dug deeply throughout his brother's body now, as some new-found power grew inside of Paul. He wanted to stop this thing from taking his brother, but he was so weak right now.

Adam looked back to Paul as the black closed in on his pupils. "I love you, little brother. Live for me." With those last words Adam pulled his knife, turned to the crowd that was piling through the broken window, and charged.

Hunching into an aggressive stance, Adam held his knife at the ready. A guttural roar poured from his lungs. The purest form of rage enveloped every corner of his mind as he screamed.

The crowd hesitated at the sound. No longer seeing faces or caring that these were people, Adam went after the closest one. The first swing of his blade plunged deep between the ribs of a 50 something black man wielding a small kitchen knife. The hatred and violence flowing through Adam didn't allow him to register the look of shock on the man's face as he gasped for breath.

Jerking the knife out with a twist, Adam used his free hand to slap him to the floor. Catching movement out of the corner of his eye, he slashed wildly. The edge of the knife bounced hard as it gashed into the cheek of a woman. The momentum carried the sharp edge across her right eye. The eyelid flayed easily, and the blade opened up her eyeball in a gorish burst of pink fluid. A horrible scream filled the air as the woman fell to the ground, holding her face.

There was no calculation or plan. No mercy. No humanity left in him. Adam plowed into the next person full bore, implanting the knife into the person's trapezius muscles. The impact halted as it struck bone. Muscles contracted around the blade as the body fell, taking the knife from Adam in the process. He didn't care. His hunger for violence blocked out all other thoughts and emotions. Without missing a beat, he spun on an average sized man trying to attack him from the flank. Somewhere in his brain a stinging pain was felt in his back. Part of him wanted to stop, to see if he was hurt, yet the rage wouldn't let go. The pain was only additional fuel for the inferno blazing inside of him.

With more force than would have been needed, he jammed his thumbs into the man's eye sockets and pushed with tremendous power.. The man's head crashed hard into a cooler door, spider-webbing the glass. He pressed harder into the man's eyes. A vile mess of pinkish white fluid spilled over Adam's hands as the man's eyes exploded under the pressure.

Something tapped Adam's back twice and he released the limp man. Turning, he found a teenage boy, maybe Paul's age, holding a broken fillet knife in his hand. Had Adam been able to see through the red, he would have seen the face of a terrified boy. He would have smelled the shit and piss blending with the growing clouds of smoke. He would have felt the smoke burning his throat. He would have heard Paul's screams, begging him to come with them, and seen Ruben trying desperately to pull Paul away while struggling to keep Madie on his shoulder. He would have felt the stab wounds in his back, and the broken blade left behind from the boy's attack that was penetrating his kidney.

He couldn't feel, see, or smell any of it, though. There was only rage. He would make all of these people suffer for coming after his family. They would fall at his hands, and it felt so good.

The kid tried to turn and run, but he was too slow. Adam had a handful of his hair before he took two steps. Using every ounce of his weight and strength, he pulled the boys head down. His feet flew forward as his head began a rapid and fatal descent towards the tile floor.

Paul clung to the doorframe, watching as Ruben urged him to run. He had given up screaming Adam's name, after watching him kill the second person. All he could do was watch in stunned disbelief, as Adam waded through the smoke and people. He recognized the boy right before his head was crushed against the floor. He couldn't recall his name, but they had had the same math class. Kid was always quiet, and he was always the first to finish tests. Adam stomped the boy's head several times, before taking a bat across the back from one of the few remaining attackers. Adam turned to the new threat like he hadn't felt the impact. Flames erupted between Adam and Paul as a large bottle of cooking oil on a shelf melted in the growing heat.

"Adam!" he tried one last time.

In that instant, an axe slashed through the smoke and embedded into Adams back. Paul's eyes bulged, "NOOOOOOOOO!"

Still, Adam didn't react to the pain, only becoming more enraged. He turned on his attacker and grabbed her by the throat, as he buried his teeth in the meat of her cheek. Her trachea cracked under Adam's thumbs, and her screams turned to a hissing squeak before stopping.

All the while, two men stabbed Adam repeatedly in the back. One finally found some vital target, and Adam dropped like someone had hit a switch and turned off the power.

Paul roared Adam's name at the sight. Sorrow-filled rage flowed from his screams. Power swelled inside him as his anger grew, pushing out into the scene before him.

In sync, all of the people murdering his brother froze in place and began to scream. Their bodies thrashed and twitched as black liquid oozed from their pores. Blood poured from their ears and noses. Then… they all fell to the ground silent.

He had judged them all. A judgement cast before their time. A judgement that killed them all, yet Paul felt no remorse.

Astonishment filled Ruben at the spectacle. He stood there, wordless. Paul kept his eyes fixed on where his brother fell, hoping that the mountain of a man would rise through the smoke and shake off the wounds. Adam couldn't die. Nothing could kill his big brother… He never stood. He was gone. Paul's heart couldn't find it's rhythm, and he choked in a gasping breath. Still he watched through the quickly growing flames. He couldn't leave. Adam wouldn't leave him. He would have stayed there and burned with the building, had it not been for Ruben screaming and pulling.

"Paul please! We need to get Madie safe!" Ruben screamed. The words breaking Paul's morbid trance.

Guilt tore at him, as he finally turned from the door. Constance was holding the back door open, as Ruben ran out with Madie. A heavy downpour had begun outside with frequent strobes of lighting.

"Come on. My car is over here," she said, motioning towards the house next door.

They took off in a mad dash towards the house when a gunshot fired behind them. The three of them ducked their heads, Ruben almost dumped Madie as he fought to keep his balance. When they turned, they saw William with his gun fixed on a man writhing in pain on the ground. A machete was a few feet from his hand.

"Dad…," Paul gasped, on the verge of breaking down.

"Are you ok?!" William asked, keeping his gun trained on the downed man.

"Adam is… they killed him," Paul cried.

William's eyes went wide as he looked to Paul. "No," he said in disbelief.

"I'm sorry, dad. I tried to save him. He wouldn't come with us," Paul said, becoming less intelligible with each word.

The man on the ground reached for the machete, and William put four more rounds into him; before the slide on his pistol locked in place. The man gasped a few more struggled breaths, before his heart gave up.

William looked back to Paul with disbelief still painted on his face, "Where is he?"

"Dad. I'm sorry," Paul sobbed.

William looked at the back door of the store, where smoke was starting to roll out. "Paul? Is he in there?!" William shouted.

"Sir. We have to keep moving. More will be coming. I'm sorry about your son, but we can't stay here," Constance said to William, an explosion inside the store reinforcing her statement. William's face went stone, and training took over while grief tore at him.

"Go!" William barked, shoving Paul forward. He dropped the empty mag from his pistol as they ran, and slid a fresh one in.

"Here!" Constance shouted, pointing to a blue SUV parked under the carport. She fumbled a set of keys from her pocket and unlocked the driver's door, quickly mashing the unlock button for the rest of the doors.

Paul helped Ruben load Madie into the backseat, while William watched the perimeter. Constance cranked the engine, as William fired two rounds into an obese man charging down the alley wielding a shotgun.

"What the hell is wrong with everyone?!" William shouted, scanning the night.

Once everyone was in the vehicle, William jumped in the passenger seat. "My patrol car is out front across the street. Drop me there, then follow me," he told Constance.

She nodded and gunned the SUV in reverse. Hitting pavement, she slammed the brakes and cut the wheel. The flashing blue and red lights of William's patrol car flashed just ahead. A man with a large pipe in his hand stood in the road staring at it with a menacing grin. The driver's window was busted out. The passenger door flew open and Frances scrambled out.

"Frances!" William shouted.

Paul's attention shot to him, "Mom?!"

"GO!" William bellowed as he trained his pistol on the man. His first shot went wide, and the man bolted towards the car. He bound onto the hood, never missing a stride. Raising the pipe above his head, he leapt towards Frances, as she stumbled backwards. Paul's flesh burned with a hellfire of anger at the scene playing out. He had lost too much already. This thing had claimed her last one of his people. He would not lose anyone else today.

"Die." he said without thought, projecting it into the world. The word exploded out of his mouth with an electric energy that almost hurt inside him. His intent reached into his mom's attacker and grabbed his beating heart, bursting it with a single crushing word. The man crashed limp onto the ground next to Frances, who had her hands up defensively and her eyes squeezed shut.

Everyone in the vehicle sat in stunned silence. The word had boomed out of Paul like it came from a stadium speaker, ringing their ears. All of their skin still tingled from the wave of energy. Madie's eyes were wide and fix on Paul.

"Frances!" William shouted, breaking the silence. Without waiting for Constance to come to a full stop, he jumped from the SUV and dashed to his wife, who was still waiting on the death blow to hit her. She screamed and flailed when William wrapped his arms around her.

"It's me! You're ok!" he said, holding her tightly.

She opened her eyes, "William?!" She burst into tears and buried her face in his chest.

"That's not possible," Constance gasped.

"W-w-what was that?" Ruben stammered.

Paul suddenly felt drained, like he hadn't eaten in days. His mouth was a desert. "I don't know," he said, just as surprised as everybody else.

Madie had seen what nobody else could. His aura had blazed with a color she had never seen. A blend of all colors and no color at the same time. Light fighting with darkness around him, before flaring into a supernova of power that exploded out of him.

"It was beautiful!" she said weakly.

She could see what it took from him, though. His light was dim, and the colors were paled. She took his hand in hers, and closing her eyes, she fed his energy with hers. Instead of draining her, she felt enlivened from the act. Color and brightness began to creep back into his aura. In her weakened state, she couldn't heal him any faster.

"How did you do that, boy?" Constance asked in bewilderment.

"I'm awake," Paul said after a moment. He felt what had been inside him all this time. In the moment he willed the man to die, it had broken free from the chains of darkness the hag had wrapped around his soul. The power was intoxicating and frightening. He felt the souls of everyone in the car like static electricity upon his skin. He could feel their emotions rolling over him. He felt the weight of their bad deeds inside them, and the joys that fed the light inside of them.

"What?" Ruben asked.

Madie smiled wide at him, feeling the true jij manifest inside. She tightened her grip on his hand, letting her feelings of love spill into him. His gentle eyes fixed on her and he returned the smile.

"The jij in him... it's finally awake," Constance said, looking at Paul through the rearview mirror. Tears streamed down her cheeks.

Ruben looked to his best friend. Something was different about him now. There was a light in his eyes that hadn't been there before. The air prickled his skin as energy coursed from Paul and washed over him. Paul met his eyes, and Ruben felt his gaze penetrate into the core of his being, seeing every part of him. Oddly, it didn't feel invasive. It was peaceful and safe.

"Holy shit," Ruben whispered.

Everyone in the car silently stared at Paul in awe, until a smack on the driver's window broke the trance.

"Let's go!" William shouted, still scouting the edges of the dark for more threats.

Constance nodded and put the SUV in drive. Once William and Frances took off, she followed.

Chapter 25

Paul looked out the window at the sky above the cemetery. The sight shook him. A swirling mass of darkness cycloned from the tumultuous storm clouds overhead. Arcs of red energy flared angrily into the night. Each flash revealed thousands of black shadowed tendrils reaching out through the town.

A peculiar sensation tickled at the hand Madie held, causing Paul to look at her. Her light had become too bright to see her anymore.

"She done grown strong, boy," Swanier's voice came from the light.

"Madie?" Paul said.

"Listen to me, child. She grows stronger wit each life taken. She has hooks in so many of da souls in this town. All da death has allowed her strength to touch dis world. You must go to her. You must send her to the darkness where she belong before she take dem all. Judge da ones dat stand in yo way. Its da only way to keep dem from feedin' her," she said.

"How do I judge her?" he asked without words.

"You will know, jij. You are awake now. Don't let her in yo head. Yo emotions can be power or yo undoing, boy. You can't let her win. If you die… everyting dies," Swanier said. With that pronouncement, the light vanished and revealed Madie rapidly blinking her eyes.

"Madie?" Paul asked.

"Yeah. What happened?" she said, clearly confused.

"Ms. Swanier, she spoke through you somehow," Paul said rubbing her arm.

"She sacrificed herself to save you. I wasn't strong enough to do it alone," Madie said remorsefully.

"Baby, Momma knew she would die tonight. Before any of that. She told me this would be her last night," Constance said.

"I'm sorry," Madie said tearfully.

"It's not your fault. Don't wear that on your soul. She is still with you, though. 'Till this is done, she will be with you. You two don't let her sacrifice be for nothin', ya hear?" Constance said.

Madie smiled and nodded. She could feel the old woman's energy in her, comforting her. "We won't," she said.

"Take me to the cemetery," Paul said abruptly.

"What?" Ruben asked. "No. We are going with Dad."

"She's there. I have to go. I have to stop this," Paul said.

"Fine, then I'm coming with you," Ruben said defiantly.

"You can't. She will use you to hurt him. She can't take over you for some reason, but she can hurt you. You think he's gonna be able to fight if he's worried about you?" Madie said.

"So, I'm just supposed to sit this one out while my boy risks his life?! Hell, nah!" Ruben exclaimed, spinning in his seat to face her. Fire was in his eyes.

"You have done your part, boy! Now let him do his!" Constance snapped, making a harsh turn onto Father Sorin Lane.

"I can help!" Ruben snapped back.

Paul rested a hand gently on Ruben's shoulder, letting the powerful emotions from his aura wash over him. His best friend was angry. Frustrated. Mostly, though, he was afraid. He had already lost Sam and Adam. Now he was supposed to let his brother march off into battle alone? How could he do that without being a coward. How would he live with himself if Paul died? Paul heard all of these thoughts screaming through his mind.

"It sucks a big fat one, huh?" Paul said.

"It sucks a whole bag of big fat ones!" Ruben almost shouted.

"Yeah… it does. I'm with you. I'm scared shitless, man. I still have to do it, though, and I have to do it alone," Paul said sympathetically.

"That's some movie bullshit. Why? Why do you have to do it alone? So you can be some fuckin martyr?! Fuc…," Rubens words stopped as Paul pushed into his mind what he saw at the edge of hell. He let Ruben feel every ounce of fear and pain he felt while he was there. After he felt Ruben's mind of the verge of shattering, he let him feel all of the power of the jij that now coursed through him.. The unyielding pull to the supernatural duty that he now held. Paul had no idea how he was doing any of this, but it had felt as natural as drawing breath, since Madie had pulled him from the nothing. In that moment, Paul saw something inside of Ruben. There was a purpose in him as well. Ruben was more than he knew. Like Paul, he had been born into a calling. He was a warrior, bound by his soul to crush anyone who would bring his Jij harm. Many people say they would take a bullet or give a bullet for the ones they loved, but Paul now saw that Ruben was the embodiment of that. Incorruptible energy flowed through Ruben's core. If Madie was Paul's shield, Ruben was his sword.

Paul released Ruben and they gasped in unison. After they recovered, Ruben looked Paul in the eye.

"You see now?" Paul said.

"Ok," was all he said.

"I need you to protect her," Paul said, touching Madie's shoulder.

"With my life, man." Ruben nodded.

Constance stopped as the cemetery came into view. All of them could see the swirling mass of darkness stabbing down from the storm. The evil was now in their realm, and hell bent on destroying everything.

Paul grabbed Madie by the shoulders. "Madie… I lo…," his words were cut short by the sound of the windshield shattering under a spray of buckshot. The gunshot was heard a split second later. Constance screamed as hot metal and glass tore into her flesh. Mr. Frazier, the gym teacher, stood solidly in front of the SUV, and as he worked the pump on his shotgun; he lined up his next shot.

"Fuck!" Ruben shouted, grabbing the wheel and straddling the middle console. He slammed the gas pedal towards the floor, sending the vehicle charging at their assailant. Another explosion lit the night as the gun fired, destroying another section of the windshield. Buckshot pelted the passenger seat headrest. Mr. Frazier had just ejected the spent shell, when the bumper smashed into his knees folding them backwards. In a blink, he was sucked under the SUV. The tires bounced, as he was crushed under their weight.

"Constance?! Are you hit?!" Paul yelled grabbing her shoulder. He knew she was hit badly before she could answer. He felt the life bleeding from her.

She responded with a gasp of pain before, struggling out of the vehicle, "Go, boy. Now!"

Paul was hesitant, but knew he had to do as she had said. With one last look at Madie's worry lined face, he jumped out of the car and bolted for the entrance.

The churning core of the darkness violently swayed the tall pines in the woods, near the path he and his brother had only dared to explore once.

The rain pelted Paul's face as he stared at the entrance to the path. His heart thumped hard in his chest. Emotions were at war within him, with neither fear nor anger being the one he needed. He needed to be focused and clear headed. Sorrow for all he had lost would have to wait. Self-pity and grief had no place here. What remained of the people that he loved would not see the morning, if he didn't get his head together. He closed his eyes and allowed his energy to expand outward. The world in this state was broken down to its pure form of energy. The dark energy snaking through the town was a pulsating black cloud filled with thousands of tendrils and red arcs of power. The sight sent fear through his core. He started to lose control of his energy, and felt it shrinking back to his body. He settled his mind for a moment and pushed his energy out further, into the woods beyond the path. He was shaken by his mind's ability to see everything at once, in all directions. Being able to process it all was amazing and terrifying. A wave of motion sickness came over him as he pushed himself out farther and faster. He could feel it already taking a toll on his body. He needed Madie for this, but that wasn't an option. With a thought, he cut off the connection to his body's senses. He prayed nothing would come after him, while he was so vulnerable. Could he snap back to his body fast enough to defend himself if something happened? He'd have to deal with that, if the time came.

What may have been an eternity or a mere moment passed before he saw it. Pouring out of the ground like an erupting geyser, he found the source. A pillar of pure darkness shot upwards and umbrellaed across the sky. It came from the ruins of the old mansion. That was where he needed to go. Sucking his energy back to his body, he dropped to his knees. The world spun for a few seconds, as he convinced his stomach that puking wasn't necessary. The sound of crunching dead leaves and twigs caught his attention, and he stood faster than his body was ready for. A shadowed figure stepped into sight a little ways down the trail. The shoulders on it were broad and powerful looking.

"Brian?" Paul whispered. No, he could feel it wasn't Brian. In a blink, the figure burst into a full sprint charging straight at Paul.

"Shit" Paul hissed.

He allowed himself to see the soul of this man. The sight hurt Paul's heart. This thing had taken his humanity away. His free will. His life. There was no light left. The evil had torn away his identity. The man's mind was only a blur of rage and visions of a war fought long ago. Flashes of bunker buddies screaming as blood pumped out of gaping shrapnel wounds. Killing Charlies as they tried to overrun his position. The darkness had covered all other thoughts and emotions in him. Just like the others, he was only a puppet of the evil that had driven the whole town mad. Arcs of red energy and those disgusting tendrils filled the space, where the man's soul should be,.

Tonight he had watched decent people become monsters like those you would see in serial killer documentaries. People he knew, trying to kill him and those he loved. He had even watched them succeed. This thing had made Paul kill and rip the souls out of people, simple people that were living out their normal boring lives only 24 hours ago. It was about to make him kill again. In his veins, traces of the intoxicating power still danced. It scared him how good it felt to make all of those people scream at the store. It felt so good, because he felt justified in ending all of them. The sight of his brother being massacred by them blinked across his mind.

Without thought or effort, Paul willed the charging man to die. With a yelp of pain, the man dropped, splashing down hard in a muddy puddle. Paul watched stone faced as the man screamed and thrashed. A flash of lightning showed his face. The face of Karl Hern.

"NO!" Paul screamed.

He tried to stop what he set in motion, but it was too late. Black liquid mixed with blood seeped from his pores. His screams became choked as the writhing tendrils poured from his mouth and burned to ash. Paul looked away, ashamed. Endless seconds passed before the screams stopped. Hesitantly, Paul looked back to Karl, who lay motionless face down in the water.

"I'm sorry," Paul said as tears were washed away by the rain.

Paul knew Karl would have killed him if he hadn't stopped him. He knew that ending his slavery to that woman was just. None of that stopped the guilt that tore at his insides.

"PAUL!" Madie's far away voice called in his head.

His focus shot back to what he had to do. Angry determination replaced guilt, as he stepped onto the trail. This bitch would take no more from him.

The ruined mansion came into view with a crack of lightning. Paul hesitated at the sight of it. He saw the vile pillar reaching up into the storm with his own eyes. It had manifested into this world. Fear tried to break down the walls of anger but failed. Paul growled and pushed on.

Thirty feet from the base of the swirling darkness, Paul stopped. His skin tingled from the sickening energy emitted from the mass. Doubt tried to creep its way in as he faced it. How could he possibly stop this? He didn't even fully understand what he'd awakened as, in that small room in Ms. Swaniers store. He couldn't do this alone. Why hadn't he let Ruben come with him? A gurgling, broken laugh came from the darkness. Pauls blood burned with anger at the familiar sound. The sound of the Hag's laughter squashed the doubt. The fire of hate took their place.

"You bitch!" Paul growled.

He pulled from the well of power within him and tried to shred the mass; the way he had done with the possessed people. Paul pushed that same power out into the vortex. Hundreds of shadow tendrils whipped out, striking into the wave of power Paul sent. A feeling like hot needles stabbed into Paul's face as the power exploded. Hundreds of the black arms disintegrated on contact, but it wasn't even a scratch on the mammoth tower of darkness.

A searing wave of power flew from the pillar with the sound of a thousand screaming souls, slamming into Paul. Hot air singed his lungs as he gasped, sending him into a fit of agonizing coughs. He screamed and stumbled back, as he raised an arm to cover his face. The smell of burning hair grew heavy in his nostrils. When he pulled his hands away, he found himself face to face with the old hag from his nightmares.

"You have failed. They will all die." she rattled.

"Fuck you, you withered old ballsack!" Paul screamed as he loosed a wave of power.

Energy rolled out from Paul's chest and seared into the hag. She shrieked in pain as her form faltered momentarily. Her hands glowed like coals, as they burned and transformed to smoke. Paul smiled menacingly at her and prepared to attack again. Silhouettes stepped from the swirling mass and were sucked into her, reforming the missing parts. A horrible croaking laugh came from her.

"Jiiiij…" she said, showing her ragged teeth.

Pulling deeper this time, Paul shot his entire being at her. Red arcs erupted from the swirling tempest behind her and collided with Paul's energy. His insides burned as the two energies collided. Shock waves of pain pulsed through him, jolting Paul back into his body.

Trembling from pain, he dropped to his knees. All of his strength was gone. He grasped his chest as his heart stuttered out a strange rhythm. Skipped beats caused pressure to engorge his skull. He squeezed his eyes shut, trying to focus on steadying the rhythm. A horrible cackling poured from the hag, like broken glass from a metal bucket.

"They belong to me now, child." she said.

Paul opened his eyes. Before him, stood Ryan and Katrina. Their eyes were clouds of swirling black. Another shape stepped out of the tornado, but when he saw this one, Paul whimpered and buried his face in his hands.

"NO!" Paul wept.

"It's ok, Paul. It's beautiful here," Sam said, monotoned.

"STOP IT!" he screamed at the hag.

"You didn't save me. You were supposed to. It hurt so much… so much. I looked for you. I wandered through the nothing forever, calling out to you. I saw you, but you wouldn't save me. You left me. Why did you leave me there, Paul? Why did you make me suffer? It's so cold there, all alone. Every second is a thousand years. I went mad with the pain, and fear, and loneliness. Then, she found me. She saved me. She did what you wouldn't," Sam said with disdain.

"I'm so sorry, Sam! I tried to let you cross. I tried. Please, Sam." Paul's words were barely coherent through the sobbing. He couldn't handle the shame that looking at her brought. He looked at the muddy ground around his knees.

"Did you?" a familiar male voice said. Paul's heart broke into infinite pieces at the sound.

"Don't…" he begged.

"You couldn't save us. You're too weak. Too afraid. You have always been afraid. I exhausted myself worrying about you. Trying to help you. Dying for you. All so you could fail again. You let my sacrifice be for nothing," Adam said.

Paul couldn't look at him. He didn't want to see those empty eyes on his brother. Seeing him die was the worst pain he had ever known.

To see him like this nearly pushed him into madness. He knew the words weren't Adam's, but they stung like wasps in his soul. There was truth in them. He was so afraid of everything, that he wouldn't wake up to his true abilities. Had he not been such a coward, he could have saved Adam. All of them. Could have stopped all of this, before it had gotten so far. Instead, he had let Sam die, killed people, and forced his brother to die trying to protect him. All of this, because he was scared and weak. Paul absently looked at the black tendrils slowly wrapping around his forearms. He felt no fear. He deserved to die.

"It's ok, little brother. You were never going to win. It's beautiful here. With her. She knows how you have suffered. Let her take it away." Adam knelt down and placed a cold hand on the back of Paul's neck. "We are all here. You can be with us forever. No more pain. No more fear. Madie and Ruben will be here soon."

"Madie…" Paul whispered.

Paul closed his eyes and put his hand on Adam's shoulder. "I love you, big brother," he said, breaking down to his core.

Paul pushed his power into the blackness inside of Adam. He felt Adam's flesh twitch as the dark inside him was burned away by Paul's judgment. The screams that came from Adam tore at Paul. He caught Adam as he fell to the ground, holding him in a final embrace. He held him until the final scream ended and Adam stilled. Gently, he lay him on the drenched earth. Sam, Ryan, and Katrina were motionless on the ground as well. It was the only thing

Paul could give them. Their souls judged and released, in an act of mercy. His heart could take no more. It was all too much loss. He felt broken.

Paul felt himself suddenly lifted into the air. The tendrils burned his skin and stretched his arms out to either side. Slowly, they brought him within inches of the old hag's misshapen form. He supposed he should be afraid, but there was nothing left. The only thing he felt was ready. He was done fighting, done feeling loss, and done being responsible for any more tragedy. He hovered in the air, limp, with closed eyes. Waiting for the killing blow.

"BOY!" a voice screamed.

Paul startled and opened his eyes. The hag's face was right there, but something was odd. Her expression was one he had never seen on her. Bright light shone from behind Paul, highlighting her horrid features. Fear. It was fear on her face. Paul craned his neck to see the source of the light. A blazing glow that should have blinded him met his eyes. The light was beautiful.

"Fight, boy! You ain't done!" Ms. Swanier's voice came from the light.

"MIIIINE!" the hag screamed as the tendrils dug in hard.

Paul wailed to the skies in agony while the hag sent the tendrils burrowing into his flesh. His thoughts were smothered by the torturous hurt ripping into him.

"Fight, boy! Fight for your love ones! For dem she done took! For your pwoteje!!"

404

Swanier's voice pushed through the all-consuming pain.

"Paul! Fight! Please! I love you! Don't leave me!" Madie's voice joined in.

She became a beacon, calling him back from the grasp of death. Her words ringing over and over in his head. Pulling every drop of will he could find, he used the pain. He let the sorrow of his brother and Sam wash through him. The sorrow became fuel that poured onto hot coals beneath, igniting them.

Paul's eyes flashed open and fixed on the hag's.

"I judge you."

Like a bomb, power exploded from Paul. The explosion became a continuously blasting wave of light. The hag screamed as it tore into her, the physical form she used dissolving into pure darkness. The force wave slammed her backwards into the swirling pillar. The entire mass quivered and squelched as it began to burn. Paul pushed harder, intensifying the onslaught. Red arcs shot outward chaotically. The glow of burning embers spread. As Paul tore away at the evil, he felt traces of light from the tormented souls she had used to fuel her power. She had no power over those, and they remained pure and untouched. He focused on that light, drawing it towards him and willing it to join the battle. The red arcs changed to white flashes and turned upon the pillar, aiding his attack.

A swelling sensation pushed outwards from deep inside of him, threatening to burst him wide open. Blood poured from his ears and nose.

His vision blurred. His skin burned. Just as he was about to stop, a hand grabbed his.

"I'm here," Madie said.

With that, he sent all of him out. In an awe-striking display of fierce color and sound, the pillar exploded.

Paul opened his eyes to find himself once again in the nothing. Before him, a young black woman trembled on her hands and knees. She looked up to Paul with sad eyes.

"No!" she gasped. Her face turned to rage, as she glared at him. The dark energy flickered weakly around her body for a moment before blinking out. She collapsed in tears.

"You failed," Paul said coldly.

"Please…," she begged.

Rage burned in Paul. "Please?" he said with venom in his voice.

"Please… don't," she whimpered. Her skin looked to be cracking as it grew pale. Black smoke seeped from the cracks.

Paul knelt in front of her, locking eyes. Her memories flooded Paul's mind. She had loved Jacob so. Paul watched them meeting for countless secret rendezvous under the cover of night. The butterflies she had felt every time she caught him staring at her, while she went about her duties. Then, the memory of Jacob sitting on a horse with a noose around his neck, as four men stood in a semi-circle around him.

"You are an abomination. Only 'cause we are kin, I'm gonna grant you the mercy of death. As for that negro whore of yours, we are gonna leave you swinging right here outside her window. She will be punished everyday till she dies," the oldest of the men said.

Jacob's eyes never left hers. He didn't look scared, only sad. Paul looked back to see her lying on the ground. Her left ankle was snapped backwards. Tears streamed down her cheeks, as she pleaded to the men to spare him or to kill her, too. One of the men slapped the horse's backside, and it darted off; leaving Jacob kicking and thrashing as his face turned shades of red and purple. She made herself watch, until he finally stilled. She felt Jacob's life leaving his body as if it were her own. A void grew in her where his presence once was. Paul felt the moment she broke. There were no more tears. In that moment, she gave herself completely over to the darkness.

In the next memory, months later, she was admiring her work as she stared at the corpse of her master, Jacob's father, and his family. There were several symbols that Paul didn't recognize, painted in blood on the walls of the house. She said an unfamiliar prayer in Haitian, before limping away from the deceased family. She stopped at the Bayou's edge and pulled a small vial from her apron pocket. After consuming the dark liquid inside, she waded out into the murky waters. Once waist deep, she clutched her stomach with a groan of agony. The memory began to grow dark as her consciousness faded and she slipped into her watery grave.

Paul was back in front of her in the nothing. As much as he hated it, he felt sympathy and pity. He placed a hand on her shoulder and said, "I'm so sorry that happened to you."

"Please. Don't send me there. Please…" she whimpered.

Paul could feel 'hell' yearning for her. Urging him to deliver her. "After all you have done, you know there's no place else for you."

Her eyes flared with blackness and her face twisted into a hag's scowl. "I'LL KILL EVERYONE YOU LOVE! EVERYONE YOU HAVE EVER KNOWN! I WILL NOT BE JUDGED BY A CHILD!"

Paul pushed his energy to his palm that rested on her shoulder. Under his touch, her form crumbled to dust, leaving her dark soul swirling in front of him.

A word he didn't know begged to be spoken.

"Koupab." Paul said sternly. With that word, her soul was violently cast deep into the nothing. Forever to feel only what this place offered. Crushing loneliness, regret, and sorrow. Maddening solitude, absence of sensation, and an eternity to yearn for anything other than the emptiness that was the Nothing. His face would be her final memory.

"Good job, boy," Ms. Swanier said, as Paul snapped back to the world. He was laying on his back, looking up to the sky. Ms. Swanier's light hovered over him. Her ethereal form glowed bright. The light dimmed and Paul could see her smiling. Her face was much younger, but her eyes told the tales of her years and wisdom.

"Is it over?" he asked. His body ached terribly. Speaking was exhausting and burned his parched throat.

"Yes, child," she replied.

"I'm sorry I couldn't save you," he said.

"I was never meant to be saved, child. Dis was my purpose. Besides, over a century in dat body was plenty fo' me. Ain't gotta worry bout pissin' when I sneeze now!" she laughed.

Paul painfully laughed with her, to his surprise. After a bit, and with great effort, he pushed himself into a sitting position and asked, "What happens to you now?"

She sighed with a smile still on her face. "Now… you judge me, jij."

Tears stung his eyes and he huffed. "I'm so tired of crying," he said.

She reached out and caressed his cheek. Her touch was like an angelic grandmother, and the pains in his body eased. "I'm sorry you lost all ya did. I can't fix dat. Take comfort knowin' dey at peace now. You did save dem, ya know. Mayhap not dey bodies, but dey souls. Dey would be wit her if not fo' you. Full of hate and sadness. Hungry to make others suffer like dem."

"Yeah," he said, but her words brought no consolation. After a long silence, he asked, "What happens to me now?"

"I don't know fo sho, child. You are sometin special. Most powerful jij I ever done seen. I have a feelin yo job ain't done yet. You will be called on again. Till den, you love dat girl. You love her with everytin you are. Never let her go. Keep dat dumbass friend of yours close. Have good times. Laugh. Love. Be alive." she said and stepped back. "It's time, boy." she said with a nod.

He stared at her for a minute. "Thank you, Ms. Swanier."

She smiled at him one last time as he reached out his energy once again on this horrible day, and he released her from this world.

"PAUL!!!" he heard Madie scream.

Other voices joined in. "PAUL! Where are you?! Paul!!!"

Paul turned to the ruined mansion. The first rays of daylight had begun to creep through the foliage. Time passed so oddly while in the nothing. Seconds there had been hours here. He let his eyes drift to where he lay his brother for the last time. There were only ashes there now. How would life go on after all this? His hero was dead. His cousin… Karl… so many more that had been part of the town's fabric. His thoughts went to those that remained. Swanier's words echoed, "Laugh. Love. Be alive." It would be hard, but that's exactly what he would do. If nothing else, as a final victory against that bitch. A smile spread upon his face and he sent himself out to Madie, showing her where he was.

A few moments later his father burst through the thicket. "PAUL!" he exclaimed with tears in his eyes.

Paul turned to him and was met by William slamming into him, as he wrapped him in a fatherly bearhug. In his dad's arms Paul felt the toll the night had taken on him. His muscles quivered and grew weak, and he allowed his dad's embrace to hold him up.

"I've got you, son. I've got you. You're ok," William voice trembled.

Ruben and Madie charged through to the clearing and wrapped themselves around Paul into a blissful group hug. Paul felt safe in their arms.

"You got the bitch, Paul!" Ruben sobbed.

Paul's strength returned enough that he pulled out of the embrace and turned to Madie. No words were needed. He placed both hands on her face and pulled her into a deep kiss. A fire of white energy and passion burned through them. They felt each other's hearts beating in sync. Their emotions flowed like electricity through each other.

Gently ending the kiss, Paul looked deep into her eyes. "I love you too," he said.

"You heard me?" she smiled at him with tearfilled eyes.

He nodded and pulled her into another kiss.

Chapter 26

10 days later:

The entire town had been cut off from the rest of the world by flooding rivers, as the chaos had ensued. The power grid failed, and phone lines were dead. It was two days before the roads were passable into Delisle. Once word of all the dead got out, people in black suits started showing up and asking questions. Areas were quarantined. Those that had been possessed by the hag and lived had no memory of what happened. Paul and everyone that knew didn't have much to say. Their story was that they got caught in the storm and hid out in Swanier's. Some people showed up trying to loot the place. Adam died defending it. Ms. Swanier died of natural causes, while the storm raged.

They didn't hide the truth about Sam… They made sure Brian's whole family would live with the shame of what he had done. Death had been too good for him. William had gone to find his and Sam's bodies after the chaos had settled. Sam's body had been pushed into the cemetery by the flood waters. Brian's body was gone, presumably swallowed by the swollen bayou. The police unit that was sent to Brian's home had found Kurt's mangled corpse in the driveway. It appeared he had been run over multiple times. Judging by the blood trail, he was alive for at least the first two passes of the car.

The news was speculating that there may have been a chemical leak from the nearby plant, and that these chemicals had caused the irrational behavior of the citizens of Delisle. That was fine with Paul. They would never believe the real story.

Paul looked at himself in the mirror, scowling at the sloppy crimson tie under his collar. "Goddamn it," he hissed.

There had been so many funerals in the past week, and he still hadn't learned how to tie the damned thing. Ms. Swanier's funeral was nice. Most of her community turned out, and did a Second Line down the streets, as they marched to the cemetery she would be buried in. That was Paul's first experience with Second Line, and he loved it. Took the sting out of death. It became a celebration of life and crossing over instead of focusing on the loss of a beautiful soul to those still here.

Sam's funeral was hard. There was no celebration. No music. No joy. There was only screams, and crying, and begging from her family. Paul's aunt pleading to God to make it not true. To bring back her little girl. She carried on until the Xanax finally kicked in. After that, she spent the rest of the day staring off at nothing. For the first time since they had known each other, Paul saw Ruben break down. After the service, when it was just the two boys remaining, Ruben dropped a rose on the freshly moved dirt before falling to his knees, lost in grief. Paul placed a hand on his shoulder, and stood with him through the tears.

It took a long time for the sobbing to ease. When it did, Ruben talked to Sam. Finally confessing how he had been in love with her since they were in middle school. How sorry he was that he hadn't been there for her and hadn't saved her. How he didn't know how life was going to work without her, but that he would make the best life he could in her honor. Once he had said his piece, Paul helped him to his feet, and the two embraced in their shared sorrow. Paul was so overcome by the onslaught of emotions that he felt physically ill. The rest of the day was spent in bed.

Today's funeral was different, though. He had to look perfect for this one. He had to make sure this final send-off was done right. Sliding the tie apart, he started the process again, trying to figure out where he went wrong.

"Cross the thick over the thin… wrap… tuck this… aaaaaand pull. Fuck!" he exclaimed, looking at the cockeyed knot around his neck.

"Language." Frances said, walking into the small bathroom.

Dark circles decorated the skin under her eyes. Sadness deeply lined her face. The knee length black dress was pretty on her, fitting her aura.

"Sorry, Mom," he said blushing. "I just can't get this tie. It needs to be right," he said. Frustration was evident in his voice.

"Let me," she said.

Stepping behind Paul, she looked at his reflection. Swiftly, she undid the tie and began the motions again. In mere moments, she had a perfect knot, and the tie sat straight on Paul's chest.

"There ya go," she said. She wrapped an arm around Paul's back and rested her head on his shoulder.

"Wow. I gotta learn how to do that," he said, examining the tie.

"You look so handsome," she said as her eyes filled with tears.

Seeing his mother breaking made his eyes sting. He turned and wrapped her in his arms. "It's gonna be ok, Momma."

"It hurts so much," she said shakily.

"I know, Momma. I miss him." Paul said as the tears broke through.

He felt her shoulders heave for a second. Her breath hitched a few times, and she pulled away. Grabbing a tissue from the back of the toilet, she dabbed around her eyes and wiped her nose.

She looked into the mirror, checking her makeup. "Thank God for water-proof mascara."

Paul joined her in the mirror. "Amen to that. Mine hasn't run at all."

She chortled and gave Paul a loving slap on the chest. "Stay out of my makeup."

The humor was only a mask, as neither of them felt any joy. They left the bathroom, and Paul walked into the living room. He found his dad with his back to him. The news chattered in the background. Something about a freak storm, riots, and mass casualties. William was staring at the portrait on the wall of his sons. Paul was a baby holding a soccer ball looking to be belly-laughing. Adam, a toddler at the time, had an arm around him with a giant smile on his face.

"Dad?" Paul said.

William sniffled and swiped a hand across his eyes. Keeping his back to Paul, he said, "Everyone ready?"

"Yes, sir," Paul answered.

"Ok. Let's load up," William said. He turned and walked out of the room, keeping his face out of Paul's view.

Paul wanted to comfort him. Wanted to take his pain away. Only time would be able to do that, though. Paul was dealing with his own hurt as well. Today would be the most difficult day of his life. He'd gladly fight the old hag again than do this.

Arms wrapped around Paul's stomach. Madie pressed her body against his back, and her warmth spread through him. Thank God for her. She was the one thing keeping him anchored through it all.

Squeezing her forearm, he sighed, "Hey, you."

"Hey," she said back.

"What did they say?" Paul asked.

"She still hasn't woken up, but her vitals are good. Everything looks good. They said she will wake up in her own time."

"Good. We'll go see her tonight after the service," Paul said.

"You sure? You're gonna be tired," Madie said, nuzzling her head against his back.

"Yeah. I'll be fine," he said reassuringly.

"Thank you," she said and kissed his neck.

After a long silence Paul said, "I guess it's time."

"Yeah. We will get through this. I'm here for you." She squeezed him tighter.

"I love you," he said.

"I love you, too," she replied, with a gentle smile.

A knock sounded from the carport door, followed by the door opening.

"Hey, Dad. How ya' holding up?" Ruben's voice came from the kitchen.

"Good. Doing good," William lied. "Paul's in the living room."

Ruben walked into the living room with a sad expression. He wore a silk black button up shirt with the sleeves rolled up, pressed black slacks and mirror shined dress shoes.

"Hey guys," he said.

"Hey Roob," Paul and Madie said at the same time.

"Looking sharp, dude," Paul said.

"Yeah. I just… borrowed my uncle's clothes. Wanted to look respectful, you know?" Ruben said.

"Adam would have appreciated it, and made fun of you for looking like a fancy bitch." Paul chuckled.

"Says the bitch in a three-piece suit," Ruben jabbed back.

"Fair enough," Paul said.

Paul turned to Madie, seeing her in the lacey black dress she borrowed from his mom. She was stunning, though he couldn't really appreciate her beauty at the moment. His mind was cloudy with anxiety and grief over putting his brother in the ground today. It would be a closed casket. His body was badly burned and beaten, from what Paul had overheard at the funeral home.

"LOAD UP!"' William's voice called from the carport.

"Ok, let's do this," Paul said to Madie and Ruben.

Chapter 27

The service at the funeral home was a blur of hugs, tears, cheek kisses, and condolences. Relatives and family friends that Paul hadn't seen in years, all showed up to pay their final respects. The sheriff popped in at some point, shaking hands and giving a politician's façade of sympathy. Once everyone had made their way past Adam's coffin to say goodbye, Paul helped carry him to the hearse along with Ruben, William, Jack, his grandfather Mitch, and Jack's son, Travis.

William sat stone faced at the graveside, fighting tears back while the pastor recited prayers and Bible quotes. His fight was futile, and tears soaked the lapels of his dress greens. Paul's grandmother held his mom, as they lowered Adam's casket into the ground. Her wails tore at Paul's heart. Ruben and Madie stood to either side of Paul, each sobbing and holding his arms for comfort.

Once the casket was lowered and the words were done, Paul, Ruben, Jack, and William grabbed shovels from the back of Jack's pick up and began filling Adam's grave. They had all agreed it would be their final deed for him and had declined to let the funeral home hire a backhoe operator. Few words were spoken as they worked. Hours later, William slung the final shovel of dirt, and the group stood silent over Adam's grave.

Paul looked at the blisters dotting his palms, then to his filthy dress shoes. Chuckling, Paul said. "Well… he would be happy to know, he got me one last time. He used to love to torture me when we were little. Remember that time he smeared mustard all over the back of my shirt on the first day of school? I walked around all day so proud of my ugly ass Hawaiian shirt thinking everyone was looking at how awesome it was."

"Yeah. You came home crying, you were so mad. Said you were gonna beat him up. Was like a rabid little badger," William said.

"But God help anyone who tried to mess with you. He was the only one that got to do that," Jack said.

"Yeah," Paul laughed.

"Who was that boy in Ohio that he picked up by the throat for stealing your bike?" William asked.

"Tim! Oh God, I freaked out! Thought he was gonna kill the kid. Ran and told on him for doing it even though he was sticking up for me," Paul laughed.

"Snitch," Ruben said.

"Hey! I was 6 years old, man!" Paul exclaimed.

They spent the next hour sharing stories of Adam's life. There was plenty of laughter and tears. The whole thing felt therapeutic, like soothing ointment on a fresh wound.

"Well… we had better get back. I'm sure your mom is about ready to pull her hair out with all the people in the house," William said.

"If it's ok, I'd like to walk back, Dad," Paul said.

William stared at Paul a moment before nodding, "Ok. Just don't be long."

"I won't. Thank you, Dad," Paul smiled.

"I'll make sure he gets home, sir," Ruben chimed in.

William turned to walk away and paused. Without looking at Paul, he said, "I love you, son. I'm proud of you."

Paul was dumbstruck, "I… I love you too, Dad."

With that, William and Jack got into their vehicles and drove away.

"So… how ya holding up?" Ruben said, wrapping an arm around Paul's shoulder.

Paul shrugged, "Today hurt, man. Felt like a piece of me went in the ground with him."

"Yeah, it still doesn't feel real," Ruben said.

"What about you?" Paul asked.

"About the same. Everything feels so fucked up. Like, what do we do now? Nothing's the same. All the shit I thought was important before just seems so stupid and pointless. Like… shit… two weeks ago all I cared about was beating your ass in pool, swimming, and staring at Sam when she wasn't looking. Now… she's dead and my best friend is some kind of superhero, or grim reaper, or something," Ruben said.

Paul thought on that for a minute. Grim reaper? He had certainly been one that night. Since the hag was defeated, he had pushed all of that far down, refusing to allow the jij to be present. He had come to terms with the shadows by his bed at night. They no longer scared him, knowing why they were there. The night Constance passed, he'd sat awake talking to her before letting her cross. He supposed it was because she grew up being taught about all of it that she was aware of what was happening and saw Paul. She was scared but anxious to see what was next. She also warned Paul to be wary of his powers. No jij had ever had the ability to will someone to die. Paul felt no sorrow sending her across. He knew she would never see the edges of hell. Her soul was bright and pure.

"I don't think I'm all that grim. Maybe the Handsome Reaper? The Wise Reaper? Oh… the Jolly Reaper!" Paul joked.

"The Dumbass Reaper," Ruben laughed.

"That doesn't really roll off the tongue, Roob. You're not very good at this," Paul said disapprovingly.

The two shared a much-needed laugh, as all of the recent days had been final goodbyes and tears. It felt good. The boys began their walk home. Paul gave one last look over his shoulder to Adam's grave and felt a little disappointment. A small part of him had hoped that he would find his brother's spirit standing by the grave, giving a movie style approving nod before fading away. Instead, it was just a fresh grave.

Paul sighed and turned back to the road. Only the road was gone. Everything was gone. He found himself floating in the Nothing, and his heart stuttered.

"No!" he screamed into the never-ending expanse.

A terrible roar rumbled through the air around him in response. His ethereal form felt the shaking, as if his body were here.

"Ruben! Where are you?!" Paul cried.

"Help me," a voice whimpered.

Paul let his senses go out in search of the source. Quickly he found it. Horror ripped through him, as he saw Jennifer. Large veins of black wrapped around her, stabbing through, rooting her into the Nothing.

"Jennifer?" he said.

"You! Why did…," the black roots tightened around her, changing her words to screams.

He watched in terror as they bored deeper into her. Hands shot out of the void and grabbed his shoulders hard.

"Paul!" Ruben shouted.

Paul blinked, and was back in the world staring at the ground in front of his face. He struggled to catch his breath and slow his heart.

"What happened?!" Ruben yelled at him as he pulled him up.

Paul wobbled to his feet and looked around, appreciating the light and air. He looked at Ruben and rubbed a hand over his sweaty face.

"What the fuck happened? You good?" Ruben asked.

"I was there again. The Nothing. Fuck!" Paul shouted the profanity, picturing Jennifer screaming.

"How? Why?" Ruben asked.

"I don't… I don't know. I was just there. And so was Jennifer." Paul said.

"Madie's Jennifer?" Ruben crunched his face in confusion.

"Yeah. She was in pain. The darkness was hurting her," Paul said.

"But, you beat that bitch," Ruben said.

Paul raised his eyes to the sky, feeling the world around him. Traces of it were everywhere, a tainted energy dragging across his skin. He reached out further. His skin still felt dirty with it. Further still, he pushed out. Again and again he reached out. There was no corner of the country that wasn't stained with it. Paul felt something...a presence within the darkness, look at him, making a river of ice flow through him.

Snapping back to his body, Paul gasped "No!"

"What's wrong?" Ruben asked, clearly concerned.

Paul looked wide eyed and panting at Ruben "It's not over. We need to get home, now!"

THE END

424

Made in the USA
Coppell, TX
24 February 2020